Victim of Honor

Rion Hall Publishing
Medina, Ohio

Victim of Honor

The Story of John Y. Beall and the Northwestern Conspiracy

By
James E. Duffey

P.O. Box 292
WestfieldCenter,OH 44251

www.RionHallPublishing.com
email: RionHallPublishing@zoominternet.net
Phone: 330-518-7440

ISBN - 13: 978-0-9790963-0-3

Library of Congress Control Number: 2006939732

Printed in the United States of America

February 2007

10 9 8 7 6 5 4 3 2 1

Acknowledgment

The writing of this book has taken more than eight years and dozens of adventures to gather information. My quest has taken me to Toronto, Canada, Washington, D.C., Richmond, Virginia, Nashville, Tennessee, Buffalo, New York, Sandusky and Port Clinton, Ohio and to Detroit, Michigan, Harper's Ferry, West Virginia, and most importantly to Charles Town, West Virginia, the home of John Yates Beall.

If it had not been for Bob Pratt and our chance meeting at Denny's restaurant, I'm not sure this story could have been told. It was he who opened up the small world of Charles Town residents to me. I would also like to thank Anne Bretsch, now the owner of John Beall's house, for her help and encouragement, and for inviting me to visit Beall's home.

There are so many people to thank that it is not really possible on these pages, but I feel I must give some recognition for their hours of help: the ladies of the Follett House museum in Sandusky, Ohio, librarian Bill Leubke at the Virginia State Library in Richmond, Virginia, the family of Martha O'Bryan in Nashville, Tennessee, and Beth Harrison, who acted as my editor. I was gratified that each of you took such an interest in my project. It was in large part that interest in John Beall's story that kept me going.

Mostly I want to dedicate this book to my family for their unwavering support through all the research and writing, especially Ann Marie, who followed me around the country and spent countless hours in libraries and museums gathering information with me.

I believed the day I began this project, and believe it even more today, that John Yates Beall was really innocent of the charges for which he was executed, and any part I can play in vindicating his life and memory was well worth the time and effort. Sleep well, John.

Jim Duffey

Dedication

To all those who seek truth and justice
and are willing to fight for it.

Contents

Victim of Honor

Forward

Why the Story Needs Telling

When each of us does a final accounting of our own lives and the way we have lived them, I am sure that we would like to think we have done some good, or at least have done no harm, that we would have done right by all. Such was the character of John Yates Beall. His calling throughout his brief life was to duty and honor in all that he did. It was a heritage passed on to him from both his grandfather and father. The Civil War created situations in which the lines that divided good and evil became blurred. Good men were called upon to do evil things as a result of war. Even the most evil of men occasionally and miraculously rose up to do good. It is the gray areas created by war and men's behavior that is a consternation to us. What are perceived to be good or heroic actions by one side in war, are often seen as villainous by the other.

In all wars the winners write the history. The Civil War is no exception. If the South had won the war, would John Yates Beall and what he did have been seen in a different historical light? I think so. Consider then, as you read, the motivations and actions of all who inhabit these pages and decide for yourself who is right and who is wrong. Who is good and who is evil. And who really upholds the traditions of duty and honor that all men profess to hold dear.

Seven years ago I began to write the story of a young man who had served the Confederate States during the Civil War in what has been called the Northwestern Conspiracy. When I began, I had hoped to write a biography of Captain John Yates Beall that would tell his story in a more accurate and honest way than it had been reported in his time.

The writing of Victim of Honor has been long and laborious. Information was difficult to find. Sadly, some of it is lost forever. Sources, located in diverse places around the United States, made research time consuming and difficult. At times I wondered if it all was worth the effort, but the more I did, the more I was driven to do. Someone had to tell this man's story. Somehow John Yates Beall had to finally get the justice denied him more than a century ago. That became my mission.

What made this book challenging to write was that so much of the story had been reported inaccurately, even by Beall's contemporaries. I have done my best to correct that, but I still admit that I have had to make some educated and hopefully sound judgments and assumptions about the facts that cannot be known, based on information that is known and has proven to be credible.

Victim of Honor is told in the form of an historical novel. I have taken the liberty of creating dialogue and scenes that never really took place, but only for the purpose of providing insight into the characters of the people involved, or to show what was reasonable to assume happened based on known facts in a way that would be as interesting and entertaining as possible. I have in every case been as true to actual facts as was humanly possible.

Victim of Honor is a story written for everyone, not just for scholars or historians. It is a story of one man's call to duty and how he committed his life to the cause for which his country fought. While many would disagree with that cause, his motives were pure and his calling an honorable one. It is that story I hope to convey.

James E. Duffey

Victim of Honor

1

The Death Watch

The Reverend Henry Joshua VanDyke arose on the morning of February 23, 1865, one half hour earlier than his usual six o'clock. He lit a small brass oil lamp and padded quietly about the bedroom as he dressed. At fifty- five his thick head of hair, once dark brown was now mostly gray. He put on a clean white shirt and buttoned up the stiff clerical collar, pulled up his trousers and buttoned his vest. Last was the black coat which fell just short of his knees. The mirror reflected a tall man, an older man with more wrinkles in his face than he cared to see. He saw a tired man, a man who had given too many sermons, had tried to save too many souls, and attended to the details of too many funerals. Now he had been asked to attend to the needs of a man facing death on the gallows. That task was not new to him either. Several times in his thirty-year career he had visited with poor souls about to be executed. To Van Dyke they were usually sullen and bitter, cruel men who felt the world had wronged them all their lives. Men who had done the vilest of things, and probably deserved to die, yet believed to the last that it was they who were the victims. They cursed society, they cursed the hangman, they cursed God himself. Van Dyke thought they deserved to meet their maker and atone for their sins.

But what of this man Beall? VanDyke knew little of him, only what

1

he had read in the New York *Times*. A spy, a guerrilla, he put innocent lives in peril, shot and robbed civilians, destroyed boats and derailed trains . He is the enemy...at least according to society. Yet his friends, Albert Ritchie and James McClure, who had come yesterday to ask his help, said Beall was a good man, wrongly accused.

How wretched it must be to face death if one really was innocent of the charges. War had created a strange set of circumstances where the line between what was right and wrong had blurred. Often, he mused, the legitimacy of one's actions depended on whose side you were on. The winning side always writes the history their way, but does that make them right? After all, hadn't Sherman march through Georgia destroying every farm and hamlet in his path...and he was a hero. So who, really, is a good man or a bad man, he thought.

Van Dyke hoped his wife would not awake. She'd insist on cooking breakfast and he just wasn't in the mood. His stomach was queasy. He didn't feel much like making small talk over oatmeal today. VanDyke finished dressing and walked quickly down the hall to his study for morning prayers. Sitting in the small dim room amid flickering light and musty old books, he prayed silently as he did each morning for troubled parishioners and the sick, he prayed for a quick end to the war, but most of all he prayed for himself, for the strength and words to help the young rebel soldier he would meet this day, the one who would die tomorrow at the hands of the executioner down on Governor's Island.

Leaving his residence by seven, VanDyke walked briskly across the dark frozen yard to the church. The crusted snow crackled beneath his feet. He unlocked the massive wooden door, and slipped into the church. He mounted the staircase and made his way down a narrow hallway to his office where he struck a match and lit his desk lamp. Messages from the previous day were read and notes were made for his secretary who would arrive about eight o'clock. "Delay all meetings until tomorrow," he wrote, "I will be gone all day and probably into the evening. If needed I can be reached through General Dix's office. I will be at Fort Columbus on Governor's Island." He signed the note Joshua, preferring the Biblical name. As he left the church and walked into the crisp morning air he shivered. The gray sky showed no signs of clearing. Wind gusted and bit at his face as he walked up the street to catch a carriage down to the battery.

The carriage made its way south on Broadway past dozens of stores and markets, some just beginning to show signs of life. By seven forty-five the carriage veered left onto White Hall Street toward the battery where a ferry, the *Henry Burdon*, waited. As he rode, staring out at New York City just coming to life, he wondered what kind of man Beall really was. The papers were full of the story and the man, but the description given him by Mr. Ritchie and Mr. McClure was so different. What was the real truth? No matter. He would soon find out. A young man was about to die, and it was his task to see that he had some spiritual guidance, some words of comfort before he departed this world. How could a man so young have done so much evil, acted in such a heartless manner as the papers had reported? What terrible power possessed men at war that would have caused this man to do the things he had done? Or had he? Perhaps, as his friends said, he was indeed innocent. Then what a tragedy, what a waste.

VanDyke's thoughts rambled into many areas he hoped to explore with the young Captain. He would simply have to hear his story and reserve judgment. He would ask him to repent, hear his confession, and offer words of encouragement and strength. No matter what he had done, no matter what price he would pay, VanDyke would assure him that God would be merciful and forgiving.

The ferry ride to Governor's Island had been uneventful save the queasiness in VanDyke's stomach. He wasn't sure if it was due more to the bouncing of the boat on the choppy waters of the harbor or the anticipation of his meeting with the condemned man. He consoled himself that his small physical suffering was nothing compared to the mental anguish the young man must be going through today. Tomorrow the good reverend would write another sermon, counsel a few troubled parishioners, and eat supper by five. The man he was about to see would have faced death by then. His upset stomach was, VanDyke thought, a small price to pay to help another human being from this world to the next, guilty or not.

Governor's Island loomed large and stony, rising sharply out of the water ahead. Its prison walls stood in dark contrast against the backdrop of the bleak gray winter sky. VanDyke could see the form of a man hunched over and pacing the dock ahead, apparently waiting for the ferry's arrival.

"Reverend VanDyke, sir? I'm Major Cogswell. I'm here to escort you to see Captain Beall." He reached out his hand to help VanDyke off the ferry and onto the long wooden dock.

"Thank you, Major." VanDyke steadied himself, regaining his land legs.

The two men walked in single file up the wooden stairway to the prison entrance with Cogswell in the lead. The wind whipped around them as they approached the gates. VanDyke pulled his collar up around his ears to protect them from the biting cold, then shoved his hands deeper into his coat pockets.

Cogswell motioned the direction. "The cells are down this way, sir. It's just a short walk. By the way, the usual procedure is that we search anyone who enters the cell block." He looked somewhat sheepishly at the Reverend. "I will forego that if you will just assure me that you carry no weapons, sir."

"No weapons, Major."

"Thank you, sir."

Major Cogswell entered the cell first. VanDyke stood in the dim corridor behind him unbuttoning his coat.

"Captain Beall, there is someone to see you." Cogswell motioned to the Reverend behind him. "This is Reverend Joshua VanDyke. He's come over from the city to see you at the request of some of your friends."

Beall rose from the small table where he had been writing letters and moved toward VanDyke. The Reverend ducked his head and slipped through the narrow doorway and entered the cell.

"Reverend VanDyke, it's good to meet you, sir. And kind of you to come." The men shook hands. Beall's hand was not nearly as cold as his own.

"Thank you," answered VanDyke, " I hope I can be of some assistance."

Major Cogswell bid them goodbye and said that VanDyke should call for the guard when he was ready to leave. There was no hurry. Take all the time you need.

VanDyke surveyed the gloomy narrow cell. Brick walls, stone floor. Cold. It appeared to be about five feet wide and eight or nine feet long. A small table and chair, a bed with a straw mattress, one small gaslight flickering on the wall. Beall offered the chair to VanDyke. He sat on the edge of the bed. There was a minute of uncomfortable silence. Van-Dyke noticed some books on the table, a *Bible* was among them, and he took that as an opportunity to begin.

"I see you have a *Bible*."

"Yes." said Beall.

"There's a lot of comfort in that book."

"I know," said Beall, "I read it every day."

"I see you've made some notes in the margins," VanDyke observed as he thumbed through the book.

"Yes, I've been making some notations on passages I particularly like."

VanDyke had often done the same for future reference, and wondered why a man with no future would take the time to do it now.

"If you don't mind my asking, why are you marking passages if you are to die tomorrow? What use will they be to you then?"

"They're not for me. I'm having my *Bible* sent to a friend. They are for her. Maybe in some future time they'll be as much an inspiration to her as they have been to me." Beall picked up the *Bible* and thumbed through it, easily finding the passage he desired. It was obvious to VanDyke that Beall was very familiar with the location.

Beall looked at VanDyke and read, "Yea, though I walk through the valley of the shadow of death, I shall fear no evil, thy rod and thy staff, they comfort me...." He put the book down. "I find that psalm very comforting right now. I'm sure that in the days ahead my friend will find it comforting as well."

"She must be a very special friend," said VanDyke, curious, but not wanting to pry.

"Yes, we were engaged to be married," said Beall. He looked at the floor and was silent.

Reverend VanDyke broke the momentary silence, "Captain Beall, I must confess that when Mr. Ritchie and Mr. McClure contacted me about coming out to see you, well, frankly I was a little confused, and hesitant. I cannot say that I had never heard of you. Your story has been in all the papers. And that is the reason for my confusion. What I read in the papers and what your friends have told me about you are worlds apart. I fully expected to come down here to confront a hardened and bitter criminal. Yet in the few moments I've been with you I can see that you are not. How does a man of your apparent refinement and religious conviction get to where you are today?"

"All I did, sir, was serve my country in the best way I could," said Beall. He looked VanDyke squarely in the eye. "That is what got me here."

"Mr. Ritchie said you are from Virginia?"

"Yes, Charles Town, Virginia," answered Beall.

"I was born and grew up on a farm in Jefferson County. Raised mostly wheat."

"Has your family been there long?" asked VanDyke.

"The land came from my mother's father, John Yates, for whom I am named. He came to Virginia many years ago from England as a boy to work for his Uncle Charles. His family had been landowners and clergymen in England. When my grandfather's father died, he was adopted by Uncle Charles. Then, when Uncle Charles died, my grandfather inherited all the land. Over the years he added some to it. About two thousand acres in all. We called the farm Walnut Grove."

"So you come from a religious family?" asked VanDyke noting the reference to clergymen in his past.

"Not particularly. Grandfather John, 'Old Yates' as everyone called him, wasn't really religious in the sense of going to church regularly or being conversant with its theology. His religion was one of belief in honor and duty, honesty and fairness in his dealings with everyone."

"Those are certainly ideals to be admired. If only more of my parishioners had them!" sighed VanDyke. "But was your grandfather a man of faith?"

"Yes, he believed in God and heaven, but he believed it was honesty, not faith, that got you into heaven." said Beall.

"And what about your own father?" asked VanDyke.

"In many ways he was similar to my grandfather. And in some ways they were quite different. My father, George Beall, had strong belief in honesty and duty. Looking back, I suppose I have been very much influenced by his beliefs throughout my life."

"You said they were different in some ways?" asked VanDyke. "How were they different?"

Beall thought about the question. It was remarkable how his family was like so many others that had been divided by the war ...brother against brother, friend against friend, father against son.

"If my grandfather were still alive, he would undoubtably have supported the Union. He was a Federalist and later became active in the Whig Party. A very conservative man. On the other hand, my father was a state's rights Democrat. A real Jeffersonian. One year, when my father ran for a seat in the Virginia Legislature, grandfather refused to support him." Beall rubbed his hands and laughed. He could still vividly remember the family arguments over that event.

"So, your grandfather has passed on." Van Dyke said, wanting to hear more.

"Yes, he has passed. When he became ill and knew he was not going to live much longer, he told us that he wanted to return to England to die. I don't think he ever cast off his English background, even after all those years. My father asked me to go with him, and I did. I was only sixteen, and very fearful of his coming death, but I sat with him until the end." Beall paused, "You know, there I sat at his bedside, terrified at the prospect of his death, yet it was he who comforted me. He was not afraid of death...I was, but not him. I've often thought how strange that was."

"Not really," answered VanDyke quietly, "I've seen many of strong faith who look forward to death, welcome it."

"Old Yates seemed to accept death as he had life. He had lived a good life, an honest life. He had done right by everyone. He believed his place in heaven was assured, so why be afraid? It was his destiny." Beall had carried that voice with him his whole life, always there in the back of his consciousness. And now as his own hour approached, he could see how it seemed strangely to apply to his own life as well.

VanDyke watched Beall as he spoke. Mr. Ritchie and Mr. McClure had been right. This was not the man he had read about in the papers. He did not seem to have the mentality of a killer, or a blood-thirsty fiend. He had welcomed the pastor into his cell as if it had been his own parlor. He appeared to be a man of refinement, of good family, good character, and apparently very well educated.

On the table next to where he had seen the *Bible* were several other volumes. He picked one up, *Manon Lescaut* , written in French. As he leafed through the pages VanDyke asked, "I see that you understand French. Where did you take your education?"

"Yes, I picked up both French and Latin at the University of Virginia." said Beall.

"What course did you study?"

"I took a degree in law there. I never really wanted to be a lawyer, never actually was licensed to practice. I did it more in deference to my father. It just seemed at the time to be the way a gentleman became properly educated. I did make some wonderful friends there. Albert Ritchie and James McClure were classmates of mine. So was Dan Lucas. Have you met him?"

"No, not Lucas."

"They are all still trying desperately to save me, now. And I suppose some of my political ideas were learned there, too. I read quite a bit of Jefferson's and Madison's writings, particularly the Kentucky and Virginia Resolutions."

VanDyke looked puzzled. His political education was weak. Beall could see that and explained.

"The Kentucky and Virginia Resolutions hold that since the states created the national government, there is a compact, or a contract between them. If a state feels that the national government has passed a law that might be harmful to the state, then the state has the right to nullify, or in effect, ignore that law. If the national government breaks that pact, then the states are not beholden to obey the laws passed. The states created the national government to help the states, not to do them harm. If that law is not changed, then the state can nullify it, and if still not corrected, ultimately the states may, upon agreement of a state convention, secede from the Union. That is what South Carolina and the rest of the southern states did."

"So you believe in a state's right to secede?" asked VanDyke.

Beall sighed, "I would have preferred that the Union stay together, but it appeared that each year the government passed laws or took actions that subordinated the southern states, putting their economies and businessmen in great peril. Many felt their livelihoods were at stake."

"Looking back at all that has happened to you, do you feel that perhaps secession was a mistake?" asked VanDyke.

"No," Beall said shaking his head slowly, "I simply felt I had to defend Virginia. If Virginia's decision is wrong in the eyes of the world, so be it. If it was a mistake, it was Virginia's mistake. I, myself, like General Lee and the others, felt a moral duty to defend Virginia. For better or worse, I cast my lot like the others with states' rights."

Though VanDyke did not agree with the issue of states' rights in principle, he agreed in his own mind at least that there were two sides to every argument. The question of who was right was unfortunately being decided at the cost of a great many young men's lives.

"So you graduated from college and went home to become a farmer?"

Beall was amused by the question, "No, not really. When I graduated, class of 1855, I returned home with a grandiose plan to move west to Iowa to make my own fortune. My older brother, Hezekiah, lived there. . . still does . . . and I thought I could go out and make money in the milling business or in land speculation. I had heard that there was a fortune to be made in buying and reselling land."

"Then you didn't go?"

"Well, I started out with my sister for Dubuque, Iowa, but at the train station in New York I received a telegram informing me that my father was gravely ill. We returned home on the next available train."

"Your father?"

"He died a few days after we returned home."

"And then what of the dream?"

"I had to give it up. I had my mother, four sisters and a younger brother to look after, as well as the farm. I still wanted to go west, but my duty was to them."

VanDyke fiddled with the paper on the table and recalled his own father's untimely death, and how that had challenged his own faith. "How did you feel when your father died, John?"

"It was a strange thing. My father was not a particularly devout man, but he, like my grandfather, died at peace knowing he had wronged no man during his life. He had lived a good life and had done his duty."

"Your father must have been a fairly young man. Did your religious convictions help you to cope with his untimely death?" asked VanDyke.

"About that time I had no strong religious convictions. I wasn't even a regular church member. I went through a time when what views I had about religion and God were challenged. I had, up until then, been very cynical about fervently religious people, and yet felt some degree of contempt for absolute skeptics. I wasn't sure what I believed. It was then that I joined the Zion Episcopal Church in Charles Town. I felt a need to become involved in the church. I had this need, not to turn away from religion, but to get some answers from it, answers about the events taking place in my own life. I became very active in the church, even acted as a delegate to the diocese convention in Charlottesville."

VanDyke stood up to stretch his legs. He had been sitting since he arrived. He took out his watch. It was a little past noon. Twenty-four hours from now this young man would die. And yet here he was calmly talking of his past, his family, his philosophy. Where did the calm, the courage come from? He wished more people could have the strength Beall had.

Van Dyke walked the length of the cell and asked, "When did you get into the service?"

"I suppose it really all began with John Brown's raid in eighteen fifty-nine." Beall recounted how Brown and his followers, encouraged by abolitionists, attempted the capture of the Federal arsenal in Harper's Ferry in the hope of arming the slaves in open rebellion. "Harper's Ferry is just a few miles from my farm. We all went over, and were there when General Lee captured Brown at the arsenal. He was Colonel Lee then. That was the sixteenth of October. The trial for treason was held in Charles Town and I attended all the sessions. I was also there for his hanging. There were many people in town for the trial. They came from all over. It became quite a festive atmosphere. Parties were thrown. People thought it was a time for celebration. For many there had been great fear that if the slaves were freed something like mass murder of whites might occur. People still talked about Nat Turner and his rebellion. And that was thirty some years ago. Can you imagine? Over sixty innocent people chopped to death with axes in their sleep?"

"So they threw parties?"

"Yes, I went to one. Actually met the actor, John Wilkes Booth. He had also been there for the trial, and performed some dramatic readings in town during the week. Seemed nice enough, though somewhat arrogant..." He didn't finish the statement. No sense getting into Booth's role in the conspiracy, he thought. Van Dyke seemed to be a man to be trusted, but Beall knew enough to remain silent. He could not let any of what he knew slip out, even to a man of the cloth. "The result of the whole episode was that my neighbor, Lawson Botts, organized a local militia, which I joined. Our duty was to respond if any other such disturbance occurred. We called ourselves the Botts Grays. When the war broke out in eighteen sixty-one we became part of Company G in the Second Virginia Regiment under the command of Stonewall Jackson."

"And how old were you then?" asked VanDyke.

"Twenty-four."

That made John Beall thirty by VanDyke's count. He looked older. War did that to men. It exacted its toll in many ways. It made boys into men . . . men into old men . . . quickly.

"John, I have been agonizing about your execution all morning. How do you feel about dying?" asked VanDyke.

Beall lowered his eyes and studied his hands as he rubbed them together slowly. "You know, Reverend, it's not that I am indifferent to life. I've had a good life. . . but I am not terrified to leave it. Many men have died in this war . . . and I suppose I can go to heaven just as well from the gallows as on the battlefield . . . or in my own bed."

"Yes, many have died, that is for sure, but most of them didn't know it until the moment it happened. Death came swift and sudden. There was no time to think about it. How do you feel, John, knowing that you are about to die?" It was hard for him to fathom that Beall was so calm, knowing exactly when and how he would die.

"I have thought about that a great deal over the last few days and nights. I. . . I am not looking forward to it, but at least I know that I died in the defense of what I believed to be right," said Beall. "Many have died for much less."

"John, let me ask you, as your clergyman, do you feel the need to confess, or repent any of the things you have been charged with?" VanDyke asked quietly. " I would be happy to listen and pray with you."

"No," Beall simply said, shaking his head slowly, eyes locked on Van-Dyke.

The minister was amazed at Beall's composure. He had come expecting to see frustration and anger. Seeing none of that in Beall, he had to ask, "Don't you feel any bitterness over the outcome of the trial, or anger toward your enemies?"

Beall shook his head. He thought for a moment and said, "I suppose I should be angry. . . I was for a while, but not now." Beall thought back to some distant past in a better place. "Some time ago, I had a discussion with the woman to whom I am betrothed, a discussion about fate and God's will." He paused remembering. "I know in my heart that my conviction was wrong . . . it was contrary to all the laws of civilized warfare. But . . . I believe in fate. If God has a plan for my life. . . if for some mysterious reason He has ordained this destiny for me, then I have to accept my fate as the will of God. I cannot change it . . . they cannot change it. I simply must accept it."

Reverend Joshua VanDyke left that day knowing he had never met at better Christian, a better man. What an odd set of circumstances this war had created, he thought. Brother against brother, neighbor against neighbor, friend against friend. Poor Beall . . . if he had been on the Union side, he would have been able to live the hero's life, but fate had assigned him the villain's role. And what a cruel fate for such a good man. It occurred to VanDyke that for young John Yates Beall's entire life, duty and honor had been his guiding principles. He'd given up his dream, first in the name of duty to his family, and then to his country. With the coming of the war he'd sacrificed his youth and freedom in the name of honor. He wondered if Beall had even guessed at the beginning of this war, what price would be exacted for adherence to those lofty principles. Here was a young man about to go to the gallows tomorrow, who felt it was his destiny. A young man whose code of honor prevented him from selling out his friends and associates to save his own life. Others, realizing the cause was lost had done it, and saved their own lives. Yet he refused, even when it meant his own death. VanDyke could not help but think that Captain John Yates Beall, tried, convicted by military commission and sentenced to die, really was in some way a victim . . . a victim of his own honor.

2

Wounded at Bolivar Heights

It had been a very mild Virginia autumn. October days were warm and sunny, the nights were just beginning to chill. Leaves had gone amber and red, but had not yet fallen. The War for Southern Independence had begun on April 12, when General Beauregard began a two-day bombardment of Fort Sumter in Charleston harbor. By the fourteenth the fort was surrendered. The war between the states was on. The North was outraged.

Abraham Lincoln, recently installed in office, called for seventy-five thousand volunteers. Three days later Virginia seceded, and was followed quickly by Arkansas, Tennessee and North Carolina. By the end of May, all of the slave-holding states had seceded except Delaware, Maryland, Western Virginia, Kentucky and Missouri, who were held to the Union by both political and military pressures brought about by Lincoln. Seven months later things were still peaceful in the northern Shenandoah Valley. Like most good things, it would not last.

On the morning of the second anniversary of John Brown's raid, October 16, 1861, the farming men of Charles Town were up at first light working in the fields harvesting their wheat. The sun shined down on the valley from clear blue skies dotted occasionally by small clusters of white clouds. Riders galloping up along the road shouted to the farmers to stop their work and get their guns. Six entire companies of Union soldiers from Pennsylvania and Massachusetts under Colonel Geary had crossed the Potomac River and had taken up positions at nearby Bolivar Heights, the hill above Harper's Ferry. In response, Colonel Turner Ashby was forming volunteer militia troops to defend the town and needed help badly.

John Yates Beall sat on the front porch of his home that morning talking with his mother and sister, Mary, about the harvest and his plans for the winter ahead. He had made all the decisions for the plantation since his father's death in 1855, but out of respect, he never failed to keep his mother informed as to the business of the farm. Today they leisurely spoke over coffee of the harvest, crop prices, and welcome news, a letter from John's brother, Hezekiah, in Iowa.

The serenity of the moment was broken by the urgent pounding of horses in the distance. One of the riders peeled off from the pack and dashed up the lane from the road, stopping abruptly in a flurry of dust at Beall's porch steps. The rider was a boy of no more than eighteen.

"Are you John Beall?" he panted, struggling for breath.

"Yes," said Beall, getting up. He could tell that something was desperately wrong. "What do you want?"

"There's Federal troops . . . came across the river late last night. Colonel Ashby's got'em pinned down over at Bolivar Heights . . . needs all the help he can get."

With the beginning of this great conflict between North and South, the Shenandoah Valley was to become a highly contested prize. It was the breadbasket of the Confederacy and would, as the war progressed, be the site of many battles over its productive farm land and railroads, but mostly its southern access to the Confederate capitol of Richmond.

Bolivar Heights stood at the top of a hill overlooking Harper's Ferry, a small town nestled on the banks of the point where the Potomac and Shenandoah Rivers merged. Harper's Ferry, the site of two Federal Arsenal buildings housing thousands of finished weapons, a cotton mill, an iron foundry, a flour mill, the extension line of Baltimore and Ohio Railroad, and a rifle factory that could produce ten thousand guns every year, would be hotly contested, and would be held alternately by

Union and Confederate forces seven times throughout the war.

Without hesitating for a moment Beall said, "You go on ahead, I'll get my horse and be right behind you! Mother, send someone over to Rion Hall to tell Dan Lucas!" Then he ran around behind the house to the stable and saddled his horse. In minutes he was headed toward Bolivar Heights full tilt.

By the time Beall arrived the local forces had repulsed the invaders, but a few remnants of Geary's troops remained and weren't giving up. John dropped from his horse and took a position among some men near a cannon emplacement. The Captain in charge was sweating and swearing, "Get back! This damned cannon ain't been used since last Fourth of July! It's prob'ly more dangerous to us than to them!" With that the muzzle of the cannon exploded sending a ball into the center of a line of Federal troops. Body parts were propelled into the air in a bloody spray and several young Union boys were on their way to kingdom come.

"Whoa, lookee there!" the Captain yelped, indicating the Federal troops under cannon fire for probably the first time. They were beating a hasty retreat toward the road down to Harper's Ferry. Beall could see that some Union stragglers had taken up a position behind old Mrs. Wager's brick house.

Beall waved to a group of volunteers who were hunched down among a grove of trees nearby, "Come on, boys, let's flush those Yankees out from behind that house!" Beall grabbed a musket and signaled for the riflemen to follow him toward the house. The Federals were quickly rousted and fired as they ran. Beall, running across open land, got off two shots, but as he reloaded for the third, a bullet hit him in the right side of the chest. He fell unconscious. When he awoke both the Federals and his militia unit were gone. Dizzy and in pain, he pulled himself up and staggered back to what had been Turner Ashby's line and collapsed.

Dr. Andrew Hunter, like many of the neighbors, had come to the battlefield to offer any assistance he could. His wagon was used as an ambulance. He approached the bloody body lying in the field looking for signs of life. Hunter was a medical doctor, but even with his training and experience, he was not accustomed to seeing men so mangled and broken. He peered down at the face and gasped out loud, "Oh, my God, that's John Beall!" Hunter carried Beall back to Beall's house.

As the wagon approached the lane to the house, Mrs. Beall was coming down the porch steps. "Mrs. Beall!" shouted Hunter, "It's John. Get some water and towels." He pulled John off the wagon and carried him into the Beall parlor. Mrs. Beall was shaking, but kept as calm as she could, pulling back his shirt and putting pressure on the open wound. She was a strong woman, and she fought back the tears. This was no time to cry, she thought.

"You keep the pressure on, while I wash my hands," said the doctor as he headed for the kitchen. Now with medical bag in hand, Hunter assessed the wound and began digging for the ball in Beall's chest. "You'd better to go outside, Mrs. Beall," he said. She looked pale. No sense having another casualty to deal with, he thought. Janet Beall, hands covered with her son's blood, walked unsteadily out to the front porch and sat on the steps, staring across the fields beyond the road.

Her thoughts raced in a dozen directions. Afterward she could not remember what she had even thought about. Finally, the doctor called her back inside.

"His right lung has been penetrated by the ball, there are several broken ribs, Mrs. Beall, and he has lost a good deal of blood, most of it while I dug for the ball. I won't lie to you, the wound is very severe." The doctor hesitated, choosing his words and tone carefully. "He. . . well, it's possible he may not make it through the night. We'll know better by tomorrow morning." Hunter saw her anguish and took her in his arms as she sobbed. He wondered how many more mothers would have to endure this pain, how long this war might go on.

The wound should have killed him, but Beall's will would not allow it. Two months later, still weak and struggling, but sufficiently recovered to travel, he went south to Tallahassee, Florida, to recuperate and visit his cousins. It was there at a Christmas party he was introduced to General Robert W. Williams and his wife Susan O'Bryan Williams. The Williams's were wealthy, middle-aged land owners and childless. They took an immediate liking to John, and from then on saw that he got all that he needed to recuperate. They both saw in John the son they never could have. General Williams persuaded Beall to accompany them to their plantation on Pascagoula Island near the border of Louisiana and Mississippi to live until he was able to return to the war.

Pascagoula Island was one of the barrier islands along the coast that was separated from the mainland by a narrow flow of water. A wooden bridge connected the mainland to the plantation. Beyond the bridge, a lane passed among the trees and brush to an expansive, open grassy yard. A stately white two-story house surrounded by tall shade trees, grass and shrubbery stood in the center of it. A porch traversed the entire front of the house, and four tall pillars rose to the second-story roof. On the porch two young women and a middle-aged Negro man stood awaiting their arrival.

As the carriage pulled up the lane to the house, Mrs. Williams said, "Well, here we are, John. Look, Robert, there are Fannie and Martha on the porch."

"Fannie and Martha are Mrs. Williams' cousins," said the General as he snapped the reins to speed up the horse. "Their father was Susan's uncle. Live near Nashville. Their brother George sent them down to avoid the war when the Federals invaded Tennessee. They'll be staying with us for a while I suppose."

As the carriage pulled up in front of the house, General Williams directed a servant to take the horse and carriage around to the barn.

"John, I'd like to introduce you to Fannie and Martha O'Bryan. The two young ladies shook Beall's hand politely and welcomed him.

"Ladies, this handsome young man is John Beall. He has recently been wounded in the war and we've asked him to come here to recuperate. I hope you will help us see he gets the best of care." The general could see by the smiles and interested looks in the girls' eyes that that would not be a problem.

"Why don't you show Mr. Beall to his room so he can unpack," urged Mrs. Williams. "Then you can get acquainted. I'll see to dinner arrangements." With that she scurried into the house, greeted the other servants and disappeared into the kitchen.

"Well, John," said General Williams, "I can see you're in good hands, so get settled while I see what's been going on in my absence. I'll be back up to the house in a few minutes."

Fannie and Martha O'Bryan were the daughters of Dr. Laurence O'Bryan and Barsha Norfleet Gordon O'Bryan, the upper echelon of Nashville high society. They had been sent south to avoid the war when it became apparent that the Yankees were going to capture Nashville. Having been on the island for a few months, and with little to do for young women who had been so active at home, a visitor was a welcome change for them, especially one so handsome. Both took a great interest in Beall.

Making the kind of small talk people do when they first meet, the young women led Beall to his room and and he got settled. Martha and Fannie stood in the doorway as John deposited his clothing in a small bureau near the bed. They didn't think it proper to enter a man's room. Then they all went out to the porch to sit in the cool evening air and await dinner.

"Well, Mr. Beall, tell us about yourself. Where are you from? What was your occupation before the war?" asked Fannie. She was the forward one of the two sisters. Never afraid to speak her mind. What you didn't ask, you didn't know, she thought.

Beall smiled. "I'm from Charles Town, Virginia, Jefferson County. It's very close to Harper's Ferry. My family owns land there and we farm."

"And what about you?" he asked.

"Nothing very exciting, I'm afraid. We're school teachers. Until we heard the Union army was coming to Nashville, we ran a school for girls. Just a small school, in my brother George's house." said Fannie.

"Don't be modest, Fannie. We had twenty-five pupils," Martha nodded toward Fannie with pride. "My sister was a teacher when she was seventeen, and the first female principal at Dr. Collins D. Elliott's academy by the time she was twenty-four," said Martha proudly. "That's really an accomplishment for a lady... to become a principal, you know."

Fannie smiled self-consciously, "Martha was actually one of my students, Mr. Beall. When our father died, Martha was sent to the academy for her education, and when she graduated we decided to open our own school. My brother offered his house for the school."

"You started teaching at eighteen? How old are you now, Martha?" Beall asked.

"I'm going to be twenty-six on January ninth."

"Well," Beall smiled, "we'll have to have a celebration." He turned to Fannie, "And how about you?"

Fannie was embarrassed. Most women her age were long married, and it was painfully obvious she was not. "I'm thirty-five," she said looking him square in the eye, "but that's not something you're supposed to ask a lady, is it Mr. Beall?" Beall sensed that in her pointed humor there was some resentment about her age. The topic of conversation should turn in another direction, something neutral, he thought.

"The Williams's said you had a brother . . . George? What does he do?" Beall asked.

"We have two brothers, George and Joseph. George runs a wholesale dry goods business in Nashville. It's called Washington, O'Bryan and Company. Right now, though, he's in the Quartermaster Corps. Joseph is still in school. He lives with George and helps in the business," answered Martha. "Before the war George was always very busy. Active in Nashville affairs, church work. . ."

"Married?" asked Beall.

"Yes," said Fannie, "his wife's name is Lucinda. They've been married about four years."

"And how about your family?" Martha asked.

"My father has passed, but my mother still lives on the farm. So do my four sisters and younger brother. I have one older brother who lives out in Iowa." He paused and thought of them, "I really hated to leave them, but when the war started I felt it was my duty to go. . . " Before he could finish Mrs. Williams called from inside the house.

"Fannie, can you come in and give me some help with the dinner?"

Fannie smiled and rose from her chair, "You'll excuse me, Mr. Beall, duty calls. . . . even for a woman."

Now with just the two of them on the porch, Martha felt suddenly awkward. "Would you . . . like to go for a walk, Mr. Beall?" asked Martha.

"Please, call me John," he said, "and yes, I would like to walk for a while."

They walked down the lane toward the road. "The island's not very big," she said, " just this plantation and some other land owned by a businessman from Pascagoula. He has land here, but he doesn't farm it."

Martha made small talk, Beall said little. He listened and took in the scenery. Trees lined the road at intervals that must have been planned, cotton fields on both sides. They stopped along the road under the shade of an old willow tree. He needed to rest, his chest ached, but he said nothing of it.

"You seem very quiet. I've been doing all the talking, Mr. Beall. Tell me something about yourself," she said.

"Not much to tell, really. I was just thinking about my mother and sisters. You and Fannie are really fortunate to be far away from the fighting. And that's as it should be. My family is right in the thick of it. Charles Town is right at the northern end of the Shenandoah Valley, where the Union army invaded, and where I was shot. They want the valley because of its farm lands. Our farms will probably feed the Confederate Army . . . if we can hold on to them. But I'm more worried my family. I've heard so many horrible stories of what the Federals do to the women when they take over the land."

"I can imagine how you must feel. George and Joseph are still in Nashville. I worry that they'll be killed, and what will happen to their business, but I'm sure those stories can't all be true. There are good and reasonable men on both sides. War can't make villains of them all. Stories like those tend to be exaggerated, too, don't you think?" she offered.

"I would hope so, but it doesn't make it any easier when I'm so far away and really don't know. I've tried to write, but the mail takes so long, and you never know if it's going to get there at all."

Martha watched him as he talked. He seemed so kind, so caring. She felt as if they had not met recently, but that she had known him for a very long time. He was so was easy to be with. They were very much the same in many ways, she thought. Like herself, he was very reserved on the outside, not one to confide in others easily about the things he cared most about. Yet, she could sense the intensity of his emotions. He cares deeply about everything, his family, his friends, but he is so guarded with what he says. Martha felt she was much the same.

"Where did you attend college?" she asked.

"I graduated from the University of Virginia with a degree in law." he said. "I don't think I'll ever use it. I really don't want to be a lawyer, it just seemed the gentlemanly thing to do at the time."

"Well," she laughed, "if I was the judge, you'd win every case that came to my court."

"Thank you," he smiled back, "I'll try to remember that."

They turned back toward the house, dinner would certainly be almost ready by now.

Two weeks passed from the time Beall arrived, and in that time Martha, Fannie and John took long carriage rides around the island, walked the beach, sat on the porch and talked, and attended several social affairs held by the Williams's. Both Fannie and Martha grew to admire and like Beall, but in different ways. Fannie was destined to be a spinster school teacher, she knew it. There was just no strong urge for a man in her life. Her work was enough, she thought. Or was it that the right man had just not come along? John Beall was a good man, a kind man. Yet, as much as she liked him, she could see something blossoming between him and Martha. At first it was the tone of Martha's voice when she spoke to him. Then it was the look in her eyes when she saw him. It was not difficult for Fannie to see what was happening, and she would not get in the way of it.

Martha had never had these feelings before. Now here was this man who had come into her life, well educated, deeply religious, caring and intelligent. Not like so many she knew in Nashville. They all seemed so shallow by comparison, more concerned about their position in society and the things they could accumulate. None of them could quote poems from memory, or speak in Latin, as he could. None of them could express the deep philosophical thoughts he did. None of them shared the commitment to life and helping others as he did. She saw in him what she saw in no other. John Yates Beall was like none of them to her. Long before anyone else noticed, she had made her decision. She would marry this man. Maybe not now. Perhaps after the war was over. But she knew that their fates were sealed together. That no matter what happened, they would be together always. And once Martha O'Bryan made up her mind . . .

John Beall was a man of quiet reserve, seldom letting his feelings show. He smiled when others laughed. He was somber when others cried. His innermost thoughts were only his. Until now. Martha was awakening something inside him he had not experienced before, something unsettling and new. Martha was bright and committed to her work. She cared about others, and he admired that. She jabbered on about anything and everything. He listened and enjoyed it. Martha was one to take life as a bull by the horns, seize it and make it do what she wanted. He was more apt to accept what happened and deal with life as it came. While they were different in many ways those differences seemed to compliment their relationship. A relationship that for him deepened as the days went on.

As days turned into weeks the sisters and John spent hours talking about their interests, values, and future plans. Fannie could see what was happening, and she found other things to do. She spent more and more time with Mrs. Williams, leaving Martha and John to themselves.

The couple had become accustomed to taking walks in the evening after dinner. It was on one of these walks that Martha decided to bring up something that had been on her mind for some time.

"John, do you believe in predestination?" she put her hand on his arm.

"Predestination? Why do you ask that?" he responded, amused.

"Well, I'm a Presbyterian, and we Presbyterians believe that in some sense our lives are predestined before we are born. That what happens to us happens for a reason, that it is part of a divine plan. Do you think that's true?" she asked.

"I never was very religious, at least not until the last few years. I'd never really given much thought to church philosophy. It seemed enough just to live a good life. When my father died something changed in me. I don't know exactly how to explain it. I had this need to really understand what was becoming of my life, why things were happening to me. That's when I began to study the faith. I'm a member of the Episcopal Church, and while I was always active in the church and its community activities, I never put much thought into its philosophy. At one time I thought each of us, by our own actions here on earth, made our own destinies. Yet, when I consider all that has happened to me, I must admit that most are things I did not, or would not have chosen myself. I suppose that predestination could explain it," he said.

"Well, I was just thinking that when you were shot, it might have been preordained. That you would have to come south to recover, and that we would meet."

In affairs of the heart, Martha saw that she would have to take the lead. John was much too shy to bring up the subject of romance. She took his hands in hers and looked into his eyes. "John, I believe we were destined to meet. I believe that there is a plan at work that says we are destined to be together." She touched his cheek and kissed him. It was just a brief kiss, a tentative kiss. She did not know what to expect.

"Miss O'Bryan!" he said in feigned surprise at such a romantic gesture, "You are a very forward young lady." She laughed at his sense of humor. He kissed her back, slowly, and looked into her eyes, "The truth is," he grinned, "I think I've fallen in love with you. I just wasn't sure how you really felt about me." He pulled her to him slowly, gently, and whispered, "I don't know if there is a divine plan for us or not, but I choose to make one with you if you'll have me."

She did not hesitate, "Yes, John, I love you, too. I'd be happy to make a plan for our lives with you."

They held each other for a long time without speaking. Each one knew the reality of their situation. He would have to return to the war soon, and she would go north, back to Nashville, back to her teaching. They would have to correspond as best they could now, and when the war was over they would be married. Their plans were announced at dinner that night, really to no one's surprise. For the next few months, Martha made wedding plans, and John grew stronger and stronger.

By April of 1862 John Beall had recovered sufficiently to make plans for his return to the war. He was anxious to get back, but at the same time, hated leaving Martha. Word had reached them that Joe Johnson's army had pulled back from Manassas in March and had moved south toward Richmond. The Union Army under McClellan had come down the Chesapeake to Fort Monroe and Newport News. It looked like he was preparing to advance on the Confederate capitol just seventy miles away. Richmond, Virginia, would be Beall's destination. He knew that at some time while he was gone, Martha would consider returning to Nashville, so he proposed an alternative, one that he felt was safe.

"Martha," he said one evening, "what would you think of getting married right now, and then you going to England until the war is over? I have cousins there, the Algionbys, who would be more than happy to have you stay with them. I'd feel better knowing that you were safe there. It's just a matter of time until the Yankees come here."

Her heart jumped at the chance to marry John now, but she knew it was not the right time. "John, I love you very much, but I don't want to get married and then have to see you off to war. If you want to marry me now, then I want you to come to England with me as my husband." She knew without his saying what his answer would be. His commitment was too deep. He would never go to England and turn his back on Virginia or his family.

"You know I can't do that. I have to return. I couldn't live with my conscience the rest of my life if I believed I had avoided my duty to my country."

" I know that," she lowered her eyes, "But you see, that is exactly why I have to stay here, too. There are people in Nashville who need me, and as soon as it's safe to go back, I will return. That's my duty, John."

He squeezed her hand and said nothing. He knew her too well to argue. Her own commitment was as strong as his. They would both do what they had to do.

"When you get back to Richmond, what will you do, John?" Martha asked.

"I'm not sure. I'll have to see some people there and find out what I can do to help. If I can, I'll try to rejoin General Jackson." he said.

"Is there some way I can know what you're doing?" she asked.

"I'll write through friends, and if I can, I'll let you know where I'll be." He gave her the address of his mother's home at Walnut Grove and that of his friend Dan Lucas' law office in Richmond. "One of them should know my whereabouts."

"John, I just don't know what I'd do if anything happened to you. But I want you to know that I will always love you." She pulled him to her and held him for a long time. He did not see the tears, but knew they were there.

"You're a very strong woman, Martha O'Bryan," he whispered

hoarsely, "and I know that whatever happens, you will prevail. Try not to worry."

"How can I not worry," she cried, "If I ever lost you, I just know there could never be another man for me. You are my destiny. . . . remember?"

They walked to the carriage arm in arm. He turned to Martha and reassured, "It won't be long until we see each other again. This war can't last much longer." He embraced her again, kissed her, and then was gone. She watched as the carriage disappeared down the lane. Then she cried. It would be two years until she saw him again.

On his way north toward Richmond, Beall heard that Jackson's army had defeated Banks and was pursuing him up the Shenandoah Valley toward Jefferson County. Beall rode desperately to catch up to Jackson and rejoin the army.

Arriving in Mansfield, Virginia, he learned that Jackson's army was up near Kernstown and Winchester. The next morning the sky was gray and overcast. By nine o'clock the heat was already stifling. The rains came early that evening, but he pushed on. Finally, as night came, torrential rain began to fall. He stopped in front of a small house and asked for shelter.

The following day he rode into the rural village of Newton and found it full of Federal troops. Held up by swollen rivers too deep to ford, they milled around and looked for ways to make trouble for local folk.If I turn around now, and they see me, he thought, I'll be arrested for sure. So he took a chance. Beall calmly rode into a barnyard and busied himself tending to the cattle. Some soldiers had seen him, and rode through the gate into the barnyard like they owned it. The sergeant, grimy-faced and naturally suspicious of all Southerners, wove his horse between the cattle and asked Beall questions as he fed and watered the stock.

"Mornin'," said the trail-worn sergeant. "We hear ol' Jackson's army has been seen in these parts. You seen any of 'em?" He fully expected this man to deny it even if he had. It just wouldn't hurt to push him a bit, and what else was there to do right now anyway?

"No, sir," answered Beall as he led a cow to the trough. "Would you mind closing that gate so the cattle don't wander out?"

The sergeant nodded to a private who moved to close the gate.

"You live here?" he asked.

"Yes, I do," Beall answered wearily, "Would I be walkin' around in the mud tendin' someone else's cattle?"

The sergeant spat tobacco juice into the mud and shook his head, "No, I reckon not."

Beall continued working with the cattle. The sergeant eyed him suspiciously. "Tell me somethin' friend. Why is it a strappin' young man like yourself ain't in the army?"

Beall pulled open his shirt and showed the sergeant the hole in his chest. " I got myself shot over near Harper's Ferry a while back. Doctors discharged me as they thought I might die of the wound. Haven't fully recovered enough to rejoin." He smartly did not say what side he had been on, and the sergeant was either too dumb to ask or so taken aback by the wound that he neglected to do so.

"Well, I'm right sorry to hear that, sir," said the sergeant, taking on an air of new respect. He looked up the road and saw that the men near the river were beginning to move. "Well, I'd best be movin' on down the road. Good day to you, sir."

The Union soldiers moved out of the yard and headed back down the road toward the river. As they did, the owner of the cattle cautiously came out the front door of the house. His wife, shaken by the confrontation, stood at a safe distance behind him, still fearful that the soldiers would return. They had seen and heard it all through an open window.

Beall extended his hand to the man and said, "I'm John Beall. I'm sorry for the intrusion onto your property. I just didn't know what to do when I saw those Union soldiers. I thought I might get arrested if I tried to double back, so I just acted like I belonged here."

The man took Beall's hand and shook it vigorously. "You cause me no trouble at all." Both men knew that was a lie. If those soldiers had found out that Beall was a Confederate soldier, or that the man and his wife might have been inclined to help him, they might have very well have all been shot right there in the barnyard.

"These damned Federals have been up and down this road for two days. They'll steal anything that ain't tied down. Where you headed for, Mr. Beall?"

"I'm trying to catch up to the Stonewall Brigade and got held up by the rain."

"Well, is there anything we can do to help?" the man asked.

"Yes, there is. I'd like to leave some things with you if you don't mind. Just some personal papers and identification. If I get caught with these I'll surely be arrested before I can get to Jackson's army. When you can, would you mail the papers to my mother in Charles Town?"

"Of course, I'll see that they are mailed out as soon as possible," said the man. That being done, the couple wished him well and he set out east in the direction of the Potomac River.

Heavy rains fell again that night forcing Beall to stop at the home of Mr. Nathan Lewis. Lewis, a widower, welcomed Beall in as he would any stranger on a rainy night such as this. Lewis was a talker and was glad for the company. He spent several hours and a pint of whiskey catching Beall up on the events in that part of Virginia.

The next day Beall found a place to cross the river, and headed for Back Creek Valley in Berkeley County. There he stayed at the home of a family friend, Mr. Griffiths, who advised him to cross the Potomac River as soon as possible. Union troops had been seen all over the valley. The next morning Beall tried to recross the river, but it had become so deep it was impossible. Riding up river, he eventually found a ferry and took it across. Beall rode on a few more miles in heavy rain, but it got so bad he had to stop overnight and dry his clothes. The next day, wearing his still damp clothing, he moved on until dark. At a boarding establishment called the Six Mile House he took a room for the night. There over supper he heard the details of General Banks' retreat.

Several days later, and completely exhausted, Beall arrived in Uniontown, Maryland. It was here he decided there was no hope of catching up with the army. Yet he knew that if he returned home he was sure to be arrested. The entire area around Charles Town and Harper's Ferry was in Union hands. There appeared no way to get home safely. Beall decided the only course of action left for him was to head west, first to Chicago, and then to his brother Hezekiah's place in Iowa. There he could rest and regain his strength. There he could decide what to do next. Beall sold his horse and bought a train ticket.

By the time Beall's train arrived in Cascade, Iowa, he heard news that the heavy rains he had ridden through in Virginia had slowed McClellan's advance on Richmond. Several battles had been fought in the vicinity of Richmond throughout June, but the city still held. With the help of his brother, Hezekiah, Beall secured a job running a grain mill using the name John Yates. There he worked from mid July until September of 1862. He read the news reports of Stonewall Jackson's victory at Cedar Mountain, and how Lee had repulsed the Union army, pushing it from the gates of Richmond to quite near the Union capitol itself. There was great fear among many Northerners of a Confederate victory. Stories were also running rampant in the North about Confederate spies and infiltrators. Most were untrue, but plausible in the minds of uneasy civilians. Any strangers or newcomers in the area became automatically suspect. It was only a matter of time until they got around to asking questions about Mr. Yates.

When rumors about Beall's own real identity finally surfaced, he said goodbye to Hezekiah, and fled to Canada. He settled in at Riley's Hotel in Dundas, in the province of Ontario. There Beall met other Confederates, mostly men who had escaped Northern military prisons. These men, many barely out of their teens, talked at great length about the terrible conditions they had had to endure before escaping from Federal prisons, starvation diets, cruel beatings for even the most minor infractions, and rampant disease brought on by the poor sanitary conditions that no human being, be he a Northerner or Southerner, should be made to suffer. It was here that Beall first conceived the idea of helping to break Confederates out of the Federal prison camps, and over a period of several months matured several ideas on how to accomplish his plan.

The Canadian papers had for many months been full of stories and discussion about the possible intervention by both England and France on the side of the Confederacy. In 1861 Confederate commissioners to England had already secured legal recognition of the Confederacy as a nation at war. That gave them the right as a belligerent nation to finance and arm privateers who could legally attack Union vessels and confiscate their cargoes. It was a bold move, but it was a time for bold moves. The Confederacy was very short on supplies. The blockade of Southern ports ordered by Lincoln had all but shut down foreign trade in the South. But by early 1863 the politics of war had changed. The papers were reporting that England had decided it would be more prudent to stay out of the war, fearing a direct confrontation with the United States government. If England was out, so was France. The

Confederacy broke off diplomatic ties with England. It was time for more drastic action.

By January 5, 1863, Beall's plan to help Southern prisoners escape was fully conceived in his own mind, and he prepared to travel back to Richmond to seek the backing of the government. He traveled south by train through Ohio, hoping to break through the Union lines into Kentucky at Cincinnati, but that was not possible. John Hunt Morgan had played so much havoc with his raids on both railroads and communications, it was not possible for Beall to get through. Union troops were swarming throughout the area. His next thought was to head for Western Virginia, but no steamboats were available. General Rosencranz's army had seized them all. Finally, he took a chance on a train to Baltimore. From there he got a ride in a small boat to Virginia and arrived in Richmond on the last day of February.

In Richmond Beall met with an old school friend, Colonel Edwin Gray Lee. Lee was a cousin to both Robert E. Lee, and Daniel B. Lucas, Beall's oldest friend. Colonel Lee had served under Stonewall Jackson and had been in command of the Thirty-third Virginia Infantry, but had been forced to resign when he developed tuberculosis in December of 1862. His fragile health, like Beall's, would not allow him to return to regular service, but he wanted to continue to fight in any way possible to him. Together they wrote down Beall's proposal and two others. Then, they contacted Dan Lucas, now a prominent Richmond attorney and friend of the President's, to arrange a meeting with Jefferson Davis.

The first part of their plan advocated privateering on the Great Lakes and levying contributions on the lake-shore cities. They also proposed a privateer action on the Potomac River and Chesapeake Bay with the intent of interfering with Union supply shipments, but most significant was Beall's suggestion about an attack on Johnson's Island to rescue approximately two thousand Southern officers held there. The Union government had discontinued prisoner exchanges. Hundreds of Confederate parolees sworn to go home and fight no more were being recaptured in subsequent battles. The Union government had lost its patience with prisoner exchanges, and seeing no good coming of them, had decided to discontinue the practice. Toronto newspapers had reported that Union prisons held thousands of Confederates who could no longer contribute to the war effort. At Johnson's Island alone there were two to three thousand prisoners, almost all of officer rank, at any given time, who were needed by the Southern Army, now sorely lacking in quality leadership.

Beall and Lee sat with the President for almost an hour discussing the proposed plans. Beall felt they were all worthy plans, but favored the Johnson's Island plan the most. He pushed it as much as he could as the one to be primarily considered.

"Mr. President, I believe that a secretly commissioned, armed and manned privateer could cruise the Great Lakes, and launch attacks on lake shore cities from Chicago to Detroit. In a surprise attack it could also overtake the *U.S.S. Michigan*, release the prisoners, and then attack cities from Toledo to Buffalo." said Beall. Beall spoke what everyone knew. "The only reason this war is dragging on so long is that the Yankees are untouched by the war. Let us give them a taste of what war is really like, and we'll soon see them begging for a settlement."

President Jefferson Davis, a graduate of West Point, but not known to be a great military thinker, listened to the plan with interest and said, "This sounds like a good plan, but I must refer it to Stephen Mallory, Secretary of the Navy. I will approve the plan only based on his recommendation. Let me speak to Secretary Mallory on this and my office will be in contact with you, probably within a few days. Let my secretary know where you two will be staying in Richmond and you will be contacted about a meeting with Mallory."

Beall and Lee left the meeting with feelings mixed between optimism and frustration. Davis had listened patiently to their proposals with some interest. Yet he asked few questions, almost as if he were tolerating them out of courtesy, but cared little for their ideas. On the other hand, they reasoned, he might not have wanted to get our hopes up, only to be dashed later. Both men had seen that the war was ruled by politics, and Davis, above all else was a politician. The political implications of their plans would have to be carefully considered. Lee understood that, but Beall argued that wars fought on the basis of politics are wars lost. Action is what won wars.

Two days later they had their answer. A messenger from Secretary Mallory's office summoned them to a meeting that afternoon at two o'clock. They arrived promptly and were received into Mallory's office exactly at two. Mallory observed the expected pleasantries and recited an overview of the plan to attack Johnson's Island, given him by President Davis. Was this an accurate account of their plan? he inquired. They affirmed it was. The Secretary silently perused the outline one more time, and peered over the top of his spectacles at the two young men, who sat on the opposite side of his massive desk. Instead of speaking, he went back to the outline for more study. Both men felt the hollows of their stomachs tighten. Did he like the plans or not? They could not tell. Finally, Mallory spoke.

"Your plan for the Great Lakes looks possible, but I am afraid that if we try it, our political relationship with England will be more injured than it already is. Until now England has been officially neutral, and while they have supported the South's cause, it has become very clear to us that England does not want to be put in a position where they would be seen as openly hostile to the United States. Any actions we might take in Canada could be interpreted by Washington as hostile action on the part of the British." Mallory paused and lit a cigar, "Do you have any other plans in mind?"

"Yes," said Beall. He was clearly disappointed at the defeat of his primary plan, but undaunted. "We've also been thinking of establishing a privateer on the Potomac River and Chesapeake Bay."

"With a few boats and some men, we could attack Union shipping and retrieve their cargoes for our government," said Lee.

Mallory rose from his desk and moved about the office puffing on his cigar. He was thinking that for now, this was the more prudent plan. He returned to his desk and butted out his cigar. After what seemed to be a long and silent few minutes, Mallory spoke with deep concern and deliberation.

"Let me just say, gentlemen, that if you choose to undertake this privateer, the government will not be able to offer much in the way of supplies or pay you a salary, but if you can procure some boats, we can give a very limited supply of money to get started, and you can keep a share of the spoils for your own uses and operation. I would be prepared to grant you both commissions as Acting Masters in the

Confederate Navy."

Beall and Lee agreed. Finally, some action. Mallory ordered the paperwork completed. As the two young men got up to leave, anxious to get started, Mallory spoke again.

"Gentlemen, don't get me wrong, now. I do like your plan for the lakes, and if at any time in the future our government would feel that it could put that plan into effect, I will see to it that you men will be assigned a part in it."

3

Privateers on the Chesapeake

Beall and Lee quickly set about the task of assembling a group of privateers. It wasn't hard to do. Richmond had many men who wanted desperately to serve. Some had been wounded, and had not been able to return to their units. Some were young and had not yet been called to serve in the army. Most were more than anxious when word was put out that a privateer was being organized. Two of Beall and Lee's first recruits were immigrant Scotsmen, Bennet Graham Burley and John Maxwell. They had been recommended to Beall through John Brooke, who had heard of their efforts through War Department channels. Burley, age twenty-two, was an adventurer at heart, and the lure of the present war in America had been too much to resist. Short and of dark complexion, Burley was the barrel-chested son of a Scottish master mechanic. John Maxwell, in contrast to Burley, was well over six feet tall with blonde hair, and very fair of face. In kilts he would have been the epitome of a highland Scot. The two men had made their way from Scotland to New York, and then had run the blockade to the Confederate capitol of Richmond. Burley carried with him the plans for a new type of bomb invented by his father. Neither felt dedicated to the Southern cause. It was a lark, high adventure, something more exciting than toiling away their young lives in a small Scottish factory.

Bennet Burley carried with him the plans for a new kind of bomb, invented by his father, Robert. It was a bomb that could be attached to the wooden hull of an enemy ship. Burley's father had served in the military in England, and become enamored with the arts of war. After his duty was concluded, he continued his interest in war-like gadgets by inventing a device he called a torpedo. Never having been able to try it out under war-time conditions, and not being able to talk Bennet out of going to America, he gave his son the plans, just in case the occasion might arise where the bomb would be useful.

First believing Burley and Maxwell to be spies, Confederate authorities had arrested and jailed them at Castle Thunder, better known to its residents as the Richmond Bastille. While incarcerated there Burley tried desperately to convince officials of his sincere desire to serve the Confederate States. When finally given a chance to demonstrate the bomb with a miniature version, he got the War Department's attention.

John Brooke at the War Department was no stranger to new weapons. He was the inventor of the armor piercing Brooke gun. Without boarding a single ship, Brooke's own invention had driven back a blockading fleet, sunk the Union ship, Cumberland, and damaged a whole fleet of Union ironclads. He had heard about the prisoner's diagrams, and when he learned of Burley's stunt with the manacles, Brooke sent for him. The warden escorted Burley and his friend Maxwell into the War Department office where they met a tall, slender man in a blue Navy coat. He greeted both men cordially, but directed his interest to Burley. Brooke had no patience for small pleasantries. He had business to attend.

"Mr. Burley, my name is John Brooke. What's this about a new weapon you have? Been hearing a lot about it."

Burley produced several pieces of paper he had stuffed in his coat pocket. He handed them to Brooke, who spread the blueprints out on his desk. Minutes passed in silence as Brooke carefully studied the diagrams.

"I like your idea, Mr. Burley, but I have some serious reservations about how successful it would be in practice. How do you propose to get close enough to a ship without being detected?"

"Sir," Burley began in his most confident Scots brogue, "too blow up a ship with my torpedo, a crew of two men in a rowboat would simply paddle silently under cover of darkness near to the side of an enemy vessel. Then, one of the men, say Maxwell here, would swim to the side of the ship, screw the bomb to its hull, and swim back to the rowboat. Now the trick is to do that without allowing the fuse connecting the bomb to its detonator to get wet. Then, rowing to a safe distance, we pull the lanyard detonating the bomb." Burley smiled and raised both hands in victory.

Brooke was amused by Burley's attitude, but skeptical. He removed and polished his spectacles. "I think your chances of success are about as good as Diogenes trying to find an honest man in Washington."

Burley and Maxwell chuckled at his remark. "That may be true, sir, but we'd sure like to get the chance to try." said Burley.

"I'll give you that chance," said Brooke, "but the assignment won't be easy. The only way this bomb will be useful, you see, is to attach it to a ship at anchor, and the only place you'll find that ship is in Union territory. How do you feel about going to New York City and blowing up a Union vessel right there in the harbor?" The idea appealed to both men instantly, and they agreed.

Leaving Richmond, Burley and Maxwell sneaked across into Union territory and took a train to New York. There were plenty of ships to choose from, cargo vessels and a few war ships, but they settled on a frigate near the end of the pier. The berth was darker than most and the ship was accessible from the port side, leaving plenty of room for escape. Several blocks down the pier they rented a rowboat from a local saying they would only have it a few hours, they wanted to do a little night fishing. Burley rowed quietly in the dark, his oars muffled with rags tied around them, while Maxwell prepared the bomb. Neither spoke, fearing that their voices would carry over the water. Burley paddled slowly, making as little noise with the oars as possible. Maxwell peered at the ship through the darkness and signaled that Burley should stop...close enough. Maxwell slipped over the side into the water, one hand holding the bomb and fuse. When he reached the vessel at amidships, he screwed the bomb to the wooden hull as quickly as possible. Twice he had to stop, thinking he heard movement near him on deck. No one in sight. It was Burley who spied the sentry moving in Maxwell's direction. If he signaled he'd attract attention for sure. The sentry paused right over Maxwell's head, and then moved on. Beads of sweat popped out on Burley's forehead. Maxwell looked up one last time for movement on deck. All clear. He sidestroked back to the rowboat, one hand holding the fuse as high as he could. He was a strong swimmer, but the water was cold, and he was tiring rapidly. It was hard to keep himself above water, let alone hold the fuse up in the air. He was exhausted and his heart was pounding as he climbed back into the small boat. Burley rowed off some distance while Maxwell reeled out more fuse. One quick pull of the lanyard and the ship would blow. The men's eyes met in the darkness as Maxwell pulled the lanyard. Silence. Their hearts sank. A few drops of water must have dampened the fuse, and it refused to ignite. Too risky to try again. They got out of there as fast as they could and headed back to Richmond.

The plan for the little device had traveled all the way from Glasgow, Scotland to the War Department on the corner of 21st and Carey Street in Richmond. Now its prototype clung unexploded on the side of a ship at dock in New York harbor at the corner of Fulton and Nassau Streets. The New York *Herald's* morning headline warned, "Curious infernal machine found attached to the bottom of war steamer on the Hudson River." New York was shocked. The Union Navy was shaken. The embarrassed sentry was questioned. He reported that he thought at one point he heard oars dipping in the water near the ship that night, but he could see nothing. Were it not for a few drops of water on the fuse, the sentry would not have been alive to make that admission.

Between mid-March and the end of the month Ned Lee and John Beall met with dozens of prospective crew members. Many were rejected due to bad health. Others because either Lee or Beall sensed they might not be trusted. Nothing sure, just an instinctive reaction. There was no sense taking chances with men you had a bad feeling about, they thought. Finally, by the end of March they had whittled down the numbers to just a few good men. It was agreed that Lee, who was still ailing from his bout with tuberculosis, would stay behind in Richmond and continue to recruit more men, and Beall would lead the newly assembled crew to the Chesapeake Bay area.

On April 1, 1863, John Yates Beall, Bennet Burley, John Maxwell and seven others departed Richmond on the York River Railroad from Tunstall's Station. They left the train near White House, Virginia, and caught the Piping Tree ferry down the bay to Mathews Court House, a small community near the southern end of the Chesapeake Bay. There, a number of citizens living along Horn Harbor and Winter Harbor, who were loyal Southerners, took them into their homes. Here, over the next month, a base of operations was set up.

On June fifteenth Beall returned to Richmond to arrange for boats of cutlass class, maps of the area, and other equipment. The Confederate government, while it supported the action, supplied only arms, uniforms, equipment, and a very small amount of money for expenses. The privateers would have to supply their own boats. They received no pay, but were entitled to keep everything they captured. All the Confederate government cared about was that they harass Union shipping and reduce supplies going to the North.

In Richmond Beall was informed that his friend and commanding officer, Edwin Gray Lee, had been reactivated and returned to the cavalry, and that Beall was now to be in full command of the operation. My goal, he wrote in his diary, is to be to the waters of the Chesapeake what John Mosby had been to the Blue Ridge, Piedmont and Northern Neck.

Beall admired General John Mosby for his courageous attacks into Union territory. Mosby had struck fear into the hearts of Union citizens and army alike with his lightning strikes on communities along the border between the Union and Confederate states. Had Beall been fully supplied that might have been possible.

On July 5, 1863, Beall returned to his headquarters in Mathews County. He sent out a squad of men commanded by Roy McDonald to capture the U.S. steamer *George W. Rogers* traveling between Cherrystone and Old Point Comfort. McDonald first hit Marapamosis Island and then went on to Cherrystone. He missed the *George W. Rogers* by twenty minutes, but so as not to waste the trip, McDonald cut the underwater telegraph cable between Cherrystone and Old Point, severing communications between these two ports twenty-five miles apart. When Beall made his report of this to Secretary of the Navy, Stephen Mallory, he enclosed a small piece of the cable.

On the first of August, Beall set sail across the Chesapeake Bay to the Devil's Ditch inlet in North Hampton County, then moved south to Smith's Island to destroy the Cape Charles lighthouse. It was ten o'clock in the morning when he and his crew landed on Smith's Island.

"You men hide in those bushes. When you hear me whistle, come running."

As the men fanned out into the underbrush to wait his signal, Beall walked casually toward the lighthouse as if this was just a social visit, not business. He checked the Navy colt tucked under his coat.

The lighthouse keeper was a rough, wiry little man. Typical of those who lived in eastern Virginia, he was a Union sympathizer. He hadn't seen Beall coming and was startled.

"Who the hell are you?" he questioned Beall. "You one of those bastards whose avoidin' service or somethin'?" he said. No good reason for this stranger being here this morning. He swaggered over to Beall. "A man your age ought to be in the army fightin' Rebs," he said with fire in his voice. He'd seen men avoiding the service hiding on the island before and had given most of them a piece of his mind.

Beall took off his hat and extended his hand. "No, sir, I'm not avoiding service" he smiled broadly, "I was just passing by in my boat and saw the lighthouse. Never have been in one or seen one up close. Just thought I might take a look. Would you mind showing me how she works?"

The lighthouse keeper was still wary, but not much company ever came his way, and he was flattered by the stranger's interest. For the next half hour the two men toured the grounds and climbed to the top of the lighthouse. The old man explained the use and purpose of all the equipment, and told Beall of how the Union government stored supplies like whale oil on the island.

"Well, sir, I'm very pleased with the way you run your lighthouse. So much so, that a group of my friends in the Confederate Navy would like to see it, too." With that Beall whistled loudly and his crew rushed out of the brush and trees toward the lighthouse.

The old lighthouse keeper gasped and looked at Beall. He was shaking both out of fear and anger. With a lot less bravado than before he said, "What're ya gonna do now, ya Rebel bastard?"

While Beall held the old man, his crew smashed all the fixtures and equipment of the lighthouse, and carried off three hundred gallons of sperm whale oil. Richmond was in short supply of oil and would be happy to have it.

Beall could see the old man was terrified. "I'm not going to kill you. You don't have to be afraid of that," Beall reassured the old man, "but I want you to promise me that if I release you that you won't leave the island for twenty-four hours? Is that a promise?" Beall let go of his arm.

Terribly shaken by the frightening turn of events, the man said, "I promise. I won't leave." With oil in hand Beall's crew sailed west back across the choppy waters of the bay to Mathews. The oil and new cache of goods was soon on its way back to Richmond by wagon.

On September 1, 1863, Beall and his party of raiders readied for a return to Mathews. Now commonly referred to as Captain, out of respect, Beall still held only the rank of Acting Master. Word of Beall's action on the Chesapeake had made the rounds in quiet conversations among those in the War Department in Richmond, and some new members volunteered.

Beall had been approached in the lobby of his hotel by George Stedman, an editor at the Richmond *Enquierer*. Stedman said that he and a few of his friends had heard what Beall was doing and would like to join him. So came George Stedman, Thomas McFarland, editor of the Richmond Whig, and a nineteen-year-old boy who worked for Stedman, William W. Baker. These new recruits joined the more experienced Gabriel Edmondson, Robert Annan, Mell Stratton, Severn Churn, Michael Fitzgerald, Walter Thomas, Robert Etter, Ralph Rankin, Paul Crouch, Bennet G. Burley, and Willie Beall, John's younger brother. These men and a few others who would come and go would come to be known as Beall's Party.

By September eighteenth Beall had a plan sketched out. He divided his men into two groups. He would take half the men in his little white boat, the *Swan*. The other half would go with Roy McDonald in a black boat named the *Raven*. Beall's group consisted of McFarland, Edmondson, Willie Beall, Annan, Etter, Thomas, and Sweeney, and Burley. McDonald took Stedman, Stratton, Churn, Crouch, Rankin, Fitzgerald, Maxwell and Baker.

The two small boats set sail across the Chesapeake the night of September eighteenth and reached Devil's Ditch inlet, Northampton County, at daybreak. There they rested all day, moving on that night to Raccoon Island near Cape Charles. They avoided all contact with other vessels by sailing at night. As the two boats passed Smith's Island lighthouse the next morning, Beall pointed it out to the new men. "That's where we got all that whale oil. If I didn't have other plans, I'd make a return trip there. I'm sure we'd find more oil there."

It was just as well he didn't. John Beall had no way of knowing it, but he had already made a name for himself with the Union government in Washington, D.C. General John Adams Dix, thinking Beall's party of raiders numbered close to one hundred, had ordered a battery of artillery placed on the island to defend the lighthouse and the island's residents.

The party sailed north up the inner channel and captured a Yankee sloop, *Mary Anne*, and two fishing boats. "I think I'm a little hungry for fish. How about you boys?" Beall laughed. "Take as much fishing tackle as you need and today we'll just fish." They spent the day on the sand shoals near Cobb's Island and that evening aboard the *Mary Anne* had the best fish supper any of the men could remember.

The next two days and nights were spent sailing up the Atlantic. Clouds were rolling in swiftly from the west. By eight o'clock in the evening, stiff winds turned to gale force and the light rain became torrential. The two small boats would be no match for a storm out on the open water. It was time to look for shelter. When Beall sighted Wachapregue Inlet, he ordered the *Raven* and the *Swan* to move in that direction.

A large schooner, the *Alliance*, had been traveling from Philadelphia to Port Royal, South Carolina. It, too, had sought to find shelter and ride out the storm. When Beall spotted her, he signaled McDonald aboard the *Raven* that they would effect a capture. He signaled McDonald to approach the vessel from the starboard side. Beall would board from the port.

The seas were high and the wind punishing. Because of the storm, the *Alliance* had no hands on deck. All were asleep in their cabins. At eleven o'clock, as the McDonald maneuvered to the port side of the *Alliance*, the stormy seas threw the *Raven* against the *Alliance* and the impact dumped him into the sea.

He managed to climb back on board, but the waves had now washed the *Raven* back away from the *Alliance*. Unable to get to starboard, McDonald moved around to port side, arriving at the same time as Beall. They boarded together.

Oblivious to the attack underway, the captain and his first mate played dominoes in the captain's cabin. His crewmen were asleep in their cabin. Not able to be heard above the howling wind and pounding rain, Beall silently signaled his men forward where they captured the *Alliance's* crew. McDonald broke in the captain's cabin door. James Ireland, Captain of the *Alliance*, grabbed for his weapon, but thought better of it when he saw McDonald's cocked pistol aimed at him. An easy capture. No one resisted and no one was injured, except McDonald's pride, which was just a bit dampened.

Beall had gone into the hold to check the cargo. He told some of his crew to bring samples of everything on deck. The men brought up food, liquor, smoking and chewing tobacco, and new clothing. The men were in good spirits as the boat rocked in the storm.

"Throw out both anchors. We need to keep this ship steady," shouted Beall. Then he moved to where the goods from below were stacked. "You boys come on over here and take what you want from this, but don't get into what's still below decks. If you need something, ask me and I'll see that you get it."

No sooner had he said that when some of the men, who had already gone below, gave in to curiosity and broke open boxes that contained Cuban cigars. They each took some as they were much better than any they already had.

Beall heard about it and shouted, "You men come up on deck!"

The sheepish men trooped out of the hold and lined up against the rail of the ship.

"McDonald, search them!" Beall was usually a kind and gentle man with his crew. He had cooked for them when he saw they were too tired, and even took his turn rowing when he saw a man was too exhausted to row anymore, but he would not tolerate disobedience from his crew.

His seldom-shown temper flared. He looked each man in line over carefully. "If I find cigars or anything else on any of you, I'll personally shoot you for disobeying orders!" There was a fine line between privateering and piracy. The men needed to know that self discipline was needed. No man under his command was going to reduce his mission to simple robbery. Beall's morals dictated that you took only what you needed to survive, the rest went to the war effort. His men needed to know that, too. Baker and a few of the others had filled their pockets with the best cigars Havana had to offer. Realizing the tight spot they were in, the men crowded back to the rail as close together as they could get and emptied their pockets into the sea. Beall knew what they were doing even though he could not see their hands in the dark.

When the search produced nothing, Beall moved up close to the men and dismissed them like a father to his sons, "Men, I am going to caution you that in the future, do not disobey me." He held a cocked Navy colt in his hand. That was all the admonition the men needed. It would not happen again.

Leaving several guards aboard the *Alliance*, and with the storm having let up, the party moved on to capture three small boats that night, the *Houseman*, the *Samuel Piersall*, and the *Alexander*. Each was stripped of all its valuables and scuttled out in the Atlantic.

On September twenty-fourth the sky was clear blue and the winds were mild and warm. All hands were now backing on board the *Alliance*. They discussed the possibility of sinking her, but Beall decided he would save the *Alliance* for future use by running it up some river if they could find one that was not too closely guarded by Yankee gunboats.

"Fitzgerald, go below and bring Captain Ireland on deck," directed Beall. In a few minutes Captain Ireland appeared.

"Captain Ireland, are you thoroughly acquainted with the channel from the inlet out to the Atlantic?"

"Sir, I know every nook and cranny of this coast," Ireland responded with pride.

"Very well, Captain Ireland," said Beall. "This is a fine vessel with a most valuable cargo which our people in the South badly need. Therefore, your crew will be placed under your command, and you will please run us, as soon as possible, out into the Atlantic. I shall stand by you, and if you should allow us to run aground I shall be under the disagreeable necessity of shooting you." Ireland did not speak. "I am sure you are aware of the gravity of the situation and will not play us false."

Under other circumstances Captain Ireland would have tried something, but he could see that this was no idle threat. He had seen Beall's Navy revolver.

"Yes, sir," he nodded. Ireland called his crew on deck and after explaining the situation to them, set sail for the Atlantic.

When they reached Cobb's Island Beall sent Burley ashore to hire a pilot who knew the bay and the Pianketank River where he intended to take the *Alliance*. Next Beall announced to Ireland and his crew that he would release anyone who promised not to tell the Union authorities his whereabouts for three days. All but twelve of the crew agreed and were set free on Cobb Island. Captain Ireland, his mate, purser, and about ten others would not agree, so they remained the reluctant guests of the Beall party.

When the *Alliance* reached Cape Charles, Ireland and his crew were divided up and put aboard the *Raven* and *Swan*, who followed the *Alliance* as far as Cherrystone lighthouse. There the party divided. Beall, commanding the Alliance, headed for the Pianketank River. He wanted to sail to the northernmost point and unload the whole cargo for shipment back to Richmond.

The *Raven* and *Swan* veered off toward Horn Harbor under the command of Roy McDonald and Ed McGuire. That night a heavy storm blew up with waves so high that the *Raven* was almost upended. At times the sea half filled the boat. About halfway across the Chesapeake, Ed McGuire, who was at the helm, told the crew he didn't know if he could keep the *Raven* afloat much longer. He took off his heavy boots, anticipating having to swim for it.

The *Raven* and the *Swan* pulled as close together as possible so that if one boat were swamped, the men could board the other. Captain Ireland and the other prisoners bailed water as fast as they could, but the churning waves continued to roll over the sides of the small boat. They fought the storm all night. By sunrise the seas had calmed. Both boats had survived.

As they sailed into Horn Harbor that morning, Captain Ireland told them, "I've been on the sea for a number of years, but that was about the closest call I've ever had. A little more wind and none of us would have seen land again." No one disagreed.

Arriving at Mathews Court House, McDonald, McGuire and their crew led the prisoners up a dirt road east of Mathews to an old church. The prisoners were tied feet and hands, and secured to a large tree near the church. Two of McDonalds's men were assigned to guard them. The crew was there only a short time when they heard cannon fire coming from the direction of the Pianketank River. Everyone waited anxiously to see if Captain Beall would return. Two tense hours passed. There was some discussion of leaving the area, but McDonald held fast. They would stay and wait for Beall. A few minutes later Beall and his crew came running out of the woods beyond the church. He gathered his crew together on the steps of the old church and told them what had happened.

"As we approached the mouth of the Pianketank at Milford's Haven we could see a Federal gunboat just to the north of us. I'm not sure whether the local pilot I hired got nervous, or was just distracted by the oncoming boat, but he ran us aground. We took off several small life boats and filled them with as much cargo as we could and took it ashore. We made several trips back and forth, but the shells were falling too close for comfort, so we set fire to the *Alliance*. She burned pretty fast, right to the water line. Then we hid the goods and made for here."

"What do you think we oughta do now, Captain? The Federals can't be too far behind," said McDonald.

"You're right." Beall said. "Here is what I want you all to do. Roy, you take a few men and escort our prisoners back to Richmond. I'll get some wagons and pick up that cargo. Once I get it, we'll head back to Richmond, too. You men who are going with Captain McDonald take the *Raven* and *Swan* down to Horn Harbor and hide them near Sand Smith's house."

Ten days later both goods and prisoners were in Richmond, and the Beall party was back in Mathews ready for more action. Beall planned an extensive raid that he hoped would net them a Union gunboat. He knew that such a boat stopped at a wharf near Chesconnessex for supplies. That would be the best spot to attack.

The prisoners from the *Alliance* capture, who Beall had released on Cobb's Island, finally made it to the mainland, where they reported what had happened to Federal authorities in Drummondtown, Virginia. Headquarters in New York was cabled and General Dix was on the war-path. Captain Beall must be captured at all costs. Dix worried privately that this pirate, Beall, was making him look foolish, and God only knew that the powers that be thought Dix was old and incompetent. He had to prove them wrong or he might soon be replaced.

The military reacted quickly. Three gunboats were dispatched to the waters around Mathews and within ten days two more steamers would arrive to assist. On September twenty-fifth a Negro infantry company boarded a ship carrying some artillery and set out to search for Beall near Hog Island. By October fifth an all-out effort under the command of General Isaac J.Wistar was under way to capture Beall and his crew. That same day eight more gunboats left Yorktown accompanied by a regiment of infantry. Detachments of cavalry directly under General Wistar headed for Mathews County. He wanted to seal off all possible escape routes by land. The gunboats would prevent escape by sea. All this by orders of General John Adams Dix, commanding general of the Department of the East, based in New York City. He was frustrated and furious.

Troop movements of that size are impossible to keep quiet. Sand Smith, who had fed and hidden Beall and his crew down on the Chesapeake, got word to Beall that he'd heard that a large complement of soldiers was up the road at Colonel Tabb's home. Beall sent Edmondson up to see if it was true. Edmondson moved quickly and quietly through thickets and trees, avoiding the road, and took up a position in the tall grass. No one was there, but he thought he ought to wait and see if any troops might arrive. He took off his coat and spread it on the ground. There he lay down and soon fell asleep. It was the sound of men's voices and horses just a few feet away that woke him. Gotta get out quick, he thought. He crawled through the grass and into the woods, leaving his coat behind.

Beall had to move fast. He ordered everyone onto the *Raven* and *Swan*. Running out on the water a short distance, Beall spotted two gunboats. He knew he couldn't get past them.

"Turn the boats around and make for Sand Smith's place. We'll get rid of the boats up Horn Harbor as far as we can go."

When they got to Smith's lawn, they shoveled sand into the *Raven* and *Swan*, sinking both. As they worked, Sand Smith ran down the sloping lawn to the water's edge.

"The Yankees are over at Mr. Tabb's place and pickets are being set up at my brother Tom's gate about a half mile up the road. They got guards in three lines all along the roads between Mobjack Bay and the Pianketank River!"

The men finished sinking the boats as the sun went down, and Beall told them that they would have to get out of there that night. Beall was concerned but felt that fate guided him. He went up to the home of Thomas Smith and knocked on the back door. Thomas' daughter, Lizzie, answered the door. She was startled. " Captain Beall," she whispered, "how good to see you." She motioned toward the front of the house, "Do you know the Yankees are right out at our gate?"

"Yes, I was told that. My men will have to leave tonight, but they haven't eaten all day. Do you think you could supply us with some provisions?"

Lizzie looked around cautiously and said, "As long as the Yankees stay out at the gate and don't come any farther, you're all welcome to have supper with us. I knew you'd have to leave here, so I prepared some extra food." Word of Yankee movements spread fast and quietly among the neighbors. "You'll all need to eat before you leave." So with the Federal troops less than a quarter mile away, Beall's crew sat down to supper with the Smiths.

William W. Baker, one of the youngest of the party, wanted the men to eat as fast as they could and make a run for it. He just about choked down his sweet potato. The others were nervous too, but enjoyed both the meal and the company of good friends.

After supper Beall took McFarland aside, "Do you think you can get out there and locate the pickets without being detected?" McFarland, formerly an Indian scout, had a tread as light as a kitten. He could do it. When McFarland returned he told Beall that he had found a way out.

"You men follow McFarland one at a time. Keep in his footsteps at all times and don't make a sound, don't even whisper." After saying their goodbyes to the Smiths, the entire company followed McFarland. He would go out ahead while the rest waited. When McFarland returned he signaled for the men to follow. When they were in a safe spot, he would go out again and repeat the reconnaissance. Then again the men would follow. They discovered that the pickets were stationed about one hundred yards apart, enough room to crawl through undetected . . . if they were lucky.

Just as they crossed the first line of pickets on the road near Colonel Tabb's house, Edmondson went to Beall and insisted that he be allowed to crawl over and get the coat he left behind earlier. The coat's pockets contained some personal letters, money, and most important, his revolver. He just had to retrieve it. Beall was frustrated and anxious to put as much distance between himself and the Yankees as he could, but he consented to let Edmondson retrieve his coat. While he crawled up through the tall grass of the field near the main body of troops, the rest of Beall's men lay in a ditch, hearts pounding, as a Yankee relief guard marched by just feet away. Edmondson was soon back and the escape resumed. By daybreak they had successfully eluded three lines of Union pickets and were resting in Dragon Swamp.

The morning after Beall's escape from Mathews, General Wistar personally led a thorough search of the area around Horn Harbor. He was furious that the neighbors in the area would not help him. Two cavalrymen rode into the yard of Sand Smith. Halting at the porch, the sergeant knocked. "Is this the residence of Sand Smith?"

Smith, who first appeared at the door said, "I'm Smith, what do you want?"

"We're lookin' for a rebel name of Beall or any of his followers. You seen 'em?"

"No," Smith answered as he came out onto the porch, "And if I did I sure wouldn't tell you!" Now Smith's daughters appeared on the porch to support their father.

The sergeant spit tobacco juice on the porch floor near Smith's feet and said, "Look, Smith, my boys have seen nothing but horses for over a week. Those daughters of yours'd look mighty good to them right now, so if you know what's good for you, tell me right now what you know!"

Sand Smith did not answer. Blind rage overtook common sense. Smith was a thoughtful man, a gentle man, who had done his part for his country as best he could, and still tried to show respect to all. Now this animal threatened his own daughters with rape? This was the final straw. Without thought to consequences, he wheeled around and through the door, emerging seconds later with a double-barreled shotgun. Smith hated the idea of war and killing. He had fought his share of it as a gentleman, and thus far had hurt no man. Now the war threatened Smith's own family.

The unexpected blast of both barrels splattered the sergeant back off the porch and onto the grass. The other soldier was so shocked he couldn't react. He just stared at the dead man on the lawn. The girls, who had been standing behind Smith, now screamed as Smith moved like a man possessed toward the other soldier, trying to pull him down out of his saddle.

The rest of the Yankee squad heard the shots and rode up to see what had happened. Dismounting and seeing the dead Sergeant, several attacked Smith with their sabers, driving him to the ground. Smith was cut in several places, but not seriously. They quickly tied him up. All the while, Smith swore at the soldiers and his daughters cried for them not to hurt their father. Several of the soldiers went to the barn and pulled out Smith's buggy. Another tied Smith's arms behind his back.

"You're going to be punished for this, Mr. Smith, but we'll do it in front of the whole command," a lieutenant barked. Then Smith and the body of the Sergeant were put on the wagon and it headed down the lane to the road. Smith's daughters ran alongside the wagon, crying hysterically, and begging to say goodbye to their father, but were pushed aside by the horsemen. As Smith was ridden out of the yard the girls screamed, "No, stop, please don't take him!" Smith heard the last of their sobbing voices as the wagon left the lane onto the road. Up between Colonel Tabb's house and Mathews Court House the squad pulled up near a grove of trees.

"Park the buggy under that tree!" ordered the lieutenant. When it was done another of the soldiers fashioned a noose out of rope and tied the other end to a sturdy branch above Sand Smith's head. Smith's heart raced in his chest, his temples pounded. "Smith, people like you need to get a message. You're our message." With that the lieutenant signaled to pull the buggy forward and Sand Smith was dragged off the seat and into the air. His feet dangled just inches from the ground. He quivered for a few moments and then was still. The war was over for Sand Smith.

"We don't have time to wait and see if he's dead. Put some lead in him and let's get out of here." said the lieutenant. The entire squad drew muskets and riddled his lifeless body. Sand Smith would be a grim reminder for all to see of what happened to rebel sympathizers. They left him hanging there.

Throughout that day the Union squad moved quickly and efficiently from house to house. They seized eighty head of cattle, burned one hundred-fifty small boats, and arrested four Confederate sympathizers who they believed might know something of Captain Beall's whereabouts. The Federal army was not about to let Beall slip through their fingers, or allow those who might have helped him go unpunished.

Beall had decided to lay low in Dragon Swamp for a few days, and sat discussing plans with the others when a young man came running into his camp. "Captain Beall," the boy said breathlessly, "the Yankees came and took Sand Smith after you left yesterday. They hung him up near Colonel Tabb's place."

"Oh, my God!" Beall's mind raced, "What about the girls? How did it happen?"

The boy recounted how the Yankees came up with questions about Beall and how Smith had gone berserk when the Yankee sergeant hinted at raping the girls if he didn't tell.

Beall could not speak. He could not find the words. For the first time in this war, he fought back tears. Had this war caused everyone to go mad? Sand Smith and his family had been so good to them. The other men sat there and searched the ground in silence for answers. There were none. None that made sense of madness. This had become an inhumane war, and was making animals of men.

Vengeance is mine sayeth the Lord, he thought. Beall vowed to himself that the Yankees would feel the force of his anger...and soon!

On November tenth the Beall party sailed across the Chesapeake in two small boats and captured a schooner. His plan was to wait aboard the schooner until night and then capture the Federal gunboat lying at anchor at Chesconnessex. Yankee patrol boats seemed to be everywhere. Beall was afraid that their two small boats might attract attention. Not many boats of that size sailed out after dark. They were sure to arouse suspicion.

"Edmondson," directed Beall, "take Baker, Fitzgerald, Burley, Thomas, Churn and Crouch, and sail the boats into an inlet and hide them. Then stay there until the rest of us come for you."

Finding a large island, Edmondson pulled the boats into a cove that in the dark looked perfectly secluded. Having hidden the boats, Edmondson left Baker and Fitzgerald to stay with the boats while he and the others went onto the island to look for a place to sleep in the brush.

The next morning the sun shone brightly, and Baker and Fitzgerald woke very early. They immediately discovered what a disastrous mistake they had made. Anyone sailing into the inlet could see them perfectly. Fitzgerald warned Edmondson when he arrived minutes later.

"I think it's dangerous to leave the boats here, too, but I think there's even more danger of us being spotted if we sail to another inlet." Edmondson told Baker and Fitzgerald just to stay with the boats where they were, and he retreated back onto the island to get some more sleep with the others.

At noon that day, November eleventh, a fishing boat appeared at the mouth of the inlet. At first it just bobbed there in the water, as if wondering if it should approach and see who these strangers were, or just pass on by. It decided to investigate. Seeing the oncoming boat, Baker asked Fitzgerald, "What are we going to say?"

"Let's just say we were hunting and rested here." answered Fitzgerald.

"But what if he reports us? Maybe we should just shoot him." said Baker.

"No, the shots would attract attention. If he gets close enough we'll grab him and hold him on the boat."

The small boat sailed closer now. Baker and Fitzgerald could see a slender man in his fifties with gray hair under his weathered cap.

"Hello," he called, not getting too close. "Who are you people? What are you doing with these boats?"

It was Fitzgerald who answered, "We're part of a hunting party. Just came down from Baltimore yesterday. We're just resting here until the tide rises. Then we're going to sail up the bay and spend the night a little farther north, near where that gunboat is anchored."

"Right! Well, have a good trip," said the fisherman. He never got close enough to grab.

They watched the fishing boat glide out of the inlet and onto the bay. Baker and Fitzgerald couldn't be sure but they thought that he just went back to his fishing. They were wrong. The fisherman sailed directly to the gunboat two miles north and reported exactly what he had seen.

At about five o'clock that evening Baker and Fitzgerald anxiously watched as two large boats entered the mouth of the inlet. In just a few minutes two barges of Yankee soldiers with guns poised and ready to fire closed in on them. It was too late to act now and they both knew it.

Fitzgerald's eyes widened. "Baker, this is sure a hot thing, ain't it?" Baker didn't answer. He just stood silently frozen and watched.

The lieutenant in command had Baker and Fitzgerald brought aboard one of the barges and asked, "What command do you belong to?" Baker started to repeat the story they had told the fisherman when suddenly the lieutenant pulled out his revolver and stuck it in Baker's ear. The lieutenant looked to Fitzgerald. He didn't have to ask again.

"We're members of Captain Beall's command, sir."

"Where are the others?" demanded the lieutenant.

"They're not here." said Fitzgerald. The lieutenant cocked his pistol and looked at Fitzgerald for answers. Fitzgerald raised his palms as if to beg for the lieutenant not to shoot Baker. "Sir, I really don't know. They left us last night."

The lieutenant didn't believe him. He thought there might be more men hiding ashore in the bush. "Take some men onto the island and see if you can scare up some rabbits," said the lieutenant.

The men fanned out among the dense brush and fired into it at random. Startled by the gunfire, the men hiding in the undergrowth lit out, but were outnumbered and soon caught. Taken aboard the barges, they were transported north to the very gunboat they had hoped to capture.

Beall and his men waited. The rest of his crew was long overdue. He had no idea of what had happened to them, but didn't want to leave without them either.

"Captain Beall," asked Rankin, "don't you think we'd better get out of here? The men are gettin' edgy. The whole area is crawlin' with troops."

"Not yet, I think if we wait a bit more we'll find out what happened. I can't just leave them here," he said stubbornly. Beall knew he should leave the area. The others were overdue and he knew that there must have been trouble. His men had pushed to leave right away, but loyalty to the others was getting in the way of good sense. Now it was too late. Horses' hooves were galloping down the path. Blue uniformed Yankees were moving through the woods in his direction. Five hundred Federal troops converged on the inlet where he sat at anchor. Seeing no way out, he ordered, "Strip the vessel. Throw anything of value overboard." The men worked quickly, heaving food, guns, and supplies over into the water. When the Yankees arrived there was little of any value left on the boat. Only then did Beall surrender to the Northern troops.

Beall and his men were escorted aboard a small boat that had arrived in the inlet and all the men were shackled. Within the hour they would rendezvous with the Federal gunboat just north of where Beall and his men had been hiding. It was there that they found out what had happened to the rest of their crew. That evening they were all taken ashore and forced to march under armed guard to Drummondtown, Virginia, where they were put up for the night in the local jail.

The next day it was back onto the gunboat and up the bay. Their destination was the prison at Fort McHenry. The entire party was herded into a large cabin on the main deck. At the front of the cabin was a large door that was opened outward onto the forward deck. Two guards stood watch just outside the door, and Beall could see a stack of muskets near the guards. He watched for a while and thought about what to do. Beall wasn't about to give up easily.

"Listen," he whispered to his crew, "when I give the signal, jump the guards and get those muskets. If we act fast, we'll be able to surprise the others before they can get their weapons." Stedman and McGuire inched over toward Beall, agreeing and ready to move.

"Wait lads," said Burley, "What if it's a trap? There might be more troops than we know around. Sure, we don't even know what's on the top deck. With all due respect, Captain Beall, I just think it's too damned risky." The majority of the men shook their heads in agreement.

Beall's frustration turned to anger. "You cowardly bastards!" he snarled through clenched teeth. He could barely keep himself from shouting out loud. "Do you want to rot in prison?" Captain Beall could not accept that his men were so unwilling to take a risk for their freedom. Wasn't it a prisoner's duty to attempt escape if he could? And so the men all sat in silence, each wondering if they really should have tried it or not.

A short while later, though, they overheard several of the crew talking outside the cabin window. There was a whole company of riflemen on the upper deck waiting for Beall and his men to make a move for the muskets. That would have saved the government the time and expense of a trial. Beall, now realizing the reality of their situation, quietly apologized to the crew, patting Burley warmly on the back for saving their lives. "That's alright, boyo," Burley said. "Sometimes discretion really is the better part of valor."

4

Criminals or Prisoners of War?

Fort McHenry stood guard over Baltimore's inner harbor. Built in 1798, it had survived a twenty-five hour bombardment by the British in the War of 1812, and its flag, still flying, inspired Francis Scott Key to pen the words to a poem that would later become the country's national anthem. By all Union accounts, it was about to receive some of the most notorious pirates the Chesapeake Bay had ever seen.

Beall and his crew arrived at Fort McHenry very late the night of November 12, 1863. The following morning they were herded in chains to a one-story building that had been converted from a horse barn into a prison where, for the most part, deserters from the Union army were kept. It also housed the office of the Provost Marshal. It was there that the processing began.

Names and ranks were duly recorded. The Provost then addressed the men. "You prisoners should know that by orders of General Lockwood, you are all to be placed in irons and put into solitary confinement." He nodded to the guard to take them away. To Beall this meant only one thing. They were to be treated as pirates and criminals, not prisoners of war. He protested.

"But we are soldiers of the Confederate States!" protested Beall angrily. "These men are to be treated as prisoners of war, not pirates! Who the hell do you and your cohorts think you are? There are laws of war, and we ought to be treated as prisoners under those laws!"

The Provost might have reacted harshly toward a prisoner so outspoken, but he privately agreed. Looking up at Beall from his desk, "I'm sorry, Captain Beall, this is just as disagreeable to me as it is to you, but until I have orders to treat you otherwise, this is the way it will have to be. General Lockwood's orders."

Beall was furious. "Would it be too much to ask for writing materials so that I may inform my superiors in Richmond what a travesty of justice is being performed here?"

"Of course, Captain, you can write your letter. Sergeant, see that Captain Beall gets what he needs to write a letter, and when he's ready, make arrangements to see that it's delivered."

The sergeant led the men back to their quarters. They had only been there a few minutes when the sergeant returned and gave Beall pencil and paper. The sergeant looked over at little William Baker, one of Beall's men, with a sly look, "You," indicating the boyish young soldier. "Some of the men out there want to initiate you into the mysteries of prison life. Come with me." Baker nor any of the others knew what to expect and the sergeant could see that in Baker's eyes. "Look, don't make any resistance, or they'll go through your pockets and steal that ring right off your finger. If you don't resist, they won't have an excuse to rob you."

Out in the prison yard Baker saw about twenty-five Union convicts. A few of them were holding a blanket stretched out between them like a fireman's net. "Hey, lil' rebel boy, jump up on this here blanket," one said.

Very wary about what was to happen, Baker jumped up onto the blanket.

"Hip..hip..hurrah! Hip..hip..hurrah! Hip..hip..hurrah!" Three times Baker was thrown into the air and caught in the blanket. "You're a good sport, sonny! That's all you get for now," laughed one of the men. The next young man they chose was not so sporting, and he was robbed of all his pocket money and tobacco. It was an introductory lesson to prison life. Go along and you'll get along. Buck the system and it bucked you back.

On November sixteenth, Beall and his men were lined up and taken from their cell and led out across the yard of the fort to a room near the horse stable. A guard working there shackled Captain Beall, Ed McGuire, and Bennet Burley with irons on both their wrists and ankles. When he came to Crouch, Thomas and Baker, he looked them over and hesitated, "These men's boots are too heavy for the shackles, sir," said the guard to the sergeant.

"Alright then, you three stand aside for a few minutes and we'll take care of these other gentlemen." said the sergeant. The three were privately congratulating themselves for their wise choice of footwear until the officer in charge said, "Sergeant, take these three men over to the blacksmith's shop and have a ball and chain riveted on each one."

The three followed the sergeant out into the yard where the he ordered each of them to pick up a sixty-pound cannon ball with a two-foot chain attached. Baker, by far the smallest of the three, shouldered his ball and almost collapsed by the time they got to the blacksmith shop. While the smithy worked on Crouch and the sergeant watched, Baker slipped his ball under a workbench and picked up a twenty-five pounder with a six-foot chain. When the smithy turned to Baker, Baker said with his best smile, "Put this one on me."

The smith looked at the ball and looked at Baker and said, "Well, since you're the smallest of the lot I'll do that for you." Then he pulled out the big ball with the two- foot chain and riveted it onto Thomas' leg. From that day on every time the men had to move somewhere, Baker would throw his ball over his shoulder and walk, but Thomas had to tie a leather thong to his chain and drag the ball across the floor. They were an odd-looking trio, Baker and Thomas side by side, and Crouch following close behind.

Once all the men were shackled and ironed, they were taken back across the yard and locked up in the cell they shared with an odd assortment of Union deserters. Captain Beall, Lieutenant McGuire, Stedman and McFarland were confined in the attic of the building above the cells, isolated from the general prison population.

The prisoners had been in irons for only a few days when it was discovered that Gabriel Edmondson had learned from a Yankee convict how to carve a key that would open his shackles. It wasn't long before all the men would remove their shackles at night and then put them back on before the sergeant's morning inspection.

The prison was segregated into sections, each holding prisoners who had committed similar acts. One section held Union deserters, a second, criminals, and two others held Confederates. Edmondson noticed that the guards would often let prisoners from the one of the other sections of the prison, who were supposed to be lounging in the exercise yard, come into the cells of the Confederates to visit their friends during the day, and then they would let them out in the evening to go back to their own accommodations. Union or Confederate, it made no difference. They were all prisoners and many on opposite sides made fast friendships. This was strictly against the rules, but for a plug of tobacco or a dollar...just about anything could be done.

Without a word to anyone but Crouch about what he was planning, Edmondson, who wore civilian clothing, rushed up to the guarded door and shouted, "Hey, aren't you going to let me out?"

The guard asked," Who are you?"

"I'm a member of the Twenty-seventh New York. You let me in a while ago to see one of my friends. If you don't hurry up and let me out, I'm going to report you to the provost for letting me in!"

With this the guard opened the door, grabbed Edmondson by the collar and threw him into the yard saying, "Don't come in here again." Edmondson was escorted across the exercise yard under a dark moonless sky, to a large wood-frame building. He was taken into a long rectangular room that held about fifty Union prisoners. There were two guards at the door and none anywhere else, including inside, that he could detect. While the Union prisoners entertained themselves by singing and dancing, Edmondson had escape on his mind. While the guards were distracted by the singing and dancing prisoners, he climbed out a window and crawled through tall grass down toward Baltimore Bay, thinking he would make his escape by scaling the fort wall and swimming across the bay toward Catonsville, or running off toward Baltimore. Just as he got near the wall, a guard approached, thinking he heard something in the dark.

"Who comes there?" he yelled. Edmondson froze. He could see the guard and his rifle on the hill just a few feet above him.

The night was pitch black, and as Edmondson lay unseen in the tall grass, he began to snort and grunt like a hog. It was one of his many talents, used mostly to entertain his friends. The guard, satisfied it was one of the many hogs kept at the fort, backed off and returned to his station. Edmondson resumed his crawl on hands and knees toward the wall of the fort. The wall extended a hundred feet in both directions.

If he could scale the wall when the guards were at opposite ends, they might not be able to see him in the dark. He watched the guards on the top of the wall walk toward each other, meet for a few words, and then about face to the extreme ends of the wall. When they were almost to the far ends, he made a fast jump for the top of the wall, pulled himself up by his fingertips, digging his toes into the rough stone jutting out of the wall, and crawled over. Neither guard saw him. Now what to do? He felt the water. Too cold for a swim tonight, he thought. Edmondson made for Baltimore on foot as fast as he could. He could get help in Baltimore. Half the city was made up of Confederate sympathizers. He could hide there if he needed, and then head for Frederick, Maryland when it was safe to travel.

Sunday night was church going night in Baltimore, and Edmondson arrived just as church was letting out. He lost himself in the streets full of people heading home after worship, and made his way across town. No sign of any army patrols looking for him. Surely by now they must know he was gone. Edmondson headed for Frederick, Maryland. He had friends there and they would surely help him with food and a railroad ticket to Richmond.

The next morning a sergeant came in to call the roll. When he got to "G. Edmondson," Willy Baker tried to cover for him by answering, "Here." The sergeant looked over to where Baker was standing and looked him in the eye. He called the name again, "G. Edmondson?" Baker now could not respond. Then all hell broke loose. The sergeant pushed his way past each man, "Where's Edmondson? he demanded. "Where'd he go?" He grabbed young Baker and shoved him against the wall. "Where is he, you little bastard?" Baker was shaken, but just stood by the wall collecting himself. He kept his mouth shut. Damned if he'd be the one to tell.

The sergeant stormed out and in just a few minutes was back. "All of you are to follow me to the provost's office." One by one the men filed out of the cell, Baker, Crouch and Thomas taking up the rear, each lugging their personal ball and chain.

The provost questioned each man separately in an adjoining room. As each one waited his turn at interrogation he had to decide whether to tell or not. Crouch and Annan refused even to answer questions.

They would not utter a word. Whether or not they knew anything that would have been of help or not, they simply refused to talk at all. For their stubbornness, the sergeant decided that he would beat a confession out of them. Each man was bound to a chair and gagged. Annan would be first. He could barely breathe. The cloth used to gag him was tied tightly through his open mouth. His tongue tasted the dry fabric and it choked him.

The sergeant assigned to administer the beating walked slowly around the chair, "Alright, Mr. Annan, you need to tell us, and quickly, where Edmondson went." Now he was behind Annan. Whack. Annan reeled. The sergeant had struck him on the back of the head with the heavy stick he carried. Annan felt the blow. His head was cut open, and he could feel the blood begin to trickle down the back of his neck. "Come on, now, Annan. You can tell me," said the sergeant sweetly. Annan saw the gloved right hand coming and tried to move his head. The blow caught him over his right eye. "Damn you, sit still!" shouted the sergeant. "The quicker you tell me what I want to know, the sooner this little lesson will be over!" Another crack to the face. Right in the teeth. Annan could feel his eye swelling shut and tasted the blood in his mouth. He gagged and coughed. The sergeant didn't waste any time. The next blow was to his body. A sharp blow to Annan's midsection. He closed his eyes and gasped. Ribs had to be broken. Annan gasped for breath, but before he could get any, another blow fell. Same place. The sergeant laughed, "You think you're pretty tough, don't you. Just tell me where Edmondson went and I'll let you go!" This time the blow came from the left. Annan hadn't seen it coming and it caught his ear full force. Everything seemed to echo. He swooned, almost passing out. If only I would, thought Annan. How long will he keep this up? Crouch sat in the other chair, watching silently and waiting his turn. He hoped he could keep his mouth shut under such a beating, and vowed to himself he would say nothing. For fifteen minutes the sergeant continued to pound Annan alternately with questions and punches. He switched off between his fists and his stick. When he finally decided that Annan probably didn't know anything, he untied him and hoisted him up from the chair, and pushed him off into a corner of the room, the gag still in place. "Mr. Annan, you're one stubborn man. Just sit there, now, while I question your friend."

Crouch was next. He sat, tied and gagged, and suffered twenty minutes of the same punishing blows as Annan. He would not say a word. After suffering long and still not confessing to anything, it was decided that they probably didn't know anything, and they were released. Both men were swollen and bruised. Annan could barely walk. The pain in his ribs was excruciating. The sergeant seemed pleased with the results of his work even if they hadn't talked.

Within hours General Lockwood heard the report of the escape. He ordered all of Beall's crew, McGuire, Stedman and McFarland and the rest, to be separated from the general population. They were moved into a tiny cell that had been built in the wall of the fort. Now locked down, Baker was first to break the silence. "This feels like being locked into a sardine can." All the men chuckled and agreed. They congratulated each other on sticking together and not telling what they knew about Edmondson's escape. They were in this together and no matter what the cost to any individual, they had to adhere to a code of silence.

Beall was held for questioning, but was able to convince his jailers that he was as surprised as they were about Edmondson's escape. When the guards had finished their interrogation, they led Beall to join his crew in the hole in the wall. As Captain Beall ducked into the small cell he was surprised to see the others. He smiled, "What brings you gentlemen to this fine hotel?" The men hooted and howled. It broke the tension. Beall was proud of his men. None had broken. They had stuck together.

Baker and the others related to him how Edmondson had escaped.

"Well, he was luckier than McGuire," said Beall. "Mac tried to bribe a guard with a ten-dollar bill and a pocket watch. They let him get as far as the steps and then captured him and brought him back."

"They didn't give the money or watch back either," groused McGuire.

Despite the brutality after the escape, the guards generally treated the men with kindness and courtesy. They were always given plenty to eat, and what they could not consume, they burned in a small stove for fear that if the food was wasted their rations would be cut.

On November thirtieth, General Lockwood, accompanied by his staff, came to call on Captain Beall. They took him to the provost's office. "Captain Beall, you and your men have caused us great annoyance recently. I just wanted you to know from me personally that as soon as a commission can be convened, you and your band of pirates will be tried. So if you can tell us anything about your organization and operations, it would be looked at very favorably at your trial." It was his smugness that annoyed Beall the most.

In the most dignified way he possibly could, Beall replied, "I do no desire any favors from the Yankee government. I have every confidence that the Confederate government is fully equal to protecting our rights."

Beall had no way of knowing how right he was. On the very day that Edmondson arrived in Richmond, he went directly to the office of Commissioner Robert Ould, who was in charge of the prisoner exchange program. He told Ould that Beall and his men were being held at Fort McHenry in irons, and that if they were tried and convicted, they would likely be executed. Ould took immediate action.

Colonel Porter, commanding officer of Fort McHenry, had a nephew who was being held prisoner in Charleston, South Carolina, by the Confederates. Ould was well aware of this. He wired Charleston, directing that Lieutenant Commander Edward P. Williams, Ensign Benjamin H. Porter, and sixteen marines be placed in irons. He further contacted Dr. Hunter McGuire, whose brother, Ed McGuire, was in prison with Beall's men. Dr. McGuire was a friend of Stonewall Jackson's, and he telegraphed General Jackson informing him of the situation. Jackson, who at the time was battling the Union General Milroy, gave McGuire permission to send a message to Milroy stating that if the Confederate prisoners held at Fort McHenry were hanged, Jackson would hang five Union captives for every Confederate man who went to the gallows at Fort McHenry.

Five days before Christmas, Lieutenant Starr came into Beall's cell. Starr was a decent sort of man. He had been friendly with Beall and his men, and had done all that it was possible to do to keep them comfortable. Starr had always regretted the war and believed that the men he fought were as decent as he was. They all just had their duty to do.

"Good morning gentlemen," he was smiling, "I believe I've got an early Christmas present for you. I just got a copy of the Baltimore *Sun*. I think you'll find some cheerful reading on page one." He handed the paper to Captain Beall who read the article aloud to the men:

> Retaliation
> Baltimore Sun, December 20, 1863
>
> Information having been received by the government that Acting Master John Y. Beall and Ed McGuire of the Confederate Navy, with sixteen men, are now confined in irons at Fort McHenry, to be treated as pirates. Commissioner of Exchange Robert Ould has directed that Lieutenant Commander Porter and Ensign Williams, and sixteen marines be confined in irons in Charleston, South Carolina, to be held hostages for the good treatment of Captain Beall and his command.

All the men chuckled and congratulated Beall and McGuire. William Baker, sitting against the wall near where Lieutenant Starr stood said, "Now, Lieutenant, y'all fellas can hang us, but those Yankees will surely swing in Charleston."

"Let's just pray nobody swings, Baker," Starr answered. He was as relieved as his prisoners. Starr's opinion was that in this war the common soldiers had become no more than pawns of the men in power on both sides. If someone died unjustly at the hands of the North, then someone had to die from the other side, to even the score. And of what were they all guilty? Just serving their countries. "Well, I hope this news improves your holidays, boys." The lieutenant passed through the cell door and it clanged shut.

Two days later Captain Beall and his crew were released from irons and put on a steamer at Baltimore. Their destination was Fort Monroe. On Christmas eve the men were taken to the Provost Marshal's office located in a hotel, the Purcell House, in Norfolk, Virginia, where they were all required to sign certificates that indicated that the irons had been removed. Stedman and McFarland were informed that they were to be exchanged for two Union prisoners and would be going home to Richmond. The owner of their newspaper had pulled all sorts of strings in Washington to get them released. The rest of the men would be confined at Fort Norfolk, about one mile east of the city.

After six weeks of uneventful captivity in Norfolk, the guard came in with a short, neatly dressed man. He didn't appear to have been in captivity long. His hair, slightly thinning, was neatly combed. His soft, white hands hadn't seen much hard work. The suit was clean, no soil or tears. He had the look of a businessman. "Captain Beall, this here's Mr. Coffin. He was arrested for helping some of you Southern boys, so we thought he might enjoy the company of his own kind."

"Captain Beall? I'm Andrew Coffin." He extended his hand. His easygoing manner and cheery conversation enabled him to join right in with the other prisoners. They all talked of the war and Coffin read-ily told the men all that he knew of its recent events. Eventually talk turned to escape. It was Coffin who brought it up. Did they have any plans he wanted to know? Could he join them if they did try to break out? He'd never been in prison and didn't much like the idea of staying. Any risk to get out was fine with him. He said he didn't intend to stay there for the rest of the war. He was really angry for the way the Union had treated his family, and wanted to get back into action against the North.

On the afternoon of February twenty-sixth Captain Beall was in-formed that his crew should prepare to move. The next morning they would be taken by boat to Point Lookout. If there was any chance for escape, Beall thought, the boat trip might be the best time to try. He began drawing up possible plans in his head. That night as the men ate dinner, Captain Beall quietly laid out a plan of escape for the men.

"Once we get on the boat each one of you will have a specific duty to perform. We will probably be guarded by one or more sentries. Baker, you and Annan will watch me for my signal. When I drop my hand-kerchief, you two will go for the guard. Baker grabs the guard nearest him by the arms from behind and Annan gets his weapon. Depending on how many guards there are, each of you working in pairs will do the same. We will wait until it's dark, about the time we're off Newport Lighthouse. If we can't get command of the ship, it's over the side, swim for it, and meet in the vicinity of the lighthouse. The channel should bring us close enough to land to make for a safe swim if necessary."

The next morning the guards came in. "Andrew Coffin? Get up and come with us." Without a word Coffin rose and went with the guards.

"Where are they taking him?" Beall asked one of the guards.

"He's going up to Baltimore for trial," was all the guard would say. Coffin waved back to the men, and wished them luck. In a moment Andrew Coffin was gone.

In fact, he was not going to Baltimore. By mid morning Coffin was in another rebel cell, joining in the conversation and asking if the men had any plans for escape. He would do anything he could to get out. Coffin was a Federal detective.

As the men boarded the steamer excitement was running high. Just the thought of being free that night was almost more than they could conceal. The trip up the the bay was uneventful until they made an unscheduled stop at Fort Monroe. There a company of Army regulars marched on board to add to the small guard force already on the ship. Beall and his men were then placed in the main cabin. Quickly, behind them followed the heavily armed soldiers, bayonets fixed and formed a circle around the prisoners.

"What's going on?" Beall asked the Captain of the guard.

"General Butler's ordered that the guard be doubled on you as he has information that you have a plan to escape," answered the Captain.

"Now where in the world did he get a story like that, Captain?" asked Beall.

"I believe the man's name was Coffin, sir." answered the Captain.

So it was that they learned that Coffin had been a detective, set among them to gather information about what their plans might be. They had been betrayed, but at least not by one of their own.

The prisoners arrived during the night of February twenty-sixth. It was frigid and the wind was unforgiving. After the usual processing, Beall and his crew were assigned to a large bell-shaped tent with about thirty strangers. Some of his men had to be split up wherever space could be found. Not long after being assigned his tent, William Baker was summoned to Colonel Brady's office. Brady was commander of the garrison.

"Private Baker, I have a letter here for you." Baker took the letter and anxiously opened it. George Stedman's sister had written. He scanned over its contents and saw that Stedman had asked his sister in Kentucky to send Baker thirty dollars and a new suit of clothes. Seeing that Baker had the information about the money and clothes, Colonel Brady said, "Here is ten dollars. I'll give you the rest later." Baker never would see the clothes or the rest of the money. It was fairly common knowledge that prisoners seldom got any or all of what was sent them from relatives. War made thieves out of men . . . or was it that men who would have been thieves anyway just got into official positions where they could steal without fear of accusation or prosecution? Baker wasn't sure. But it really didn't matter. He was in no position to complain.

Beall and his men had been at Point Lookout for about two months, and prison life was wearing on all of them. Possible ways of escape were explored on a daily basis, and most evening meals were punctuated with newer and more desperate plans. As the days wore on, it didn't seem to Beall or the others that any plan would really work, and most had by now resigned themselves to just doing their time and hoping for an end to the war. That or escape now seemed their only way out of prison.

One afternoon, Will Baker was visiting Dr. Emmet Stratton, a physician prisoner who helped out in the infirmary. Both from Richmond, the two had become close friends. There Baker overheard two Union doctors discussing the imminent exchange of five hundred sick prisoners. They were soon to be sent south. Returning to his commander, Baker told Beall what he'd heard about the prisoner exchange.

"I really doubt if we could all pass for being sick, but go ahead and try it, Will. Maybe you'll get through." At this point anything was worth trying, Beall thought.

Baker went back to the infirmary to discuss the possibility with Stratton.

"I'd really like to help you, Will, but I'm afraid the head surgeon won't pass you and it will look bad for me. You look too healthy." Stratton really felt like he should help Baker, but if they got caught, Stratton might not be trusted to work with patients in the future. He had been compromised by the system and he was just slightly ashamed about that. But not enough to help. Will Baker had an idea, though, and if it worked he'd soon be a free man. It was worth a try. What did he really have to lose?

During the days of wearing his ball and chain, Baker had developed a severe sore on his leg where the cuff rubbed against his leg. The sore had never really healed, so Baker scuffed it up until it bled. Then he rubbed all the blood on his leg and limped over to one of the doctors who was attending those being released.

"Doctor, I don't know what's the matter with me, but if I stay here I'll never get well. Please let me go." He held his leg out to show the doctor and winced in pain.

"What's wrong with you?" the doctor questioned gruffly. He was too busy to be bothered with what looked to be a minor problem.

"I don't know, but I'll never get well if I stay here." Baker winced again, as if in pain.

"Get over in that line," he scowled. The doctor indicated the line of men who were healthy enough to stay. Baker saw two lines, and by sheer mistake, got in the wrong line. In his nervousness, and the confusion that surrounded him in the infirmary, he had joined the ranks of the sick who were being sent home. The doctor was too busy to notice.

Inching his way toward the front of the line, Baker soon found himself on a steamer bound for Varina, Virginia. He would very shortly rendezvous with Colonel Robert Ould and an equal number of anxious Union prisoners about to be exchanged. Within hours of daybreak, April twenty-seventh, William Washington Baker was back in Richmond, a free man.

By the luck of the draw, John Beall was exchanged nine days later, but the rest of his command, including his brother, Willie, remained in prison until October when they were scheduled to be exchanged. As much as he detested prison, Beall hated to leave his men behind. Yet, he had no choice. He could be more help to the Southern cause on the outside. And, he feared that if he stayed in prison much longer, his lungs, which had never properly healed from his wounds, might just fail him. His coughing had increased greatly during his imprisonment, but only he knew how much it bothered him.

5

Return to Richmond

On Sunday morning, May 12, 1864, war came to Richmond. At five a.m. General Phil Sheridan's artillery began blasting northeast of the city along the Mechanicsville Road. By six o'clock many of Richmond's citizens were up and preparing for church services.   They heard the roar of the cannons in the distance. Some expressed concern, but most felt that Richmond was impregnable. After all, there had been other attempts by the Yankees to take the city. All had failed, and so they busied themselves preparing for their weekly religious sojourn. After all, God had seen them this far in the war. He would take them the rest of the way. It was out of their control, but not completely out of their minds.

As the residents of Richmond moved into the tree-lined streets that sunny spring morning, they were shocked. It was only nine o'clock and already long lines of wagons carrying the dead and wounded were streaming into the city. Until now there had been no serious threat to the safety of the city or its people, so well had the city been defended, but today U.S. Grant had finally mounted a full-scale attack on the Army of Northern Virginia. Richmond began to have its doubts.

John Yates Beall, droop-shouldered and exhausted, lips compressed in sadness, wended his way south along the road through the parade of dead and wounded as he made his way toward Richmond. He stopped in humble reverence as a litter carrying the lifeless body of General

Jeb Magruder passed by. When he saw men were needed, he joined in with Gregg's troops, who were attempting to drive back General Phil Sheridan. The battle lasted most of the day, and he camped that evening with his adopted unit, glad for some food and a place to sleep, and feeling lucky again just to be alive.

The next day he broke camp with Gregg's men, and when they moved out, he continued on toward Richmond. Just north of the city he happened upon the encampment of the Engineer's Corps. He knew the Henderson brothers from back in Charles Town were with the Engineers so he stopped to inquire about them. A young private pointed toward several neat rows of canvas tents.

"Lieutenant Henderson is in that tent over there, sir," said the private, indicating the first tent in a row of three.

As Beall approached, Henderson appeared out of the tent. Seeing Beall his face lit up. "Well, I'll be! How are you, John?" The men shook hands vigorously. "Where have you been?" Henderson took in the full view of the man before him, haggard and worn, pale, thin and somewhat stoop shouldered.

"I've just been released from Fort Delaware in a prisoner exchange. Got out on May fifth and headed here."

Billy Henderson was troubled that John was looking so poorly. "If you don't mind my sayin' so, John, you don't look any too good. Have you had anything at all to eat today?"

"No, I'd sure like something, but only if you can spare it."

"How about coffee?" Henderson asked."

"That sounds good." Beall said rubbing his hands together. His chest ached, but he tried not to show it.

The men sat and ate and talked of old times, and caught up on as much as they knew of mutual friends back home. Beall told Henderson that he was trying to get to Richmond, but Billy Henderson could see that his friend needed rest more.

"If you'd like, you can stay with us. At least we'll feed you...although we don't have too much to offer," said Henderson. "Our rations are pretty limited right now. Not as bad as it's been in Richmond though. Lot of the food has been diverted away from the civilian population to feed the army."

"That's a shame. What this war has done to a proud people..." said Beall shaking his head in dismay.

"You hear about the bread riot in Richmond last April?"

"No, I've not gotten much news for a while." said Beall. "What happened?"

"Well, it all started when food got scarce and the dealers raised their prices on flour. The poor people had no bread. Some lady named Mary Jackson riled up some other women and they demonstrated in Capitol Square. One thing led to another, and they decided just to go into the stores and take what they couldn't afford. Didn't stop at bread either. Dry goods, dresses, jewelry, stole everything they could get their hands on. Not a merchant on Carey Street was left untouched."

"What did the authorities do?" asked Beall.

"Well, finally, as I hear it, Governor Latcher went out and read the riot act and told'em that if they didn't all go home, he'd order the soldiers to shoot 'em down in the street."

"Would he really do that?" asked Beall.

"Probably not. Latcher's too kind-hearted to shoot women and children."

Beall was saddened to think what had become of good people because of this war. Reduced to the lowest level by deprivation and starvation. Look what we are capable of, he thought.

Henderson continued, "President Davis also came out and told everybody that if that kind of behavior continued, they'd all be in worse shape because farmers would quit bringing produce to the city for fear of losing it. Merchants would close their shops and there'd be nothing to buy at any price."

"Did the crowd break up then?"

"Yes. The women all went home. Not much was done about it, but it hasn't got any better since, so don't be surprised what you see when you get there."

"It would seem to me that Latcher or Davis should have seen that coming. Why didn't they do something to see that people had food before if they needed it so desperately?" asked Beall.

Henderson cocked his head to the side and said with a wry smile on his face, "Latcher and Davis don't really see how those people live. The wealthy of Richmond can afford things at any price. They're just out of touch with how the rest of the people are having to live. Other than making her own hats, I don't think Varina Davis has gone hungry, do you?" Henderson could see Beall was thinking about what he had just said.

"Well, like I say, John, if you're of a mind, you're welcome to stay with us."

"I think I might do that, Billy, at least for a while," Beall responded. "Thank you." He tipped his cup as Henderson poured more coffee. Beall coughed sharply and grasped his chest, obviously in pain.

"John, are you all right?" Henderson asked.

"No, not really." He coughed hard again. "I've never really gotten over this wound in the chest I got back at Bolivar Heights. It got my lung and I've never been able to regain full strength. If the war doesn't kill me, this cough might," winced Beall. He coughed again. "But what can you do? Just take whatever fate deals you and live with it."

As they finished eating, a tall young man of about eighteen approached them. "Excuse me, sir, are you Captain Beall?" he asked.

Beall looked up a little surprised and said, "Why, yes. What do you want?"

"There is someone who'd like to see you for a few minutes. His tent is down there. I'll show you the way," he offered.

"Who is it?" asked Beall. Who even knew him, or that he was here? Someone must have seen him come into camp earlier.

"Pardon me, sir, but he just said to request that you come to see him." answered the private. Henderson and Beall looked at each other a shrugged. Neither had any idea who this man could be.

Beall extended his hand to Henderson and said, "Billy, I'd better go see who this mysterious person is. I'll see you a little later. Thank you again for the hospitality. It's good to see you again."

Beall followed the young man down the row of tents until he gestured, "Over there, sir. Just go right in."

Beall ducked into the tent. The man inside half rose and stuck out his hand. "Captain Beall?" It was Jeremy Gilmer, Chief Engineer of the Confederate Army. Beall had a passing acquaintance with him back home before the war as a resident of Jefferson County. "Please, sit down." he offered. "You're probably wondering how I knew you were here." Beall shook his head. "My aide came in a few minutes ago and said a Captain Beall had come into camp. He was pretty impressed. You've made quite a name for yourself over the last few years up there on the Chesapeake. I've been in to Richmond, and you're being talked about quite a lot around the War Department."

"Well, I suppose I have caused a stir up there, but I've recently spent a good bit of time in a Yankee prison because of it."

"That I've heard, too." said Gilmer as he pored over maps laid on a small table. "What are your plans now, Captain?"

"Well, I was released about a week ago, and I'm heading back to Richmond."

"I figured as much. I'm sure they'll be glad to see you at the War Department."

Beall was surprised. "Really? Do they have something in mind?"

"Not really...at least not anything I'm at liberty to talk about now. What are your plans? Going right down to Richmond?"

"Yes, but I'm going to take a little time off and rest," said Beall. "I did just get out of prison, and my health has been a bit of a problem."

"Sorry to hear that. It'll do you good to take some time off. You look like you could use some rest." Gilmer paused and looked intently at Beall, "But when you get back to Richmond be sure to see Secretary Mallory over at the Navy Department. He may have a project you'll be interested in."

Two days later, long before daybreak, Beall packed his bag and left camp for Richmond. If there was a plan in view for him, rest would have to wait. He needed to find out what Mallory had in mind.

That morning Lieutenant Henderson came as usual to call at Beall's tent. He was not there. All his things were gone. Billy Henderson was puzzled. Surely, if John was leaving, he'd have come and said so, he thought. Henderson would not see John Beall again.

6

Secret Service in Canada: Northwestern Conspiracy

In early May of 1864 Ulysses Grant marched his armies south of the Rappahannock River into the wilderness area, hoping to defeat Lee and capture Richmond. General William Tecumseh Sherman drove hard from Chattanooga toward Atlanta. Both had decided no matter what the cost, they must crush all resistance. And it was to be costly. After seven days, Union losses would be thirty thousand. And still Lee held the line.

John Beall left Richmond for Columbus, Georgia, on the same day the Battle of the Wilderness commenced. Prison life had taken its toll on his already frail health. His coughing spells were more frequent and painful. Too much time had been spent in damp prison cells, and he needed rest badly. But mostly, he needed to see Martha O'Bryan, who was now staying with friends in Columbus.

The trip from Richmond to Columbus took five days by rail. Union troops had to be avoided, tracks had been torn up, and scheduled departure times were changed without notice. War made travel in the South almost impossible. Talk on the train and at each new station was more discouraging. Yet General Lee held on.

The train station in Columbus was crowded with travelers, many of whom were headed further south to avoid an ever more threatening situation in Virginia and the Carolinas. She spied him as he stepped off the train and ran to him. Two years had been a long time.

"John, John," she cried, tears of joy. "I've met every train this morning. I wasn't sure which one you'd be on and I didn't want to miss you. I got your telegram the day before yesterday and I just couldn't believe it was true you were coming."

He hugged her tightly, "Oh, God, how I've missed you," she cried. "I've thought about you every day for the last two years. I didn't think I was ever going to see you again. Did you get all my letters?"

"Yes, your mother, God bless her, and Dan Lucas have been so thoughtful toward me. I've even gotten letters from them whenever they had news about you."

They walked out of the station to a waiting carriage. "I've arranged for some friends to put you up. There probably isn't a hotel room in town that's available anyway. Columbus is full of people desperate to avoid the war."

"What have you heard?" he asked.

"The latest news is that Grant is headed toward Spotsylvania and that General Jackson and General Lee have beaten Hooker at Chancellorsville."

Beall was pleased. He knew that Lee's army was probably half the size of their opponents. It showed what good leadership could do. But for now that would all have to wait. They had too much time to make up.

For the next ten days John and Martha spent as much time together as they could. They pieced together the vacant spots in their lives since Pascagoula and talked again of marriage.

"Are you still thinking of going back to Nashville?" he asked.

"No, my brothers tell me it's still too dangerous to return. I'll probably wait here until the war is over. I just hope I don't wear out my welcome." she said.

"You could still go to England and stay with my cousins," he offered, hoping she'd accept this time.

"No, you know I can't do that. This is where I belong. Besides, it will be easier to get mail from you if I'm here and not in England." He knew there was no changing her mind. She was stubborn, and when she made up her mind, there was just no chance of a reversal.

"That is true," he said. It was just that he knew she'd be safe in England, and he dreaded the thought that anything might happen to her. He pulled her close to him and whispered, "We've missed so much of each others lives since we've been apart. I wonder every day what you're doing and if you're alright."

"What we really should do is keep a diary of our daily activities. Then when we're back together, we can share what we've done." Martha suggested.

"I like the idea, but I don't always have room to carry a diary with me."

"It doesn't have to be a large one. We can get small ones, small enough to carry in your pocket." It was agreed. They would keep up a diary until after the war with all their thoughts and feelings and experiences. There would be no lost time. The following day Martha presented John with a small leather-covered diary that fit neatly into his coat pocket.

Two weeks passed quickly. May twenty-first arrived, and it was time for John to go. Martha had thought about this moment for days. She had almost made up her mind to ask John if they could get married now and both go to England, but she knew he could not do that. Instead, she made him promise to write as often as possible. He told her he would, but not to expect too much. The way the war was going, the mail might be more difficult to get through. She knew, but hoped he'd try. He would, but mostly it would be through friends. He feared writing her directly. He didn't want any more people to know who Martha was than needed. The fewer the better, for her own safety.

By the time Beall reached Richmond on May twenty-sixth, there was news that General Grant had fought Lee at Spotsylvania. Though no one was a clear victor, Grant had whittled Lee's troops to dangerously low levels. Sherman had also defeated Johnston with an army of one hundred-ten thousand, but Johnston was able to effectively retreat with what was left of his small army intact.

Beall contacted Congressman Alexander Boteler, a friend and neighbor from near Charles Town, who arranged a meeting with Secretary of the Confederate Navy Steven Mallory. Beall was impatient for a new assignment. Mallory was definitely interested.

"Mr. Beall, it is indeed a pleasure to see you again, sir" He pumped Beall's hand vigorously. "I've heard a good bit about you over the last year. Quarter million in captured cargo up on the Chesapeake they say?" Beall didn't know. He hadn't stopped to count it. "How have you been?" Mallory did not stand on formality. He waved Beall to a chair near his desk. Mallory sat back in his oak swivel chair and pulled some papers from his desk drawer. Then, as if an afterthought, he got up and closed the inner office door. Too many people wandering in and out of these halls and offices. Don't even know who they all are. In a voice much lower in tone he said, "I have something that you might be very well suited for, John. May I call you John?"

"Yes, sir." answered Beall.

"We have just organized a Secret Service. It's under the direction of Major William Norris. I'd like you to go and talk to him. Your experience and success on the Chesapeake indicate that you would be well suited to such an organization."

"Yes, I would like to talk to him about it. I have some ideas of my own that I would like to propose if you think he'd be receptive." said Beall.

Mallory tapped the newspapers on his desk and looked toward the window. "The way this war is going lately I think Norris would be glad to hear any new ideas. I'll arrange a meeting if you'd like." Beall nodded his head. "By the way," he said, "you come highly recommended. I received a letter from Dr. Andrew Hunter indicating that you were dedicated to the cause and highly reliable. I just thought you might like to know that."

Two days later Beall found himself in the halls of a nondescript office building on the southwest side of Capitol Square on Bank Street. It was the headquarters of the Confederate Signal Corps, but what few knew at that time, was that it also housed the offices of the newly created Secret Service. Its director was a refugee from Baltimore, forty-year-old Major William Norris. Norris, a successful businessman and lawyer before the war, gave it all up to join the Confederacy. His first experience in espionage was when he worked with General John B. Magruder developing a system of signals and military correspondence on the peninsula around Yorktown, Virginia. That experience introduced him to the value of intelligence operations by signal corpsmen who would report back information they had gathered in the field on enemy troop movements.

The Secret Service office was nestled away at the end of a series of long narrow corridors near the extreme rear of the building. The location was not elegant, but it served the purpose. If necessary, the office could be entered or exited via a door to an alley that ran between two adjacent streets. Beall was directed to knock before entering. Having traversed the maze of corridors he came to the door, and found it half opened. He entered.

The outer office was small, not more than ten by ten. Its wood plank floors showed much wear and the walls were in need of fresh paint. But then so were most of the offices he had seen lately. Decoration could not be a priority now when even food for soldiers was scarce. Beall didn't really know what to expect, perhaps a secretary or sentinel. The tall man he faced was William Norris himself.

"Excuse me, I am John Y. Beall. I have an appointment with Major William Norris."

Norris eyed him up and down, sizing up the man, wondering if he really was as good as the stories about him indicated. War had a way of exaggerating both the good and the bad. Norris had learned to be skeptical. He'd seen quite a few frauds come and go in this business.

"I'm Norris. Come into my office." He led Beall through a door at the back of the room. The inner office was more spacious. A large desk covered with maps was placed against the far wall between two small windows. Several chairs were buried under piles of papers, folders and documents, and various small machines sat in crates on the floor. Beall surmised that they must be the cipher devices that were used to encode and decode messages carried by couriers to and from Richmond.

Norris was six feet tall, and easily one hundred-eighty pounds. He had dark hair and a wavy full beard beginning to show gray. His military coat, the traditional Navy with two descending rows of gold buttons, hung neatly over the back of his chair.

"Captain Beall, It is indeed a pleasure to meet you. I've heard of your success over on the Chesapeake. You know, I spent some time there early in the war myself, in and around Yorktown."

Beall smiled and shook his head affirmatively. "Major Norris, let me get to the point. As you may or may not know, I have recently been released from a Yankee prison because of those escapades on the Chesapeake. I'd like to get back into service. I went to Secretary Mallory because I have a plan I have been wanting to put into effect on the

Great Lakes." Beall looked for a response.

Norris stroked his beard thoughtfully. "Go on," he encouraged.

"There are two parts to my plan. As we both know, this war is dragging on because people of the North are not touched by the war. I propose a privateer on the lakes that would cruise from one end of Lake Erie to the other. We would attack coastal cities, hit their shores and exact financial tribute from them. We should be able to disrupt Yankee trade very effectively."

Norris was interested. He leaned forward and wrote a few notes. "Go on."

Beall continued, "Another problem we have right now is that so many of our best officers are in Yankee prisons. I propose a plan by which we break them out. The one prison I have in mind is on Johnson's Island. It's an island located in a bay of Lake Erie just off the coast of Sandusky, Ohio. They are holding about two thousand prisoners, mostly of officer rank. There is also a Federal gunboat assigned to guard the island, but if we could disable and capture it, we could release the prisoners, and use the boat to threaten the coast afterward from Toledo to Buffalo."

Norris was silent. He was very aware of everything Beall was saying. He knew well the location of Johnson's Island, and the approximate numbers. The plan, in principle seemed sound. And he had heard it before, about a year or so ago. He just didn't know it was Beall who had originally proposed the plan.

"Personally, Captain Beall, I like your plan, and I think it could work. However, as is usually the case in government, I do not have the ultimate authority to grant you the permission or the funding you need... and it will be considerable, will it not?" Norris thought for a few moments as Beall sat and waited. "I think the best course of action is for you to see the Secretary of War. James Seddon is the only one who can authorize this type of activity. I'll send over a letter of introduction this afternoon." With that said, Norris was on his feet and escorting Beall back to the door. "I really do like the idea, Beall. I hope you can be as convincing with Seddon."

The following day Beall appeared at the offices of the Honorable James A. Seddon, Secretary of War. He watched an amazing array of messengers, secretaries, soldiers and officers come in and out of the office that served as ante-room to the offices of both Seddon and his assistant secretary, John A. Campbell. He had been waiting for about an hour when Captain R.G. Kean came to him and said that the Secretary could see him now.

James Seddon, a fellow Virginian himself, indicated that he had been briefed about Beall's plan the previous evening by Norris. "Mr. Beall, this secret service is a pretty new thing for us. We need good young officers who have proven they have what it takes. There is no question in my mind about that where you're concerned!" he said firmly. "I understand you currently hold the rank of Acting Master in the irregular Navy. What I'd like to offer you is a commission as Lieutenant in the Secret Service." He waited for Beall to accept.

"Mr. Secretary," he began, "I am certainly honored that you think so highly of me, so please do not misinterpret what I am about to say." Beall rubbed his hands together as he thought of the right words. "Throughout this war I have seen the most horrible actions taken by men, either by order of their commanders or on their own. If, by taking this commission, I would be under the command of a superior, would it not be possible that I could be given a command that I morally could not obey?"

"I suppose that could be true, Captain Beall." He waited to hear Beall out, not sure of what he was getting at.

"It's not that I don't want to take orders, sir, or to be subservient to someone else. It is rather that my strong moral convictions about how this war has been conducted . . . on both sides . . . might be compromised. I do not want to sacrifice my moral beliefs for the sake of obedience. I've already seen too much immorality in this war."

"Am I to understand that you are turning down my offer, Mr. Beall?" he asked.

Beall pondered the question. As Acting Master in the irregular service he had the backing of the Confederate government, and still the freedom to make his own moral choices. If he took this assignment, much as he wanted it, he would be responsible to someone else's decisions. No, he had seen too much depravity, too much robbery, vandalism, uncalled for destruction, and even murder, justified as acts of war. Acts ordered by men who thought that war gave them authority to do whatever they pleased. No, he could not be put in that kind of position.

"Sir, I very much appreciate the offer and the confidence that you have in me, but unless I can act independently, I will have to decline. I am truly sorry."

Seddon was clearly disappointed, yet, somehow gratified. He felt a spark of hope through Beall's comments that the best in some of the South's young men had not been destroyed by the war, and in part, he agreed.

"Very well, Captain Beall. If you should choose to reconsider, the offer stands. But, as for now, there is still something I can offer you by way of service. It will involve a trip to Canada. There are plans afoot up there that we can discuss if you'd like. Perhaps they will be more to your liking."

Beall's comments about the immorality of war were quite accurate, as James Seddon would find out. In the first days of June 1864 General Grant, despite horrible losses, continued to pound at Lee's defense at Cold Harbor. Grant had already lost sixty thousand men. Even Southern generals were calling it murder . . . not war.

Undiscouraged, Grant began his siege of Petersburg. By August, Union Admiral David Farragut had successfully closed the ports at Mobile and New Orleans. Yet the South was not without victories. Johnston's forces had turned back Sherman at Kennesaw Mountain and Jubal Early had gotten so close to Washington that he could see the flag flying over the White House. Successes on both sides were paid in the carnage of tens of thousands of young men's lives. So much for morality.

James Seddon's letter was received at the office of the Confederate Commissioners to Canada in Toronto about one month before Beall's arrival. Jacob Thompson read the letter with interest. He would inform his fellow commissioners, James P. Holcombe and Clement C.Clay in the morning. Clay was in Montreal and Holcombe had left the office for the day. Holcombe was preparing for a trip to England to consult with Confederate representatives in London. The letter informed Thompson of the decision by officials at the highest levels in Richmond to launch an attack on Northern lake cities, and of the plan to break prisoners out of various prison camps in the North. Thompson was to report back, advising Richmond as to the feasibility of such a plan. He tossed the letter on his desk. It was old news to him. Finally Richmond had given the go ahead. They had talked about it for months, but politics had held things up as usual. Thompson anticipated that Seddon and his people would eventually come around. He had already begun laying the ground work for such a mission weeks ago.

Jake Thompson was born rich in Caswell County, North Carolina. An honor graduate of the University of North Carolina, he settled at age twenty-five in Mississippi, practiced law and made a fortune in cotton planting and shady real estate ventures. With the money he built a twenty-room home complete with offices, servant's quarters and a carriage house. He had served six terms in the U.S. House of Representatives, lost an ugly Senate race to Jefferson Davis, and later accepted appointment to James Buchanan's cabinet as Secretary of the Interior. By age fifty-four he was a highly respected politician, certainly one of the most visible in Mississippi politics. He drank heavily and often. Jefferson Davis and Thompson had had their differences in the past, but Davis knew that Thompson had a way of getting the job done. On April 7, 1864, Thompson had received a telegram from President Jefferson Davis.

> If your engagements permit you to accept service
> abroad for the next six months, please come here
> immediately.
> .   Jeff. Davis

Thompson's assignment had been to go to Canada and set up a headquarters from which the Confederate States would support insurrection by militant anti-war groups in Northern states. His office was to work to free rebel prisoners now held in Northern camps, and if possible buy up Northern newspapers in the hope of influencing the coming Presidential election. Newspapers and their opinions could go a long way to defeating the increasingly unpopular Abe Lincoln. If a peace candidate won, the South felt it could negotiate some type of political settlement to the war that would allow for their independence.

On May third, Thompson and his co-commissioner Clement Clay had left Wilmington, North Carolina, for Canada. They were chased for five hours by a Federal blockade steamer, but finally outran it. On

May twenty-ninth they were met in Nova Scotia by their other co-commissioner, James P. Holcombe and Captain Thomas Henry Hines, who was to be Jake Thompson's aide and chief planner of the action about to begin.

The twenty-three-day trip had completely worn out the elder Clay, and by the time they reached Montreal, he flatly refused to continue on to Toronto. Clay didn't care what the others were doing. He was getting a room at the best hotel Montreal could offer. Captain Hines argued vigorously against it. Montreal was full of Federal agents and it was not a safe place to conduct business. Cantankerous old Clay would not believe it. Nothing could change his mind. Captain Hines was extremely annoyed. If Clay's health was so bad, Hines thought, why was he even chosen for this mission? Finally, Thompson gave in and deposited ninety-five thousand dollars in a personal account for Clay at the Bank of Montreal. Hines could not believe that Clay could act so childishly, or that Thompson was so cavalier with his use of the nine hundred-thousand dollars he had been given in Richmond.

Major Charles H. Cole had arrived like so many others in Toronto, and presented himself to Jacob Thompson, offering his services. He claimed to have been a prisoner of the Yankees, recently paroled, and told Thompson that he had served in Kentucky under the command of Nathan Bedford Forrest. Rumors circulated around Toronto intelligence circles that Cole might not be who he said he was. Some suggested he was a deserter from the Union army while others said he had deserted both armies. These were times when one did not know what or who to believe. The only population larger than that of the citizens of Toronto, were the swarms of both Union and Confederate agents who constantly kept the rumor mills churning. Thompson, not known to be a good judge of character, had decided to put his trust in Cole, and gave him his first assignment.

Charles Cole booked passage on a steamer bound for Toledo. The steamer would make stops in Buffalo, Ashtabula, Cleveland, Sandusky and Toledo. Cole posed as a rich oil executive from Mount Hope, Pennsylvania on a business trip. His assignment was to observe and ask questions, careful questions so as not to arouse curiosity or suspicion.

He noted supply depots, arms caches, the number of large vessels capable of defending a city from attack, and the strength of Federal troops present in each location. Larry McDonald, a personal friend of Jake Thompson's, had previously spent a goodly portion of Confederate funds cruising the lake, but with results that were vague, lacking in sufficient detail, and, as was later be proven by Cole's assessment, downright inaccurate. Charles Cole's report to Thompson appeared to be detailed and accurate, and included Cole's own narrative on the chances for success of such a mission should it ever be undertaken. He reported that Buffalo and Cleveland were excellent targets. Both had large stores of food and weapons that could easily be taken. Neither city was well defended.

Cole reported that he had traveled from Detroit to Chicago where he met with a man active in the anti-war movement, who told him that tug boats docked in Chicago were available that could be fitted with guns. They could easily be run up the river to Camp Douglas, destroying drawbridges, and freeing Confederate prisoners. His report stated that while most cities on all the Great Lakes were vulnerable, actions on Lake Erie had the best chance for success. None of its major cities were adequately defended. He added that he had made the acquaintance of Captain Carter, the commanding officer of the U.S.S. Michigan, the gunboat guarding Johnson's Island. Cole described Carter as an unpolished man who was offended, that with all his military experience, he had not been given a larger responsibility in the war. Despite his unhappiness, Cole did not think Carter could be bribed. By all accounts, Carter was an honorable man who quietly did his duty. Other means would be necessary to take possession of the Michigan.

Thompson decided to trust Cole and expanded his part in the mission. In July of 1864, he dispatched Cole to the city of Sandusky. His job was to lay the foundation for an attack on the Union prison at Johnson's Island and determine how to effect a capture of the Michigan.

By August 14, 1864, John Beall had reached Dundas, a small town on the outskirts of Toronto. The plan was already in motion. It was a plan of sabotage and liberation so widespread that Thompson and the other commissioners felt it would force the North to negotiate a settlement to the war, a settlement that would allow the South to go its own way, free from the domination of Northern bankers, abolitionists and politicians. Free to make its own way as an independent country. People in the North had already begun to tire of the war. The Copperheads, Sons of Liberty, and others had organized opposition groups and had become engaged in protest of the war and outright sabotage. Thompson had even been in contact with Ohioans who would be willing to help if the Confederates launched an offensive out of Canada. If, through these attacks, the people of the North were suddenly and violently touched by the war the way the South had been, Thompson believed there would be tremendous pressure on Lincoln to negotiate a settlement. Better yet, with the Presidential elections coming, Old Abe might just be on the way out.

The Queen's Hotel was a beehive of activity in Toronto. Not far from the harbor on Lake Ontario, it housed an amazing assortment of guests. Families of many wealthy Confederate leaders lived there waiting out the war until they could return home. Parolees from Federal prisons who had gone to Canada until they could safely book passage back south, and escapees from those same prisons, who fled to Canada to continue their fight against the Union, lived there, too. It was the unofficial office and residence of the Confederate Commissioners. It was the place where deals were made and plans were hatched. It was the place where large sums of money were dispensed to the visiting leaders of the Copperhead movement in the Union states. There were dozens of transients on a daily basis, business men, travelers, foreign diplomats, prostitutes, pickpockets, and it crawled with snooping Federal agents sent there by Lincoln's chief detective, Lafayette C. Baker. All living under one roof, ostensibly unknown to each other.

John Yates Beall walked into the Queen's Hotel and asked the desk clerk if Mr. Thompson was in. The clerk eyed him suspiciously up and down. His clothes were dusty and he carried only one small valise. What business could he have with Mr. Thompson? he thought.

"Whom shall I say is calling, sir? the clerk asked.

"Tell Mr. Thompson that Mr. Yates would like to see him," Beall answered.

The clerk called a boy over and told him to take a message to Mr. Thompson's room and wait for a reply. In a few minutes the boy returned and instructed Beall to follow him. They climbed one flight of stairs and stopped at the door to Room 207. Beall knocked, and as quickly as he did, the door was opened.

"Mr. Beall? Please, come in. Mr. Thompson's been expecting you." Thomas Hines quickly closed the door. "I'm Captain Thomas Hines, aide to Commissioner Thompson. It's good to meet you."

The suite was spacious and lavishly decorated. Ornately carved cornices over the windows, a marble mantelpiece over the fireplace, and highly polished mahogany tables with brass lamps adorned the room. Several expensive oriental rugs covered the oak floor. It was obvious that Commissioner Thompson had gotten used to the finest that money could buy in Toronto.

"Mr. Thompson, may I introduce you to Captain John Yates Beall," said Hines. Thompson, who had been sitting in a large overstuffed chair nursing a drink, rose and walked to Beall.

Captain Beall, how are you? I understand that you are looking for some action. I think we can provide plenty of that for you, right Hines?"

Thomas Hines nodded cautiously and said, "I'm sure that can all be discussed in due time. Right now it would appear that Captain Beall might like to wash off the dust of the road. Am I right, Beall?" Hines was not sure that this was the best time to get into details. Thompson had already had a bit too much to drink and tended to get loud in his speech. Discussions of this nature were best conducted quietly and more importantly, sober.

Thompson wasn't one to stand on titles. "Tom, fill Beall in on the plan so far. Then we'll let him go for tonight. He does look like he could use a bath and some sleep. Hines could see that Thompson did not catch his subtle suggestion, so he took Beall over to a large round table where various papers had been strewn about. He gathered them into order.

"To be brief for now, there are several phases to our operation. We intend to send agents into several Northern cities and set fires in public buildings. While the locals are distracted by the fires, we will attack various Union prison camps and attempt the release of our soldiers. We have already been in contact with key men in those prisons and they are ready to uprise at our signal."

"What prisons will you be going after?" Beall asked.

"Camp Chase, Camp Douglass, and Johnson's Island," Hines answered.

Beall shook his head. "I proposed this very plan back in sixty-two and the government didn't want to try it. They were afraid of what effect it would have on British relations. What's changed?"

"Well, for one, the war situation is much more desperate now. Over two thousand officers are in prison right now just at Johnson's Island. And the Yankees have stopped exchanging prisoners altogether. We need those men." said Hines.

"A second reason," interjected Thompson loudly as he poured another bourbon, "is that if we don't open a second front against the Yankees, all the pressure will still be on our armies in the South. They're having a tough time of it now. An action like this could force the Union armies to turn some of their attention away from the South to defend their own states."

"What about British reaction?" Beall felt they were sidestepping that issue.

"That, admittedly, is a sticky situation," said Hines. "The Canadians are giving us tacit support now, but neither they nor the British want to overtly come out against the Union government. Any actions we take must be taken strictly on U.S. soil."

"Then the Canadian and British governments can claim neutrality." said Thompson as he sat back into his chair.

"What exactly will be my role in this?" asked Beall.

"Your job will be to assemble a crew of men, gather what equipment you will need, and work in conjunction with our man, Major Cole, who is now in Sandusky, in the capture of the *U.S.S. Michigan*. Once you have done that, you will assist in helping our prisoners at Johnson's Island to escape." said Hines.

"What plan do you have in mind for them when they are freed?" asked Beall.

Thompson was now up again and back at the table. He pulled hard on his thin Havana and blew a narrow stream of smoke into the air. "We haven't decided yet. There are two options. One is that we can take them aboard the *Michigan* and bring them back to Canada." He paused, and moved to the other side of the table. His finger picked a place on the map of the north shore of Lake Erie. Beall's eyes followed as Thompson traced southward from Sandusky to Cincinnati. "We may launch an offensive down through Ohio. There is a hell of a lot of sympathy and support for us there. That could have a great effect on the outcome of this war."

Hines took Beall by the arm. "That's enough for now. We've arranged for a room for you." He handed Beall the key. "Get some rest tonight and keep low. There are more Federal detectives in this town than there are Canadians."

He wasn't too far from wrong. "Bennett Young, one of our operatives, should be back from Sandusky by tomorrow. He delivered some money to Charles Cole."

Thompson joined them as they walked to the door. "I wanted to go myself, but Hines thought I might be recognized. I told him I could disguise myself as a woman." He laughed out loud, "How do you think I'd look in petticoats?" They all laughed heartily, and then Beall began to cough. It was a deep hard cough. Tears came to his eyes.

"What's the matter, man?" Thompson was very concerned.

"I was wounded, shot in the lung a few years ago, and sometimes I just start coughing. It will pass," he assured them, "I'll be alright."

The men said good night and Beall made for his room. He felt weak, almost sick. Maybe with some rest he'd feel better.

The next morning Beall waited in the hotel lobby for word from Thompson. A good night's sleep had done him good. The coughing had subsided and he felt rested for the first time in a long while. At about nine o'clock Hines appeared in the lobby and bought a newspaper. Beall watched him from across the room. They did not speak. Hines folded his newspaper and his eyes met Beall's. He nodded toward the door. Hines wanted to be sure they were not going to be followed. He strolled several blocks down the street, and then turned the corner. Beall followed at a safe distance. Hines stood against a lamp pole as Beall approached. "Good morning. Feel any better today?"

"Yes, thank you." Beall questioned Hines about the plans for the day.

"Wander around town till one o'clock this afternoon. Get some breakfast, see some of the shops. Bennett is arriving on the noon train from Niagara Falls. We'll meet in Mr. Thompson's room like last night. See you about one o'clock." He was off in the opposite direction. You just couldn't be too careful. There really were spies everywhere.

Beall breakfasted at a small restaurant on King Street and wandered around taking in the sites. At twelve thirty he arrived back at the Queen's Hotel. He carried a Toronto paper under his arm. It reported that Lincoln had relieved General Burnside of his command. In an apparent attempt to place mines at a Confederate fortification, there had been a mistake, a horrific explosion, and Burnsides' own men suffered four thousand casualties. There was also talk of McClellan's campaign against Lincoln for president. It looked to the Canadians like Abe was on his way out if McClellan got the nomination of the Democratic Party. He'd have to be careful, because it would be necessary to pull the Peace Democrats and the War Democrats together.

Hines and another man Beall assumed to be Bennett Young arrived in the lobby about twelve forty-five. They did not acknowledge Beall and separated from each other. Hines went to the desk to inquire about mail and Young went into the bar. At precisely one o'clock Hines crossed the lobby and headed up the stairs. He nodded for Beall to follow. Young followed two minutes later.

By one-fifteen, Room 207 had taken on life. Drinks were being served generously. They were being consumed that way, too. Hines toyed nervously with his slender mustache and worried about that. Thompson had invited two of his close friends to the meeting, one W. Larry McDonald, and the other Godfrey Hyams. Both served as couriers for Thompson on occasion, but mostly they took great advantage of his gracious and generous hospitality.

Several rounds later Thompson called the men to the large table that last night had held the map of Ohio. "Gentlemen, I think by now you've all been introduced, so let's get on with the business at hand." He indicated Bennett Young, "Bennett, here, has just gotten back from Sandusky, Ohio. He tells me that Major Cole has become well established with the local community as well as with the officers and crew of the *Michigan*. He has also gotten to know some of the guards at Johnson's Island who come to wet their whistles at the West House, a local hotel and saloon."

Hines asked, "What did he say about how many locals could be counted on to help if we decide to invade Ohio?"

"He has maintained to me that forty or fifty local people can be called upon for help," said Young.

"Will that be enough?" asked Larry McDonald.

Don't seem like it'd be enough help to me." Hyams agreed. He always agreed, Hines thought. He never offered an opinion of his own. He just sat and listened to the others and agreed. Godfrey Hyams made Hines uneasy, but he didn't exactly know why. He ate, drank and lived well at government expense, but contributed nothing. What purpose did he serve except to consume Confederate resources?

Thompson continued, "Cole will handle all operations on the Sandusky end. I have every confidence in him." Thompson turned to Beall. "You wanted some action, son, well here is where you get it. I want you to go to Buffalo and get a room at the Genesee House. Bennett will come in by another train in a day or so. He will bring twenty-five hundred dollars with him. You take the money to Sandusky for Cole. Be very careful that you are not being followed. The area is swarming with Federal detectives. Take a room at the West House. It's right downtown, just across from the wharf. Cole is staying there. Then the two of you can decide your plan of action. He will get word back to me through a woman who is there now as to what you decide."

Clement Clay departed Montreal by train. By the time he arrived at the Clifton House Hotel in Niagara Falls, the guests had been milling about for an hour. He liked parties, and this was a big one. Many of the old Southern aristocracy were there, glad for another evening of social gaiety to wile away the days until the war was over and they could all go back home. Guests mingled in small groups, laughing and chattering about life in Canada. Clay wandered among the guests, smiling and shaking hands, sharing pleasantries. Sarah Douglass, late of Virginia, had been talking to Jacob Stone, a displaced Southern aristocrat from Alabama, when she saw Clay.

"Why, Mr. Clay, how good to see you. Do you know Jacob Stone?" she asked.

"No, I don't believe I've had the pleasure," Clay said, shaking Stone's hand.

"Mr. Clay has recently been to a peace conference here in Niagara Falls with Lincoln himself. Is there any good news to report?" she asked.

"No, I'm afraid not," said Clay. "All I got was a taste of Yankee impudence!" He could feel his anger rising just at the mention of it.

"What did Lincoln have to say?" asked Stone.

"About all Father Abraham said was that if we abolish slavery and abandon everything else, that then we can come to Washington and talk peace," answered Clay.

"What do you think the prospects are for peace?" asked Mrs. Douglass.

"Not very promising, I'm afraid. I'm going to give peace talks one more chance. Then if nothing comes of it, we're going to take the war to the White House." He looked around hoping he had not spoken too loudly. They drifted on to other topics as George Sanders approached.

"Clement, how good you could be here. May I have a word with you in private?

"Yes, of course, George. Mrs. Douglass, Mr. Stone, would you excuse me for a few minutes?"

"Certainly," smiled Sarah Douglass, "you go right along, now. We'll see you a bit later, I'm sure."

Sanders led Clay to an adjoining room where a group of men had gathered. Among them were Clay's friends, John McGill, William H. Carter, and Robert Cobb Kennedy. The others had come by invitation of Sanders, and included select group of Confederate soldiers who were refugees, and two couriers for the Confederate Secret Service, one of whom Clay knew to be the actor, John Wilkes Booth. Cigars and drinks were plentiful, but the mood was somber. The subject of the meeting was what to do about Lincoln. There had been talk for some time about possibly kidnapping Lincoln and holding him hostage, but Clay knew Lincoln to be a western man. He would not allow himself to be captured without a fight. And then there were the questions of where and when. Lincoln was not a creature of habit. Kidnapping could prove to be too difficult to plan. Clay knew that if something big wasn't done soon, all this fruitless political babbling would be the South's undoing. He was tired of pussy footing around with bureaucrats.

"These raids we have planned are one thing," began Clay, "and, if they are effective, they'll accomplish a great deal for the South in terms of manpower and political clout with the Copperheads and other

Northern anti-war men . . . could even turn public opinion toward a political solution to the war." The men all murmured their agreement. "But something more dramatic is needed." He looked into the eyes of each man in the room and waited until all were silent. He spoke deliberately in slow even tones. "We have to kill Lincoln." The room was silent. After a momentary pause, Clay continued. "And it will be risky business. But if we're successful in killing 'Old Monkey Abe,' and get back to Canada, we'll all be rich men."

Clay's reference to Lincoln as a monkey broke the tension. The men laughed at the notion and tipped their glasses in a toast. "However, if we fail . . ." he waited to regain their attention, "we'll all be hung." Each man knew the risks and knew what was expected. Kill Lincoln, and his cabinet if possible, a clean sweep. Grant, too, if he could be gotten. Why not? That for sure would leave the Union reeling and ripe for a settlement. Details of the plan would be outlined later by George Sanders. Before he left, Clay gave them all expense money, and said that more was available at the Ontario Bank if needed. Clay quickly returned to the party, leaving the details to Sanders.

A few days after the party, Clement Clay called at the home of James and Sarah Douglass just a little outside Toronto. The Douglass home had on many occasions been the local meeting place for Confederates. Some of the raids had even been planned there.

"Why, Mr. Clay, what a surprise. Won't you come in?" Clay removed his hat as he entered the door, and stood in the spacious parlor. There with Mrs. Douglass stood another rather attractive young woman.

"Mr. Clay, this is my friend, Mary Knapp. She's also from Virginia. We were just talking about old times in Richmond."

Mary Knapp smiled and said, "Mr. Clay, I'm glad to meet you."

"What brings you to see us, Mr. Clay?" asked Sarah.

"Is your husband at home, Mrs. Douglass? Clay inquired.

"No, not right now. He's in town tending to some business. Have you got any news for us today?"

"Yes, and I'm afraid none of it good." Clay shook his head and said, "I'm just so sick of this war. Just want it to be over. And if the boys in Washington can do their jobs and escape, it probably will be over soon."

"What job is that?" asked Mary Knapp solemnly.

"Well, madam, they're going to kill Lincoln." he said flatly.

Clay had breeched secrecy, and he knew it. He had only met this woman, and had uttered words that should not have been said to a stranger. Yet, she was a friend of Mrs. Douglass, and Clay assured himself that it would be alright. Clay was not known for his discretion or good judgment.

"What? What if they get caught?" asked Sarah Douglass. She was horrified.

"Let's hope they don't. It should be such a surprise that the Yankees won't be able to react quick enough." He tried to downplay the possible consequences. "It's my feeling that if they are caught, and I'm sure they won't be, that they will be treated as prisoners of war," said Clay. "I believe that Lincoln intends to hang all Confederate leaders after the war anyhow, so what have we got to lose? There's no more harm in taking his life than in him taking ours. After all, Mrs. Douglass, Yankee spies have already tried to kill President Davis and his family by setting fire to his home, and I fully believe it was done on Lincoln's direct order."

Mrs. Douglass was visibly upset. "I'm sorry, Mr. Clay, but I must really disagree! Lincoln may be many things, but a murderer is not one of them. I cannot believe he would order the killing of Mr. and Mrs. Davis."

"Well, Mrs. Douglass, with all respect to your opinion, you may not have heard that during a recent attack on Richmond, a Yankee colonel named Dahlgren was killed. On his body they found papers that gave him the authorization to burn Richmond and kill President Davis and his cabinet. So it is my opinion that anything must be done to these scoundrels to facilitate the end of the war."

That said, the door opened and James Douglass entered. Sarah and Mary excused themselves and left the men alone. They made their way to the kitchen. What had her husband gotten into? thought Sarah.

The men spoke quietly for a few minutes and then Douglass called from the parlor, "My dear, I'm going out on some business with Mr. Clay. I don't expect to be long." She heard the door close as the two men left the house. Mary and Sarah looked at each other not knowing what to say or what to think.

7

Confederate Eyes in Sandusky

Major Charles H. Cole, at age twenty seven, was of fair complexion. His light sandy hair fell just over the ear. He stood five feet-four inches tall, and wore the most expensive tailor-made suits Confederate government money could buy. Of slight build, verging on frail, the only things large about him were his imagination and sense of self importance. He had told Thompson at their first meeting that he had been a lieutenant in the Confederate Navy. The truth was that he had been a lieutenant in the Fifth Tennessee Infantry and had been cashiered in December of 1863. His commanding officer, Major R.J. Persons, knew him to be a thief and a consummate liar, certainly not someone to be trusted with men's lives or large amounts of Confederate money.

Cole was a native of Harrisburg, Pennsylvania. He had been in both the Union and Confederate armies at one time and another. For a short time he served, or at least drew pay, under Nathan Bedford Forrest's command. He had been taken prisoner and later paroled, promising to return to Harrisburg, where his parents lived, and to report to the Provost Marshal there. He did neither. An adventurer with an eye to excitement, Cole had no political cause. He had little sense of duty or honor. All Major Charles H. Cole had was thousands of dollars in Confederate money to spend on lavish living and expensive aged bourbon. This was the man Jacob Thompson had decided to trust.

The West House was the finest hotel in Sandusky. It had been built in 1846 at the foot of Columbus Avenue across from the docks by a group of Sandusky investors who wanted to develop the city as a major port on Lake Erie. To attract business and people you had to have the proper accommodations. The West House, complete with thirty-five rooms, a bar, and perhaps the best restaurant west of Cleveland, had become the social center for Sandusky's burgeoning population. Everyone who was somebody in Sandusky, and a few who wanted to be, could be found haunting the saloon or lobby at one time or another. It was a gathering place for local politicians, businessmen, and the various officers and men who administered the Johnson's Island prison just across the bay. Even the crew of the *U.S.S. Michigan* was known to purchase an occasional beverage during their frequent trips ashore. It was fertile ground for a conniver like Charles Cole, Executive Secretary of the Mount Hope Oil Company. And he was sure to point out that his boss, the president of Mount Hope Oil, was none other than Millard Fillmore, former President of the United States. Cole preferred to refer to him as Judge Fillmore, however, an appellation that suggested a very close and personal relationship with the former President. The truth was that Charles Cole had never laid eyes on Fillmore, much less knew him. But the story was impressive to the locals in Sandusky, especially after a few rounds at the bar, so graciously and generously purchased by Cole. And he did more than impress the drinking crowd. Cole made so many large deposits in the Sandusky bank that he was given the privilege of withdrawing in gold if he so desired. He had done a very effective job in establishing himself as a free-wheeling, high-living, and very generous oil tycoon, one whom everybody wanted to meet and be seen with. No one bothered to check his story.

Cole had registered into the West House with a woman he introduced as his wife, Annie. Annie Cole had used any number of other names before. She had been Annie Brown, Annie Davis, and on occasion Belle Brandon. She was, in fact, a Confederate Secret Service courier and sometimes-prostitute from Buffalo, New York. Her real name was Emma Bison. Aside from posing as Cole's wife and providing such services as he might require, she acted as the conduit of information between Cole and Jacob Thompson, making trips back and forth to Toronto as the need arose.

One evening as Cole and Annie were finishing dinner in the dining room of the hotel, an Army officer whom Cole had become familiar with came over to the table with another man.

"Mr. Cole, excuse me, but I thought you might be interested in meeting my friend here." He touched the man on the arm. "This is Ensign James Hunter." Nodding politely to Mrs. Cole, he continued, "Ensign Hunter, may I introduce Mr. Charles Cole and his lovely wife." Annie smiled and nodded politely without speaking.

Cole remembered a conversation the previous week he'd had with his army friend. They had discussed the difficulty of shipping oil to Europe what with the war going on. And it was difficult to get reliable captains for his ships. James Hunter's name had come up.

Annie Cole began to rise, "Well, I can see this conversation is turning toward business, so if you will excuse me, Charles, I think I will go on back to the room for the evening." Annie made her exit as if on cue and the men adjourned to the bar.

Several drinks into their conversation, Cole suddenly changed the topic. "Say, Hunter, I have a proposition for you. You said before the war you had been a salt sailor, right? How would you like to come to work for me? Our company owns a schooner, the *Fremont*, and we need a dependable captain that can operate between the states and Liverpool, England. It pays well. What do you make as an Ensign on the *Michigan*, anyway?"

Hunter was both surprised and impressed by Cole's offer. And it was tempting. He was sure the pay would be much more generous than his salary as a lowly ensign on the *Michigan*. It would also be a welcome change to get off the lake and back to the ocean. There was just something about Cole that puzzled him. He had so much money, and threw it around so freely. Hunter wondered if he could be a counterfeiter.

"Well, Mr. Cole, you've caught me a little off guard with your generous offer. I'd have to think about it for a while, what with my responsibilities here and all, but thank you for asking just the same. I will think about it. Can I let you know later?"

That was fine for Cole. "Of course. I have a good bit of other work to do in the meantime." He smiled. "Oh, barman, get up two cases of wine for Mr. Hunter here." He looked back to Hunter and said, "You take some wine back to the officers on the *Michigan* with my compliments."

Hunter was impressed, "I thank you very much, sir." He lifted his glass to Cole in a toast.

Over the course of the next week Cole made the most of his time in the bar. He made the acquaintance of another Ensign from the *Michigan* by the name of Michael Pavey. He was the ship's engineer and was in charge of the engine room. Pavey had joined the Navy more as a way of making a steady living. He had no strong feelings about the country's political troubles. Pavey came from a working-class background where money had been scarce. Cole sensed that given the opportunity to make some real money, Pavey might not be so loyal to the Navy. It occurred to Cole that if the *Michigan* ever needed to be disabled, Pavey could be very useful. And he struck Cole as a man who could be bought. Cole made a mental note to cultivate Pavey's friendship.

The first week of September started out mild and sunny, but as Tuesday passed to Wednesday, the temperature dropped rapidly and great black thunderheads rolled across the lake from the northwest. By the time John Yates Beall got off the train in Sandusky and made his way to the West House it was pouring. Droplets of water clung to his moustache, and his clothing was soaked as he entered the hotel lobby.

The clerk arranged for his room, suggesting a hot bath might be in order. Beall agreed. Though he did not know it yet, his room was directly across the hall from Cole's. That morning Cole had told the hotel clerk that a business associate of his by the name of Yates would be arriving, and to save the room as it would be more convenient for them to be close to one another.

Usually, by late afternoon the hotel was beginning to buzz with people coming in for a drink or early dinner. This afternoon, the weather had rendered it unusually quiet. When Charles Cole arrived for dinner with his wife, there were only a few diners in the room, most of whom Cole knew by name. The gentleman at the far table in the corner of the dining room was John Beall. Cole had not met him, but had been given a general description by his wife, direct from Jacob Thompson. Cole approached his table.

"Mr. Yates?" asked Cole.

Beall looked up and nodded. "Yes, and you must be Mr. Cole." They shook hands.

"Why don't you join my wife and me for dinner," he nodded in the direction of his table. "We can talk business later." Dinner conversation consisted of the usual pleasantries for the benefit of anyone who might be listening. They also talked of the events of the war, careful not to talk too loudly, or suggest strong feelings one way or another about them. You couldn't be too careful.

The main topic of their conversation was General Sherman. He had taken Atlanta on September second, after Hood's withdrawal. "Practically the entire city has been destroyed," said Cole, holding up a copy of the Sandusky *Register*. "It's in all the papers." Beall hadn't had time to see a newspaper. "He is now marching two hundred and fifty miles across Georgia toward Savannah. His men have been ordered to pillage and burn everything in sight over a path sixty miles wide. They say even civilians will not be exempt from Sherman's wrath."

"I can't believe that," Beall said quietly. "I don't understand why the Northern government would do such a thing. Until now both sides have respected civilians and their property." Cole looked around, afraid that someone would hear. No one was in earshot.

"It would appear that Old Abe and his generals don't share your opinion, Mr. Yates," said Cole with a smirk. "If it were up to me, I'd probably do the same to them." He wondered if Beall might just be a bit too proper for this line of work. He handed the paper to Beall, who quickly scanned the front page.

"It says here that Sherman's men are destroying homes, barns, crops, and businesses, even if they had no importance at all to the war. It's just destruction for destruction's sake," said Beall. "Is this what the war has come to?"

Cole shrugged as if he really didn't care. It made Beall sick inside to see what this war had done to men. Seeing that Cole didn't share his heartfelt sentiments troubled him. What was a man like Cole capable of, if he had no heart for the suffering of others? Or was his attitude just a part of his cover? Beall couldn't be sure.

With dinner concluded, Cole and Beall agreed to meet at eight o'clock in Cole's room. That was two hours from now, and he needed some fresh air. Beall decided to take a walk.

The rain had stopped, but the wind had not died down. It came off the lake and cut through his coat as he walked the fifty or so yards from the West House to the pier. He noted that the West House sat on Columbus Street which ran perpendicular to the wharf. It came to a dead end at the water's edge, where Water Street intersected, running east to west directly adjacent to the wharf. Beall had a clear view of Sandusky Bay and, despite the weather, thought he could make out lights on both the *Michigan* and Johnson's Island. It was too dark to get a clear view of the entrance to the bay. That might be a problem. He had heard that the channel was narrow.

The meeting at eight o'clock was fruitful. For over two hours the men pored over the details of the plan. Cole was to meet the evening of September eighteenth with local men, Rosenthal, Merrick, Williams, Strain, Brown, and a Dr. Stanley, who would help the escapees from the prison with guns and supplies once they got into Sandusky. Cole would make arrangements to visit the prison and inform key Confederate officers of the plan. Cole decided a signal flare might be the best way to let the prisoners know to start the breakout because it could be seen simultaneously by the prisoners on the island, and by Beall approaching the *Michigan* by boat.

To divert the attention of the crew of the *Michigan*, Cole would arrange a dinner party and drug the wine. That way most of the officers and crew would be off the ship and unable to respond. The skeleton crew still on board would be easy to subdue once Beall and his men boarded the *Michigan*. Beall would travel to Windsor, Canada, and recruit a crew of Confederate soldiers. There should be no trouble with that, thought Beall. A fairly large community of them lived there openly, much to the chagrin of the citizens of Detroit just across the river.

"When you get to Windsor, there will be money deposited in the name of Yates at the Ontario Bank," said Cole.

"Good, who made arrangements for that?" asked Beall.

"One of our men brought it down from Toronto. A courier had delivered it to him direct from Richmond." answered Cole.

"That must have been pretty risky. . . to move money through the Northern states to Canada," said Beall.

"Not for this courier. Ever heard of an actor named Booth?" laughed Cole.

Yes, there is a whole family of them, all actors," said Beall. "I met John Wilkes Booth in Charles Town back in eighteen fifty-nine."

"Well, he's your man. He's able to move just about anytime and anyplace he wants, and no one asks questions. Always going someplace to do a play. Sometimes he carries medicine south, sometimes its messages between Toronto and Richmond. I read where he's doing a play in Buffalo this week. Wouldn't surprise me if he made a little side trip to Toronto. Maybe you'll even see him in Windsor when you get there. He's been pretty close with Clement Clay up in Montreal, but meets with Colonel Thompson when he's in Toronto."

At about ten-fifteen the men concluded their work, wished each other well, and parted. Beall left for Windsor on the six forty-five train the next morning. He made mental notes about the number of weapons and other equipment he would need to get for the attack on the *Michigan*. He still had mixed feelings about Cole.

8

Assault on Johnson's Island

Windsor, Canada, sits across the river from the city of Detroit. The Detroit River itself flows from Lake St. Clair, between the sister cities and down into Lake Erie. Since the beginning of the war, Windsor had become the haven for various and sundry scoundrels, deserters and Confederates who had escaped prison. The people of Windsor, like an increasing majority of Canadians as the war dragged on, were Southern in their sympathies. It was the perfect place to recruit a crew and obtain all the supplies needed with little danger of being reported to Federal authorities.

Beall's first stop in Windsor was the home of Samuel Overfield. John had stayed with Overfield during his visit to Canada in eighteen sixty-two, and it was Overfield who would handle any correspondence Beall had. Overfield also knew the community well, and would be much help in rounding up a good crew for the impending mission. Within a few days he proved to be as good as his reputation. A crew of volunteers had been assembled and brought in to meet Captain Beall.

As the men entered the room they could not know how shaken Beall was. He kept what was in his heart to himself. The Detroit papers that day carried reports that in two separate battles, Jubal Early had been defeated by Phil Sheridan's forces. Despite heavy losses, Sheridan had driven Early out of the Shenandoah Valley. The Union army now had control of the valley from Harper's Ferry south to Winchester. What had happened? Were his mother and sisters alive? Did Sheridan plan to destroy the valley the way Sherman had done in Georgia? In his heart he wanted to leave immediately for home no matter what the cost. After all, everyone else seemed to take duty so lightly. Why shouldn't he? But there was his father's ever-present voice. He had been raised to accept duty, to put responsibility above self. He hated that feeling right now, but over two thousand prisoners craved freedom, and his country needed them desperately. That would all depend on him. Personal concerns had to be put out of his mind for now.

As the men filed into the room their voices mixed in an undistinguishable buzz, except for one. Beall was jostled from his personal thoughts by a Scotsman's brogue. As Bennet Burley entered the room he saw Beall and shouted, "Boyo, am I glad to see you, lad!" He clapped Beall hard on the back and gave him a big bear hug. Beall, his chest in pain, winced, but managed a laugh and smacked Burley on the back with both hands.

While Overfield prepared whiskey for everyone, Burley took the floor and introduced the others to Beall. "My good fellows ... ahm ... , " Burley was in good humor, and about to turn an introduction into a speech. "This here's my friend and commandin' officer from those excitin' days of yore on the Chesapeake, pirating against his majesty, Abe Lincoln." Beall was pretty sure that Burley knew the difference between being a pirate and a privateer, but to Burley it didn't seem to matter. It was all just high adventure to him.

"Captain Beall, may I introduce you to your crew." Burley waved his hand in theatrical fashion. "This gentleman's name is Henry Barkley, here's Robert Smith, David Ross, Richard Drake, and Big Jim Brotherton," Brotherton, actually very small in stature, drew a laugh from all, and a slap on the back from one of the men standing next to him. Burley continued, "William Byland, Robert Harris, William Holt, Tom Major, Nathan Johnson, John Bristol, and Harley Dugan, a good Irish lad ... if there is such a creature! ... but I'll forgive him for that!" The men all laughed as Burley move across the room to some men he had not yet introduced. With his forefinger he enumerated, "Willie Key, Francis Thomas, John Odoer, Joseph Clark, and last but not least, the distinguished surgical magician, Dr. John S. Riley."

Now Beall took the floor, thanking Burley for the introduction. He explained to the men at first a general overview of the plan, and then went into specific details of how each man would be expected to perform. He reminded them of the political implications that were present in what they were doing, and stressed that no laws of war were to be violated . . . strictly none! There was no room for error on this mission. The worst thing that could happen would be to create an international incident that would put the Canadians and British in an untenable position. All this being understood, the men would be assigned their roles by Burley. He would also make the final arrangements for a boat, and Beall would acquire the supplies and weapons. Until then, he admonished them to keep quiet and wait for further instructions. The meeting was over.

After the others had gone, Beall and Burley sat down and caught up on what had happened since their escapades on the Chesapeake. Burley, ever the story teller, recounted how he himself had been appointed Acting Master and conducted raids on the York and Potomac Rivers.

"We got into a terrific gun battle with squad of Union men. I got shot in the leg . . . . thought I'd likely bleed to death. We were in a real pinch and couldn't get away. When we surrendered, the Union officer took two of my men and had them shot in cold blood. Can't barely stand to think of it as we speak, lad! Then, as I lay bleedin'. . . like to die. . . they set upon me and went through me. . . robbed me blind, they did! Then they took us down below Philadelphia about forty miles to Fort Delaware. What a God awful place!"

"Yes, I know," agreed Beall. "I was there too for a while."

"I can't recall how many weeks I was there," Burley continued, "when it occurred to my feeble brain that there was a way out. I was gettin' some fresh air out in the prison yard one day when it struck me that the long sewer that ran through the center of the yard must leave under the prison wall and flow down to the Delaware River. The sewer was about three feet wide and covered over with wooden planks. I imagined that if a soul was to be able to climb into that sewer drain, he could swim undetected right under the wall and out to the river. The only problem was that the water level came right up to the supporting beams on which the planks were nailed. That meant I'd have to dive under water about every ten feet where the beams crossed the ditch. There was a damned air space between the support beams, but it was only big enough to raise my face out of the water to gasp for air. And gasp I did, laddy! Did you ever swim over seventy-five feet through piss water and floatin' turds?"

Beall smiled and shook his head. He had to admit he hadn't, but there were times when he had felt neck deep. Though he never drank anything stronger than soda water, Bennet Burley acted like he was on his third or fourth drink. He rambled on with his story, fully enjoying the retelling of it. "Six of us started out in pairs, a good swimmer paired with one not so good. We tied canteens around our waists to buoy us once we got to the river. I really wasn't sure I could make it, and I was in pretty good shape. Sad to say, some o' the others were not. Two of us made it out into the river where we got picked up by a passing boat. The others didn't make it. Two drowned in the river and we heard shots . . ." Burley shook his head sadly, "I think the other two lads never made it out of the sewer."

Beall was curious. "What did you say to the men on the boat who picked you up? How did you explain why you were out there in the river?"

Burley cleared his throat and waved his hand, "I was just gettin' to that. We told them that we'd been fishin' and our boat capsized. I'm not sure they believed us, but they took us all the way to Philadelphia. From there it was on to New York and then here." Burley paused and took a long look at Beall, his eye lids narrowing, "So my lad, and what have you been doing?"

9

Capture of the Philo Parsons

On September 15, 1864, Captain John Yates Beall took a small front room on the first floor at the Windsor Hotel, not far from the Detroit River. It seemed a safe haven from Federal detectives and had been well used by Confederate refugees and operatives for some time. The hotel's manager, Charles Smith, was a short stocky man with hairy arms and a deep scar on his chin. He was about thirty years old, but his craggy face made him look to be fifty. His bald head, except for a few thin wisps that never stayed in place, was the only thing neat about him. He wore the same white shirt, verging on yellow, sleeves rolled to the elbows, and black silk tie every day. His only trousers were baggy and badly in need of pressing. Smith never said much. Kept to himself, and for good reason. To those who thought they knew him, he had arrived in Windsor from Toronto in 1862 to run the hotel. In truth, he was a Confederate escapee himself. Disillusioned with the war, all he wanted was an end to it. Smith had relatives on both sides, and mostly out of the luck of living in the South when the war started, not because of any strong belief, he had joined the Confederate cause. The hotel was a good place to hide until the war ended. He didn't much care how it came out, he just wanted it done, and soon. But now the South was trying something new. He had seen a great deal over the last few years, and overheard more than he let on. He kept it all to himself, but now he was having doubts.

It was through Charles Smith that John Beall ordered three dozen hatchets and four grappling hooks. They would need to be delivered to the hotel by seven a.m. on Monday, September nineteenth. Beall also requested that any messages for him be delivered first through Bennet Burley. On Friday, September sixteenth, Beall sent another message saying that so far everything was satisfactory, but that the goods should now be delivered on Sunday to Room 101 at the Windsor Hotel. It was Burley who invited Smith to come along with them. Smith initially declined, saying he had too much responsibility for the hotel, but he would think about it.

On Saturday morning, September seventeenth, Lieutenant Colonel Benjamin H. Hill, acting assistant provost marshal at Detroit, received a note from an anonymous source that a party of men from Canada were leaving Windsor intent on capturing the *U.S.S. Michigan* in Sandusky. Hill was skeptical. For over a year rumors of such an attack had been rife all around the lakes. He dismissed it as just another rumor. Then on Saturday night, an overweight, balding man appeared at Hill's hotel room.

"Colonel Hill, I'm sorry to bother you so late in the evening, but I am the man who sent you the note this morning." Smith did not bother to identify himself. He looked around secretively, "May I step in?"

Hill opened the door and allowed the man to step inside. "What information do you have?" he asked.

"Jacob Thompson is in Windsor and intends to send a party of men to Sandusky tomorrow to take the *U.S.S. Michigan*." He added that he knew for a fact that some of the *Michigan's* crew had been bribed.

"How do you know all this? Hill asked.

"I was asked to be a member of the party. I, myself, he hesitated..."am an escapee of one of your prisons, and I told them I would go along."

Hill was still skeptical, but felt there might be something to it. Otherwise, why would this man take the trouble to come to him now? Hill pressed the man for more.

"All I know right now is they plan to leave tomorrow morning on the *Philo Parsons* and that Mr. Thompson's paid a great deal of money to some members of the *Michigan's* crew. I'm supposed to meet with them again on Sunday for full instructions. I could see what I can find out and come back on Sunday night?"

Hill was impressed with the man's earnestness. He told Smith to go ahead and see what else he could ferret out about the plan. As soon as Smith left the hotel, Hill went directly to the telegraph office. He sent a warning to Captain Carter of the *U.S.S. Michigan* in Sandusky.

On Sunday evening, September 18, 1864, two men with different but related purposes moved through the streets of Detroit. The sun was beginning to descend in the west, and rays of crimson blazed behind the city skyline. One man would keep an appointment with Lieutenant Benjamin Hill as he had promised. The other was making his way down to the wharf where the *Philo Parsons* rested at dock.

Charles Smith appeared at Hill's hotel room about nine o'clock. He told Hill that he had agreed to participate in the raid, and that the party of Confederates planned to board the *Parsons* down river at Malden, on the Canadian side. He had also heard that a man named Cole in Sandusky had bribed both the Captain and crew of the *Michigan*. If Cole's intentions were carried out, he would drug the crew to effect the takeover of the ship.

At almost the same hour that Hill received his visitor, Bennet Burley approached the gang plank of the *Philo Parsons*, a 220 ton sidewheel steamer that made daily runs between Detroit and Sandusky, Ohio, carrying both passengers and cargo. Burley stood on shore for a few moments studying the boat carefully, noting the decks, location of the cabin, wheelhouse and cargo holds, needing to know it all. He'd been there several times before to look the boat over. No room for mistakes. Burley noticed the young man on deck watching him and casually walked on board. Walter O. Ashley, part owner and clerk, was alone on the aft deck.

"Evenin' to ya, my good fellow," Burley said with all the Scottish charm he could muster. "Name's Bennet G. Burley." He extended his hand to Ashley. "I understand this boat makes trips to Sandusky each day. Some friends and m'self were thinkin' we'd go down to Kelley's Island for the day. Sort of a holiday, ya know? Maybe get in some fishin'. But can ya tell me, lad, does the boat stop at Sandwich on its way?"

"No, sir," said Ashley. "It doesn't. Why?"

"Well, some of me friends would find it most convenient to get on there if at all possible, as one of them is a bit lame, and finds it hard to go too far by foot." Sandwich, a small town on the Canadian side of the Detroit River, was just a few miles south of Windsor. "Could ya make an exception, as a favor to me, and pick'em up there?" Burley grinned.

Ashley hesitated. He didn't like making unscheduled stops, especially for strangers. But Ashley had seen this man several times before on the docks. Seemed a friendly sort. Probably would be all right. "Yes, I suppose I could do it," he said, "but you'll need to board right here at this dock in the morning so I know for sure to make the stop. And I'll only touch at the dock in Sandwich just long enough for your friends to board. Be sure they're ready. I won't wait." That was just fine with Burley.

As Charles Smith left the hotel, Bennett Hill debated what to do. Was this just another hoax? If it was, he'd look like an alarmist, a fool. If it wasn't, and something did happen, he'd be seen as derelict in his duty. He debated with himself for almost an hour. Do something before it's too late, he thought. It was near midnight now, and Bennett Hill was once again making his way, more quickly this time, to the telegraph office.

The operator keyed in the message:

Captain Carter: *U.S.S. Michigan,*

> It is reported to me that some of the officers and men of your steamer have been tampered with, and that a party of rebel refugees will leave Windsor tomorrow with expectations of getting possession of your steamer.

Captain Carter replied:

> I am ready. I hope they will come; it is not true as regards my officers and men.

In Detroit it was now almost two o'clock in the morning. Colonel Hill read Carter's reply and prayed he was right.

Seventeen-year-old Mary Stephens and her friend, Amanda Roberts, had come from rural Perkins Township to Sandusky to start high school in early September of 1864. Mary had two brothers there, Washington Stephens, a lawyer, and Jefferson Stephens, a guard at the Johnson's Island prison. Mary had planned to stay with Washington Stephens and his wife, but when Mary arrived with her friend, her sister-in-law balked at the idea of boarding both girls. She had agreed to only one. The other came as a surprise. So it was that the girls, wishing to be together, took a room at a boarding house on Madison Street. The house was full of boarders, mostly men, but Stephens was assured by the proprietor that these were men of good reputation. The girls would be safe.

Mary and Amanda went to their room Saturday night happy over the prospect of starting school. Late that evening they heard several men talking downstairs. Soon more men came. It wasn't long until fifty or so had arrived. They were drinking and talking loudly, becoming more boisterous. The girls, curious as to what was going on, sat in the dark at the top of the stairs and listened, amused by the men's behavior.

A man named Cole, who seemed to be their leader, was talking with the others about how someone was going to capture the boat . . . the *Michigan* . . . and then go over to the island. . . capture all the guards. . . and then release all the prisoners. Cole also talked of capturing Sandusky and conducting a raid down through Ohio. Words like burn, loot and rape drifted up to the top of the stairs where the two sat silently horrified, eavesdropping in the dark.

The girls were panicky, but didn't know what to do. They wanted to get out of the house, but were afraid if the men discovered them, they might be killed. Quietly, the girls crept back into their room. They looked out the second-story window. It was too high to jump, so they huddled together on the floor and kept silent, too frightened to sleep.

Late into the night the tired and drunken men left. As day broke Sunday morning, the girls slipped quietly out of the boardinghouse and ran to Mary's brother's house on Columbus Avenue. He wasn't home. Stephens had gone to his law office very early that morning. Mary's sister-in-law was shocked as she listened to their story. She told them to say nothing about it to anyone because rebel sympathizers in town might try to kill them. When Mrs. Stephens reached her husband, he notified his brother on Johnson's Island, and the authorities in Sandusky.

Now two separate sources had confirmed Captain Carter's worst fears. He immediately dispatched Ensign C.C. Eddy to get a room at the West House to keep an eye on Cole. Next, Carter made arrangements for Ensign James Hunter to go to Detroit to more fully investigate the matter. Before he was able to leave another telegram dated September nineteenth arrived from Colonel Hill in Detroit.

Captain Carter: *U.S.S. Michigan,*

> The parties will embark today from Malden, on board the steamer *Philo Parsons,* and may seize another boat running from Kelley's Island. Since my last dispatch I am again informed that a man named Cole is to be introduced on board in the guise of a friend of the officers. I consider the matter as serious.

Captain Carter immediately sent his orderly to fetch Ensign Hunter from his cabin. Hunter was fully aware of the rumors that had been circulating for more than a year. On more than one occasion he had secretly been sent to Detroit and Canada to investigate. Until now the rumors had been just that, rumors.

"Mr. Hunter, here is a telegraphic dispatch that says the rebels are coming on the steamer *Philo Parsons* from Detroit, and that some of our ship's officers are traitors. It says that a man named Charles Cole is a spy." said Carter.

"Captain, I know these men very well. I don't think any of them could be traitors."

"Do you know this man Cole?" he asked.

"Yes, sir, I do." answered Hunter.

"What do you know about him?"

Hunter related that he had met Cole at the West House, and that he was an oil company executive. He told Carter that Cole had family in Philadelphia and that he had been dealing in oil stock lately in Enniskillen, Canada.

"He also recently asked me if I'd resign from the Navy and go as

Captain of the schooner *Fremont* to Liverpool, England with a load of oil for him." said Hunter.

"Mr. Hunter, get your sidearms on and come with me. We're going over to the island to see Commandant Hill at the prison." Carter knew there was no time to lose.

Lieutenant Colonel Benjamin Hill had arrived at the docks just before six a.m. It was still dark and he stood well back in the shadows. Less chance of being seen. He knew that the *Philo Parsons* departed Detroit promptly at eight. Looking her over, he decided that she was too small to be of any danger if she was seized, so after some consideration he came to the conclusion that if the plot was real, it would be better to let the steamer go, and put Captain Carter on guard. That way the whole rebel crew could be caught in the act. Satisfied he had made the right decision, Hill left. He arrived at the telegraph office before sunrise and dispatched another warning to Carter. Then he went back to his hotel.

At seven forty-five a.m. sharp a stocky, barrel-chested man of dark complexion joined the line of people waiting to board the *Parsons*. His brown hair was partially covered by a woolen cap with a net peak. But for a small moustache, he was clean shaven. The man spoke to several of the women and their children. Small talk mostly, nice weather, he hoped the trip was a smooth one for the tykes. The children were intrigued by his accent. Each of the passengers stopped as they reached the deck to pay their fares to young Walter Ashley. In return each received a little blue ticket which Ashley said would be collected after departure.

"Good marnin' to ye, lad. Remember me?" Yes, Ashley remembered. "We will still be able to stop at Sandwich, won't we?" smiled Burley. Yes, they would. Ashley didn't forget. He continued to collect money and pass out tickets.

The last man aboard was the captain of the boat, Sylvester F. Atwood. The *Parsons* always ran on time, but Atwood never got there too early. He marched past Ashley with a curt good morning and made his way quickly to the wheelhouse. One would have hardly guessed by the stiff greeting that Walter Ashley was Atwood's son-in-law. Three short blasts on the horn and they were under way.

As the boat pulled away from the dock, Burley ambled casually forward making small talk with the passengers, especially the women, who particularly enjoyed his complimentary attentions. He noted the approximate number of passengers, thirty-five in all, the location of the wheelhouse, the boat's office, the ladies salon, and the entrances to the hold below decks. There seemed to be quite a lot of cargo aboard. Some of it would have to go.

As the *Parsons* approached Sandwich, Captain Atwood issued two short blasts on the ship's horn and they touched the dock. Three men jumped aboard while the boat was still in motion. All three were dressed neatly as gentlemen. One, shorter than the others at five feet -seven inches, wore gray pants and a black cloth coat buttoned over his chest. What showed of his white shirt exposed a rolling collar and a black silk cravat. His hair was dark brown covering half his ears. Forehead high, nose straight, his lips were thin and compressed. His complexion was pale. He had a light moustache and beard, neatly trimmed to a point under his chin. He smiled as he boarded and limped over to Ashley to pay his fare. He spoke softly and pleasantly as he greeted Ashley and nearby passengers. The limp soon disappeared. Ashley didn't notice. He was too busy with other things. John Yates Beall slowly and cautiously moved forward and up to the helmsman's deck, striking up a conversation with the Parson's mate. They both admired the weather. The sky was blue and the temperature unseasonably warm, although it was still early and the breeze had a nip in it. The other two men who boarded with Beall moved throughout the boat sizing up the situation. They struck up a conversation with a rather talkative Scotsman near the stern, out of earshot of the other passengers. Orders were given. Be at your stations when Beall moves toward the wheelhouse.

Malden, Canada, twenty miles below Detroit, was the next scheduled stop. Sixteen passengers came aboard, all men, and pretty roughly dressed. Walter Ashley sized them up and commented quietly to Captain Atwood that he'd bet they were skedaddlers, local jargon meaning draft dodgers. They'd seen a lot of those in recent weeks. Almost every stop in Malden picked up such men who could not find jobs in Canada, and were forced to return home and take their chances with the law. None of these men had any luggage, except for an old black pinewood trunk tied shut with a rope. Two of the men carried it aboard at the stern. Few seemed to notice it at all. Everyone was talking, enjoying the sun and air, and thinking what an enjoyable excursion today would be. By nine thirty a.m. the *Parsons* was again headed for Sandusky.

The meeting of Carter, Hunter and Commandant Hill on Johnson's Island produced an agreement that the *Michigan* would continue to guard the entrance to the harbor and watch for the arrival of the *Philo Parsons*. An armed force would be sent to watch all railroads and telegraph lines around Sandusky in case the rebels came by train, or attempted to cut the wires. James Hunter then hurried back to the *Michigan* and told Executive Officer Martin to get ready for action. Hunter quickly prepared to go ashore to arrest Charles Cole. This would have to be done as quickly and quietly as possible. Hunter didn't want to alert any accomplices.

As Hunter climbed off the barge at the Sandusky dock, he met crewman Richard Gregory. Gregory had been waiting for the barge to go back out to the *Michigan* to see Hunter.

"Ensign Hunter, I just now left the West House. That fella Cole was asking about you. Told me he wanted to see you. I told him if I saw you I'd let you know," said Gregory.

Hunter turned to Coxswain Peter Turley. "Turley, turn this barge around, and keep the crew ready at their oars." He then told Turley to follow him. "Gregory, you stay with the barge." As they crossed the street toward the West House, Hunter said to Turley, "Now, there may be some trouble shortly, and I want you to stand by to help me. If you hear me give out a long whistle, you come right away. I'm going upstairs in the West House to arrest Charles Cole."

Hunter reached Cole's room and knocked. No answer. He opened the door and found the room empty. Thinking Cole had already fled, he ran downstairs and asked the desk clerk, "How long since Cole left?"

"He's ready to leave, sir, but he hasn't. Just now he's in parlor B," the clerk answered.

Hunter found Cole putting on his shirt. His wife was sitting, already dressed for travel, and their trunks were packed and ready to go. Cole's face lit up, glad to see Hunter. "So...you did receive my message from Mr. Gregory?"

"Yes," Hunter answered, trying to appear as calm as possible. Don't want to give anything away, he thought. "I met him at the dock just a few minutes ago."

Cole pointed to a large wine bottle encased in wicker. "Have a drink, Hunter, that's a very fine vintage, there."

"No, thanks," he said.

"Oh, come now, man, just one little nip won't do you any harm, have one," Cole insisted. Cole continued dressing, adjusting his tie.

Reluctantly Hunter poured a glass and took a sip. He didn't swallow, afraid it might be drugged. Pretending he had a chew of tobacco in his mouth, Hunter choked and coughed, then went to the spittoon and spat the liquor into it.

"I'm afraid I almost swallowed my chew," Hunter explained sheepishly.

Cole laughed, "Take another one, Hunter."

"After you," replied Hunter. He held his empty glass high as if to propose a toast.

Cole took a drink, so not to make him suspicious, Hunter poured himself one. If Cole could take it, he thought, the wine must be all right.

Cole told his wife he had some business to attend to, and that he would be back in a few minutes. Cole and Hunter left the West House and headed up Columbus Avenue to the bank. Turley followed them at a distance, dodging from lamp post to doorway, keeping out of sight.

Cole drew out nine hundred dollars in gold which he placed in a small valise, and then he and Hunter returned to the West House. There they ran into an army officer who invited them into the bar for a drink. They all had one, and Hunter bought another round. When they'd emptied their glasses, Hunter took Cole by the arm in a very friendly way, and motioned toward the door. "Can we speak privately, Mr. Cole?" he asked.

"Yes, of course." Cole answered. "You will excuse us, sir?" he said to the officer. "Let's give this man another drink on me," he said to the bar man, and he left with Hunter. They headed down the street toward the docks. Hunter spoke first.

"What's up, Mr. Cole? Gregory told me you wanted to see me."

"Why, yes...I'm going to have a little party this afternoon out at Seven Mile House, and I want you to go along and have a real good time." He winked at Hunter, implying that women who aimed to please would be there.

"Well, I can't go without the executive officer's permission, but if you'll wait at the dock, I'll go aboard and get it."

That was just what Cole wanted. "See if any of the others can come. They're all welcome, you know." If he could get some of the officers away from the ship it would be that much easier to disable it.

When they reached the barge, Hunter still had Cole by the arm, with Turley tagging close behind. At the edge of the dock Hunter gave Cole a quick push and he fell off the dock into the barge. Hunter and Turley jumped in after him, and Hunter ordered the barge away from the dock.

"No! No! Put me back! What the hell is going on here?" shouted Cole as he fumbled to pull himself off the bottom of the barge.

"You're all right where you are, Cole, and I guarantee you, we will have a good time this afternoon. Give way men!" Hunter yelled, and the barge pulled away.

About mid morning, the *Philo Parsons* made a brief stop at Middle Bass Island to drop Captain Atwood off at his home. It was Atwood's custom to stop there once each week, stay overnight and be picked up again on the return trip. Until then the ferry would be in the able hands of Walter Ashley. They steamed past South Bass Island and on toward Kelley's. At Kelley's Island the *Philo Parsons* docked to take on more cargo and four more passengers. One of them, who had been posing as a sewing machine salesman on the island the past four days, sought out the familiar face of the Scotsman. The others drifted off to other parts of the boat. Burley knew that if the plan had to be aborted at this point, they would all get off at Kelley's Island and catch another ferry back to Canada. The very presence of these men told him that so far, all was probably well. A very brief and hushed conversation ensued. No word one way or the other from Sandusky. The sewing machine salesman wasn't quite sure what to make of it. Passengers approached, and the salesman walked away. As he did, Walter Ashley confronted Burley and reminded him that he and his friends had wanted to get off. Burley told him they had changed their minds, and would go on to Sandusky.

Beall ambled along the deck and ducked into the salon. Passengers milled around talking. As he studied them, he bumped into a young woman holding a baby.

"Oh, excuse me, m'am. I am so sorry." He reached to steady her and the child.

"Thank you," she said. It was obvious that the baby was fussing.

"You have a beautiful baby there," he said. "He or she?"

"It's a she," the woman said, "and right now she's not feeling very well. She seems to be congested. I hope it's nothing serious." He could tell she was very concerned and tried to reassure her.

"They're stronger than you think. Probably just a little cold," he said tousling the baby's small head gently with his hand. "Perhaps you'd be more comfortable if you sat down." He looked around for a chair. "You know, my lungs bother me quite often, too. It's troublesome. This damp air doesn't help matters either."

The woman smiled and sat down. "Thank you so much for your concern." She turned her attention to the baby and rocked it in her arms.

"Well, I hope you'll have a pleasant journey, m'am," Beall said. "Now, if you'll excuse me?" He tipped his hat and smiled as he turned for the door.

Burley made his way into the ladies' salon and in a short time acquired the pleasant task of turning pages for one of the female passengers who was playing the piano. He sang along, which was great cause for hilarity among the women. What he lacked in talent, he made up for in volume. But he was very amusing, and they were pleasantly distracted. Burley pulled out his pocket watch and noted the hour. It was almost four o'clock.

"Ladies," he bowed graciously, "I have enjoyed your company immensely, but now I must take my leave. Would one of you be so kind as to take my place at the piano and assist this fine lady in turning her pages?" He bowed theatrically, and moved out of the salon to the aft deck leaving laughter and applause behind.

Shaken and confused by what was happening, Charles Cole did his best to pull himself together. His mind was ticking off all the possibilities. Had he really been discovered? Did they know about Beall? Best to be cool. Wait to see what they knew. "Pull lively then, and I'll treat you all to a drink when we get back to the dock," he said with unconvincing confidence.

As the barge pulled alongside the *Michigan*, the sentry told Hunter to bring the prisoner into the Captain's cabin. By now, Cole, a rather fragile man, had lost his nerve. Hunter took hold of his arm and almost dragged him into the cabin. Captain Carter, seated at his desk, looked up at Cole and said, "I suppose you know why you were arrested, Mr.Cole?"

"Captain, if you'll give me just a few minutes of private conversation with you, I will explain everything," pleaded Cole. He knew if he had Carter alone he could kill him, then maybe make a break for it. He had a small pistol concealed in his hip pocket. It would be useless to try anything with Hunter in the room. He was too big.

Carter replied, "No, I think not. Mr. Hunter here is an officer, and he has arrested you. Search him, Hunter."

Hunter patted Cole down. He felt something. Lifting Cole's coat, he pulled a small caliber revolver from his hip pocket. He cocked it as he stared at Cole. Hunter handed the revolver to Captain Carter. "Please cover Mr. Cole while I search him," said Hunter.

Hunter stripped Cole naked as Carter watched, gun in hand. Cole stood silently, his mind looking for some angle, some tack to use as an explanation. As the minutes passed, none came to him. Charles Cole was without a good lie for the first time in his life. After searching Cole's pockets and taking all the letters, papers and valuables, Hunter told Cole to get dressed. Carter then called the Sergeant of the Marines and told him to put Cole in irons.

Among Cole' s papers were his commission as a Major in the Confederate Army, the names of some Sandusky men who were obviously accomplices, and the name of a U.S. Army Captain stationed in Columbus, Ohio. Some of these men were to cut telegraph wires and others were to spike the artillery guns at Sandusky. Within the hour Carter and Hunter took the documents to Commandant Benjamin Hill over on Johnson's Island. Hill telegraphed Columbus, Ohio, to have the officer named in Cole's documents taken into custody, and then ordered the men from Sandusky to be rounded up and arrested.

Returning quickly to the *Michigan*, Captain Carter sent his Executive Officer, Edward G. Martin, to the West House to confiscate all of Cole's bags. Martin hurried to the West House and made a thorough search of Cole's room and the salon where Cole's bags sat waiting for departure. Mrs. Cole was not there. The desk clerk said she had left a few minutes earlier, but said she would return shortly. Martin instructed the clerk not to say a word to Mrs. Cole when she returned. The search produced more information on Cole. He had been a prisoner and was paroled by General Hurbut at Memphis, Tennessee. He also had written to rebel refugees at Windsor, Niagara Falls and Toronto, Canada. At about four p.m. Carter sent for Commandant Hill. He wanted Hill present when Cole was interrogated.

Before Hill arrived, Captain Carter asked Cole, "What do you know about rebel conspirators coming down from Canada to seize the Michigan and release prisoners at Johnson's Island?"

"I don't know a thing. Haven't got any idea of what you're talking about," he answered with as much bravado as he could muster.

Carter then read a dispatch that had been found on him during the search, 'I send you today by messenger the thirty shares of Mount Hope Oil Wells purchased as you previously advised.' "What is this all about, Cole?"

"I'm in the oil business," he lied. "That is a private dispatch." said Cole.

"Well, I'll tell you what I think it means," said Carter. "I think it means that thirty conspirators are coming on the *Philo Parsons* to try to capture the *Michigan*. And I'll tell you something else I know. If you tell us everything you know, name names and such, I can see that it will be taken into consideration when you are tried." said Carter.

Cole knew it was all over. The best thing he could do now was to cooperate. They were on to him. Time to make the best deal he could for himself. "All right," he said, "It's true." Cole laid out the entire plan. "Some men are coming on the *Philo Parsons*. Others will be coming into Sandusky by train later today."

"Do the prisoners on the island know of the plot?" asked Carter.

"Yes, they are to wait for a signal flare fired by me. That would start an uprising on the island. Once the prisoners got free they were to begin an invasion of Ohio from Sandusky down to Cincinnati."

"Who else is involved? Any here in Sandusky?" asked Carter.

Cole named names, Rosenthal, Merrick, Williams, Strain, Brown, and Dr. Stanley. They would be coming on the train with the others from Toledo that night.

Events moved rapidly now. Colonel Hill put a detachment of soldiers on the island for extra security, and sent men out to meet all incoming trains. They were to arrest anyone who even looked suspicious. Rosenthal, Strain and the others were arrested. All vigorously protested they were innocent. Carter ordered Ensign Pavey to fire up the *Michigan* and be ready. The *Philo Parsons* should arrive between five and six o'clock. Carter would be waiting.

Mrs. Charles Cole had returned to the West House and sat waiting for her husband. His delay did not concern her. He was probably out at the Seven Mile House making arrangements for the party. She had no idea that he would not be coming back until the authorities came for her. In the parlor of the West House, Annie Cole was arrested and taken to the headquarters of Colonel Hill on Johnson's Island. Hill had no reason to believe that she knew of the plot, but he suspected she did.

"Mrs. Cole," Hill told her, "we have arrested your husband in connection with a Confederate plot to board and capture the *U.S.S. Michigan* and to break prisoners out of the prison on Johnson's Island. We are now holding him in the brig aboard the *Michigan*. We think you might be able to tell us something about his activities."

Hill had no real evidence on which to hold her, but thought if he was careful, he could get her to divulge something that would help with the investigation.

"That is absurd, Colonel!" she said with an air of disgust. "My husband is in the oil business. He has no interest in that prison or any other. The only thing Charles is interested in regarding this war is making money."

"What do you know about your husband's business? Do you know the names of any of his associates?" asked Hill. She stuck to her story.

"I know nothing about my husband's business. I don't bother myself with those

details. Charles has always been an excellent provider and I just don't get involved. I am frankly shocked and perplexed by these allegations.

Surely there must be some mistake."

The questioning dragged on for several hours. Hill hoped that by continued questioning, she'd slip up somewhere, give up some detail they could use. He probed for dates, names, places they'd been. She kept to the same line. She was sure this was all a mistake. Her answers never varied. Keep it simple, she thought. If I don't know anything, I can't tell anything. They'll wear out eventually. She was tough.

If she does know something, thought Hill, she wasn't telling. He began to almost believe that she really didn't know anything. One thing was sure, Hill thought, if she is somehow involved, she certainly has more guts than her husband. Lacking any real evidence of complicity on her part, Hill knew he could not charge her. He eventually would have to release her. That could wait until tomorrow. For now, let her stew.

Bennet Burley could see that all the men were in place. He moved quickly toward the black trunk at the stern of the *Parsons*. In just a few minutes they would be off Marblehead, within six miles of the entrance to Sandusky Bay. Beall was on his way toward the wheelhouse. Men were gathering around the Scotsman. Burley opened the trunk and handed out pistols. Each man knew his job and moved quickly and silently to his own position, fore and aft decks, wheelhouse and engine room. Beall climbed up to the hurricane deck. DeWitt Nichols, first mate and pilot, saw him coming and nudged the wheelman to look. Beall was about thirty years old, in a Kossuth hat and black coat. He entered through the pilot house door.

"Are you the captain of this boat?" he asked calmly.

"No, I'm the pilot," Nichols answered, wondering what this was about.

"But you are in charge of her now, are you not?" ventured Beall.

"Yes, sir." Nichols was puzzled.

"Will you step back here for a minute?" Beall indicated a spot near the smoke stack behind the pilot house. Nichols told Michael Campbell, the wheelman, to hold present course, and he followed Beall.

"There are about thirty of us, and we're well armed. I am taking possession of this boat in the name of the Confederate States. If you don't resist, you won't get hurt." Nichols stared at Beall in disbelief.

His mouth gaped open, his eyes questioned. Was this some fool joke? Beall quickly pulled his Navy colt from under his coat and stuck it along side Nichols' temple. It was no joke. Nichols could feel the cold steel against his cheek. His palms began to sweat.

"You are now my prisoner, and you will pilot this boat as I direct you." Nichols could feel Beall's breath on his ear. "Right now I want you to run down and lie off that harbor." He indicated a place dead ahead near the Marblehead lighthouse.

At the same time three other pistols were pointing at Walter Ashley. Before the astonished Ashley could ask for an explanation, Bennet Burley came aft with fifteen of his crew and told Ashley, "Get into that cabin or you are a dead man." Burley, with pistol cocked, counted, "One, two...." Ashley did not wait for three.

On the upper passenger deck, Frederick Hukill, a Cincinnati businessman, and his associate Joseph Skinner, had just settled into deck chairs to enjoy the cruise. Hukill lit a match to his long Cuban cigar and offered a light to Skinner. Mr. Thaddeus Werk, a wealthy wine dealer, and his daughter sat next to them on the left. Werk dozed as his daughter gazed across the glittering waves. To their right, Mrs. Elizabeth Faran, wife of the editor of the Cincinnati *Enquirer*, talked animatedly to her friends about her Canadian trip and how anxious she was to get back home. Hukill had just started to ask Skinner when the little blue tickets they were issued would be collected, when the commotion began. Shouts at first and then gunshots. As the startled Hukill looked for the cause of the commotion, he saw out of the corner of his eye the long black barrel of a revolver pointed at his head.

"All of you, get up and get into the cabin!" the stranger demanded.

"Oh! My God!" shouted Mrs. Faran. "What is going on here?"

"Yes," demanded Skinner, "What is the meaning of this?"

"It means," replied Captain Beall, "that this boat has been taken over by the Confederate Navy, sir. Now, if you please!" He motioned his pistol in the direction of the cabin door.

Captain Beall moved down the deck through the passengers. "Lieutenant Burley, line these men up and search them for weapons." Burley went down the line frisking each man and asking the woman if they were carrying weapons.

"Are you armed?" asked Captain Beall as he came to Fred Hukill.

"No, sir, I'm not!" snapped Huckill nastily. His short temper had gotten the best of the little man.

"I asked that in a gentlemanly way," Beall answered sternly, "and it deserves a gentlemanly answer."

Hukill didn't debate the matter with him. Cocked pistols spoke eloquently. The frisking continued. No weapons were admitted to and none were found.

The *Philo Parsons'* engineer, James Denison, heard the noise from the fireman's room. Gun shots, women screaming, and men swearing in fear and frustration. As he came out on deck, he saw Michael Campbell climbing desperately up the ladder from the main deck to the upper deck.

"Stop and get down into the fire hold!" shouted one of the Confederates.

"Go to hell!" Campbell yelled back, continuing to climb. When he didn't stop the man shot at him. The bullet richoched off the bulkhead between Campbell's legs. He got to the top of the ladder and found five more gunmen forcing passengers into the upper deck cabin. Other gunmen were frisking male passengers. Were they after money or what? he wondered. Now at gunpoint, he, too, was being forced into the hold with the rest of the crew. The Confederates then quickly closed the hatches and piled pieces of the pig iron cargo on top to keep any of them from escaping.

Michael Campbell's captivity did not last long. When the Confederates realized they needed him to steer the boat, they forced him back up to the pilot house where he joined first mate Nichols, Beall and Burley.

Women were screaming and men were being backed up to the cabin walls of the upper deck with hands in the air. "Ladies, ladies! We are Confederate gentlemen! We aren't here to harm you!" yelled one Confederate above the commotion. "I promise you, we'll treat you as if you were our own sisters." Two of the sisters promptly fainted. Quickly all passengers were stowed away in the cabin. Guards took their places on both sides of the door to be sure that no one got out.

Inside the cabin the captive passengers sat in a semi-circle, both in chairs and on the deck. Women cried in fear. The men talked quietly and cautiously. Something ought to be done, but what? No one wanted to take a chance for fear of being shot. The guard swore at them to be quiet. No one will get hurt, he said, but he kept waving his gun around and swearing at the passengers. He made suggestive and insulting remarks to the women, who cowered in absolute terror. At any moment this man might just start shooting. Hukill whispered to a young woman near him, "If someone could just go get the officers of the boat, I'm sure they would protect us from this guard." He thought for a minute and said, "It might be better if a woman went. They certainly wouldn't shoot a woman," he said.

A young women sitting near him agreed. "I'll try it," she said. She got up shakily, gripped with fear, and walked about ten feet, and then she fainted. Hukill could see that wouldn't work. Without thinking, he sprang to his feet and headed for the door. The guard, taken aback by the girl fainting and Hukill's attitude, was not as much a menace as he appeared. He stood mute and offered no resistance as Hukill bolted through the cabin door. Hukill hadn't gotten far when he ran into Lieutenant Elbert.

"I demand to talk to your commanding officer!" he shouted.

"What's the problem?" asked Elbert.

"Lieutenant, one of the guards has been making outrageous remarks to the women in our cabin and scaring the hell out of us all with his pistol!" said Hukill. "What can you do about it?"

Elbert didn't answer. He led Hukill back into the cabin. "Which one?" he asked. Hukill pointed him out. Elbert grabbed the guard angrily by the shoulder and threw him out the door. That was the last the passengers saw of him.

Little James Brotherton pulled a Confederate flag out from under his coat and hoisted it up the mast on the aft upper deck. The *Philo Parsons* was now officially a Confederate vessel. The old black trunk was brought forward. Hatchets and grappling hooks were removed and readied for use.

Up in the pilot house DeWitt Nichols' temples pounded. What could he do? Things were moving so fast. There had to be something he could do. He didn't want to die. Nichols protested weakly to Beall. In a polite and calming voice, Beall reassured him.

"Just remember what I told you. If you just obey my orders, you won't get hurt." His pistol was still trained on Nichols' head. Nichols was not convinced.

Burley and the crew began clearing the deck of freight, throwing most of it overboard. Twenty-five barrels of coal tar sat near the rear area. "Keep those barrels of coal tar. We might be able to use them," instructed Burley. If they didn't think they could board the *Michigan* by force, they could use subterfuge. They would set the *Parsons* on fire, and when the *Michigan* came along side to their aid, they would attack.

Beall called down, "Find a key for the baggage room." He wanted to know what was stored in there.

When no one offered a key, Burley snarled impatiently and said, "I'll make a key." He took a fire axe that had been hanging on the bulkhead and smashed the baggage room door open. Then he went forward and smashed in the saloon door, where more cargo was stored. Finding a black trotting sulky, he chopped it up and had it thrown overboard. He and the crew continued to unload cargo. Tobacco, household goods, and pig iron destined for Sandusky all went into the water. The entire capture had taken one half hour according to Burley's watch.

Having stowed the passengers and gotten rid of the cargo, Beall went to Walter Ashley, "Mr. Ashley, where are the ship's books and papers?"

Ashley hesitated. "Why do you want them?"

"The reason I need them, Mr. Ashley, is that I am an agent of the Confederate States government and I have seized this boat. Since this boat is now ours, I will require its papers and books. Now, will you get them, please?"

Ashley walked quickly into the office to get the papers with Beall and Burley right behind. "What do you intend to do with the boat?" he asked.

"We intend to go down and take over the *U.S.S. Michigan* and free the Confederate prisoners on Johnson's Island." answered Beall.

As he got out the papers, Ashley said, "Whatever use you have for the boat, when your done, I just ask you not to destroy it." Beall nodded, understanding the man's concern for the boat. Ashley was young and a part owner. It would be a great loss to him.

"Mr. Ashley, what if you were a United States officer and had seized a Confederate vessel. Wouldn't you destroy it?" Ashley did not answer. He didn't need to. He knew what Beall intended to do. "Now, Mr. Ashley, how much money do you have in that drawer?" asked Beall.

Ashley reached into the cash drawer and pulled out about forty dollars in greenbacks. Burley took it and shoved it into his pocket. "Come, now, my good man, you've certainly got more than that. What have you got on you?"

The clerk gingerly reached into his vest pocket and pulled out a wad of cash. It amounted to about one hundred dollars more, passenger and freight fares from the morning plus some petty cash for making change. He laid the bills on the desk, and Beall and Burley picked it up. "I have some personal notes, too. Do you want them?"

"No, "Beall answered, "all I want is the boat's money, not yours."

"Besides, lad," laughed Burley, "how would we collect them personal notes anyhow?"

Ashley did not hear the last two comments. He was distracted by the door bursting open. A Confederate, agitated and out of breath, told Captain Beall the news.

"Sir, there does not seem to be enough wood on board to fire the engines for the rest of the trip. We're likely to run out before we get away. What do you want to do?"

Beall left the office and headed for the wheelhouse with Burley and Ashley right behind "Mr. Campbell, where can we get wood?"

"The closest place is Middle Bass. There's a wooding station there." he answered. He knew he dare not lie.

"Then get us turned around and run up there right now," ordered Beall.

They reached Middle Bass about dark. From the dock they could see the lights of the Golden Eagle winery just fifty yards or so up the hill. The wooding station, a large brick building set just to the left of the dock, was manned by several island men and a boy, the son of one of the men. As soon as the *Parsons* was fastened to the dock, Beall yelled to the men to begin loading wood. The men were suspicious and hesitated. Where were Ashley and Captain Atwood they wanted to know. Why are you coming in here at this late hour? No, they would not load wood. A few well-placed pistol shots in their direction changed their minds. Frightened, the boy ran up the hill and off in the direction of Captain Atwood's house, just beyond the winery. Atwood had heard the shots from his porch, and was already running down the lane. He met the boy half way.

Breathless, the boy yelled, "Captain Atwood! The *Parsons* is back! They're tryin' to kill my father! Come quick!

Who's doin' the shootin', boy?" asked Atwood. "Why is the *Parsons* back?"

"Heard someone say they was Confederates, they brought the boat back," the boy yelled as he ran on ahead of Atwood.

Sylvester Atwood marched onto the dock and shouted, "What in hell is going on here?" Four cocked and ready pistols pointed at him all at once.

"Come aboard!" one of the men shouted.

"No, I won't. I'm the captain of this boat!"

Two of the men grabbed him and shoved him toward the gang plank. He walked aboard. As he walked toward the cabin two of the men followed him. Atwood could see the passengers sitting inside guarded by two other men with pistols. Then he saw Ashley.

"Walter, what's the meaning of all this?"

"The boat's been seized by Confederate rebels," he said, exasperated, "there's no use resisting."

Now another Confederate approached Atwood. He appeared to be the oldest of the Confederate party. "Captain Atwood, I'm Dr. Riley. Why don't you sit down here with me."

"What is this all about, doctor?" Atwood asked.

"I'm sorry, I can't tell you. I can only tell you that I am a surgeon in the Confederate Army. I know this is an unpleasant affair for you, but we have our duty to perform. Just be cool and I can assure you that you won't get hurt."

Atwood was exasperated. "Look, man, can I go see my wife? I promise that I'll come right back. She's probable terrified at what might be going on here."

"No, I can't let you do that." said Riley.

"Then I'd like to see your Captain," countered Atwood.

"Be patient, I'll introduce you to him in a few minutes. I know he wants to see you, too."

"What do you people intend to do with my boat?" asked Atwood.

"I think you'll get your boat back after this is all over," assured Riley.

It was half past seven when they all heard the shriek of the *Island Queen's* whistle. Captain Beall was ordering that some of the *Parsons* crew be brought up from the hold to help load the wood when one of his men caught him by the arm, "Look, Captain, a boat's comin' in."

Beall barked out the order, "As many as can be spared from the cabin, come out this way!"

The *Island Queen* was a 173-ton sidewheel ferry similar in design to the *Philo Parsons*, but somewhat smaller. It made regular runs between the Sandusky, the Bass Islands and Toledo. Today she carried among her passengers thirty United States Army soldiers of the 130th Ohio Volunteer Infantry, who had completed their tour of duty and were on their way to Toledo to be mustered out. They were unarmed.

Captain George Orr of the *Island Queen* didn't know what to make of it. He had seen the *Parsons* earlier in the afternoon heading toward Sandusky, and then saw her turn back toward Middle Bass. She had arrived just ahead of the *Queen* and taken Orr's usual dock space. Orr made ready to pull along side and tie off on the *Parsons*. When he got close enough to see that something was desperately wrong, Orr rang the full-steam reverse order to the engineer, but it was too late. The Confederates jumped aboard the *Queen* fore and aft with hatchets and pistols. The soldiers put up a fight but were no match for the surprise attack in the dark by Confederate hatchets and guns. The Confederates had the element of surprise and darkness on their side.

While Beall's men scuffled with the soldiers and crew of the *Island Queen*, Captain Orr signaled the engineer again to reverse engines full. Henry Haines, below decks in the engine room, was trying to set the engine to pull out away from the *Parsons*. One of Beall's men yelled down to Haines, "Stop those engines immediately!" When Haines did not comply, someone else yelled, "Shoot the son-of-a-bitch!" Haines looked up into the darkness of the open hatch, and caught a bullet in the face. The ball passed through his nose and out his left cheek near his ear. A painful and ugly wound, but not life threatening. Engines were now at full stop and Henry Haines, bleeding and in shock, pulled himself up onto the main deck. Two men stood before him in the dark, one with a globe lantern and revolver, and the other with two revolvers. Haines was holding his cheek. The second man asked, "What's wrong with you?" He couldn't see the wound in the dark. The gunman didn't know that he had hit his mark. The shot was only intended to show the engineer they meant business. He handed Haines over to one of the others aboard the *Philo Parsons* and told him that this man was a prisoner.

"Hey, you can't take him aboard the *Parsons*. He's the engineer. He's got to stay aboard the *Island Queen* to tend to the boilers." said Clarence Woolford, one of the *Queen's* passengers who knew Haines.

"All right, put him back over here," said the man with the lantern.

Again Beall ordered, "Bring the Captain of that boat up to the pilot house. Make sure it's tied fast, we're taking off as soon as all the wood is loaded."

At about eight-thirty Beall, Burley and some of the others got together and decided that they'd have to get rid of most of the passengers before they left.

"Get all the women and children off this boat now. Males passengers later, and then those soldiers. Bring Captain Atwood up to his room. I want to see him privately," ordered Beall.

Dr. Riley brought Atwood to Beall. Beall shook his hand. "Captain Atwood, I'm Captain John Beall, Confederate States Navy. I'm sorry for all the problems we're causing you, and I hope it will be over soon. I'm going to let you go ashore with the others. I don't want you on the boat, but I do want you to promise me that you won't leave the island for twenty-four hours, unless your boat comes back. I also want you to take charge of these women and children while they are on the island."

"Can I take some of my clothes?" Atwood asked.

"No, but don't worry. Nothing in your cabin will be disturbed." Beall said.

"What are you going to do with the *Island Queen*?" Atwood asked.

"We'll have to get rid of her, probably we'll have to burn her." said Beall.

"And my boat?" asked Atwood.

"You'll probably get her back, Captain," answered Beall. Atwood felt relieved but not entirely certain.

Once the women and children had all been lined up with their luggage, Beall told them he was releasing them all so long as they promised not to send word of what had happened for twenty-four hours. They all agreed, more than happy to be freed unhurt. Atwood led them all up the road past the winery and wood station to his house under a clear, bright moonlit sky.

When the women were made as comfortable as possible, Atwood

walked back down near the dock, standing in the shadows to avoid being seen. Other passengers were being led off single file, the male passengers, and last the soldiers.

As the male passengers lined up on the gang plank to go ashore, Burley asked the name and residence of each passenger. The men from Cincinnati headed the line.

"In return for your freedom each of you must swear that you will not divulge what has happened to you for a least twenty-four hours."

When he came to Joseph Skinner there was trouble. Skinner spoke up, "I'm sure glad to be rid of you rebel slave drivers!"

"And ye must be a god-damm black abolitionist!" Burley spat.

There was no time for argument. When Burley came to Frederick Hukill he said, "And who might you be?"

"Fred Hukill, of Cincinnati."

"Oh, another god-damm black abolitionist!" repeated Burley.

Hukill fumed. "No I ain't . . . not by a frigging far sight!" he shouted.

Caught off guard by the remark, Burley was at a loss for words. All he could get out was, "I thought not!" He moved on to the next man.

As they prepared to land, Fred Hukill noticed that the ladies' luggage had been put ashore. One of the Confederates gave him a shove toward shore, but he hung back.

"Ain't you goin' ashore? a rebel guard asked.

"I want my baggage," Hukill protested.

"Well, you can't have it," countered the rebel condescendingly.

"C'mon, Fred, come ashore," cried Skinner from the dock, afraid Hukill might get himself shot.

"Well, when can I get my bags?" he persisted.

"When we're finished, we'll run the boat aground somewhere. You can get them then."

Hukill stood fast. If anything, he was stubborn. Skinner thought he was being stupid.

"I want to talk to an officer!" Hukill demanded. "Those other people have theirs, I want mine!"

The Confederate shook his head in disbelief and marched back onto the boat. "I'll ask an officer," he called back.

In a moment he was back. "Take my arm and follow me." They climbed with lantern in hand back to the aft deck of the boat over pieces of machinery and found the baggage. Hukill picked up both his and Skinner's bags and headed back to the dock. By now all the rest, with only the clothes on their backs, had left the boat. Skinner shook his head and breathed a sigh of relief.

Atwood heard the order to shove off, and he watched the *Parsons* towing the *Island Queen* as far as Ballast Island. Just before he lost sight of them, he could see the *Parsons* and the *Queen* separate. Then the *Parsons* disappeared into the darkness.

10

Mutiny

Middle Bass Island was now out of sight. Captain Beall ordered his men to board the *Island Queen*, sever her pipes, and then cut her loose. She was of no use to them now. Captain Morgan climbed over the *Parsons'* rail and onto the deck of the *Queen*. He climbed down the ladder into the engine room where Henry Haines sat, still nursing his wound.

"Haines, I'm Captain Morgan. Where are the valves on this boat?" Haines took Morgan into the hold and showed him the pony pipe. Morgan picked up a fire axe and quickly began chopping. Haines winced. As he chopped at the pipe, Morgan asked Haines, "How are you voting this year?"

"I guess I'll be votin' for Old Abe," Haines replied, holding a rag to his wound.

"What do you think McClellan's chances are?" asked Morgan lifted the axe to strike again.

"I don't think he's got any chance at all," said Haines. He shook his head in dismay as Morgan took a large sledge hammer and broke the big water cock off the side of the boat. Water began pouring into the hold. It was filling up rapidly. Ought to go down fast, thought Morgan. Quickly, both men climbed up to the main deck. Back on board the *Parsons*, Morgan and some of the others cut the tethers loose and the

Island Queen drifted away into the night.

"I want all members of the *Parsons'* crew put in the hold," Beall told Burley, "with the exception of just those needed to run the boat."

"It'd be my pleasure, sir," nodded Burley.

"And pull in those running lanterns. I want total darkness. I don't want them to see us coming."

Burley and a few others busied themselves rounding up the rest of the crew and forcing them into the hold. The *Parsons* continued to steam down toward the mouth of Sandusky Bay in pitch darkness with Michael Campbell at the wheel. Captain Beall kept his gun on Campbell, but his eyes were on the opening of Sandusky Bay, some six miles away. The night sky was moonlit and black, blending into the lake, interrupted only by an occasional white cap breaking over a reef, and the dim glow of the lights of Sandusky on the horizon. Beall strained into the darkness, hoping to catch the blaze of a lone signal flare. One by one the men on deck and at their various stations were watching, too. Where was the flare? The more they watched and saw nothing, the more tense they became.

Small quiet conversations developed among the men, in two's at first, then in small groups. Where was the flare? Had something gone wrong? Minor doubt turned to anxiety, and then to outright fear. The only man of real confidence was John Beall. He was sure the plan was working, maybe not exactly as anticipated, but it was working.

As the *Parsons* closed in on Sandusky Bay, their talk turned to the narrow entry channel. Was it possible to get through in the dark without running aground on a sand bar? The channel was so narrow. The night was black. One small error and they would all be stranded and caught. And Captain Orr was piloting the boat. He had everything to gain if they got stuck.

That wasn't the way Orr figured it. He was nervous. If he ran the *Parsons* aground he was certain they'd shoot him. He didn't relish the thought of trying to pass through the channel this night at all.

The lights of the *U.S.S. Michigan* were now clearly visible. They would soon be in range of her fourteen guns. If they ran aground, they'd be sitting ducks. Beall had no time for worry. He concentrated on the night sky. It was Burley that entered the pilot house and spoke first.

"Captain Beall, I think ya should come down on the main deck. There's a bit of a problem with the men."

"What kind of problem?" puzzled Beall.

Burley didn't want to say it out loud. He eyeballed Campbell and indicated for Beall to step outside the pilot house. His words were for Beall only. Beall left one of his men to keep an eye on the the man at the helm, and he followed Burley down to the main deck where most of his crew had assembled.

"Captain, with all due respect, the crew has decided to refuse to go any further with this mission." Dr. Riley, an army surgeon and the oldest man in Beall's crew, acted as spokesman for the rest. He handed Beall a bill of lading. On the back was written a statement of the crew's intention not to go through with the attack on the *Michigan*.

Beall quickly read it over:

> We the undersigned, crew of the boat aforesaid *Philo Parsons* take great pleasure in expressing our admiration for the gentlemanly bearing, skill and courage of Captain John Y. Beall as commanding officer and a gentleman, but believing and being well convinced that the enemy is already apprised of our approach, and is so well prepared that we cannot possibly make it a success, and having already captured two boats, we respectfully decline to prosecute it any further.

J.S. Riley, M.D.	Wm. Byland
H.B. Barkley	Robert G. Harris
R. F. Smith	W.C. Holt
David H. Ross	Tom S. Major
R.B. Drake	N.S. Johnston
James Brotherton	John Bristol
M.H. Duncan	F.H. Thomas
W.B. King	J.G. Odoer
Joseph Y. Clark	

Beall couldn't believe it. "You mean you refuse to go further...after all we've done to get this far?" Beall rubbed his hands together and thought. His mind was racing. Have to make sense to these men. "I don't know what to say to you. What the hell are you thinking? We've come this far ...why stop now? Have you all suddenly become cowards?" He was absolutely shocked. Rarely did Beall ever express strong emotions, but so much was at stake here. He was frustrated and furious.

"Captain," said Doctor Riley, "the men feel that it's too dark. If we hit a sand bar and run aground we'll all be caught."

"And there hasn't been a signal," said Duncan. "What if Cole's been caught?"

"That's nonsense. I'll be damned if I've come this far and will now just turn around and run like a pack of scared weasels. Are you men cowards or just fools? Have you lost your nerve? What is it? There are two thousand men over on that island, and any one of them would be happy to take the chance to help you."

David Ross took off his hat. He ran his fingers through his hair and looked at the deck. "You know, sir, we've all come a long way here, but that's the point. If there's no flare, then somethin's gotta have gone wrong. If we get caught, we'll all be in that there prison with those men, or worse. If we play it safe now we can go back to Canada and fight the good fight on another battle field. If we lose now, we're through."

Heated argument went on for almost an hour. Finally, Beall folded up the mutiny statement and put it in his pocket. He said nothing as he turned away from the men and headed back up to the pilot house. Seventeen men's names were on that list. He could continue on, but could he do it with only the help of Burley and a few others? No. Where the hell is their pride? They had a duty to those men on Johnson's Island. Beall was angry and frustrated but he held it in. He had to keep control. He slipped through the pilot house door and quietly ordered Michael Campbell to reverse course and head for the Detroit River. . . full speed. In the dark privacy of the pilot house, he stood back of Campbell. His jaw was taunt, his eyes were bright with tears. No one saw.

Captain Jack Carter stood on the bridge of the *Michigan* and strained his eyes to catch a glimpse of the *Parsons*. If she entered the channel she'd be within a mile of him, and he was certain he could overtake the

Parsons. No sense even considering using his guns, there were civilians on board. What could that idiot Provost Marshal in Detroit have been thinking to even let the boat go with all those civilian passengers aboard? He checked his watch. The *Parsons* should have arrived. Even if she had decided to turn around, he should have been able to see her running lights. And still no orders from Washington. Wasn't that always the way, he thought. We've got a serious threat on our hands here and the bigwigs in Washington won't let us make our own decision to give chase. Probably afraid we'll go into Canadian waters and create an international incident or something like that.

Carter was right. Late that afternoon, General Dix had received the telegram about the takeover of the *Parsons.* His first impulse was to order Carter to go out on the lake and look for the *Parsons* before she even got near Johnson's Island. But that would leave the prison undefended, except for the small complement of guards on the island. And if the *Parsons* tried to make a run for it and got to Canadian waters, there would be international consequences to consider. Not sure what to do, Dix sat on the telegram until he heard more. If the *Parsons* showed up and caused trouble, he'd order the *Michigan* out after her. Play it cautious for now, he decided.

Through the evening hours Commandant Hill prepared the prison for a possible attack from within and from without. He ordered all prisoners into their barracks and steadily increased the guard complement with troops brought over from Sandusky.

The prisoners on Johnson's Island knew something was up. Something had gone wrong. Cole had told them over several visits to the prison that a group of Confederates were coming by water and he would signal them when they had arrived. Under the leadership of General Isaac Trimble, the prisoners had quietly divided into companies and created a set of plans about how best to rise up against the guards. With that accomplished, they would make their escape to Sandusky. The Sons of Liberty would have guns and horses for them, and they'd head south toward Cincinnati. Along the way they'd show these Northerners what the war was really like. But something had gone wrong. No one knew just what.

By ten thirty p.m. the *Philo Parsons* had not been spotted. A ferry boat, the *Princess,* arrived at the *Michigan* with Cole's accomplices on board. They joined Cole in the brig. Colonel Hill received a telegram from Detroit informing him that the *Philo*

Parsons had left on time. By his count, she was long overdue. Even if the *Parsons* had gotten near the bay, he surely would have been able to spot her running lights. Something had gone wrong, he just didn't know what, or why.

Below decks in the *Philo Parsons'* cramped hold, the passengers and crew were frightened and disoriented by all the course changing and the fear of what might happen to them. Around midnight the boat lurched as it struck something in the water. DeWitt Nichols, mate of the *Philo Parsons,* could hear the engine running full out, but the boat had stopped almost dead in the water. Suddenly the hatch was thrown off and a lantern appeared. "Nichols," a voice commanded from above, "you're wanted by Captain Beall on deck right now!" It was an emergency. As soon as he reached the pilot house Nichols knew exactly what had happened.

"You've run the boat onto a fishing net," he said.

"Can you get us off?" asked Beall.

"I think so," he answered looking warily down at the water. With a gun pointed to his head, Nichols gingerly slid the boat back off the net and moved around it.

"Maintain course for the Detroit River, Mr. Nichols," ordered Beall.

Several long hours passed in silence. As the *Parsons* entered the mouth of the Detroit River, Beall stood watch over Nichols and Campbell. They saw several boats along the river. They'd be easy pickings, thought Beall. At least we could get something for our trouble tonight.

"Whose territory are we in, Canada or the United States?" Beall asked.

"We're in Canadian waters," Nichols replied.

"They're safe, then." Beall allowed, "If we were in American waters, I'd board them."

Just before dawn the *Parsons* reached Malden. They were ten miles below Detroit. Beall touched Nichols' shoulder. "Steer into the Canadian channel on the right." A few more miles up river Beall ordered Nichols to land on the Canadian shore. "We're going to unload some of the cargo. Once we've done that I want you to make for Fighting Island."

On Fighting Island, a long stretch of land located in the middle of the river, Beall released Captain Orr and a few crew members. The sun was just coming up. The last stop was a small dock at Sandwich, Ontario. They tied up there and removed passenger trunks, mirrors, deck chairs and even the piano from the salon where Burley had sat turning pages that morning. A few sleepy people milled around the dock that morning, but none seemed at all interested in what was happening.

Now Beall ordered one of his men to go down and cut the injection pipes. Water began to rush in, filling up the hold. As the *Parsons* slowly filled with water, Beall released the crews of the *Parsons* and *Island Queen*. He told them all to begin walking toward Windsor. One by one as they walked north, Beall's crew split off from this odd parade until none was left. By the time the crews of the *Parsons* and *Island Queen* reached the city, the *Philo Parsons* had sunk at the dock, with only her hurricane deck and pilot house showing.

The men of the *U.S.S. Michigan* had remained on alert throughout the night, but nothing of the *Parsons* was seen. Commandant Hill wanted to send the *Michigan* out to look for her, but was still waiting for orders from Washington. None came.

Shortly before dawn Hill lost all patience, and sent Captain Carter out with the *Michigan* to look for the *Parsons*. By sunrise the *Michigan* reached Kelley's Island where Carter found some of the *Parsons'* passengers. The passengers told him what had happened aboard the ferry and that the Confederates had used the name John Robinson, referring to someone from Sandusky who had given one of the Confederates a message.

The *Michigan* steamed on past Middle Bass to the mouth of the Detroit River, arriving at ten a.m. Carter hailed several boats to ask if they had seen the *Parsons* on the river or at Malden. The *Parsons* had not been seen. Failing to locate the *Philo Parsons*, Carter set his course for Put-in-Bay at South Bass Island. At one-twenty p.m. they spotted the *Island Queen* resting in three feet of water, grounded on a shallow reef. By three p.m. Carter was steaming back into Sandusky bay. By three-fifteen, John Robinson, who had been used by Cole as a messenger between himself and his contacts in Canada, was taken into custody, and joined Cole and the others.

Annie Cole was released on Tuesday morning. She caught the first train for Toronto an hour later. By Thursday she was in the office of Jacob Thompson. She related the whole story to him. Thompson fired off a letter to President Jefferson Davis informing him that Charles Cole had been involved in the plot to get the *Michigan* and the prisoners at Johnson's Island, and that he was being threatened with trial and execution. Thompson claimed that Cole was a very useful man to the Confederacy, and that President Davis should take strong retaliatory measures.

By Wednesday night, while U.S. and Canadian authorities argued heatedly about what to do, most of Beall's men had made it the forty miles to Belle River, and were on a train headed east for Toronto. Most of them eventually found themselves in Halifax, Nova Scotia, far from the reach of United States authorities.

Bennet Burley headed for Guelph, Ontario, where he had been living with relatives before the raid. Within a few days he was arrested by Canadian authorities and held for extradition to the United States to face charges. For a short time the police thought they had captured Beall. And Burley relished in their confusion. John Beall made a wiser choice. He traveled northeast of Toronto to Balsam Lake, and spent the next few weeks laying low, camping and fishing.

When he returned to Toronto the news of Bennet Burley's arrest was in all the papers. The authorities thought they had Beall, and Burley hadn't told them differently. Beall discussed what to do about the situation with friends. He felt like he should turn himself in. It wasn't fair that his friend Burley should take the brunt of the punishment. After all, Beall was the commander in charge of the operation. His friends disagreed. It was likely that the Confederate government would take some action to block any attempt by the Union government to extradite Burley, they thought. If that happened, it wasn't likely that the Canadian government would do anything. If they let Burley go, what would be the point in Beall turning himself in? He could be more help out of prison than in. Beall finally agreed, but he still did not feel good about it. It didn't seem the right thing to do.

11

A New Plan

The news of Beall's attempt on the *Michigan* hit the Toronto papers quickly. Both accounts of the event and editorials throughout Canada decried the event as both outrageous and illegal. Editors loudly and angrily proclaimed that Beall and people of his ilk were abusing their presence in Canada, and their actions ought not to be tolerated. Reading these accounts, Beall, too, became angry. He wrote a personal letter to the editor of the Toronto paper:

Mr. Editor:
You condemn the conduct of those who captured the two steamers on Lake Erie as infringing the laws of Canada. Cognizant of the facts, I wish to present them to you, hoping to win you to reserve your decision. The United States is carrying on war on Lake Erie against the Confederate states, either by virtue of right or sufferance from you, by transportation of men and supplies on its waters; by confining Confederate prisoners on its islands, and lastly, by the presence of a 14-gun steamer patrolling its waters. The Confederates clearly have the right to retaliate, provided they can do so without infringing your laws. They did not infringe those laws; for, first, the plan for this attack was matured, and sought to be carried out in the United States, and not in Canada; there was not a Canadian, or any man enlisted in Canada. Secondly, no act of hostility was committed on Canadian waters or soil. Any man may lawfully come into, or leave Canada as he may please, and no foreign government can complain of the exercise of this right here. These

men embarked on an American vessel from Detroit, or sprang on to it while in motion from Canadian wharves. The boat did not properly stop at Sandwich, or Malden at all, as the Customs will show. It touched at two American ports, and was not captured until within range of the 30-pounder Parrott guns of the 14-gun steamer. What act of hostility had been committed up to this time? Another boat containing thirty or forty United States soldiers was captured in an American port. After wooding up, the *Philo Parsons* proceeded to the mouth of Sandusky Bay for the purpose of attacking the *Michigan*, when six-sevenths of the crew refused to do duty, and thus necessitated the abandonment of the enterprise. Thirdly, what is this *Michigan* that she cannot be attacked? Is the fact that she carries thirteen more guns than the treaty stipulation between the United States and England allows, a sufficient reason why she is not subject to attack? England allows this boat to remain guarding Confederate prisoners, though she carries an armament in violation of the treaty. Before these men are condemned, judge if they have broken your laws. No murder was committed, indeed not a life lost. There was no searching of prisoners, no robbing. It is true the boats were abused; but, sir, they were captured by Confederates, enemies of the United States, and however questionable the taste, the right is clear. These men were not burglars, or pirates, or enemies of mankind, unless hatred and hostility to the Yankees be taken as a sin against humanity, or a crime against civilization.
J.Y. Beall

By the time Beall returned to Toronto, Jacob Thompson already had a new plan in motion. Immediately after the failure of the Johnson's Island plot, Thompson had begun the delicate process of acquiring the *Georgianna,* a boat he wanted Beall to crew and equip for attacks on all major cities on Lake Erie from Buffalo to Toledo. It was for this venture that Robert Martin and John Headley were called to serve.

Colonel Robert Martin and Captain John W. Headley had been summoned to Richmond from the field in July of 1864 by Secretary of War, James A. Seddon. Both men were experienced in the arts of irregular warfare. Colonel Martin had served under General John Hunt Morgan, and had participated in most of his raids into Kentucky and Ohio. Captain Headley had served as a Confederate raider under both Morgan and Cantrill. In Richmond they were given a letter from Secretary of State, Judah Benjamin, outlining their mission. The letter was to be presented to Jacob Thompson when they arrived in Canada. That mission, stated in very cautious terms, was to lead raiding parties on several northern cities.

With one hundred-ninety dollars in greenbacks between them, Martin and Headley left all Confederate identification behind, and headed in the direction of St. Louis, Missouri. They knew that if caught and identified, they would surely be killed. At Abingdon, Virginia, they sold their horses for seventeen hundred dollars and took a train south and west to Mississippi. By the first of September, their travel slowed by the war, the men passed through the town of Meridian, Mississippi in the safe company of Nathan Bedford Forrest's cavalry. Then it was on to Corinth by rail. There they left the train and walked to Jackson, Tennessee, where they bought a horse and mule, and rode to Hickman, two miles south of Charleston, Missouri. After selling the animals, they walked eighteen miles to Cairo, Illinois, where they boarded a steamboat loaded with Federal infantry bound for St. Louis. They treated themselves to a shave and haircut, and it was on to Alton, Illinois. From there they traveled to Chicago by rail. The night after they reached Chicago they caught another train for Detroit. The morning of September twenty-second, just three days after Captain Beall abandoned his raid on Johnson's Island, they crossed by ferry into Canada and caught another train for Toronto.

Their journey had taken them two months. Now in Toronto, Martin and Headley went to the Queen's Hotel, headquarters of the Confederate Commission. Jacob Thompson occupied a suite of rooms with his secretary Walter W. Cleary on the second floor. Many other Confederates and wealthy Southern refugees lived there, too. Among them was Dr. Stuart Robinson, a well known minister from Louisville, Kentucky, some of the Breckenridge family, and about one hundred other prominent Southerners.

The lobby of the hotel was alive with people coming and going. It was midday and the city was bristling with all the normal city business. Porters carried bags from carriages in the street, women attired in their finest dresses stood about cheerily talking of their plans for the day. Men lounged in the lobby's comfortable over-stuffed chairs, reading the daily papers. Some had already found their way into the hotel bar. The sounds of their voices drifted out into the lobby. Dozens of people came and went constantly throughout the day.

Martin and Headley attracted little notice except for one young man who watched them closely as they ambled across the lobby to the desk. Each registered in a separate room, so as not to attract attention. As they signed the guest register, the clerk recognized the names. He leaned down and quietly said, "Mr. Thompson's been expecting you. Take Room 315. Mr. Headley, you'll be in Room 317, right across the hall."

"Thank you," said Martin. "Would you let Mr. Thompson know we are here?"

"Yes, sir, I will. Dinner is a six, sir. You may want to clean up." The dust and smell of the road was apparent. "I'll send a messenger to fetch you when Mr. Thompson is ready to see you."

Martin and Headley welcomed a hot bath and clean sheets. Martin decided on a nap. Headley went out for a brief walk through the neighborhood around the hotel. A thin young man of about eighteen watched him cross the lobby to the door. He followed at a respectful distance. One block down the street Headley heard a soft boyish voice behind him.

"Captain Headley?" Headley turned, a bit startled. "George Anderson, sir," he grinned. "I thought it was you and Colonel Martin when you came through the lobby this afternoon, but I wasn't sure. Decided to wait and get a better look later." Headley clasped his outstretched hand and shook it firmly. "Well, of course! How have you been? We'd heard you were captured."

"I was, but I escaped off the train in Ohio. Heard you and Colonel Martin had come to Canada, so that's where I headed, too. Don't happen to need a good courier, do you?"

"Right now I'm not sure what I need. I'll know that better by tonight.

Are you staying at the hotel?"

"Yes, sir, I am." said Anderson.

"Well, just sit tight and I'll see if I can use your help. What is your room number?"

"It's Room 212, sir." answered Anderson.

"Fine. I'll call on you tomorrow." Headley looked up and down the street. Never know when someone's watching. The men shook again and parted, Anderson back to the hotel for dinner, and Headley on down the street. He'd circle around the block and back to the hotel. Martin would be surprised. It was a strange coincidence. Anderson had been Martin's courier, too, at different times and in different companies. And now they were all in Toronto together. When he returned to his room a note had been slipped under the door. Dinner was at seven with Mr. Thompson. Headley knocked. Martin let him in and Headley told him about how he'd been approached by George Anderson on the street that afternoon. They discussed how they might be able to use him, and read the papers until it was time to meet with Jacob Thompson.

Walter Cleary answered their knock. "Mr. Martin and Mr. Headley, I presume?"

"Yes, we're here to see Mr. Thompson," said Martin. Cleary led them into a second room where a number of men stood about smoking cigars and drinking bourbon.

"Colonel Martin, Captain Headley, how good to see you." Thompson walked over quickly and shook their hands. "Gentlemen," he said to the men gathered in the room, "let me introduce you to Colonel Robert Martin and Captain John Headley." He took the men around the room and introduced, "my friend and associate Larry McDonald, Godfrey Hyams, another good friend of mine, Captain Thomas Hines, my aide, late of Morgan's raiders, and of course you've just met Walter Cleary, my secretary." The men were greeted all around and supplied with good Cuban cigars and generous glasses of bourbon.

"Captain Hines, I understand that it was you who designed the plan of escape for Morgan from prison in Ohio." Godfrey Hyams drew deeply on his cigar. "Tell us, how exactly did you accomplish that? We've heard accounts of it, but I'm afraid that they are all different, and probably quite exaggerated," said Hyams. He was always asking questions, pushing for details. A bit of a pest, thought Cleary as he poured another round. "It's a pretty damned long story. Are you sure you want to hear it?" Hines laughed. He didn't mind telling it, really. But he didn't want to take away from the reason they were there. He looked to Thompson for a cue.

"By all means," Thompson agreed. "Our business here won't get started until after dinner. Go ahead, I'd like to hear it, too."

The men settled into chairs about the room, smoked, drank and listened.

"As you know, I was with General Morgan in Ohio. When we were captured they took us to the Ohio State Penitentiary, not with the criminals, though. We were separated from them by a wooden wall that cut the cell block in half at the middle. There were five ranges of cells in all. General Morgan, his brother, myself, and a few others were on the first range. The rest who were captured with him were on the second range. The cells were only three feet wide and six feet deep. We each had our own cell, but during the day we were allowed out, and could visit in the corridor that traveled through the center of the cell block. It was about twelve feet wide and one hundred-sixty feet long. At night we would be put back in our cells and locked up."

McDonald interrupted, "How did you come up with the plan to escape?"

"From the day we were first imprisoned, we all tried coming up with escape plans, but none that showed much promise of success. I, myself, began thinking of ways to escape on our very first night there. Oddly enough, I was inspired by two books I was reading, *The Count of Monte Cristo* and *Les Miserables*, but I didn't know enough about the design of the prison to even know how to proceed." said Hines.

"Then how did you discover what to do?" prodded McDonald.

"Well, first we thought about bribing the guards, but there were civilian guards and military guards. They were more suspicious of each other than they were of us. We were afraid of even trying, because if we got caught it meant solitary confinement in the dungeon in total darkness. Nobody wanted to chance that. Finally, I decided that the only way out was to dig a tunnel. I had noticed that in my cell, which was on the ground floor, there was no dampness or mildew on the floor or walls. That could only mean that there must be some kind of air passage under the cells. If we could break through down into that passage, we could tunnel under the cell block wall and out into the prison yard."

"That's fine, but how did you know where you'd be? How far you'd have to go?" asked Thompson.

Hines leaned over and drew some imaginary lines on the floor. "This is the cell block. Down here at the end was a window. It was right up at the top of the wall. There were five tiers of cells, so I estimated it was thirty feet up to the window. There was a ladder attached to the wall that was used by someone who wished to occasionally open the window for ventilation, but if we tried to climb it, we would surely attract attention. So, one day the assistant warden came walking through, as was his custom. Apparently not a very bright man, we told him we'd made a bet that one of our men could not go up the ladder hand over hand and back down again without using his feet. The warden didn't think he could do it either, and wanted to see him try. So our man went up the ladder to the top. He looked out the window and memorized the shape of the yard, placement of the wall, and location of the guards. Then he came back down again." The men all laughed at the Yankee stupidity, and ordered another round. Cleary obliged.

"But how far did you have to tunnel once you got into the air passage?" asked McDonald.

"We weren't sure at first. When we broke through the floor in my cell by digging at night with a dinner knife, we had to judge the approximate width of each cell and the thickness of the walls between, and mark a center point for each cell from which men would be escaping. Then we cut holes from inside the air shaft into each cell."

"How did you cover up the holes?" asked Hyams.

"Yes, and what about the dirt and concrete?" questioned McDonald.

Headley was mildly amused by the story, but was more amused by the interest of McDonald and Hyams. The liquor was working on him, though, and he sat back and indulged the rest of them. Those Yankee guards must have been idiots, he thought.

"We dug at night, working in shifts. It took several months to accomplish. Once the guards did their bed check at ten p.m. they didn't come back until the morning. If by some chance they did come back, we developed a series of knocks to signal the men in the shaft to stop digging until the guard passed. We carried some of the dirt out into the exercise yard in our pockets and deposited it when no one was looking. The biggest part was left in the air shaft. We covered the holes by pulling our bunks over them. I used a satchel I had with me to actually cover the hole in case a guard would move my bed. During the time it took to dig the tunnel, General Morgan's brother, C.C. Morgan, wove a rope in links from the bed ticking. And from the iron poker in the hall stove, we fashioned a hook. We used those later to ascend the wall."

Thompson raised his hand, "Now, you're getting ahead of yourself, Hines. Where did the tunnel come out? And how did you get past the guards on the wall?"

"We had to cut a tunnel through five feet of solid brick wall. The tunnel surfaced a few feet outside the cell block wall in the yard, and about thirty feet from the prison's outside wall. Once we got into the yard, we waited in the dark for the guards to march to opposite ends of the wall. Their custom was to start from the corners of the wall and march to the center. There they would exchange a few words, turn and march back to the extreme ends of the wall. That was when we threw up the grappling hook and scaled the wall." said Hines.

Cleary interrupted, "Colonel Thompson, dinner is ready, sir." The men adjourned to the dining table where Cleary served another drink and two waitresses from the hotel made sure that all were served. Then Cleary ushered the women out of the suite. Once the room had been cleared of strangers, Thompson said, "Well, Hines, on with the story." As the men consumed generous portions of potatoes, green beans and roast beef, Hines continued.

"Once we all scaled the wall, we got to the station and jumped aboard the train for Cincinnati, figuring if we got that far, we could get across the river into Kentucky where some of our people would help us."

"But, if they took everything away from you when you were taken into the prison, where did the money come from to purchase the tickets?" asked Hyams.

"There was a convict that was trusted to go out of the prison to make deliveries. They called him Heavy. I convinced him to take a letter and mail it to my sister in Kentucky. I instructed her to mail a number of books to me for reading, but to remove the backing and enclose greenbacks, regluing the backing over them. It was those books I sat and read while watching for guards as the others dug the tunnel. Heavy also picked up a local newspaper from which we got the train schedule.

We figured we had about six hours before the guards would discover we were missing, and that should be enough time to get into Kentucky, which we did. It was afterward that we split up, and later I heard that General Morgan had been killed."

"Captain Hines, that was some story. But I've heard that Morgan referred to you as the Count of Monte Cristo. Is that true? Why?" inquired Headley.

Hines smiled, "My idea about the escape I owe to Victor Hugo. If you recall the escapes in *The Count of Monte Cristo* and *Les Miserables*, you'll see where my ideas came from."

Dinner was now over and Cleary sent down for the hotel staff to clear the table. The men all moved to an adjoining room where Cleary made sure that all glasses were full. More cigars all around. Jacob Thompson now took the lead.

"Gentlemen, tonight's little get together has been very pleasant, but now it's time to get down to the business for which we're all here. Cleary, make sure those women are gone."

Cleary left and shortly came back waving his hand with an all clear. He closed the door behind him.

"Let me fill you in," continued Thompson, "on the progress of our next venture to date." He directed his remarks toward Martin and Headley. "Captain Hines, John B. Castleman, Vincent Marmaduke and Bennett Young have spent the last few months putting together teams of raiders to go to Chicago, Columbus, Ohio and Rock Island, Illinois to set fires. The fires are primarily to divert the attention of local authorities, so that the teams can then aid in the release of our prisoners being held in those cities. As you may or may not know, negotiations for peace have become stalled. We're still attempting to negotiate for peace, but feel that the prospects are pretty dim right now. Perhaps if McClellan is elected in November our chances will improve. We've had to hold off for the present on those plans, especially in Chicago. The Democrats are holding their convention there, and if there's any trouble, it might hurt McClellan's chances of getting the nomination. Therefore, we've developed an alternative plan. I have purchased a steamer, the *Georgianna*, from Dr. J.P. Bates, of Kentucky. Captain John Beall, who I'm sure you've all read about in the papers, is now getting a crew organized. He will steam across the lake shelling lake cities east to west, from Buffalo to Toledo. If he finds at Johnson's Island that the *U.S.S. Michigan* is vulnerable, he has my authority to attack it, and to do what he can to release prisoners on the island. Right now we have between three and four hundred men committed to this little venture. I'd like you two to join him." Thompson waited for a response.

Martin spoke first. "Sir, I would certainly like to join Beall, and I'm sure Captain Headley would, too, but there's another man we'd like to include if it meets your approval. He's a young boy who acted as a courier for me when I was with Morgan on his last raid into Kentucky. He also served Captain Headley in the same capacity with Cantrill. Name's George Anderson. He was captured by the Yankees, but managed to escape from the train while on route to Camp Chase. Says he heard Headley and I had gone to Canada, so he came looking for us. Captain Headley met up with him purely by chance this afternoon out in the street."

Thompson put his hand on Martin's arm. "If he rode with Morgan and Cantrill, and you two know him, I'm sure he can be trusted. Fine. Get together with him tomorrow and see if he'll go along."

The message was short and simple. It had apparently been slipped under the door late the night before after the Provost Marshal's office in Buffalo had closed.

> Scroggs, watch the steamer *Georgianna* in Port Colburn. Beall and company will arm it for attacks on lake cities. Notify proper authorities now.
> G.H.

Scroggs lost no time. He wired General Dix in New York and the War Department in Washington. Reaction was swift.

> Get detectives on a round the clock watch of the *Georgianna*. Give descriptions of possible Confederate suspects to all detectives. The *Georgianna* must not be allowed to sail.
> General John Adams Dix

General Dix was furious . . . and frustrated. He fumed about his office giving orders. "You get a cable to the Canadian authorities as fast as you can. I want that ship watched very closely. Get a description of Beall up to them as well. We have got to get this man. He's dangerous and a serious threat to the lakes."

"Yes, sir," his aide replied. "Do you think the British authorities should also be notified?"

"Certainly, though I'm not sure how much good it will do. Those people seem to like to turn their heads when it comes to Confederate activity, but do it anyway."

The aide retreated from the office and headed for the telegraph room. Dix lit a cigar and walked to the window. Damn him, thought Dix. It's like this Beall is out to embarrass me, personally! First on the Chesapeake, then on Lake Erie, and now one more attempt. He's been lucky so far, but his luck has to run out sooner or later. I will get this man, he vowed, if it's the last thing I do!

The *Georgianna* was moored at Port Colburn, a small town fifteen miles west of Buffalo on the Canadian shore. Martin, Headley and Anderson went there to meet with Beall, but when they arrived he was not there. They waited two days. Beall was one day over due, and the men were mystified. They returned to Toronto to see if Jacob Thompson had any answers. He did.

"Gentlemen, the Canadian authorities have been watching the *Georgianna* so closely that we have been unable to get guns and supplies aboard. Also, the U.S. authorities somehow have found out about our plan and are, as we speak, arming every tugboat from Buffalo to Cleveland with artillery to destroy her. The *Georgianna* plan has been abandoned. I was afraid to cable you at your hotel for fear the telegraph wires were also being monitored." Not yet undone, Thompson had several new plans in mind, but an event beyond his control surfaced and he had to deal with it first.

12

Complications in St. Albans

On the morning of October 20, 1864, every Toronto newspaper carried sensational reports of a Confederate raid on the sleepy village of St. Albans, Vermont, just about twenty miles south of the Canadian border. Lieutenant Bennett H. Young, who had been Thompson's connection with Cole in Sandusky, had led the raid, setting fires and robbing a large sum of money from three banks. Several citizens were shot. One was killed. Some of the citizens of St. Albans had chased the raiders back into Canada. Now angry residents were calling for the U.S. Army to give them protection.

Colonel Thompson had known nothing about the raid. "What the hell is going on here?" he shrieked at Walter Cleary. He paced the floor of his sitting room pounding the rolled up paper against his leg, finally slamming it down on the table. "Cable Clement Clay in Montreal, Mr. Cleary. I want to know what the hell is going on up there, and why I wasn't told about this." He pounded the table, knocking over his coffee, and stormed into his office, slamming the door.

Cleary knew what to do. He beat a hasty retreat to his own room, got his coat and headed for the telegraph office. His message was cautious. In vague phrases he let Clay know that they had heard about the fiasco of late and that Mr. Thompson desired a meeting in Toronto, immediately. Two days later Clement Clay arrived from Montreal, and went directly to the Queen's Hotel. The meeting was anything but cordial.

It was all Thompson could do to keep from striking the elder Clay. "Clement, what in God's name were you thinking? This damned raid was your idea, and now it's creating an international incident that could get us all kicked out of Canada. Give me one good reason why you didn't at least check this out with me first!"

Clay wasn't about to justify his actions to this sanctimonious bastard. He hadn't wanted to be in Canada in the first place. Clay looked hard at Thompson and spoke deliberately, his words measured and short, trying to hold back the anger he felt for being called on the carpet by a man more intent on spending Confederate money on lavish living than on winning the war.

"Mr. Thompson," he said, "in case you have forgotten, our whole reason for being here is to bring the war home to the Northern states, is it not? That, my dear sir, is why this war has dragged on so long in the first place. You people in Toronto are so caught up in observing diplomatic niceties that you've forgotten that this is a war we're fighting." By now Clay lost all desire to be polite. "And as for checking with you before I take action, well, you can go to hell! I was making decisions in the Senate of Alabama when you still wore pimples on your face. I am your equal in this commission, sir, and don't you forget that! I shall not seek your approval every time I wipe my ass!"

Thompson flushed, but always the politician, he could see that his tough approach would get nowhere with Clay. Better just get the information. He directly changed tone as if none of what he'd just heard had been said. He sat down and spoke, "What, exactly happened up there, Mr. Clay?"

Clay was somewhat satisfied by Thompson's change of mood. Apparently he'd seen the error of his ways. At least that is what Clay preferred to believe.

"First of all, the raid, for which I take full responsibility, mind you, did exactly what it was intended to do. The Northern states have been largely sheltered from the war. They read about it in the papers, and make a good deal of money from it, too. It never really touches them. Now they are all in a state of panic, screaming for protection from the government. A few more raids like this and they'll be suing for peace for sure."

"I don't need a sermon on politics, Clement, just tell me the details," demanded Thompson, but more cautiously.

"Well, some time ago, Bennett Young, a nice young man, only twenty-one I think, came to me with the idea. He took twenty men across

the border on the night of October eighteenth. They came from separate directions on trains into St. Albans. They spread out into different
hotels, and wore civilian clothes. The next morning the men stayed in
their rooms while Bennett went out and scouted the banks and livery
stables in town. At about three o'clock that afternoon the men all gathered at the town square and took off their civilian coats, you see they
wore their uniforms under them, and announced to the townspeople
that the Confederacy had just taken over their town." Clay chuckled.
Must have been the damnedest thing, he thought. "Most of the citizens
laughed and thought it was a joke until our boys started shooting at
people." Clay could see he had Thompson's attention. "Can a man get
a drink in this place?" Walter Cleary took his cue and filled a glass
for Clay. "Three men went to each bank, while the others set fire to
stables and other buildings. Used Greek fire I believe. Then they got
the horses Bennett had arranged for that morning. By now, what with
the shooting and all, just about all five thousand townspeople were arriving at the center of town in the company of a few Federal soldiers.
Suddenly a hail of bullets came from windows. Three of our men were
wounded. Bennett and the boys beat a hasty retreat with an odd assortment of citizens and soldiers in hot pursuit!" He chuckled again as
he told the story. Wished he'd been young enough to be there himself,
he thought. Hell of a good time!

"I assume the men got back into Canada?" asked Thompson.

"Yes, but not without incident. They are being held by Canadian
authorities now."

"Have you been in contact with Young?"

"Yes, one of my operatives interviewed him not long after he was
brought in. He got the whole story."

"What happened on the way back?" asked Thompson, he took
notes.

"Jacob, that boy's got spunk. He's got some fight in him for one so
young. Bennett took the road to Sheldon which was eight miles away.
There at the bridge that traverses the Black River they were delayed by
a hay wagon slowly crossing the bridge. This delay allowed his pursuers to catch up, and he was forced to open fire on them. He stopped
the hay wagon, turned it across the bridge and set it afire, destroying
the hay, the wagon, and the bridge." Clay slapped his hands together

in glee. "Having eluded his pursuers, the group got to the Canadian border about nine o'clock that night, and put their civilian coats back on and headed out in separate directions, Young going off on his own. The next afternoon he heard that several of his men had been arrested in Phillipsburg. He decided that as commanding officer, who held written authority to make the raid, he would give himself up, too. On the way, Young stopped at a farmhouse to get warm. When he entered the home, he left his weapons in the parlor and went into the kitchen to sit by the stove. As he sat getting warm, twenty-five people from St. Albans, who had somehow heard that there was a stranger in the home, rushed in and captured him before he could defend himself."

"What did they do then?" prodded Thompson, now unable to contain his impatience.

"The crowd beat the tar out of him, but they knew they had to take him back to St. Albans alive. They put him in the back of a wagon with two guards who kept threatening to shoot him. He protested and argued that they were violating British neutrality ... I don't think they really cared." Clay said that more for Thompson's benefit than because it was his own thinking. Thompson worried too much about the politics of this whole thing to suit Clay. "As the wagon moved down the road, Young swung his arms up quickly, hitting both guards, and seized the reins of the wagon. He headed for Phillipsburg. His captors, momentarily surprised, pounced on him again and beat him. Luckily for Young, a British officer happened by and stopped the fight. Young told the officer that he was a Confederate lieutenant and was entitled to protection. His captors were American civilians who had not the authority to arrest him. They were violating British neutrality."

"And how did the officer respond?" Thompson asked, taking more notes.

"The officer told the Americans that five others had been arrested in Phillipsburg and two at St. Johns. They were all to be sent back to St. Albans the next day. Reluctantly, the men agreed to let the officer take Young to Phillipsburg. Arriving there, Young did find that five of his men had been arrested, but no arrangements had actually been made to return them to St. Albans."

Thompson lit a cigar, rose and circled his desk. He looked out the window down into the busy street and thought of the repercussions.

Clay might think this was just exactly what the doctor ordered, but Thompson knew that all it would do was incense the U.S. government and make it harder to negotiate. God forbid the next time a Confederate operative gets caught. The Yankees would string him up and ask questions later.

Clay drained the last of his whiskey and continued. "I heard just before I left that the prisoners were brought to Montreal, but I had not time to see them," he frowned in mock dismay, "so urgent was your request for my presence."

Jacob Thompson lost no time in checking with Canadian authorities. No sooner had Clement Clay left, and Thompson was out the door and on his way up Yonge Street and over to Parliament. He was assured that his men had violated no Canadian laws, nor had they abused Canadian hospitality. He then brought up the subject of the jailed raiders in Montreal.

As a result, Bennett Young and his men would be treated more like honored guests than prisoners. Thompson quickly retained lawyers for their defense. It soon became apparent to the Confederates that the real issue in their case was that in the eyes of the U.S. government, Young and his men were not real Confederate soldiers. Since the United States government did not recognize the legitimacy of the Confederacy, this would not be treated as an act of war. Washington was demanding their extradition on criminal charges. Thirteen of Young's men had not been caught, and the Canadian government did not seem predisposed to look for them. The treatment of Young's men as guests, and the seeming lack of interest on the part of the Canadian government to arrest the others, created tremendous tensions in both Washington and New York.

Nowhere was that tension more obvious than in the New York office of General John Adams Dix. The old soldier, at age sixty-six, had been relieved of his field command, and was promoted to Commander of the Department of the East, a military desk job in New York City. Though no one said as much, the promotion was due more to lackluster performance in the field than to his age. He chafed privately at what he perceived to be a horrendous slight to his good name. Why, he'd fought as a boy in the War of 1812. He'd wept at Chrysler's field when ordered to the rear to escort prisoners, wanting to remain in the thick of battle. His life was one long road of action. What did he have to do to prove his competence? He'd become a lawyer, a power in the New York Democratic party, had served in the United States Senate, for God's sake, not to mention having been president of two railroads, and Secretary of the Treasury for Buchanan. Why, he'd even been mentioned recently for the Governorship in New York. What the hell more did he have to do?

Now, this damned young upstart of a general, Ben Butler, had come to New York, and he just knew Butler was after his job. Well, maybe he could have it. In September it had been the raid on Johnson's Island. He had personally gone to Sandusky to interview and interrogate all those involved. His report had been as complete as was humanly possible. Now this attack on St. Albans. Those damned Confederates in Canada ... and the Canadian government, too, for that matter. It seemed a clear violation of the laws of nations that they would harbor these fugitives. Why couldn't Washington see it that way and just go up there and clean house? He knew the British sympathized with the Confederates, and likewise the Canadians. Just go up there and get the whole thing over with at one time. Well, Lincoln was just too wishy-washy, and that priss McClellan was a shame on the Democrat party. Maybe I should be running for president, he thought. Be careful, don't step on any British toes. Bull! Dix had been having dinner with Lord Lyons the night he got the message about the St. Albans raid and ordered troops to go to Canada to get them. If it had been up to Dix, he'd have told'em to stay there until they got those Confederate bastards. But no, Lyons went squealing to Lincoln, and Lincoln had slapped Dix's hands. If it was up to me, he thought, we'd have those people right now. To hell with what the Canadians and British think!

Feelings were running high in Washington as well. In the office of Edwin Stanton, Secretary of War, sat General Benjamin Butler, the young rising star of the Union Army.

"General Butler, I'm afraid that Dix is a real threat to our relations with the British. That chase he ordered across the Canadian border proves to me what a loose cannon he is. Too old, but maybe worse, unstable. His bull-headedness is playing right into the Confederates hands. They'd like nothing more that to rupture U.S. and British relations. If Dix goes off and invades Canada again, the British are almost certain to retaliate, and that will be that."

"I don't disagree, Mr. Secretary," said Butler, "but I'm not so sure that I'm ready to leave my field command, yet. And besides, it may not be a good thing politically, to relieve Dix just yet. He's pretty popular up there. Being talked about for governor of the state by both Democrats and Republicans! With all the Copperheadism up in New York, it could cause more problems than it solves." said Butler.

"Just the same, I want you to go up there. For now you'll be in command of the troops, but be prepared to take over when the time is right."

Dix pushed paper across his desk and wrote off an order dated October 28, 1864. It would be sent out from his office to all the papers that day:

> By order of General John Adams Dix Com-
> mander of the Department of the East:
>
> As of this date all people who enter the U.S.
> territory must register or be regarded as an
> enemy spy.

For once he sought Stanton's approval and got it. Dix also requested that more troops be placed along the Canadian border, and that General Green, commander of the New York militia, be arrested for disloyalty. After all, he was a known Copperhead.

Both requests were denied. Dix was angry. He fired back a letter to Stanton requesting to resign and go back to civilian life. Why fight it, he thought. These people don't want to fight this war, they just want to play politics.

And it was politics that Edwin Stanton used when he replied to Dix. Stanton played to the General's own political hopes, saying he felt sure that if Dix stayed on for now, the people of New York would probably elect him Governor next time. As Commander of the Department of the East, he was in a very visible position, much more so than he would be in private life. By now Dix's anger had subsided and he decided to stay on. But it was not the last he would hear of Confederate raiders.

13

Rescuing the Generals

On the morning of December 9, 1864, low gray storm clouds were moving in over Toronto. Through the night a cold rain fell that at times flurried. Jacob Thompson, his eyes swollen and red from the previous night of drinking, paced the floor as he awaited the arrival of Martin and Headley. His head was pounding. Godfrey Hyams, who had arrived promptly at seven for his ritual breakfast with Thompson, sat quietly in the corner sipping coffee.

"You seem mighty fidgety this morning, Jake. Something on your mind?" he asked.

"Yes, I have a meeting with some of the men this morning. I've gotten word that some of our generals are being transferred from Johnson's Island to Fort Warren, in Boston. I'm sending a group down to New York state to see if we can rescue them." He looked to Hyams, "I'm afraid I'm going to have to ask you to leave before they arrive. I don't want any information about this known to anyone. Even the men will only know what they absolutely need to know."

"I can understand that, Jake, there's an awful lot of information being passed around these days by a little slip of the tongue, what with all the detectives lurking about. It's probably best I go now, before I hear too much," he laughed. He'd heard enough already. He picked up his coat, said his goodbye and was gone. None too soon, thought Thompson. He wasn't in the mood for Godfrey's good humor this morning. His head was killing him. He vowed to himself to cut down on his drinking. He did that several times a week. Nothing changed.

It was only eight o'clock, not yet time for their arrival, but Thompson was impatient. He glanced at the mantle clock in the sitting room and then out the window to the street. People, bundled against the bitter wind off Lake Ontario, were moving slowly, carefully, as a glaze of ice formed on the brick thoroughfare. His headache was beginning to ease up.

Martin and Headley finished bacon and eggs in the hotel dining room and ascended to Thompson's suite. Breakfast talk had centered on old times and family. Both were eager for the war to be over, to get back home. They passed Godfrey Hyams as he hurried down the stairs, but did not speak. Never knew who might be watching. Walter Cleary let them in. "The Colonel's expecting you," he said, indicating the adjoining office.

Thompson greeted them, "Good morning gentlemen," he said. "I hope you slept well." Enough pleasantries, he thought, get to the point. He motioned for Martin and Headley to sit down across from his desk, and he began. "I have gotten information that seven Confederate generals are being transferred by train from Johnson's Island to Fort Warren in Boston on the fifteenth of December. I don't think I have to tell you how important it is to rescue these men. It is a risky venture to be sure, but I thought if anyone could do it, you two and a few others can. Now understand, it is risky, and all I am asking is for you to volunteer. I won't order you to do it." Without a moment's hesitation both men agreed. "Good," said Thompson, "I'll contact Captain Beall, and you men secure a few others you can depend on. We're going to keep this operation as close to the vest as we can. Too many Federal spies around, and if even our own men know too much they might spill something we don't want known to the Federals."

It was agreed that with the exception of Captain Beall, the other men would only be told what they needed to know to carry out the mission. Martin and Headley chose Lieutenant James Harrington, Captain Robert Cobb Kennedy, Lieutenant John T. Ashbrook, Charles C. Hemming, W.P. Rutland, Forney Hold, and George S. Anderson.

Thompson outlined the plan for Martin and Headley. "You will take the train to Buffalo. Perhaps it would be better if you all arrived at different times. Make arrangements to travel west along the railroad tracks to a point where you can stop the train, board and capture it.

The area around Dunkirk might be the best because of its remoteness. But you will have to determine exactly how that can best be accomplished at the time. Once you have stopped the train and are aboard, arm the generals with revolvers and hold the passengers and crew until Beall and a few others can secure all the money in the express car safe. Once that is accomplished, give some of the money to the generals and instruct them to scatter into Ohio or New York. Be sure...and I can't emphasize this enough...not to take anything from the passengers."

"And what if a passenger interferes?" asked Headley.

"Shoot him," Thompson said curtly.

The meeting was now over. Martin and Headley knew what to do and how far to go. Secrecy was the rule. As far as Kennedy, Anderson and the others were concerned, they were out to rob the express car. Only Martin, Headley and Beall would know the real object of their mission.

Very early on the morning of December tenth, Godfrey J. Hyams slipped out of the Queen's Hotel and made his way to the train station. At six he was on the train for Buffalo. By eleven he was sitting in the office of G. A. Scroggs, provost marshal of Buffalo. Scroggs, overweight and in his early fifties, sat drinking coffee and struggling with a report as Hyams entered.

"Mr. Scroggs, I have some news from Toronto that should be of some interest to you." he hesitated, relishing the suspense in seeing Scroggs' anticipate. Tantalizing Scroggs was one of Hyams small pleasures in this ugly business. The other small pleasure was dispensing information to the U.S. government in bits and pieces. Just enough, but not too much all at once. After all, it didn't pay to tell the whole story all at once. He could make much more money by dribbling it to them a little at a time. By the time the war was over, Godfrey Hyams would have been paid more than sixty thousand dollars for what he knew. But after the Union government had taken his land, he felt they owed it to him.

Scroggs was not in the mood for his game, but he put aside his paperwork and closed the outer door to his office. "And what would that be Mr. Hyams?" Hyams was such a pain in the ass, he thought. But in all the time he had been dealing with Hyams, his information had always been reliable.

"It appears that in the next few days a group of Confederates from Canada will be coming into this area. I couldn't find out what they plan to do or exactly when they will come. I just know they have a plan to help free some Confederate generals."

"How did you come by this bit of information, Mr. Hyams?" asked Scroggs. He knew that Hyams had access to some very reliable sources, but never would he discuss who they were.

"Let's just say I have had the good fortune of overhearing some interesting conversations in a Toronto hotel." he said. Not a good idea to tell too much. He doesn't need to know how I get my information, thought Hyams. He should just be glad to get it. If his relationship to Jake Thompson was ever discovered, he'd be a dead man, and he knew it. Playing one end against the other was dangerous business.

That was good enough for Scroggs. By noon he had wired every local law enforcement agency in western New York. Get officers into all train stations and watch hotels for any groups of unknown men registering. He especially wanted heavy surveillance in Niagara Falls and Buffalo. Anyone coming from Canada would undoubtedly stop in those cities first, he thought. The day shift police were put on overtime. Security for Buffalo would have to be doubled until the raiders were caught. His last telegram was to Washington. Who were the generals and where were they being transported?

Colonel Martin's men were finally gathered and briefed. They traveled in pairs by train to Buffalo, some on Saturday, the thirteenth, and the rest on Sunday the fourteenth of December. Martin and Headley left on Saturday night and got off in Hamilton, Ontario to meet with Beall. They arrived at his hotel very late that night, and found he was already asleep. Martin and Headley would have to wait until morning to meet Captain Beall.

Neither Martin nor Headley had known Beall before, but both took an instant liking to him. Martin saw in Beall a modest, unassuming man, a thinking man, not prone to jabbering for entertainment. All business, he thought. The three spent Sunday in Beall's hotel room honing their plan. First, stop the train, surprise the guards, and disarm them. Next, while Beall and his group attended to the express car, Martin and Headley would have the generals change clothes with passengers of like size, and compensate the passengers for the value of their clothing. Then they would disconnect the passenger cars and leave them behind on the tracks. After cutting the telegraph wires they would all head to Buffalo, as it was close, and scatter on trains heading in different directions.

On Sunday afternoon snow blanketed the ground, and the skies were beginning to clear to a crisp blue. They caught the train over the Suspension Bridge and connected to Buffalo. The Genesee House dominated the corner of Main and Genesee Streets in the heart of downtown Buffalo. Built in 1842, it rose five floors above street level and was one of the busiest hotels in the city. It had plenty of rooms, a restaurant and a bar. Several stores occupied space on its first floor level. Hundreds of people trafficked its corner daily. It was easier to blend in than if they had chosen a smaller hotel. There was less chance of raising suspicion. Martin and Headley went directly to the hotel on arrival and arranged for their room. Then they set out to look over Buffalo.

George Anderson was in the reservations office arranging for his room when Martin and Headley returned. Headley signaled for Anderson to follow him outside into the lobby and upstairs to their room. Martin briefed Anderson on the plan to raid the train's express car. He said no more. Anderson was a good soldier, but he was only about eighteen years old. It was best not to entrust him with any more information than he needed to know. The other men were contacted throughout the evening and arrangements were made to leave the next morning for Dunkirk, New York. They needed to be there in enough time to meet the eastbound train from Cleveland.

Picking up the paper the next morning, Headley quickly scanned the telegraphic dispatches. The one that caught his eye was datelined New York City, Headquarters, Department of the East, sent by General John A. Dix. The dispatch stated in short that the St. Albans raiders had been released by Canadian authorities. In case of further attacks by marauders acting under commission of Confederate authorities, said marauders were to be shot down. If need be, Federal authorities were authorized by Dix to chase said rebels into Canada.

The stakes had just gone up considerably, thought Headley. If we're caught, they'll shoot us or pursue us back to Canada, and we'd be brought back to face Court Martial. He knew they were playing a risky game, but now it was even more dangerous. He told only Martin and Beall for the moment. There was already enough for the rest of the men to think about.

When their train pulled into Dunkirk everyone got off except Colonel Martin. He traveled on to Erie, Pennsylvania. Martin would pick up the eastbound train there and ride with the generals. While the rest of the men killed time in Dunkirk, Beall and Headley made some quiet inquiries of people in town to see if the generals had already passed through. Then the men went back to the depot and watched for Martin's arrival on every train heading east. He came on the second train.

"The generals have not yet been sent east." said Martin to Beall and Headley. "There's been a delay, but I couldn't find out why."

"What do you think we should do now?" Headley asked Martin.

They discussed heading to Buffalo and watching the trains coming from Sandusky. Martin could get on the train carrying the generals when it left Buffalo.

"No," said Beall, "I think that would be too risky, too much possibility of being spotted."

After some discussion Beall said to Martin, "I don't think it's safe to stay in any one place too long considering General Dix's dispatch."

They decided to tell the men about the telegraph message Headley had seen in the paper. Beall took Anderson and his group aside, as did Martin and Headley with theirs. Beall still did not tell the real reason for the raid, just that an alternative plan was in the works and their job was unchanged, he and Anderson would relieve the express car of its cargo while the others would guard the passengers and crew. Anderson believed that it was the train with the express car they were looking for. He still had no idea about the generals.

Headley and Martin explained the change to their men. "If the right train doesn't come along by tomorrow morning, we'll go out in sleighs away from town and block the path of the next train. We'll just tell the trainmen that we've come out from town along the road because there's trouble on the tracks ahead." On Martin's signal the men would jump the guards.

"What if there's too many guards for us?" asked one of the men.

"Then go for the officers and try to get them to order the others to give up." said Martin. It was something he had not really thought about, and didn't think his response made much sense, but they all seemed satisfied with the answer. Once the generals were released, they would run the train as far as Buffalo's outskirts where Martin would get off with the generals. Some of the party would back the train up and out into the country and block the tracks. Then they would all scatter and meet back in Toronto. A few of the men would take the sleighs back to the city and catch the Niagara train.

The men spent a restless night in Buffalo. The next morning the generals again had not been sent, so Beall, Martin, Headley, Hemming and Anderson rented a double-seated sleigh and rode west out of the city to scout out a secluded place to stop the train. The others stayed behind in Buffalo. Four miles west of Dunkirk they found a place where a narrow country road crossing the tracks showed little traffic. There were no houses nearby, only woods to the north and fields to the south. It would be a good spot to stop the train.

Returning to Buffalo, they rented two more sleighs and set up a meeting for five o'clock that evening. Martin and Headley rode out together with their team and once again reviewed the plans...break into the express car, detach the passenger cars, get the generals back to Buffalo ahead of the train and everyone else. Beall, riding in the other sleigh with Anderson and Hemming, discussed only the procedure of breaking into the express car. When they arrived it was dark. As Hemming and Anderson hid the sleighs in the woods, Martin decided to put an iron rail they found across the tracks, securing it in a fence that ran parallel to the rails. Then they would cover it with snow. If the train did not stop when they signaled it with a lantern, then this would surely get the train to stop. Their practice run was poorly timed. They had not known a train would be coming by within minutes. There was no time to remove the bar. They all ran for cover.

As the train roared passed by, it hit the bar and threw it about fifty yards down the tracks. Jarred by the impact, the train stopped and the forms of two men with lanterns began walking back, carefully inspecting the track to see what they had hit. Afraid they'd be spotted, Martin and his company hid in the woods until the train left, and then headed back to Buffalo. The plan would have to be abandoned for now. There was too much risk of being caught. They would catch the next train back to Canada at the Suspension Bridge. They'd been in the area too long already.

Arriving at the bridge, Martin, Beall and Headley decided it was best to split up the group. Martin and Headley would walk across the bridge and wait for the others to arrive by train in Canada. An hour later when the train arrived, Martin and Headley boarded it and looked for their men. Beall, Anderson and Hemming were not on it. Thinking this might be the wrong train, they got off. Reluctant to leave without Beall and the others, they missed the last train and spent the night in a hotel. By morning the missing men had still not shown up, so Martin decided that he and Headley had better go back to Hamilton, Ontario where Beall had left his baggage. Beall had not come there either. Finally, returning to Toronto, they found Ashbrook, Kennedy, Holt and Rutland. They had been on the train the previous night, but had gone into a sleeper. Charlie Hemming arrived a few hours later. He had been spotted and chased by police before he could cross the bridge, and ran to Fredonia, New York, where a widow, Mary Cummings, had taken him in. Beall and Anderson had still not returned. Jacob Thompson was concerned. He sent a messenger to the Niagara train station to see if he could find them. They were not to be found.

14

Arrested in Niagara Falls

As Martin and Headley walked toward Suspension Bridge, John Beall and George Anderson entered the train station and purchased tickets. The others would follow their lead a few at a time. They had all agreed to sit separately in the station and meet on the train. The New York Central station was bustling with people, and Beall soon lost sight of Anderson. He busied himself by reading a newspaper someone had left on the bench. The lead article rejoiced at Sherman's march from Atlanta to Savannah. It reported that the Union army had fanned out over a sixty mile wide path, and was moving in rapidly on Savannah, Georgia. They had destroyed farms, homes, entire towns. Beall found it hard to imagine how Sherman could be seen as a hero, when so many poor civilians were being left homeless or worse, dead.

The train arrived shortly before nine o'clock. Beall boarded and took a seat. The others followed a few at a time. Anderson did not show. Worried that the train would pull out before Anderson could get on board, Beall hurried off the train and back into the station. He found Anderson asleep on a settee. Beall sat down to wake him up. Then he heard, "All aboard going east. Last call!" He aroused Anderson, and the two headed for the train. Suddenly they were seized from behind by two policemen. Beall immediately thought of the Navy revolver under his coat. He was an expert shot and knew he could easily put those two away even at eighty yards. Beall quickly looked around. There were more than a hundred bystanders. Thoughts raced through his head. If he tried to make a break for it he probably wouldn't make it. If he drew and fired and missed he might hit some innocent bystander. The only decision left for him and Anderson was to give up without a fight.

The two detectives led Beall and Anderson at gun point away from the crowd and into the telegraph office. David Thomas, one of the two detectives, searched the men. "What is your name, sir?" asked Thomas, referring to Beall.

"Beall." he replied.

Thomas asked him again for his full name. Now realizing his mistake, Beall replied, "Baker... W.W. Baker."

Thomas corrected him, "Didn't you just say Beall?"

"No, W.W. Baker," answered Beall.

As the policeman searched him, Beall asked, "What are we being arrested for?"

The policeman replied, "We're looking for two men who are escaped rebel prisoners."

Beall asked from where. Detective Thomas said it didn't matter. "Was it from Point Lookout?" Beall asked.

Thomas looked surprised. "Yes, it was from Point Lookout."

Then Beall said, "That I will acknowledge. I am an escaped prisoner from Point Lookout."

Thomas found Beall's Colt and some money, two ten-dollar American gold pieces, two Canadian four-dollar notes, six dollars in American scrip, and a small amount of silver coins. "Why do you have Canadian money?" Thomas asked.

"After I escaped from Point Lookout I went to Baltimore. Some friends gave me the money to go to Canada," lied Beall.

Next, Thomas went through the carpet satchel Beall and Anderson had with them. A rumpled shirt previously worn, a pair of socks, five tallow candles, some matches wrapped in paper, and a box of paper collars spilled out onto the table. From Beall's vest pocket Thomas pulled a bottle of laudanum. It reminded Beall of the toothache he'd had for several days. Thomas turned to the bag and its contents.

"Whose bag is this?" The bag had been sitting on the floor between him and Anderson when they were arrested.

"It's not mine," stated Beall.

Thomas turned to Anderson, "Why do you have the candles?"

Anderson was plainly frightened, "I ... I sometimes need them when there is no other light."

Now Thomas turned back to Beall as he picked up the small vial of laudanum off the table, rolled it around between his fingers and studied it. He looked at Beall.

"I've been having problems with a toothache," he replied, anticipating the question.

Thomas nodded and returned the bottle to the table. He looked to Anderson, indicating the things on the table, "Put all this back in your bag. We're going to take you down to the police station." He placed handcuffs on both Anderson and Beall.

Now Detective Saule moved. He'd been the silent partner until now, just watching and observing the prisoners. "All right, now, boys, move toward that door and no funny business. We'll be right with you and our guns are at the ready."

The police station at Niagara Falls was a spare and decrepit little place. It appeared to have an open room with several desks in front. There were several doors on the back wall, one of which Beall was taken through into an interrogation room. Anderson, accompanied by Detective Saule was taken to a separate room. Beall did not know where. David Thomas told Beall to sit down, indicating a small wooden chair next to a cluttered oak desk. Thomas moved behind the desk and slowly pulled Beall's gun from inside the detective's coat. "Very nice weapon . . . what about it?" he asked.

Beall smiled. "You and Mr. Saule are lucky you caught me by surprise, because I had made up my mind that I wouldn't be taken alive again. Either I or Saule or you would be a dead man if I had seen you." Thomas was indifferent to the remark.

"What regiment were you in?" he asked.

"I'm a sergeant in the Second Virginia Infantry," answered Beall, looking Thomas directly in the eye.

"When did you escape from Lookout Point?"

"Several days ago," answered Beall.

Anderson was shaken by the surprise arrest and Detective Saule could see it in his face. Since they could get nothing from Beall, the detectives began to work on Anderson, who was placed in an adjoining room.

"What is your name?" asked Saule.

"George S. Anderson, sir," said Anderson. His voice shook.

"Anderson, this could go easier for you if you tell us the truth. What is the name of your partner?"

Anderson hesitated, his eyes darted around the room. He could taste his fear. It seemed futile to lie, he thought. What's the point? And he was really afraid of what the burley Saule might do to him. "Uh ... It's Captain Beall." His head lowered and he stared at the floor. The two detectives looked at one another. Could that be true? Federal agents were scouring Canada looking for Beall. If Anderson was telling the truth, they had the man who had attempted to attack the *Michigan*. They also knew that a man in Canada had already been arrested who was thought to be Beall, and he had turned out not to be. If their informant had been right they just might have him this time. They had to be sure. Anderson needed to be pressed for details. Perhaps a deal could be reached, perhaps clemency for testimony? But they knew that Washington would have to approve that.

On Sunday, December eighteenth, Beall was delivered to the Mulberry Street jail in New York City, still insisting he was W.W. Baker. He had no idea where Anderson was or what happened to him. The turnkey at the jail, Edward Hays, led him to his cell. Hays unlocked the iron door and motioned for Beall to step in. His cell was eight feet by five feet, walls of brick, and a stone floor. A small sink was mounted on the wall and an empty pitcher sat on a small table next to it. No water was provided with which to bathe. A mattress lay on the floor. Hays handed Beall a blanket as he banged the door shut. Neither man spoke. The door was solid except for a window at the top covered with heavy steel grating. Across the corridor some six or eight feet away Beall could see three more cells and a window, also heavily grated. The corridor outside the cell was dimly lit with gas lamps mounted at intervals on the walls.

Over the next twelve days Beall would be subjected to a dozen different police line-ups. Each time the police would come to his cell, escort him to a room where he was told to line up against the wall with an assortment of other men, most of whom were police detectives. Unshaven and unwashed, Beall stood out in the crowd. Witnesses were brought in and asked if they could recognize anyone. A small band of rebels had invaded New York recently and set fires at several hotels. P.T. Barnum's museum had even been a set ablaze. Police officials were anxious to see if this man Baker, or whoever he was, might be one of them. None of the witnesses could identify him as a participant in those arsons.

After several more days of sitting in his cell watching a procession of petty thieves come and go, Beall was again taken to a police line-up. As he entered the room Beall saw about thirty people. One of them was the young clerk and part owner of the *Philo Parsons*, Walter Ashley. The police did not ask Ashley to point him out, only to see if Ashley recognized any of them. Ashley and Colonel John Ludlow, a member of General Dix's staff, stood near the door and scanned the room, taking in the faces of all the men who slowly milled around the room. Mostly pickpockets and petty thieves, they all looked like a sorry lot to Ashley. They stayed only a few minutes. It was a nerve-wracking affair for Ashley. Beall, trying to be as anonymous as possible, kept to the rear, but he knew when their eyes met that Ashley remembered.

After leaving the room, Ashley signified to Ludlow, who had accompanied him to the police station, that Beall had indeed been in the room. The only difference Ashley noted was that Beall now wore a full beard.

The next day Beall was again aroused and taken to the same room in which he had seen Ashley. This time a woman was brought in. At first Beall did not recognize her, but she spotted him immediately and walked right over to him.

"Captain Beall, you probably don't remember me, but I want to thank you for being so kind to me aboard the ferry in Ohio. My baby was sick. Do you recall?"

"M'am, I'm sure you must be mistaken. I've never met you before, and I've never been to Ohio." Beall lied.

"No, I'd not forget your kindness to me then. Remember, my baby was so sick and I was terrified? You talked to me in the salon and made sure that the baby was comfortable. I can never thank you enough for your concern."

Beall smiled at her and said, "I certainly hope that your baby is now fine, but I'm sure that it is not I who you met."

The police detective took the woman by the arm and led her away from Beall and out of the room. Two positive identifications. They had their man. Washington would have to be notified for further instructions.

Beall settled into the daily routine of jail life. At first he talked to his cell mates, taking an interest in their cases. Each had a different story. He soon came to see that they all felt a row with the law was just a mere skirmish, one they repeatedly had. They had no sense of morals, no ethical values. Whether they were men, women or children, he saw them all in jail. They all told him to go back on his friends and save himself. But that Beall could not do, no matter what the price. He had sworn he would protect the identities of his friends and his government's plans. A man was only as good as his word, and he was honor bound to keep that word. It was all he had left to contribute to the cause.

As the days passed Beall tired of the inane stories and attitudes of his cellmates, so to pass the time and avoid the rabble he was forced to live with, he began to set down his thoughts in his diary. He also found a copy of the New Testament in his cell and asked the turnkey, Hays, if he could get him a copy of the Episcopal church's Book of Common Prayer.

Christmas came and went. In jail it was just another day, no different than the one before or the one after. He wrote down his feelings that Christmas day.

> The Christmas of '64 I spent in a New York prison! Had I, four years ago, stood in New York, and proclaimed myself to be a citizen of Virginia, I would have been welcomed; now I am immured because I am a Virginian. . . tempora mutantur, et cum illis mutamus. As long as I am a citizen of Virginia, I shall cling to her destiny and maintain her laws as expressed by a majority of her citizens . . . if her choice is war or peace. I go as she says. But I would not go for a minority carrying on war in opposition to the majority, as the innocent will suffer and not the guilty; but I do not justify oppression in the majority. What misery I have seen in these last four years, murder, lust, hate, rapine, devastation and war! What hardships suffered, what pri-

vations endured! May God grant that I may not see the like again! Nay, that my country may not. Oh, far rather would I welcome Death, come as he might; far rather would I meet him than go through four more of such years. I can now understand how David would trust to his God, rather than to man.

Beall's thoughts were interrupted by the approach of jail turnkey, Edward Hays. Hays periodically walked the corridor to check the cells. As Hays approached, he stopped and to see if there was anything Beall needed.

"It's pretty cold in here this evening," Hays said. Beall replied it surely was. Indicating that the old man who had shared Beall's cell the night before was gone, Hays said, "The old man was lucky to get out of here today. He wanted me to take a letter out for him, but the amount he offered was too small. I couldn't do it for that."

Beall recalled overhearing the conversation as he wrote in his diary. "Would you take a letter out for me? I'll pay you well for it."

"There's a good deal done for money," said Hays, "Money does a good deal." Hays looked back toward the office, then to Beall. Locking eyes with Beall he said, "Where do you want the letter sent?"

"To Canada," answered Beall.

Hays then asked, "Don't you think the letter would have a hard time getting through?"

"Indeed, it might. I've heard that your government is opening and reading all the mail going to Canada now. But if it did get through, my government would know I am in prison and might be able to do something to get me out."

Again, Hays shifted his eyes toward the office. "All right, I'll do it." Hays returned to the office to get some paper and a pencil.

In the office Hays mentioned his conversation with Beall to chief detective Kelso. He said nothing of his agreement to send a letter. Kelso told him to see what information he could get out of the prisoner, particularly his real name. He was still calling himself Baker.

At seven p.m. Hays went back to Beall's cell and told him there were several detectives in the office and he'd have to wait until the office cleared out to get the paper. Beall spoke quietly, his face close to the door grating, "Hays, I'll tell you what you can do for me. You can let me go."

Taken aback by this surprise request, Hays said, "No ... no, I can't do that."

"If you do I'll give you one thousand dollars in gold."

Hays got interested. He cleared his throat and swallowed hard. "Do you have that much money with you?" he asked.

"No," replied Beall, "but if you take my word, I'm good for the money. When I get back to Canada, I can contact a man who is holding my money. I'll send it to you from there as soon as I'm back."

Hays thought for a moment and then spoke, "Mr. Baker, did you set any of those fires in New York?"

"No," replied Beall, "but I know who did. They're in Canada."

Hays shook his head and said, " No, I don't think I can let you go for any money. It really would put me in a bad position. It's too risky."

Beall understood, "I know your position. You're afraid you'll be blamed ... but I'm probably going to be found guilty. Can't you run a little risk for me?" Beall persuaded. Hays was thinking, staring at Beall's face through the door. He had a feeling that he might be getting somewhere with the jailer. If Hays wasn't interested he might just as well have walked away. "Look, Hays, I was arrested before ... some time ago ... and some of my friends got a letter through. When the Confederate government heard I was in prison, they imprisoned the son of one of General Meade's officers and eleven other men until I was released."

"I suppose if your government found out that you were in prison here now that they would try to get you out in some way." Hays said.

"No. I don't think they would. I was arrested on a different charge now from what I was then. I also don't think my government is in a very strong bargaining position right now."

Hays hesitated, looked again down the hall toward the office. "Listen, I, uh ... I'll have to think about this ... uh, ... do you still want to write a letter?"

"No, it would probably take too long to do any good. It would be better if you'd just release me. You know you can."

Hays thought for a while and whispered, "If I could do this, what time would you want to leave?"

"I think it would be best to go in the early part of the night," Beall said. "I have two friends up on Thirtieth Street. If I could get to their house no one could see me then. I'd be able to get a gun. I know well what would happen to me if I was caught again and brought back."

Hays replied, "Would your friends be able to give you the money to give me before you leave New York?"

"Yes, probably part of it. Say half in greenbacks, maybe gold before I leave. If not, I promise to send it from Canada."

"How do you think you're going to get from New York clear to Canada? Will your friends help?" asked Hays.

Beall confided that he would first go to the house of the man on Thirtieth Street. Then he'd start for a friend's home in New Jersey about five miles from Jersey City who did business in New York. He could safely travel out of the city with him.

Hays was more curious. "Well, just who is this gentleman on Thirtieth Street? Where does he live?" Beall would not tell. Hays questioned further. "When you came, you said your name was Baker. Is that your real name?"

"No," answered Beall, "they don't know my real name."

"I think you're a real smart man, and you must have done a good deal of harm to our government since this war commenced," said Hays.

"Yes, I have," Beall said. "I've taken hundreds of prisoners. I've done Lincoln a good deal of harm, and they know it."

"Did you take those prisoners on land or sea?" asked Hays.

Beall leaned forward against the grate and whispered, "That is my secret." He smiled as he toyed with Hays.

"Come on, man, what is your real name?" Hays pressed.

"No." Beall shook his head. Beall tried again, "Mr. Hays, I know something that would be worth thirty thousand dollars to anyone in the detectives' office. I know things that would be worth millions to your government, but I'd die before I'd tell." Beall paused and looked down, "Hays, I caught a ball in the side back in sixty-one and it still bothers me. I don't think I'll live very long. I'm going to die one way or the other."

Hays moved closer to the door and looked into Beall's eyes. "I'm glad you like to keep secrets because if I let you go, you'd have to remember that," he said hoarsely.

"You can rest assured that you'd get the thousand dollars, and get it in gold. I owe you more than that myself," Beall whispered back.

Hays glanced furtively in both directions, fearful that someone might hear. "I'll see what I can do," he said. "I'll come back tonight. If I can let you out I will, but I can't say when. If I can't come back tonight, I'll see you tomorrow evening." Hays returned to the detectives but said nothing to Sergeant Kelso. Hays was thinking hard about what a thousand dollars could do for a man in his position.

On New Year's Day, 1865, John Beall celebrated his thirtieth birthday in his cell with another entry into his diary.

> Thus far on life's way I have lived an honest life, defrauding no man. Those blows that I have struck have been against the society of a hostile nation; not against the society of which I am a member by right, or vs. mankind generally. Today the thought has obtruded itself again and again to become an 'Ishmail.' Your country is ruined, your hopes dashed--make the best bargain for yourself. Today my hands have no blood on them (unless of man in open battle); may I say so when I die. I saw my grandfather and father die; they both took great comfort from the thought that no one could say that they had of malice aforethought injured them. Better the sudden death, o'er all the loathsome corruption of a lingering life, with honor and a pure conscience, than a long life with all material comforts and the cankerworm of infelt and constant dwelling dishonor; aye a thousand times.

Hays arrived at about three p.m. and made his way to Beall's cell. He had made up his mind. Best do it quickly before he lost his nerve. He gaped into the grated window in the cell door. Beall was gone. Quickly retracing his steps to the office, Hays asked Kelso, "Where is Mr. Baker?"

Kelso did not look up from his paperwork. "They came up early this morning and took him to Fort Lafayette. Why do you ask?"

"No reason," replied Hays, "just surprised that he's gone." Hays hoped the disappointment didn't show in his voice.

15

Imprisoned at Fort Lafayette

It was just before six a.m. January 5, 1865. John Beall lay huddled half asleep on his straw mattress trying unsuccessfully to keep warm. The night was unusually cold, and he awoke several times with an uncontrollable fit of coughing. If the Yankee government doesn't kill me, this jail just might, he thought. My lungs can't take much more of this dampness and cold. Beyond the cell door and up the corridor he could hear voices moving closer. A moment later the iron door opened and the police sergeant entered his dark cell followed by several soldiers.

"Mr. Baker, these men have come up from Fort Lafayette to remove you from this jail today. Please get up." It was an order, not a request.

"May I ask what's going on, Sergeant?" asked Beall.

"I don't rightly know," he said, "just come on duty myself. Paper here says by order of General Dix you're to be taken to Fort Lafayette prison. These here men come up to get you."

Beall saw two guards in the doorway and two in the corridor outside. The first two entered the cell and quickly clamped wrist and leg irons onto Beall. He was escorted out of the cell, a guard on each arm, with one additional guard in front and back.

Outside it was still dark and cold. Beall was hoisted into the back of the prison van and the door was locked shut. The black horse-drawn van moved into the foggy morning down Mulberry Street and then right onto Chatham, past City Hall. Traveling south on Broadway, the van veered left onto Whitehall, and then right at South Street. At the wharf across from Castle Garden the steamer, *Henry Burdon*, lay waiting to carry the prisoner eight miles down the harbor to Fort Lafayette.

Beall shivered as he was helped down out of the police van. His leg chains were too short to allow stepping down, and the guards almost dropped him as he hit the street. He half-stepped up the gang plank to the deck of the steamer and was led to a room on the first deck near the stern of the boat. One of the guards unchained his leg irons, but left the chains on his wrists. The room had a small bed, a table and a basin of water, and one small round window that looked out on the city as they headed south toward the fort. Beall had finally begun to warm up. He lay down on the mattress, not much better than the one he had in jail, and dozed. He had slept fitfully that night and the warmth and movement of the boat lulled him to sleep.

At the same hour that Beall boarded the *Henry Burdon*, Sergeant Billy Reilly entered the steamer's ward room. "General Warren, the prisoner is aboard, sir."

"Thank you, Sergeant. We'll let you know when we're ready for him."

No time was being lost. The government was satisfied that they had identified Beall. A military court had been assigned to his case, and the members had assembled in the wardroom shortly before Beall came aboard. Judge Advocate John A. Bolles, the government's military prosecutor, briefed them.

"Gentlemen, you should all have copies of the details of this case, and I trust you've read them already. As you know, the purpose of our meeting today is to arraign Captain Beall. I'm fairly certain he has no counsel as yet, but as you know, procedure calls for this arraignment regardless. Do you have any questions?"

The seven men sitting around the table looked at each other. Each had been through this many times over the past four years, but this case was not like the rest. General Dix had taken a personal interest in this case. Captain John Yates Beall had been a thorn in his side since Beall's days as a pirate on the Chesapeake. His successful destruction of Union shipping and property had been a personal embarrassment to Dix. He spared no efforts in capturing him, only to have him exchanged. Now he was back. Accused of spying and guerrilla warfare, destruction of property and putting civilian lives at great risk. Yes, they were ready.

General Warren polled each member for questions, "Morris? Howe? Day? O'Bierne? Williams?" None answered in the affirmative. "Very well, then, I think coffee is ready in the galley." With those words uttered, the formality of the room turned to congeniality. The officers all rose and filed out of the room chatting, the case put to the back of their minds for the moment.

Of the men serving on this court, only two were outstanding jurists, General Fitz Henry Warren and Lieutenant Colonel Robert F. O'Bierne. Before the war both had had long and distinguished careers on the Federal bench. General Morris was neither a good lawyer nor a good general. He had been more interested in running his import-export business than the military paper shuffling position he held in New York City. Wallace and Day were the youngest on the court. Before the war Wallace was an up- and-coming lawyer who had not lost a case, but Day was a hack. He entered the service in 1861 more to collect a steady paycheck than to uphold the law. Had it not been for the war, he would have left the practice of law and gone into business working for his father-in-law. The war, however, had provided him with a way to use his legal experience to convict a steady stream of rebels.

Two hours had passed since the boat departed the city. It was now almost quarter past ten. General Warren excused himself and left the galley to speak with the captain of the *Henry Burdon*. He wanted to wait until the boat docked a Fort Lafayette before beginning the arraignment.

Captain Virgil O'Malley stood at the bridge next to the wheel man. As Warren entered the cabin to ask for the time of arrival, O'Malley pointed ahead out the window. In his best Irish brogue he anticipated Warren's question. "Thar's the fort, General. We should be dockin' about ten forty-five."

"Good, Captain. Let me know when the boat is secured and we'll begin the arraignment." Warren was a man of few words, and he liked punctuality. The court would convene at eleven a.m. Beall would plead and Warren would be back home by six to celebrate his wife's fiftieth birthday.

The motion of the boat hitting the dock and the voices of men calling orders awakened Beall. Before he could shake the cobwebs from his brain, the door to his room was unbolted and Judge Advocate Bolles stood in the doorway. Bolles was fifty-two years old and a native of Maryland, a state that, if it had not been for Lincoln's arrest of the entire state legislature, might have voted to secede from the Union. Half the state were secessionists, and even more so in Baltimore where Major Bolles practiced law before the war. Unlike most of the men on the court, Bolles had mixed feelings about the departure of the Southern states. He was a Union man, but his brother and two close cousins fought for the South. While he was personally torn about the war, he felt duty bound to uphold the law, a belief he had inherited from his father, grandfather, and great grandfather, four generations of lawyers who had seen all the trials of the nation from the Revolution to the present war.

From behind Bolles a young guard entered the room. Bolles held his hand up, motioning for the guard not to chain Beall just yet. "Captain Beall, I'm Major Bolles. I'll act as Judge Advocate at your arraignment in a few minutes."

"What arraignment?" Beall was surprised.

"An arraignment was set for you as soon as we docked a Fort Lafayette. Didn't they tell you?"

"No. I was picked up at the Mulberry Street police station at six o'clock this morning and no one told me anything. I haven't even talked to a lawyer yet!"

Bolles felt sorry for Beall. He looked terrible. Grimy and unshaven, his hair matted and dirty.

"Guard, let Captain Beall wash up before we go." Bolles indicated the basin. "There are some towels on the shelf under the table. Just be quick because General Warren does not like to be kept waiting."

Beall was led in chains along a narrow corridor to the rather spacious ward room. He sat at a small rectangular table. Next to the table, about four feet away, Major Bolles took his seat. The only other man in the room was the court stenographer, James E. Munson, who sat silently at his own table and stared at the blank pages on which he would take notes of the proceeding. Across the front of the room was a large table with six chairs. It was the semblance of most courtrooms except for the occasional rocking of the boat as it moved in the choppy waters of New York harbor.

Snow began to fall quietly outside as the members of the military commission entered the room single file through the side door. Bolles, Beall and Munson all rose to their feet. General Warren took his place at the center of the table. To his right and left stood Morris, Howe, Day, O'Bierne, and Wallace left to right according to rank. General Fitz Henry Warren, President of the Commission, directed himself to Beall.

"Captain John Yates Beall, you have been brought before this military commission on a number of charges, but before those charges are formally read I will ask you if you have any objection to any man sitting on this tribunal?"

Beall rose and spoke quietly, "I do not." How could he? He had never seen any of them and knew nothing about them. "However, I do wish to protest my trial by military commission."

General Warren looked to the stenographer and said, "Mr. Munson, take special note of Captain Beall's protest for the record." Warren then directed his remarks to Beall. "Captain Beall, it is my duty as the President of this commission to inform you of the charges being leveled against you. You, sir, are charged with acting as both a spy and a guerrilla in commandeering a vessel on Lake Erie and for attempts to derail trains outside of Dunkirk, New York. How do you plead?"

Beall stood. "Not guilty on all charges."

Now Judge Advocate Bolles rose and spoke to Beall. He knew the answer before he asked the question, but it was one of those formalities. "Captain Beall, are you ready to proceed with the trial?"

"I am not, sir. I will need time to acquire the services of a lawyer and to prepare my defense. Would it be possible to delay the trial for one week? I should be able to secure counsel and be prepared by then."

General Warren nodded his agreement and looked to Major Bolles for any objections. Seeing none, Warren said, "This proceeding stands adjourned until eleven o'clock a.m., Wednesday, January twenty-fifth." With that, he and the other members of the commission rose and filed out of the room followed by the stenographer.

Major Bolles pushed his chair away from the table and walked over to Beall. Putting one hand on Beall's shoulder he asked, "Captain Beall, do you know who you would like to act as your counsel?"

"Yes," replied Beall, "I have a friend in Richmond, Daniel Lucas. I'm going to contact him. Other than Dan, I have no idea."

Bolles looked across the room and thought for a moment. "I doubt very much if General Dix will permit that, but I'll propose it to him this afternoon." He paused, "If your request is denied, I'd be happy to suggest someone who would provide excellent counsel here in New York. His name is James Brady. If you'd like, I can contact him myself."

Beall rubbed his hands together nervously, "Thank you, Major, I would appreciate your doing that for me." Bolles patted Beall firmly on the shoulder and left the room quickly. He had much to accomplish this afternoon.

As Beall shuffled out of the courtroom escorted by two guards, he thought about his would be prosecutor. Bolles seemed a fair man, genuinely concerned for Beall's well being. Was it Bolles' sense of fair play or compassion? Beall had never heard of James Brady, yet he was trusting the man who might send him to the gallows to potentially choose his own lawyer. The oddity of the situation was perversely amusing. There was still a slim hope that Dan Lucas might be approved as counsel.

At four-fifteen that afternoon Major Bolles walked through the door to the inner office of General John Adams Dix. Bolles well knew Dix's attitude about all rebels. After all, Bolles was married to Dix's sister. He wasn't likely to allow one rebel to be defended by another. Dix was a fair-minded man on most issues, but he had absolutely no sympathy for the Southern cause.

Dix was working on some papers and motioned for Bolles to sit down, indicating he'd be a few minutes. It was almost four years ago, but Bolles could still recall the speech Dix made about shooting anyone who pulled down the American flag, and people were still referring to it whenever his name came up in conversation.

Dix pushed back from his large mahogany desk and lit a cigar. As he gave it a long pull, he eyed the Major. He was a good officer and an excellent lawyer, thought Dix, but he lacked the killer instinct. Though they were family, the difference in their ages, and for that matter their respective feelings about the war, had prevented any real closeness between the two men. Both were comfortable with the military formality of their meetings, and saved first names for family gatherings.

"What's on your mind today, Major?"

"Sir," Bolles began, "I'm sure you are aware that the trial of Captain Beall started today. It could not proceed because he does not have counsel. He has requested the representation of a Southern lawyer from Richmond, a close personal friend. I told him it would be necessary to get your permission."

Bolles saw the irritation in Dix's eyes as he said "Southern lawyer." Dix butted out his cigar and looked across the room to the window as if seeing something in the distant past. He rose and slowly walked to the window. Bolles felt the tension as Dix turned to him. "Out of the question, Major. These damned Southerners caused this whole war. You know that as well as I do. Now, when they get caught, they want special consideration. If I gave in to every prisoner's demands, I'd be a pushover for every rebel who came through those gates." He pointed out the window toward the gates of the fort. "As long as I'm in charge there'll be no Southern lawyers defending any prisoner. I don't care who he is or what he's done. Beall will have to make other arrangements." He shot a stare at Bolles. "Will that be all, Major?"

"Yes, sir, that will be all." Bolles rose quickly. He gave a salute and beat a hasty retreat out the door.

Dix walked over to his desk and picked up a letter. It was from one Daniel B. Lucas of Richmond, Virginia. He claimed to be a close personal friend and had heard of Beall's arrest, and was requesting to represent his friend. Dix opened a drawer and slid the letter inside. The letter would go unanswered.

At almost the same moment Bolles left General Dix's office, Colonel George Burke arrived at the New York law office of James T. Brady with a letter. He was met by Emil Traphage. "Mr. Brady is not here at the moment, sir. I am his associate, Emil Traphage. Is there anything I can do for you?"

Burke spoke quickly, "Mr. Traphage, a Southern officer by the name of Captain John Yates Beall, is now held at Fort Lafayette answering to charges of being a spy and guerrilla against our government. He has no counsel at present and Mr. Brady was recommended by Major John Bolles, judge advocate on the case. Do you expect Mr. Brady back very soon?"

Brady was in court and Traphage knew there was no telling when or if he'd be back in the office today, but sensing the urgency of the situation, Traphage said, "Let Major Bolles know that Mr. Brady or myself will either take the case or secure suitable counsel. One of us will go down to Fort Lafayette and consult with Captain Beall." "Thank you, sir. I have a pass to the fort for either your use or Mr. Brady's." Burke was gone as quickly as he had come. Traphage began at once to gather legal materials that might aid in the defense of Captain Beall. He knew that Brady would be interested in this case and best the groundwork be laid immediately.

The *Henry Burdon* had been docked at Fort Lafayette, the arraignment held, and now the infamous prison prepared to take in its newest guest. Lafayette, known throughout the South as the Union Bastille, housed both military and political prisoners. As the war commenced, Lincoln had thrown out the writ of habeas corpus. Many men who were merely suspected of illegal activity on behalf of the South were summarily imprisoned until evidence could be attained on them. Though the government lacked sufficient evidence for trial, they remained locked up, despite the clear violation of their Constitutional rights. President Lincoln said it was necessary. If he hadn't torn a few holes in the Constitution now to defend the Union, he said, there might not be a Constitution, or for that matter, a Union to defend in the future.

Fort Lafayette, located on a shoal in lower New York harbor, was a low, flat, five- sided stone building. It had been built at the time of the War of 1812 to defend New York from the British. A wooden stairway led up from the dock to the fort's gates. At the top of the stairs the walkway divided in two directions. To the left was the block that housed the officers and guards. It also led the way to the offices of Colonel Martin Burke, commandant. Martin Burke, older brother of

George, who had gone to seek James Brady's help, had a reputation for running the prison smoothly. He was strictly a by the book man. He stood at the top of the steps to meet Beall. After a brief introduction, Burke led Beall and his guards over the path to the right, to the cell block for prisoners. As they walked Burke told Beall about the fort and its history, acting more the guide than the prison keeper.

"You'll be housed with several other officers, so I'm sure you'll feel right at home. I'm putting you in with General Roger Pryor. He's from Virginia, too. Do you know him?"

Beall answered that he did not, but he had heard of Pryor. Before the war Roger Pryor had been one of the best lawyers in Richmond. Beall knew him by reputation only. Burke and Beall slipped through massive double wooden doors into a wide corridor with rows of iron doors about twelve feet apart on both sides. At the sixth door on the right Burke stopped. He smiled and motioned to the narrow door with the iron grated window.

"This will be your new home, Captain Beall. I hope you enjoy the companionship during your stay." A twinge of sarcasm bordering on vindictiveness was laced in Burke's voice. Beall was caught off guard by the sarcasm and looked at Burke, puzzled.

The guard opened the door and Beall peered in. The room was larger than he imagined and dimly lit by two gas lamps fixed to the wall. Four cots, a table and a wash stand were spread neatly around the room. Three prisoners arose as Beall entered.

"Gentlemen, this is Captain John Beall. He's taken up residence with us today, and I trust you will all be amiable companions," Burke announced.

The graying senior officer stepped forward. "Welcome to Hotel Lafayette, Beall. I'm General Roger Pryor. We've been reading about you in all the papers. You've been a busy man." Pryor indicated a shorter man. "This is Colonel Amos Oaks," and pointing to the other, "This is Major Tom Buell." Beall extended his hand to each and eyed them all. Pryor had arrived a month before and looked fit for his age. The others showed signs of longer captivity. Both were pale, but mostly it was a drawn and haggard look of despair due to lost hope.

"Have a seat, John," Pryor indicated the cot on the outside wall.

"Thank you, General," Beall said as he headed toward the cot.

"And there's no need to call me General. Roger will do just fine. In here we've given up standing on ceremony. In some sense captivity makes us all equals."

Beall lost no time. "Is there some writing paper and a pen here? I need to write some letters and prepare my defense. These boys are losing no time trying to put a noose around my neck. They actually held an arraignment on the boat as we docked and wanted to know it I was ready to go to trial."

"You're lucky to be getting a trial," said Buell, moving a plug of tobacco from one cheek to the other, "Some's been in here for two years and ain't had a trial yet."

"That's true enough, Tom, but those boys'll go back home after the war. Beall here has earned a reputation the Union government can't ignore." Pryor looked at Beall and grinned, "Your reputation precedes you, my boy. I've read about you in the *Times* ... Johnson's Island, Dunkirk railroad, and setting fires in New York. That was some job!"

"I was never in New York. I had nothing to do with that one." Beall answered.

"That might be the case, son, but I hear by the grapevine that General Dix thinks you did, and that's good enough for him. Ever since he was relieved of his field command and moved upstairs he's been tryin' to prove he's not old and soft. I heard the guards talking that Lincoln slapped his hands for ordering his troops into Canada after the St. Albans raid. They say he didn't take it too well. You and your people in Canada must have him pretty frustrated by now, so don't look for him to do you any favors."

Beall pondered that thought and set aside the idea of the letters for the moment. He lay back on the cot to think, and fell into a deep sleep. At five-thirty p.m. he was awakened by a hand on his shoulder. It was Pryor. "Dinner time, Captain. Don't want to miss the feast."

The table was set with four tin plates and cups. Beall was famished. It was the first meal he'd had all day. Cold carrots, two pieces of brown bread and a cup of cool beef broth. Hardly a feast, but better than nothing.

After dinner the four men sat and talked of the war and their lives before it. Beall took an instant liking to Roger Pryor and asked him about his law practice. The discussion ran on until nine p.m. when

Oaks and Buell turned in. Beall and Pryor talked for several more hours about the raid on Lake Erie and his attempts to stop the trains. Pryor questioned him in exacting detail as to the things he said, and precisely how he spoke to the captives on the *Philo Parsons*. No details were left uncovered. After lengthy consideration of all the facts, Pryor became convinced that in a real court of law Beall would not be guilty of the charges being leveled at him.

"I spoke with a Major Bolles aboard the ship and asked him if my friend, Dan Lucas, from Richmond could defend me," said Beall. "He didn't think that Dix would approve it."

"Lucas, you say? I've heard of him," said Pryor. "I seriously doubt Dix will give permission though."

"What about you, Roger? Do you think Dix would let you defend me?"

"I don't know, but I'd be happy to do it for you. Why don't you write him a note and request me as your counsel. We'll see what happens."

That night Beall wrote the note to Dix and three other letters, one to Dan Lucas, one to Jacob Thompson and the third to Colonel Alexander R. Boteler. He asked Lucas not only for help in representing him, but also to personally contact Thompson and Boteler to get papers that showed his actions on the lake and in New York State had been sanctioned by the Confederate government. That information was vital to his defense.

Setting the completed letters aside, he went to his cot and pulled out his copy of the Book of Common Prayer, given to him by the jailer Hays, and read until he fell asleep.

The next morning Beall asked the guard who delivered breakfast if he would give the note and letters to Colonel Burke, and ask him to forward them to the appropriate authorities. By Wednesday, January twenty-fifth, no answer had come.

On that morning at eleven a.m. the military commission reconvened in a makeshift courtroom at Fort Lafayette. The record of the previous proceedings were read by Judge Advocate Bolles and approved by the commission. Bolles turned to Beall and asked as he had before, "Captain Beall, are you ready to proceed with trial?"

"No, sir. I have requested counsel through Colonel Burke and have received no answer."

Bolles directed the commission's attention to a letter he received from James Brady that very morning. He read it into the official record.

> Major John Bolles
> January 23, 1865
> My dear sir:
> I am very much obliged to you for your courtesy and con-
> sideration in regard to the case at Fort Lafayette. Unfortu-
> nately the trial I have in Superior Court has commenced, and
> I must attend it day to day. I have sought to procure counsel
> for Mr. Beall, but cannot at present obtain any whom I can in
> all respects commend. I trust it may not be inconsistent with
> the public interest to postpone the trial at Fort Lafayette for
> at least one week. I send you this by my friend William H.
> Ryan, Esq.
> Yours truly,
> James T. Brady

Having read the last line of the letter, Major Bolles indicated the presence of Mr. Ryan in the courtroom. William Ryan arose.

"Mr. Ryan," asked General Warren, "will Mr. Brady be able to be
present and act as counsel for Captain Beall if the commission were to
postpone this trial for one more week?"

"Yes, sir," replied Ryan.

"Thank you. You may be seated, Mr. Ryan."

Major Bolles turned to Beall, "Captain Beall, I have in my possession three letters purported to have been written by you to Colonel
Thompson in Toronto, Canada, to Mr. Daniel B. Lucas and Colonel A.R.
Boteler, both of Richmond, Virginia. It would be helpful to the court if
you would by our next meeting reduce to a statement in the form of an
affidavit the facts you hope to prove by these witnesses or documents
so as to save yourself the trouble, expense and delays of getting them
here for trial." Bolles handed the letters to Beall. He was dumbstruck.
Why had they not been sent? Who kept them? Why?

"Major Bolles, I wrote these letters on January twenty-second. Why
have they not been sent to the parties?"

"I don't know why they weren't sent, Captain." But Bolles had a good idea. The letters sent to Burke had been immediately forwarded to General Dix's office. Dix apparently was not going to make the job of Beall's defense an easy one for him, but Bolles did not say as much to Beall.

Beall handed the letters back to Bolles and said, "Yes, I'll have an affidavit prepared as you ask." Beall knew in his heart what Bolles knew. It was Dix. The old bastard wanted to see him hang! There would be no such thing as a fair trial for him.

Major Bolles took the letters and faced the commission. "If it pleases the court, and if Mr. Brady can have Captain Beall's defense ready, I would like to proceed to trial on February first."

Directing his view toward Beall, General Warren asked, "Will you be ready on February first?"

"I believe that will be possible, General."

"Very well. This court stands adjourned until eleven o'clock a.m. Wednesday, February 1, 1865."

James Brady's law office was located at 111 Broadway on the second floor. Two large floor-to-ceiling windows looked down onto the street. Brady stood at one window, his hand holding back the drapery, peering out at the evening traffic. Ten days to prepare for trial. Not much time. He had met with Beall that morning and was struck with the sincerity of the man. Beall had told him of how he volunteered to lead the assault on the *U.S.S Michigan,* and how the crew was assembled in Windsor. He recounted how the men had boarded as passengers and at the earliest opportunity had announced that they were Confederates and commandeered the boat. Brady listened in amazement as Beall recounted how the crew, faced with what they thought was a broken plot had refused to go forward, and how they had retreated to Canada. Brady took copious notes as Beall told of the second plot to help Confederate generals escape from an east bound train outside Dunkirk, New York, and how Beall and Anderson had been captured and interrogated in the Niagara Falls train station. The interview had taken over an hour and a half. At no point in the session had Brady felt anything but admiration for his client. There was not the slightest sense of bravado in his retelling of the events. Beall genuinely believed he was doing no more than his duty as ordered by his commander-in-chief. Brady had the strong sense that the man he sat with was not the same man as described in the documents provided him by the government. To be that man, one would have to have no character, no morals at all.

Ira Cooper, Brady's clerk, entered the office with several large law books, both criminal and military law. He placed them on the desk and quietly turned to leave, not wishing to disturb Brady's thoughts.

"Ira, wait," Brady said, returning to his desk. He sat his large frame delicately into the swivel chair and motioned for his assistant to sit. "This case down at Fort Lafayette is very unusual. Not a normal case. Beall is charged with being a spy and a guerrilla. Now, by definition a spy is a person out of uniform who portrays himself as someone other than a soldier. A guerrilla is someone who acts in a warlike manner without authorization of a legitimate government. You've read the material on the case. How would you approach it?"

Ira shook his head. Brady loved to ask his opinion, but when it came to action, Brady did what his heart told him to do anyway. Ira never saw Brady take his advice unless he was in total agreement with it in the first place, but Ira spoke anyway.

"There is no doubt in my mind that Beall is guilty of the acts described in the indictment. The real issue to me is whether he can be seen as a spy or guerrilla in doing them."

Brady shook his head in the affirmative. "I agree," Brady poked into the air, "but the big question is ... how badly does General Dix want him dead? I've had many cases that I just knew I could win when it seemed like it was a lost cause to everyone else. I've even won cases that by rights I should have lost. In all those cases I had to convince a jury of citizens that there was some reasonable doubt, and in some of them that was no easy task. But with a military commission, I don't know. It would seem to me that they could be predisposed to convict, don't you think? I've never had the sense like I do in this case that no matter what I say, it's a lost cause from the start. Hell, this morning I met with Beall and never was so impressed with the forthrightness and honesty of a man. He's a lawyer, himself, did you know? Never actually practiced. He was a deacon in the Episcopal Church. Comes from a very prominent family in Charles Town, Virginia. He's about the last person I'd think of as a villain or fiend. But that's the way Dix wants to paint him. Dix wants to see him hang for sure."

Ira thought for a moment. Brady's pessimism about the case was typical. He was always that way before a difficult case. Yet, as Ira recalled, Brady had argued about fifty capital murder cases and had won them all. With that record, if Beall had only Brady in his corner, he was in the best of hands.

"The charges say he stole money from the boat's captain," said Ira. "Do you think he did?"

"That's another good question. The law says taking personal money is forbidden, but if a man is authorized by his government as a privateer, and takes money or goods from a ship, it is a legitimate act of war. It's just a matter of whose money was taken."

"Well, what do the depositions taken at Sandusky say?" asked Ira.

Brady's eyes closed to slits, "An astute question, sir. The clerk of the *Parsons* stated in his deposition that it was the ships money, probably taken from passenger fares. Later he stated, or someone else did, that it was personal money. There seems to be a god-awful lot of conflicting evidence, but my money is still on Beall. I can usually read people pretty well, and he seems to be an honorable man. Almost to a fault."

"Why do you say that?" asked Ira.

"Well, in our discussion of the facts and charges I told Beall that one avenue we should explore is that in return for dropped or reduced charges he might testify as to the activities of his government in Canada, name names and so on. He flatly refused. Called it a coward's way out. Told me he saw his grandfather and father die with clean consciences and if he is to live or die, it won't be at the expense of his friends or his country." Brady looked across the office beyond his clerk and spoke, more to himself than to anyone else, "Personally, I think he's deluding himself about the integrity of this court. He may well wind up a victim of his own honor."

16

Trial as a Spy and Guerrilla

At eleven o'clock sharp on February 1, 1865, the six-man military commission convened for trial. Judge Advocate Bolles had arrived at ten forty-five. At ten-fifty Beall was led into the courtroom accompanied by James T. Brady. The stenographer was seated and Bolles took his place to the right of Beall's table. No one spoke.

As the commission filed in, all present in the courtroom rose to their feet. General Warren took his chair and motioned for everyone to be seated. He looked to Bolles indicating he should begin.

The Judge Advocate rose, "Captain Beall, are you now ready for trial?"

Both Beall and Brady stood. "Yes, I am ready," answered Beall.

Directing his remarks to Beall, General Warren said, "Major Bolles will now read the charges against you in this case." He looked to Bolles.

Again Bolles was on his feet and looking at Beall. "Captain Beall, you are charged with violations of the laws of war.

Specification 1--In this that John Y. Beall, did on or about the nineteenth day of September, 1864, at or near Kelley's Island, in the State of Ohio, without lawful authority, and by force of arms, seized and captured the steamboat *Philo Parsons*.

Specification 2--In this that John Y. Beall, a citizen of the insurgent State of Virginia, did on or about the nineteenth day of September, 1864, at or near Middle Bass Island, in the State of Ohio, without lawful authority, and by force of arms, seize, capture and sink the steamboat *Island Queen*.

Specification 3--In this that John Y. Beall, a citizen of the insurgent State of Virginia, was found acting as a spy at or near Kelley's Island, in the State of Ohio, on or about the nineteenth day of September, 1864.

Specification 4--In this that John Y. Beall, a citizen of the insurgent State of Virginia, was found acting as a spy on or about the nineteenth day of September, 1864, at or near Middle Bass Island, in the State of Ohio.

Specification 5--In this that John Y. Beall, a citizen of the insurgent State of Virginia, was found acting as a spy on or about the sixteenth day of December, 1864, at or near Suspension Bridge in the State of New York.

Specification 6--In this that John Y. Beall, a citizen of the insurgent State of Virginia, being without lawful authority, and for unlawful purposes, in the State of New York, did in said State of New York undertake to carry on irregular and unlawful warfare as a guerrilla; and in the execution of said undertaking, attempted to destroy the lives and property of the peaceable and unoffending inhabitants of said state, and of persons therein traveling, by throwing a train of cars and the passengers of said cars from the railroad track on

the railroad between Dunkirk and Buffalo, by placing ob-
structions across said track; all this in said State of New
York, and on or about the fifteenth day of December, 1864,
at or near Buffalo.

Bolles paused, sipped some water, and continued to read,
"Charge number two. Acting as a spy.

Specification 1--In this that John Y. Beall, a citizen of the
insurgent State of Virginia, was found acting as a spy in
the State of Ohio, at or near Kelley's Island, on or about the
nineteenth day of September, 1864.

Specification 2--In this that John Y. Beall, a citizen of the
insurgent State of Virginia, was found acting as a spy in the
State of Ohio, on or about the nineteenth day of September,
1864, at or near Middle Bass Island.

Specification 3--In this that John Y. Beall, a citizen of the
insurgent State of Virginia, was found acting as a spy in
the State of New York, at or near the Suspension Bridge, on
or about the sixteenth day of December, 1864. The above
named Beall is to be brought to trial before a military commission of which Brigadier General Fitz Henry Warren is
President.

Bolles laid the charges on his table and sat down. General Warren
spoke, "Captain Beall, how do you plead to the charges that have just
been read?"

Beall rose slowly, scanning the eyes of each officer on the commission. "I am not guilty of all charges, sir."

"Very well," said Warren, "Major Bolles, you may call your first witness."

Bolles stood again and looked to the commission. "I call Walter O.
Ashley."

Walter Ashley was ushered into the room and directed to the witness's chair. He stood before General Warren and was sworn to tell the

truth. Then Ashley sat, looking tired and a bit unnerved by the whole proceeding. It had been a long trip from Detroit, and he dreaded reliving that day again.

Bolles walked out from behind his table and stood just to the left of Ashley.

"Please state your name, place of residence and occupation."

"My name is Walter O. Ashley. I am both clerk and part owner of the *Philo Parsons*. I live in Detroit, Michigan."

Indicating Beall, Bolles said, "Look at the accused. Have you ever seen him before?"

Ashley shook his head, "Yes, I have. Last September nineteenth I saw him for the first time."

"Mr. Ashley, state for the court the circumstances under which you saw him. And also tell the court about the transaction that occurred on the eighteenth of September."

Ashley looked at Beall and began talking slowly and carefully. "On Sunday the eighteenth of September, at about six o'clock in the evening I was on board the *Philo Parsons* which was docked at Detroit.

I was alone in the cabin that evening when a man came aboard to inquire about passage to Sandusky. You see, our boat regularly sails between Detroit and Sandusky, stopping at Amherstberg and sometimes Sandwich on the Canadian side. The man, who I later found out was a Mr. Bennet G. Burley, came in asking for Ashley. I told him I was Ashley, and he said that he and three friends intended to go down to Sandusky in the morning. He also asked that the boat stop at Sandwich where those friends would get on. I told him it wasn't customary to stop at Sandwich, but he asked as a personal favor that the boat stop to pick up his friends. I then agreed, as long as he, Burley, would take the boat at Detroit and let me know for sure that his friends would be ready to get on at Sandwich. He then went away. The next morning, being Monday, the nineteenth of September, the boat left Detroit at eight o'clock in the morning. As the boat was pulling away from the dock, Burley came to me and reminded me that I promised to stop at Sandwich. So, we stopped and took on these friends of Mr. Burley."

"Who were they?" Bolles asked.

"Well," said Ashley, "the accused was one, and there were two others."

"Coming on board, did they report their names?" Bolles made a quick notation on his pad.

"No, they did not. It had been my custom to record passenger names on long routes, but this time I did not."

Bolles continued, "Please describe the dress of the accused when he came on board. Was it military or civilian?"

"They were all dressed as civilians, the entire party. They were very gentlemanly in their appearance. I asked it they had baggage, but they said no. It was just a little pleasure trip, they might stop at Kelley's Island. Said they didn't know exactly where they'd go, but paid their fare to Sandusky. The boat then proceeded to Malden, Canada, about fifteen miles down the river. At Malden about twenty five men came aboard and paid their fares. Malden is the port for Amherstberg. When the men came aboard all they had for baggage was an old trunk tied up with a cord, a rope tied around it. It was taken on at the after-gangway by the roughest looking men in the party. Most of the men were roughly dressed in civilian clothing."

Bolles moved back to his table and looked at his notes. "What did you come to find were the contents of that trunk?"

"Later, I found it contained revolvers and hatchets."

"After you left Amherstberg, where did you go next?"

"We started down toward the lake," answered Ashley.

"What time was that, Mr. Ashley?" Bolles asked.

"About half past nine." answered Ashley.

"What happened next?"

"Nothing really," shrugged Ashley. "Everything went off smoothly until about four o'clock in the afternoon. The boat stopped off at a number of islands transacting business and taking on passengers."

"What type of business?"

"We took some cargo to be shipped to Sandusky. We haul both cargo and passengers, you see. At four o'clock in the afternoon we had just left Kelley's Island."

"Where is Kelley's Island, Mr. Ashley?" asked Bolles.

"It is an island in Lake Erie about six miles from the American shore. It's almost due north of Sandusky."

"State what occurred next." directed Bolles.

"Well, we were about two miles out from Kelley's Island heading for

Sandusky. I was standing on the main deck of the boat."

Bolles interrupted, "Where was Captain Atwood at this time?"

"The captain had gone ashore at Middle Bass Island. He had a house there. It was customary for him to stop off there on trips to Sandusky."

"Who was in charge of the boat then?" asked Bolles.

I was in charge of the business of the boat, but I am not a sailor. The mate was at the wheel."

"What happened next, Mr. Ashley?"

"As I said before, I was standing on the main deck in front of the office and the ladies cabin. The passengers were all in the upper cabin. Three men came up to me, drew revolvers and leveled them at me, said if I offered any resistance they'd shoot me."

"Who were these men?"

"They were three of the party who got on at Sandwich." answered Ashley.

"Captain Beall was not one of them?"

"No, neither was Mr. Burley. But then Mr. Burley did come from the forward part of the boat with fifteen or twenty men. He had a revolver in his hand. He pointed it at me and told me to get in the cabin or I was a dead man. He commenced counting ... one ... two ... three. He never got past two and I was in the door. I was in the cabin for about an hour. Mr. Burley stationed two guards with revolvers at the door, presumably to keep me in. I looked out the door and saw the whole party gather around the old trunk. They cut the cord and opened it. They had revolvers and hatchets inside, and all the men armed themselves."

"What took place next?" asked Bolles.

"Well, Burley got an axe he found on board and smashed the saloon door open. Then he went with the axe and smashed a racing sulky to pieces. They threw it overboard. From that he and his men commenced to throw the freight overboard."

"What kind of freight?"

"Some of it was household goods, some tobacco and pig iron. They threw the iron over first. I won't say I saw the household goods thrown overboard, the iron was...perhaps the household goods weren't. I don't recall."

James T. Brady was annoyed. He whispered to Beall, "What does he remember clearly. His deposition is quite a bit different from his testimony so far." Beall nodded agreement.

"Mr. Ashley, when did you next see Captain Beall?" Bolles indicated the accused.

"Almost an hour after the boat was captured, Captain Beall came to me and asked me if I was in charge of the office. I told him I was. He then asked me if I was in charge of the boat's papers. He took me to the office and I gave him the papers and he took them with him."

Bolles looked at Beall and asked, "At the time he asked you for the papers, did he indicate to you who he was, or what his purpose was?"

"Not directly. I asked him not to destroy the steamboat, and he said something to the effect that if I was a United States soldier and had seized one of their vessels, that I would probably destroy that vessel. He did not say to me that he was a Confederate officer." Ashley paused, "Some of the others did say so ... that they were Confederate states soldiers, and that the expedition was in the charge of Confederate States' officers."

"Mr. Ashley, try to recall for the court where you were at this time on the lake," said Bolles.

"By this time we were heading down the lake for about a half hour, but then we turned off from the Sandusky course and headed up the lake again to Middle Bass Island to get wood and to put passengers ashore."

"So you went to Middle Bass. Did you get wood and were the passengers put ashore?"

"Yes, sir." answered Ashley.

"Please tell the court to the best of your recollection what happened then." directed Bolles.

"Well, we had been lying there for about fifteen minutes when the *Island Queen* pulled in along side. She is a steamboat that also makes runs from Sandusky to the islands every day. The party from the *Parsons* went over to the *Island Queen* and seized her, making prisoners of all the passengers on board. Some of them were put in the cabin of the *Philo Parsons* and the rest were put into the hold. The passengers of both boats were later put ashore on Middle Bass Island. We had been at Middle Bass for about an hour when Captain Beall came to the door. He told the man and two young ladies who were with me that they could go ashore."

"What did you do next?" asked Bolles.

"I started to follow them, but went back to my desk to get the ship's books and papers. Captain Beall came back and Burley with him. I was standing at my desk. Beall was on one side of me, Burley on the other. I asked Beall if I could take the boat's books. He said that I should not take anything that belonged to the boat."

"Was that all, Mr. Ashley?"

"No, I told him I had some private promissory notes, and could I have them. Burley asked to see them, but said I could keep them because he couldn't collect on them. Then Captain Beall said, 'We want your money.' I opened the cash drawer and pulled out eight or ten dollars and they took it."

"Is that all they got?" asked Bolles.

"No, Burley said, 'You've got more money than this, let's have it!' I put my hand in my vest pocket and pulled out a roll of bills . . . about one hundred dollars, and laid it on the desk."

"What did they do with the money?" inquired Major Bolles.

"They took it." said Ashley.

"Who exactly took it?" pressed Bolles.

"They took it between them. I'm not sure which one actually picked it up, but they both demanded it."

The Judge Advocate glanced at the documents on his table and continued, "According to your deposition, you then went ashore. Please state for the record what you observed."

"Yes, sir. After about a half hour the *Parsons* and the *Island Queen* started for Sandusky. They were lashed together. At about two miles out I noticed the *Queen* drifting. What they did was scuttle her and set her adrift to sink."

"Did she sink?" Bolles asked.

"No, not completely. The next day I was on my way to Sandusky and saw her. She had taken on about four feet of water but was resting on a reef."

Bolles asked, "Do you recollect anything else from that night that might aid the court in this case?"

"No, sir, I think I've stated everything that would be of account," answered Ashley.

"Did you see Beall at any time after that?"

"Yes, in New York City, after his arrest."

"Thank you, that is all I have. No further questions." Bolles sat down.

"Your witness, Mr. Brady," said General Warren.

Brady hesitated momentarily to gather his thoughts. He knew when he took this case it would not be easy. Ashley was a convincing witness. His only hope at this point was to create some doubt in the minds of the court about Ashley's memory of the events. Brady rose. His large head nodded to Ashley in a friendly way.

"Mr. Ashley, how long were you the clerk of the *Philo Parsons*?"

"Two seasons. This is only my second season."

"And what positions had you held before that?" asked Brady.

"I had been a clerk on other steam boats for nine years before that."

"Any occupation before that?"

"Well, I clerked in a store and helped my uncle at the post office. Before that I was in school."

"So in all of your working life you've been in a position to handle money. Have you ever been accused of taking any?" Brady didn't think that he had, but if it made the court think about it, so much the better.

The question ruffled Ashley. "No, who told you I ever took money?" he asked indignantly.

"No one, Mr. Ashley, its just seems to me that a young man whose always handled money must have been tempted at one time or another. Had you ever seen Beall or Burley before that day?"

"Only Burley. He came to make the arrangements for the trip." said Ashley.

"Was Beall with the group of twenty-five who came aboard at Sandwich?" Brady asked.

"Only three men came on at Sandwich. The others got on later at Malden." answered Ashley.

"Very well, was Beall one of the men who got on a Sandwich?"

"I don't recall." Ashley answered.

"But you do recall that Burley and the men said it was a pleasure trip?"

"Yes."

"Did Burley say at any time that he was a Confederate officer? Or what his rank was?" asked Brady.

"No, sir."

"But you have stated that some of the men said they were Confederate officers and soldiers?"

"Yes, some did say so. The men who were guarding my door said they were going to capture the *U.S.S. Michigan* and free their friends from Johnson's Island."

"You stated before that Burley was the spokesman for the party. When did you first become aware of Captain Beall?"

"It was about an hour to an hour and a half after we were under way when Beall came to me and asked for the ship's papers. He said he was in charge."

"So you can remember when the men came on and pretty close to how long you were underway, but you can't remember seeing Captain Beall before he came to your office?"

"Yes, sir," Ashley said, somewhat confused by the question.

"What did Captain Beall say when he came to your office?"

"He asked if I had the ship's papers. I told him I did and that I was part owner of the boat. He told me he was in charge of the party and wanted the papers. I asked if he intended to destroy the boat."

"What did he say to that?" asked Brady.

"He said if I was a United States officer and had seized one of their vessels that I would probably destroy it."

"Did he actually say he would destroy the boat?" prodded Brady.

"No." Ashley rubbed his arm slowly and looked around the room.

"Mr. Ashley, you have stated that revolvers were pointed at you. Was your life threatened at any time by the accused?" asked Brady.

"No, he had a revolver at the time of the meeting in my office, but I don't recall if he pointed it at me." answered Ashley quietly.

"You don't recall someone holding a pistol to you and demanding a key, and Captain Beall telling the men to kill you if you moved? That he'd make a key himself?"

Brady was referring to statements made by Bennet Burley, but now Ashley was confused. "I don't really recollect anything like that. Beall may have been present, but I don't recall."

Brady pursued. "You testified that Captain Beall wore citizen's dress. Did he have a hat or a cap on?"

"I don't know. I don't pay very close attention to people's clothing."

"There was nothing peculiar about any part of his dress that you observed?"

"No, nothing peculiar."

"How about on his hat? Any insignia or gold braid?"

"No, there were none."

"Mr. Ashley, just a few minutes ago you testified that you could not remember if Beall wore a hat or not. Now you say he had no insignias on his hat. Just how much do you recall?" Brady did not expect an answer. He just hoped the court would note the inconsistency of the testimony. He looked at the court, drew his breath and went back at Ashley.

"Mr. Ashley, let's go back to the cash drawer. You stated there were eight or ten dollars in it, and that Burley and Beall took it away with them. Is that correct?" asked Brady with an air of feigned frustration.

"Yes," he answered.

"Had this sum of money been collected from the passengers?"

"Yes."

"Was any other money collected from the passengers after the capture of the boat?" asked Brady.

"No, not to my knowledge."

"And what about the money you produced from your pocket. Where did that come from?"

"It was money collected from the passengers. I had not time to put it in the cash drawer. When the boat was seized I handed it over to Beall and Burley."

"Who took the money?" pressed Brady.

"I laid it on the desk. I cannot say for certain who took it," Ashley admitted.

"So it is possible that Beall took none of it?"

"I suppose, but they both asked for it."

"And it was the boat's money, not yours personally?"

"Yes," Ashley hesitated and looked away from Brady, "that is correct."

"Mr. Ashley, when the *Island Queen* was attached to the *Philo Parsons* were there any soldiers aboard the *Island Queen*?"

"Yes, there were about twenty or twenty five unarmed United States soldiers going to Toledo to be mustered out."

"What happened to them?" asked Brady.

"At first they were put in the hold with the other passengers. Then we were all put ashore at Middle Bass Island."

"And when was it you say you saw Captain Beall again?"

"In New York City at the police station."

"Was he alone?"

"No, he was with twenty or thirty others." answered Ashley

"Did he look the same as he does today?" asked Brady.

"Yes, sir."

"I have no further questions of this witness." Brady sat down.

General Warren directed himself to Walter Ashley. "Mr. Ashley, was there any military or naval mark, or badge on the accused while he was on board the *Philo Parsons*?"

"No, there was not, they were all dressed as civilians, paid their fares and were treated as passengers." said Ashley.

"Did Burley and Beall divide the money you laid on the desk?" asked Warren.

"They were taking the money when I left. I laid it on the desk when they both demanded it and took it between them. There was an actual division of money. I saw that."

"Thank you," Warren looked to the Judge Advocate, "Major Bolles?"

Bolles rose and strode over to Ashley. "At the time the boat was captured how far was it from Johnson's Island?"

"I would judge it to have been six miles."

"How far from Kelley's Island to Johnson's Island?" Bolles asked.

"I should say thirteen or fourteen miles." Ashley said.

"Have you ever seen the *U.S.S. Michigan*?" asked Bolles.

"I've seen her, but I've never been on board."

"Do you know where she was at the time of this affair?"

"Yes. She was lying off Johnson's Island about a mile ... and also I stated I was not on board ... but about six or seven years ago I was on board her, but not since the war." Bolles sat and nodded to General Warren.

General Warren spoke, "Thank you, Mr. Ashley, "Any recross,

Mr. Brady?"

Brady slowly arose and rubbed the back of his neck, "Mr. Ashley, you've previously stated that the soldiers on the *Island Queen* were unarmed. Were there any arms aboard?"

"Not to my knowledge." he answered.

"Did you examine to see if there were?"

"No."

"Isn't it true that the Beall party ran up a Confederate flag on the *Philo Parsons*?"

"Not to my recollection."

"No further questions, your honor." Brady returned to his seat.

General Warren thanked Walter Ashley and excused him. Then Warren looked to Bolles. "Call your next witness, Major."

Judge Advocate Bolles said, " I call William Weston to the stand."

Weston took his seat on the witness stand as Major Bolles walked to him. "Please state your name, place of residence and occupation."

"I am William Weston. I live in Sandusky, Ohio, and have been a fireman for five years."

"Have you ever seen the accused, Captain Beall before?" asked Bolles, pointing toward the accused.

"Yes, sir. I saw him on the *Philo Parsons* last September nineteenth."

"Please state for the court, Mr. Weston, what you saw and heard on that date."

Weston was nervous. His voice quivered as he told of the capture of the boat. "We were all a little excited after the capture. Captain Beall came forward and told us what they were going to do with the boat. He said none of us would get hurt and that he'd land us as soon as possible. He also told me he was an escaped rebel prisoner from Johnson's Island and that they intended to use the *Philo Parsons* to capture the *Michigan* and liberate prisoners from the island, and destroy commerce on the lakes, as best I recall."

"Did you see what they did with the freight?" Bolles asked.

"I didn't see them do anything with the freight, but they did throw out some boxes near the shore of Middle Bass Island."

"Did Captain Beall have any weapons on him or not while on the *Philo Parsons*?" asked Bolles.

"I'm not sure. I didn't see any," answered Weston.

"How was he dressed?"

"He had on citizen's dress."

"Did he wear a hat or cap?" asked Bolles.

"He wore a low crowned hat."

"When did you next see him?

Weston thought for a few seconds, "I did not see him again until I was brought down to Fort Lafayette to identify him."

"Did you hear the others refer to the accused by name that day?" asked Bolles.

"Yes, they called him Captain Beall." answered Weston.

"You heard them call him Captain Beall?"

"I can't say for certain he was the person or not. I heard someone called Captain Beall."

"Who seemed to be in command of this party?" asked Bolles.

"I don't know," said Weston.

Bolles began to feel that if he went any further with this line he might hurt his own case. Weston was not as clear in his recollections as Bolles would have liked.

That fact was not lost on James Brady. He rose and walked around his table toward the witness' chair. Putting both hands on the rail in front on Weston, he spoke softly and looked into Weston's eyes. "Mr. Weston, when you were brought down to Fort Lafayette to identify Captain Beall, did you point out this man?" Brady indicated Beall with a wave of his hand toward Beall.

"Yes, sir, when I saw him."

"Who was with him?" asked Brady.

"I really don't know who they were. I'm a stranger in New York."

"Isn't it true, Mr. Weston, that you actually identified another man? A man who turned out to be named Smedley?" Brady smiled as he asked the question.

"No sir! That's not true!" retorted Weston indignantly.

"Didn't you testify that the first and last time you saw Captain Beall was on the forward deck of the *Philo Parsons* on September nineteenth?"

"Yes," answered Weston, wondering where Brady was going.

"Mr. Weston," Brady paused, "do you mean to tell this court that you saw a man one time on September nineteenth, and that among twenty or thirty others, you could identify him in December, a full two and a half months later? I find that very difficult to believe!" Brady walked abruptly back to his seat hoping the court found it so, too. As Brady sat he turned back toward Weston, "By the way, did you notice what kind of cord he had on his hat?"

"I don't know."

"Was there a tassel on it?"

"I can't say."

"Was there gold on it?"

"I don't know."

"Oh," almost as an afterthought Brady asked, "did you see a Confederate flag on board?"

"No, sir."

He sat. "No further questions of this witness." Brady had established the idea that Weston might not be a credible witness, but the faces of the court gave no reaction that they agreed. William Weston was dismissed and walked quietly out of the room.

Bolles called his next witness, "David H. Thomas."

"Please state your name, residence and occupation for the court," Bolles
directed.

"My name is David H. Thomas and I live at Niagara City, New York, and I am a police officer with that village." He spoke with the confidence of one who had spent time in court before.

"You arrested the accused?" tendered Bolles.

"I did."

"When and where?"

"We, Officer Saule and myself, arrested the accused in the depot of the New York Central Railroad on the sixteenth of December between nine and ten o'clock at night." Thomas spoke matter of factly.

"Did you arrest anyone else at that time?"

"Yes, a young man calling himself Anderson."

"Were they together?" asked Bolles.

"Yes."

"Did they have any baggage?"

"Yes, they had a small carpet bag. It had some shirts, socks, five or six candles, some matches and a box of paper collars," stated Thomas.

"Did you search the accused's person?" questioned Bolles.

"Yes, we found a bottle of laudanum in his pocket."

"What type of clothing was he wearing?"

"About the same type he has on now, except for an overcoat and cap." said Thomas.

"Did he have any arms?" asked Bolles.

"Yes, he had a Navy Colt revolver secured on his hip under the coat."

"Was it loaded?"

"Yes, fully. It was a six shooter."

"Did you ask him his name?"

"Yes, while I searched him I asked his name and he said Beall. A few minutes later I asked him again to learn his full name and he said his name was W.W. Baker. I corrected him saying he told me his name was Beall, but he denied it." recalled Thomas.

Bolles made a notation and asked, "Did he have any money on him?"

"He had about thirty-six dollars. Some of it in U.S. currency, some in Canadian.

"Did the accused account for himself in the train station? Why did he say he was there?" asked Bolles.

"When I arrested him, he asked what he was being arrested for. I told him he probably knew as well as I did why. He said he did not. I finally told him he was arrested as an escaped rebel prisoner. Then he asked me from where. I told him it didn't matter. He asked if it was from Lookout Point. I told him it was. He said, 'That I will acknowledge. I am an escaped prisoner from Lookout Point'."

"Did you ask him how he got the Canadian money?"

"Yes, he said when he escaped from Lookout Point he got to Baltimore where his friends gave him money to go to Canada."

Bolles now turned his attention to Beall's luggage. "In regard to the carpet bag, could you tell who it belonged to?"

"When we arrested them, it was sitting on the floor between them. Anderson carried it into the room where we questioned them. I asked whose bag it was and Anderson said it belonged to Beall."

"Did the accused hear this remark?" asked Bolles.

"Yes, he denied it was his."

"Did you ask why they had candles and matches in the bag?"

"Anderson said they carried them in case there were no other lights."

James Brady looked intently for some reaction from the commission. He hoped the commission wasn't tying the matches and candles to the fires in New York City. The commission members' faces gave away no signs at all. Brady scribbled a few notes for future reference.

Bolles looked toward Beall. "And what about the laudanum?"

The detective smiled, "Beall said he carried it because he had a tooth-ache."

"What did the accused say about having a revolver?"

"He said it was lucky we surprised him because he had been in pris-on so much that he had resolved never to be taken alive."

"Thank you, Mr. Thomas. I have no further questions now." Bolles returned to his seat.

General Warren looked at his pocket watch and spoke to James Brady.

"If your cross will be lengthy, I think we should adjourn for today."

"I'll be brief, General. I think we can finish up the witness in a few minutes."

"Very well, then," Warren waved, "proceed."

Beall watched Brady rise and move toward Officer Thomas. His tooth was aching and his chest hurt. He wished he had the laudanum now. He coughed quietly twice and several members of the court glanced his way.

"Mr. Thomas," Brady began, "was Beall alone when you arrested him?"

"No, he was sitting along side of Anderson on a settee."

"And when was this? What time of day?"

"Night, some time between nine and ten o'clock, closer to ten o'clock."

"You said an Officer Saule was with you. Did he take part in the ar-rest?"

"Yes. He arrested Anderson, I arrested Beall."

"And about the laudanum. How big a vial was it?" Brady had a feeling the court might be thinking the laudanum was to be used as a poison. It worked very well as a pain deadener for toothaches, but used in enough quantity, it was a deadly poison.

"I believe they call it a two ounce vial. It had very little left in it." answered Thomas.

"In the conversation you had with Beall at the train station did he tell you about his being a Confederate officer?"

"No, he said he was a sergeant in the Second Virginia infantry."

"And he told you he escaped from Lookout Point?"

"Yes," said Thomas.

"Did he say when?" asked Brady.

"Not exactly, just that it had been a few days before his arrival in Buffalo."

"What kind of cap did he wear?"

"It was a cloth cap, a citizen's cap." answered Thomas with assurance.

"Thank you, Mr. Thomas, no further questions."

General Warren pulled his papers together and noted the time was late. "We will adjourn this court until eleven a.m. tomorrow morning." He rose and led the commission members out of the room. The two guards moved toward Beall to escort him out. Brady patted him on the arm as he left and gathered his papers into his bag.

James Brady left the court room knowing that the worst was ahead. So far he'd tried to pick apart the recollections of the witnesses hoping to cast some doubt on their reliability, but he wasn't confident he'd impressed the court. Most of these trials were a forgone conclusion the day they started. If General Dix wanted Beall found guilty, then he would be despite any efforts by Brady. He hadn't voiced his beliefs to Beall, but in his heart he felt Beall knew it, too. Every officer on the court owed his future in the military to General Dix, and it seemed to Brady that what Dix wanted was a fair trial and an execution.

Beall returned to his cell at Fort Lafayette and sat in semi-darkness. Tomorrow he'd be hearing from Hays, the crooked doorman of the Mulberry Street police station. He was sure he'd convinced Hays to help him escape. He came so close. If only they had not come that morning to get him. He'd probably be back in Canada by now. He also wondered what lies Hays would tell to cover himself. It wouldn't really be hard. Who'd take the word of a Confederate over a loyal police doorkeeper?

Beall's thoughts wandered back to that jail and all the advice he'd gotten from every pickpocket and burglar who had shared his cell. Save yourself! Sell out your friends! That's what every one of them said. But if Beall told what he knew, the whole effort in Canada would fail. What point was there in saving your own hide by selling out your friends, he thought. He could not live with that thought, and pushed it out of his mind. He'd just have to accept whatever came his way ... and then he thought of Martha, and he anguished about his decision. Sleep came, but slowly.

On Thursday, February second, the court reconvened. General Warren had the court stenographer read the previous day's proceedings and Judge Advocate Bolles called Edward Hays to the stand.

Bolles approached the witness. "Please state for the court your name and occupation."

"Edward Hays, doorman at the police headquarters on Mulberry Street."

Motioning toward Beall, Bolles asked, "You see the accused sitting here. Have you ever seen him before? And if so, when?"

"Yes, sir, I have. At the Police Headquarters on Mulberry Street."

"It is my understanding that Captain Beall asked you to help him escape. Tell the court your recollection of that incident," said Bolles.

Hays glanced almost sheepishly at Beall. "He asked me to carry a letter out for him and have it mailed. He said he wanted it sent to Canada. I asked him if he didn't think it would have a hard time getting there. He said it would probably be hard. The government was opening all letters going there then, but he thought if he could get the letter to Canada, word could be sent to his government in Richmond and they might help to get him out. When I went to get the paper, I told Mr. Kelso, who was in charge of the office about the letter. Kelso told me to go back and tell him that there were too many detectives and I couldn't get the paper. I told him I'd have to wait until the office cleared out before I could get it without being seen."

"What did Beall say when you told him this?" asked Bolles.

"He said, 'Hays, I'll tell you what you can do for me.' "I said, 'What?'
He said,

'You can let me go!' When I told him I could not, he offered me one
thousand dollars in gold. At first I thought it was just a joke, and asked
him if he had the money on him. He said no, but if I took his word, he
would see that I got the money when he got to Canada."

"Did Beall say anything about participating in the recent fires here in
New York City?" asked Bolles.

"I asked him about that, and he said no, but he knew who did. They
were all back in Canada."

"What did you say to his offer of one thousand dollars?"

"I told him I didn't think I could let him go, but he persisted. He told
me he'd been arrested before under different charges and his government had helped him, but they weren't as powerful now. He was afraid
his government might not be able to help him now."

"What did you do next?" asked Bolles.

"I told him I'd think about it and left back to the office. When I got
there I reported what he said to Mr. Kelso."

"What did Kelso say?"

"Mr. Kelso told me to go back and see what else I could find out from
the prisoner, so I went back and I told him it would be pretty hard for
me to get him out without getting caught myself, but if I could, when
would he want to go? He told me sometime after midnight would be
best." Hays paused.

"What did you do next?" prodded Bolles.

"I asked him how he intended to get back to Canada if I got him out,
and he said he had two friends living up on Thirtieth Street who'd help
him get back to Canada. I then asked him if those friends could get me
the money before he left New York. He said maybe they could furnish
part of it, and he could send the rest from Canada."

"Did you ask the location or address of this house on Thirtieth
Street?"

"Yes, and I even asked their names, but he would not tell me. Said he
wasn't sure of the house number." answered Hays.

"Mr. Hays, at the time did you know Captain Beall's proper name?"

"No, Mr. Kelso told me he thought Beall was using a fictitious name
and to see if he'd tell me his real name."

"And did he tell you?" asked Bolles.

"No, he said he knew many things he would not tell. Told me he knew plenty of things that would be worth millions to the government, but he'd die before he'd tell. I told him I was glad because if I let him go, I hoped he'd remember that in my regard, too."

"Did he say anymore?" asked Bolles.

"Yes, he made the thousand-dollar offer again. I told him I would see what I could do, and if I could come back that night I would. Then I left him. When I came back the next day, he had been taken to Fort Lafayette, and I haven't seen him since."

Bolles walked back to his table. "I have no further questions of this witness."

General Warren made a notation on his pad and looked across to Brady, "Any cross, Mr. Brady?"

Brady motioned with his finger for a few seconds as he scratched down some notes. He rose slowly, still intent on the content of his notes.

"How long have you been the doorkeeper at the Police Headquarters?" Brady asked, still intent on his notes.

"Since last April."

"And what were you engaged in before that?"

"I worked at the Navy Yard as a laborer."

"Did you do anything before that?"

"Yes, I worked in a liquor business on Madison Avenue," said Hays.

"Why did you leave the liquor business, Mr. Hays?" asked Brady.

Hays did not answer. He gazed at the floor and collected his thoughts. He had not expected the question.

"Mr. Hays, I asked you why you left the liquor business," Brady pressed.

"I ... I was fired," Hays said quietly.

"And would you explain to the court why you were fired?"

Before Hays could respond, Judge Advocate Bolles interrupted. "Mr. Hays' past occupational problems are not in question here."

Brady smiled at Bolles who knew what was coming next. "If it pleases the court, Mr. Hays' job problems are relevant to this proceeding. It is my feeling that he is not a reliable witness."

"Mr. Hays, you must answer the question," said General Warren.

Brady spoke again, "Mr. Hays, explain to the court the exact circumstances under which you lost your job."

"Some liquor had disappeared from the warehouse on the day I was in charge and I was blamed ... but I didn't do it!" Hays protested.

Brady was patronizing, "I am sure you didn't, Mr. Hays." Brady winked at Bolles and smiled. Then he turned back to Hays and continued, "Mr. Hays, can you recollect when you first met Captain Beall?"

"It must have been a week before New Years, I think. It was the night before New Years that our conversation occurred. I'm not positive, but I think so ..." Hays was flustered.

"Do you say all these conversations happened on the same night?" asked Brady.

"Yes," Hays responded.

"So for a week you checked on Captain Beall and fed him and yet never talked to him before the night before New Years? Doesn't that seem unusual, Mr. Hays? Suddenly Beall blurts out all of this so called plan, and you do all the thinking, and reporting back to Kelso ... all on the same night?" The question did not need to be answered. Brady moved on.

"How did you happen to have this conversation with Captain Beall?"

Hays cleared his throat, "Mr. Kelso asked me to see if I could find out what the prisoner's real name was and on what charges he had been arrested." said Hays, trying hard to gather his composure.

"When did you find out his name?"

"About seven o'clock that evening." answered Hays.

"Mr. Hays, Captain Beall was arrested and held at Niagara Falls, New York. Mr. Ashley has already testified that he identified him at the police station. How is it that by the time Captain Beall got to your jail in New York City that no one knew his real name?"

"Ah ... I don't know."

Brady walked slowly across to his table and turned, "Where were the police commissioners at the time you had this conversation with Captain Beall?"

"I don't know if they had gone home or not."

Brady was incredulous. "You mean to tell this court that you came from Kelso's office and did not know if any of his superiors were still in the building? If my memory of the Police Headquarters is accurate you should have been able to see them. Is that not right, Mr. Hays?"

"I ... I ... just don't remember," stammered Hays.

"But you do remember that Kelso told you to do it and what time it was?"

"Yes."

"Mr. Hays, I want you to repeat exactly what Kelso said to you when he expressed a wish that you should see this man and ascertain his name." said Brady.

Hays was becoming agitated. Brady liked that.

Hays continued, "Mr. Kelso said to me when I could get the time to go to his cell and see if I could get his name and the charges he was arrested on."

"Were there more prisoners than Beall in the jail that day?"

"Yes, several."

"Then how did you know the prisoner Kelso referred to?" asked Brady.

"He referred to him as Baker, he told me to go see Baker and see what I could learn from him."

"Did Kelso give you a reason as to why he wanted the information? Hadn't the police commissioners told him?"

"No, he did not tell me why," answered Hays. He wasn't very comfortable with where the questions were going.

"Had you ever before given Beall any reason to think you'd help him escape before that night?" Brady knew that Hays would deny it, but the idea would be planted with the court just the same. Brady was pretty sure that Hays and maybe even Kelso might have considered helping Beall for the money. What Brady had to do was to get the commission to think it, and then Hays would lose all credibility as a witness.

"Mr. Hays, it seems remarkable to me that Captain Beall would take you into his confidence about a possible escape so readily. Can you recall anything you might have said previous to that night that might have made Captain Beall think you'd help him?"

Hays was uneasy. ""No, I do not."

"What exactly do you recall of your conversation with the accused on that day?"

Hays measured his words carefully, "There was a man in the cell with Beall earlier that day, an old man who wanted me to deliver a letter for him. When I told him I couldn't take it, he offered to pay me, so I asked how much. He said ... I don't recall how much ... well, I told him I could not take it for that. That evening when I returned to the cell about eight o'clock, Captain Beall was alone. I said, 'It's pretty cold in here this evening,' and he agreed. I said it was lucky the old man got out before night as it was so cold. Then he said, 'Would you take a letter for me? I can pay you well.' I told him there was a good deal done for money."

Beall smiled and rubbed his hands together slowly. He knew hungry little Hays would have helped him if he'd only had more time. He'd probably never seen a thousand dollars in his life. And now he sits up there acting so innocent, and not a very good actor at that.

Brady shifted away from Hays a few steps and stood in front of the commission. He looked back to Hays.

"Mr. Hays, is it customary to search prisoners at your jail when they are brought in?"

"Yes, of course."

"And all their goods confiscated?"

"Yes."

"Then why would you assume that Beall could pay to have the letter delivered?"

"I didn't know if he could or not." answered Hays.

"And during that conversation did Captain Beall tell you his name or on what charges he was arrested?"

"No, he did not. He said that was his little secret," answered Hays.

Brady wheeled around and raised his voice. "So you didn't know if he had money or not, you didn't know the charges against him, but you expect the court to believe that you were convinced he'd give you one thousand dollars on his word if you released him. That is incredible! No further questions." Brady returned to his seat and Hays was dismissed.

The members of the court glanced silently at each other and then General Warren spoke, "Call your next witness, Major Bolles."

"I call George S. Anderson, sir."

As Anderson was sworn in Beall stared at him intently. He couldn't believe that Anderson would turn on him. If it hadn't been for Beall, Anderson would have been caught by himself in the train station that night. To save himself, Anderson had turned state's evidence. Now it was Beall's life that was in Anderson's hands. A cruel irony, thought Beall.

Bolles approached the witness stand and placed his hand on the rail. Anderson was visibly frightened. With all the effort he could muster, he avoided eye contact with Beall. This was not his proudest moment. George Anderson was just a boy, not quite eighteen. Yet war had sent him to do a man's job. It had made a poor choice. Anderson had joined the army at age fifteen. The tall gangly boy had been reliable when he served as courier for Colonel Robert Martin in Kentucky, and thus was chosen to help in the rescue effort when they met again in Toronto. But now it was different. The chips were down. A deal had been offered. If he accepted, he was told, he'd spend a few months in prison. If he did not accept, he would probably be convicted as a spy and sentenced to death. It was too much to ask of a boy, and the boy did not have the courage to say no. Despite his religious nature, he was not ready to meet his maker so early. Testify against Beall and your life will be spared, they had said. The war will be over soon. Why risk death when all is already lost for the South they told him. It was just too much to resist. The deal had been made. He felt ashamed. He was a coward and a traitor. He would remember and regret what he was about to do for the rest of his life.

"What are your name and age?" asked Bolles.

"George S. Anderson. I'll be eighteen this month."

"Have you ever been in the Confederate service?"

"Yes, sir. Since the fall of 1863."

"How long have you known the accused, Captain Beall?"

"I first met Captain Beall on the day we went out on the railroad toward Dunkirk, New York. I don't know what day it was, but it was five or six days before we were arrested."

"Were you and the accused arrested at the same time?"

"Yes."

"Please state where that was," directed Bolles.

"It was at the New York Central railroad station near the Suspension Bridge at Niagara Falls," said Anderson.

"Would you please state the circumstances which led you to meet the accused out on the railroad, and all that transpired afterward in connection with your movements and his." Bolles indicated Beall.

Brady stood quickly. "Your honor, will this testimony be related to the sixth specification of charge number one against my client?" This charge accused Beall of acting as a guerrilla in attempting to derail trains outside Dunkirk, New York, a charge that Brady thought was incorrectly brought to the court.

Looking to Major Bolles for an answer, General Warren asked, "Major Bolles?"

Bolles looked up, "Yes, it will relate to that charge."

"Then I object," said Brady, "I object to any proof Mr. Anderson might offer in regard to that charge on the grounds that it relates to a transaction which, if perpetuated as stated in the specification, would be an offense against the laws of New York, and not within the jurisdiction of this military tribunal." If the court ruled his way on this point, the whole issue of guerrilla warfare would be removed from the case, literally half of the charges against Beall. And if the charges were not supported, and Beall was tried as a citizen and not a guerrilla, he might face time in prison, but not death if found guilty.

General Warren momentarily considered his objection and answered, "Over-ruled." Brady sat down shaking his head. He scratched some notes on a pad. Bolles repeated the question and Anderson began his testimony.

"I got to Buffalo on the Sunday before my arrest. It was about an hour or two before daylight on Sunday morning. I went to a hotel, got a room and went to bed. I got up at about eight o'clock and went out and walked around the street for a while. Then I came back to the hotel."

"Did anyone meet you at the hotel that you had known in the rebel service?" asked Bolles.

"Yes, I met Lieutenant Headley. I knew him from when I served under Morgan's command. When he saw me, he signified for me to come outside. I waited a few minutes then followed him. He told me to follow him back into the hotel and upstairs to his room."

"And you did? Anderson shook his head in the affirmative. "What occurred next?" asked Bolles.

"I followed him up and in his room I met Colonel Martin who also had been an officer in the rebel service."

"What was said between you and them?" asked Bolles.

"They said they were glad to see me and that they had a plan in view but needed more men, and they'd like to have me join them."

"What did they say about their plan?"

"They said they intended to capture a train. I was told to stay at the hotel that day, and that they were going to Dunkirk on Monday. Then on Tuesday night they would capture the train." said Anderson.

"Where did you get the pistol that was found on you when you were arrested?"

"Lieutenant Headley gave it to me when we went out to Dunkirk."

"Did Headley or Martin tell you where they had come from?" asked Bolles.

"No, sir, they did not."

"They didn't say they were from Canada or any other place?"

Anderson thought hard, "I think they might have said they'd been in Canada."

"Did they tell you anything about what they planned to do after they captured the train?"

"No, they didn't say. They expected to go back to Canada, but what they intended to do they did not say."

Bolles studied his notes. "What happened next?"

"On Tuesday evening I went out to Dunkirk. We were supposed to capture the train coming from Dunkirk to Buffalo that night." said Anderson.

"Did you go to Dunkirk alone?

"No. Headley and Martin went at the same time, but we did not travel together so as not to arouse any suspicion."

"Did anyone else go?" asked Bolles.

"Not that I know of," responded Anderson, feeling a little more at ease.

"What happened when you got to Dunkirk?"

"Martin and Headley told me that they were not going to try to take the train that night. I was told to be at the depot in Buffalo at two o'clock the next day. When I got to the depot on Wednesday, I saw Headley and Martin and they told me to follow them out along the railroad toward Dunkirk, which I did.

When we were three or four miles from Dunkirk we met Captain Beall."

"Did Captain Beall become one of your party at that time?" asked Bolles.

"Yes, sir. He was one of the party. " Anderson hesitated and looked over at Beall.

"Continue. " directed Bolles.

"Well, we went on a few miles, the four of us, and we tried to pry a rail off the track."

"How did you do that?"

"With a sledge hammer and a chisel," answered Anderson.

"Who had the sledge hammer?"

"Captain Beall."

"And who used it to try to pry up the track?"

"Colonel Martin."

"Anyone else try?" asked Bolles.

"I don't think anyone else tried. We all tried to pull up the rail but couldn't do it so we went back to town." answered Anderson.

"Did you stay in Dunkirk or Buffalo?"

"Neither. We went to Port Colburn in Canada. We stayed there two nights and one day, and then went back to Buffalo."

"Then the four of you went back to Buffalo?" asked Bolles.

"We went back to Buffalo, but a new man had joined us in Port Colburn so there was five."

"Who was this new man, Mr. Anderson? asked Bolles.

"I don't know who he was. He never said his name as I can recall."

"Was he a rebel soldier or not?"

"He was a soldier."

"How do you know he was a soldier? Was he in uniform?"

"No, he was in citizen's dress. All I know is that he said he was an escaped prisoner from Rock Island," answered Anderson.

"So you five came to Buffalo. What did you do then?" asked Bolles.

"Colonel Martin told me to go with this Captain Beall and stay with him, which I did. The colonel said he'd meet us at some bridge with a sleigh."

"Did Colonel Martin meet you there?"

"Yes, sir. And Lieutenant Headley was with him."

Bolles looked at his notes and was puzzled. "You said there were five of you. Where was the fifth man?"

"He came with Captain Beall and me, but he left us to look for the road to the bridge. We missed the bridge, and by the time we came back, Martin and Headley were already there."

"What did the five of you do at that point?" asked Bolles.

"We went to a place on the railroad about five miles from the city and waited for the train."

"Did you see it?"

"No. We missed it, so we all went back to Buffalo and tried again the next day."

"What happened out on the railroad the next day?" Bolles asked.

"Colonel Martin and I stayed with the sleigh. The other three went up the tracks to get a sledge hammer we hid there the day before." said Anderson.

"What next?"

"When we saw the train coming, the Colonel took an iron rail that was laying near the track and laid it over the tracks."

"Now, by this time it was almost dark?" questioned Bolles.

"Yes." said Anderson.

"What happened when the train hit the iron rail on the track?"

"It hit the bar and I heard the whistle blow. Then the train stopped about two hundred yards from there."

"What did the people on the train do?" asked Bolles.

"Two or three men came back with a lantern to see what they hit."

"What did you five do?"

"We got back in the sleigh and returned to Buffalo." said Anderson.

"What did you do with the sledge hammer?"

"We threw it away."

"And what about the chisel you carried?"

"We threw that away, too."

"How had you carried the chisel previously?"

"We carried it in a carpet bag."

"The same carpet bag you and Beall were arrested with?"

"Yes, sir."

"When you first saw the carpet bag, who had it?" asked Bolles.

"Lieutenant Headley had it."

"How did it come to be in your possession at the time of arrest?"

"I supposed it just belonged to the group." said Anderson.

"When you got back to Buffalo, what did everyone do?"

"We decided to leave for Canada so we took the train for Suspension Bridge."

"Who carried the carpet bag?"

"I did, most of the time."

"Did the five of you arrive at Suspension Bridge together?" asked Bolles.

"No, only Captain Beall and myself. The others left Buffalo separately and I never saw them again."

Beall sat listening and wondering if he'd even been in the same place as Anderson. His story sounded good, but was not at all correct. Events he described to the court over a period of several days were all mixed up. He didn't even remember who he was with accurately.

"Mr. Anderson, let's go back to the time of your arrest. Near as you can recollect, what was said and done at the time of arrest?" asked Bolles.

"Captain Beall told the officers we had escaped from Lookout Point and we were making for Canada. I can't really remember much else of what was said."

"The two officers arrested you, according to the record, between nine and ten o'clock in the evening. You and Captain Beall were seated together in the depot. Were you and Captain Beall awake when they arrested you?" asked Bolles.

"No, I was asleep. I don't know if he was."

No, you were asleep, I awakened you and we were arrested as we headed for the train, thought Beall. How could he not remember these things?

"What happened next, Mr. Anderson?"

"Well, the officers awoke us and arrested us. They took us to a room and questioned us. Captain Beall said we were escaped prisoners from Lookout Point. I didn't say anything about myself."

"Did Colonel Martin or Lieutenant Headley or Captain Beall at anytime state that they were under orders, or acting by someone's direction?" asked Bolles.

"No, sir, I don't think they did."

"Did they at anytime tell you what they expected to do with the train between Buffalo and Dunkirk?"

"Yes, the Colonel told me that he expected to capture the express car and the money that was on it."

"Is that all he told you?" asked Bolles.

"That's all I recollect," answered Anderson.

Bolles turned to the commission. "No further questions."

James Brady rose slowly. There were a number of small holes in Anderson's testimony. He was going to have to open them up. Speaking from behind his table, Brady asked, "Mr. Anderson, where were you born?"

"In Pittsylvania County, Virginia."

"When did you first enter the service of the Confederate States?"

"Last May, I think."

"In whose command were you?"

"I was with Morgan as a private in the cavalry."

"And how long have you known Captain Beall?"

"The first time I ever saw him was on the railroad."

"When did you become acquainted with Colonel Martin?"

"I met him when we served under Morgan."

"How did you come to work with Colonel Martin?"

"I was his courier."

"How long did you serve as a courier?"

"I think it was a week or two."

"Mr. Anderson, does it occur to you ... as it does to me ... that you are not very sure of your answers. You think quite a bit, but seldom in your testimony do you know much of anything!" Brady began his sentence softly and crescendoed to the end, putting the most emphasis he could without shouting on anything. He wanted to startle Anderson, maybe even scare him. He feigned impatience hoping to rattle the witness.

"When you first met Lieutenant Headley in Canada, was he with anyone?" asked Brady.

"Yes, sir," said Anderson, trying to sound sure, "he was with Colonel Martin."

"You had seen him and knew him personally?"

"Yes, he was attached to my company about three weeks."

"When you went to the hotel with Colonel Martin, it has been said that there was a plan in view. Who said that there was a plan in view?" asked Brady impatiently.

"It was first Colonel Martin. He and Lieutenant Headley both spoke to me about it at the same time."

"Was anything said about there being a number of Confederate Generals on the express train who were being moved from Johnson's Island to Fort Warren, Massachusetts?"

"No, sir, there was not." said Anderson.

"Who had command of this expedition?" asked Brady

"Colonel Martin did, sir."

"And Headley and Captain Beall acted under his orders?"

"Yes, sir, that's the way it appeared to me."

"Was Captain Beall present at the time of your discussion of the plan with Martin and Headley?"

"No, he was not."

"Was Captain Beall present at any conversation between Martin and Headley when you were present?"

"No, I don't think he was."

Brady rolled his eyes at the answer. Again he could not be sure. He hoped the court saw this, too.

"Who introduced you to Captain Beall?"

"Lieutenant Headley."

"Did he or anyone else tell you that Beall was an officer in the Confederate service? his rank? or anything of that kind?"

"I don't think they did."

Brady saw some cracks in Anderson's already stressed demeanor. He picked up the pace of questions and continued to act annoyed that Anderson could not be more positive of his answers.

"How did they address him, did they call him Captain?" Brady scowled.

Anderson could feel himself beginning to sweat. His voice was weak. He needed a drink of water, but was too frightened to ask. He just wanted to get this over with and get out.

"I cannot remember how they addressed him."

Again Brady reacted in feigned frustration and anger. His voice took on even more of a menacing edge. He spoke each word with clear emphasis, each one louder than the one before it.

"Did ... Captain Beall ... give the order ... to put the rail ... across the tracks?" Brady's head was down, hands on the rail, eye to eye with the unnerved Anderson.

Anderson quivered, "No, sir, ... I ... I don't think he did."

"Well, then," smirked Brady, "who do you think did it?"

"Colonel Martin," he said in a voice just above a whisper.

Brady had pushed the boy far enough for now. He backed off, took a new, almost friendly tone.

"And where were the five of you when the train hit the rail?"

"Colonel Martin and I were hiding in the woods. The others were up the road a piece."

"Did you all get back together?" asked a friendlier Brady.

"Yes, we all got in the sleigh and went back to Buffalo." Anderson began to relax.

"At about what time did you arrive?"

"I'm not sure. I think it was about an hour after dark."

Did you go to a hotel together, or did you separate back in Buffalo?"

"I don't recollect whether we went into any hotels or not." Anderson knew it was coming. Brady was instantaneously furious.

"Do you mean to tell this court," he shook his finger toward the commission and looked Anderson right in the eye, " that you remember all the things you have so far testified to, but you can't remember if you stayed in a hotel that night?!" Brady was the consummate courtroom lawyer, full of drama, but Anderson really was beginning to make him angry. Acting for effect was beginning to give way to true emotion. This young man could cost Beall his life, and he wasn't sure of anything, damn him! Anderson started to answer the question, "Well ..." but Brady did not wait. He moved on quickly, his point made.

"What arrangements had been made about the five of you meeting in Canada?"

Beall knew the boy didn't know of a plan. He had only been told what he needed to know ... but that was the problem. His story made the mission sound very different than it really was.

"There was no plan. We were all to go, I think, to Toronto."

"Why did you not all go together?" Brady questioned.

"There was nothing said to me that I recollect about why we did not go together."

"On the train from Buffalo to Niagara were you all on the same train?"

"I suppose we were, but I don't recall seeing them after we left Buffalo."

"Why were you and Beall waiting in the depot at Niagara?"

"We were waiting for the train, the eleven o'clock train … I think it was the eleven o'clock train." Anderson looked nervously at the floor. It was so hard to remember all the details. It seemed so long ago.

Brady paced across the room past the commission and moved toward where Beall was sitting. "It does not surprise me that you aren't sure of the time. It does surprise me that you even knew it was a train you were waiting for! That will be all of my questions." Brady sat down in disgust. He had walked a fine line with Anderson. His tactics might have broken the witness, or at least caused the commission to doubt his testimony. But it could also have caused the commission to sympathize with Anderson. His hostility toward the boy could just as easily backfire on him. He had to take that chance.

General Warren looked to the other officers on the commission. "Are there any questions of this witness by members of the commission?" None were forthcoming, so Warren asked, "When you referred to the express car, did you understand that to mean the express train, or the express car on the train?"

It was an important distinction. If Beall and the others were after the train to rescue prisoners that was one thing, but if all they were doing was robbing the train of its money, that was another issue entirely.

Anderson answered, "As I understood, it was the express safe we were after."

A knot formed in Beall's stomach. That was what Anderson had been told. Martin and Headley and he had agreed to tell the others no more than what they needed to know, and that was what they had told Anderson.

"What did Captain Beall do at the time Colonel Martin laid the rail across the tracks?" asked Warren.

"He did nothing, sir. There was nobody that did anything except Colonel Martin."

"Thank you, Mr. Anderson, you may step down," said General Warren.

Anderson quickly moved out of the chair, his eyes on the door, and left the courtroom as fast as possible. He looked at no one, save one guilty glance at Beall. Beall felt sorry for him. Anderson had been reduced almost to tears. Fear was in his voice and it trembled at times. I forgive you, Beall thought, because God will judge your actions here, and in some way you will have to make amends for the wrong you've done today. I may die for what I've done, but it will be with a clear conscience. You will have to live with the guilt for the rest of your life.

With all the prosecution's testimony complete, Judge Advocate Bolles rose and read into the record three letters written by Beall that were respectively addressed to Colonel Jacob Thompson of Toronto, Canada, Mr. Daniel Lucas of Richmond, and Colonel Alexander R. Boteler, also of Richmond. The three letters were those written by Beall and turned over to Colonel Burke at Fort Lafayette. Had they been sent, they would have provided the proof that Beall needed to defend himself.

Warren asked, "Are you ready to proceed with your defense, Mr. Brady?"

Brady rose and spoke for Beall, "We are not ready at this time. I would ask the courts indulgence for adjournment until next week."

The commission agreed to postpone further proceedings until Tuesday, February 7, 1865, at eleven a.m.

17

James T. Brady: In Defense of Beall

News of the war had come in bits and pieces to Beall and his fellow prisoners at Fort Lafayette. By the first of February rumors were circulating throughout the prison population that Grant would be making a move on Richmond. General Grant had been trying unsuccessfully for months to take the Confederate capitol. On February fifth he sent his army south and west of Petersburg in an attempt to cut off the city's line of supply. He hoped to force Lee to over-extend his already thin defenses. Grant would be finally victorious two days later at Hatcher's Run. Roger Pryor felt that it was now only a matter of time until Richmond would fall. Then it all would be over.

Through the week that followed the presentation of the prosecution evidence, James Brady prepared his defense. Mornings found him ferrying down to Fort LaFayette to meet with his client. Details of the case were gone over again and again. Perhaps there was something Beall was missing, or had forgotten. Anything, some small fact, a shred of evidence or new recollection that might help his case. Roger Pryor was invited to join these sessions, and provided additional legal advice where he could. By mid-week it appeared to Brady that his best, and really, only defense was to base his case on the law itself, law that at best was vague on the subject at hand.

By late afternoon Brady was back in his law office poring over every treatise on military jurisprudence he could find. Brady's thoroughness bordered on fanaticism, but that was his style, and that was why he won cases. No stones left unturned, not even pebbles. By week's end Ira Cooper had been worked to a frazzle, but Brady's case was assembled. All that could be done now was pray that his arguments would work. Cooper felt hopeful, but without witnesses for the defense, Brady had only the law to depend on. He did not share Cooper's optimism.

On the morning of February 7, 1865, the Commission reopened promptly at eleven o'clock. The clerk read a summary of the proceedings from the previous session and they were approved by General Warren.

"Mr. Brady, are you prepared to go forward with the defense?" asked Warren.

"Yes, sir," Brady nodded. "We have no witnesses, but I would like to submit into evidence two exhibits. The first is a warrant that certifies Captain Beall as Acting Master in the Confederate States Navy signed by S.P. Mallory, Secretary of the Navy, on December 23, 1864.

The second exhibit I offer is a letter written by Jefferson Davis, President of the Confederate States, dated December 24, 1864, that affirms that the actions taken by Beall and the others in an attempt to capture the U.S. Steamer, *Michigan*, and subsequent actions outside Dunkirk, New York, were under the direction of the Confederate States government." Brady handed the two exhibits to Warren and stepped back.

"Your submissions are duly noted, Mr. Brady." Warren handed the letters to the clerk in order. "Mark these exhibits E and F." Warren looked back to Brady. "You may begin your summation."

Brady surveyed the court slowly, taking in the gaze of each man sitting before him. He knew that of all the cases he had ever tried, none was more critical than this. None in his heart of hearts was more important, and none was as close to a lost cause as this. But he was resolved to do his best for John Beall.

"Mr. President and gentlemen of the commission. Since I had the honor of appearing before this court last, there has been published in all the newspapers, accounts relating to the success of our detectives in ferreting out ... as is now supposed ... the perpetrators of the attempt to set fire to the city of New York. That, of course, you gentlemen have all read, and being gentlemen of intelligence, reading it has made some impression on your mind." Brady ran his tongue across his lips, pausing to let his words be absorbed by each man. "In ordinary cases, a lawyer seeking every advantage for his client, lays great stress on the fact that jurors may have their minds so impressed by these publications, that it is frequently a reason for dismissing a juror. I have never, as a lawyer or individual, attached much importance to that system. However, I would be very sorry though, if any man claiming to be intelligent, should read any accounts of the fires, and say it did not produce some kind of impression on his mind." Brady paused again, and moved deliberately toward Beall. "I only allude to it now for the purpose of saying that while Captain Beall's name has been mixed up in that ... and there are many inaccuracies in those stories ... that there is not a hint nor suggestion that he was either connected, or could be connected with the attempts to set fires in New York City. Any suggestion that he may have somehow been involved is utterly without foundation. In fact, if the court has any idea that he was involved, both Captain Beall and I beg you ... to charge him and put him on trial for that!"

James Brady paused and put his hand on Beall's shoulder. "Captain Beall is a soldier and a gentleman. He has the utmost confidence in the fairness and integrity of this commission, but like any man in his position, he is concerned about the possibility, no matter how remote, that someone may have been insensibly affected by these newspaper accounts."

Brady patted Beall's shoulder firmly, and then removed his hand to the table. He leaned forward slightly and looked into the eyes of the court. "I wish to assure Captain Beall, and say to this court that I have no such fears." As he mouthed the words Brady knew that he was no surer of the integrity of the court than Beall. Maybe he could shame a few into mustering up some integrity, but in his heart Brady knew that General Dix wanted a conviction, and these men were under his command, they were the instruments of his desire. Their military futures ... in his hands. Brady sipped some water and continued.

"As you may have already ascertained, Mr. Beall is of highly respectable origin. His ancestors migrated to Virginia many years ago from the north of Ireland, and he is a man of considerable property. He entered into the fight which is now going on impelled by as high motives as any man in the north. Like ourselves, he is dedicated to his cause ... no matter how deluded we may believe it is ... as any man on our side."

With all the years of courtroom performance he could muster, Brady moved forward, toward the commission. He paused near the judge on the far left and placed his hand gently on the rail that divided the commission's table from the rest of the room. He gazed down the row of officers sitting in judgment. They were intent on his every word.

"While each of us in this room believes that the sacred cause we are engaged in should continue until our government has reimposed all the power and authority it had in all the territory we once possessed, we would be wrong to believe that all those who fight on the other side are hypocrites and fanatics ... or are driven by the bad motives of those who commit crimes. I cannot believe the Almighty would permit such men, led by such intellects, to act entirely from blind, unreasonable ... and wicked impulses."

He moved away from the court. He could see their eyes following him. Brady paused and looked back to Beall.

"No matter what civilians may think or do, soldiers will never look at an enemy like the one we contend with as utterly bereft of reason. Captain Beall, as you have learned from his diary, is intelligent and educated. He has received a sound moral foundation from his mother, so often referred to in that diary. He is a graduate of the University of Virginia, and as a man of education, has his own views about this case which I will present to this court as he has communicated them to me."

Brady smiled and put his hands in his trouser pockets. His voice was less formal now.

"I have never had the pleasure of addressing the members of the court except as a private citizen. My friend, Major Bolles ... I hope I may call him so ... and I have never been associated, or opposed each other in any previous matter. And for that reason ... and at the risk of sounding egotistical ... I have never argued with the view that an advocate for the accused should go any further than to present honorably whatever any man who is accused should have a right in truth to say for himself, and no more. With that view of the duty which I am attempting to discharge on this occasion, I present in the first place the accused's proposition that this court has no jurisdiction in the matters which are being investigated here.

My client believes that the trial of these offenses should take place in a general court martial according to the will of established laws of war. A military commission, though it may exercise power over the citizens of the government which established it, cannot take cognizance of the specific accusations presented here."

Brady hoped the commission would recognize the fact that Beall was a citizen of another country, not the United States, and therefore not subject to the commission. He should be treated as a prisoner of war, and tried as such, not as a common criminal. But both he and Beall realized that to do so would be to recognize the South as a separate government, and Beall as a legitimate citizen and soldier of that government. Neither was sure the officers of the commission would concede that point.

"Gentlemen, these issues are new to me," Brady continued. "This is the first case of this type I've tried, but looking through the history of law related to spies as recently as 1863, I find that they are to be tried by a general court martial. This military commission would seem to be an improper place, then, to try this case."

Bolles stood abruptly, "If I may interrupt! Mr. Brady is obviously not aware that in 1864 Congressional action extended the jurisdiction in spy cases to military commissions."

Brady nodded, "Thank you for that lesson, Major Bolles. I apparently do not have those changes in my library. I'll move along to my next point." He paused, glanced at John Beall. "Captain Beall, in these charges seems to be treated in two different ways. One, as a mere individual perpetrating a crime against society, and another as a military man violating the laws of war. If the evidence presented here shows he has committed a crime against society at large, then under the Constitution he should be given a jury trial. That right is given to all citizens.

Since our government does not recognize the Confederate States right to secede, then Captain Beall should be treated as a citizen and afforded his right to a jury trial. The law ... as it is currently constituted . . . says that citizens may only be tried in time of war by a military commission if no civilian court exists. That, gentlemen, is not the case in either Ohio or New York where these offenses are alleged to have been committed. If one of our soldiers should straggle into Richmond or any of the towns along General Sherman's path and commit burglary, he would not be liable to court martial, but rather would be tried in a civilian court. We should apply that same principle to a Confederate soldier."

He waited to see the reaction among the commission members. They glanced briefly at each other. O'Bierne and Wallace scratched notes on the papers before them. Colonel Howe studied his fingernails, Morris tapped his finger on the table. Warren simply watched Brady for his next statements. None gave any indication of agreement, or for that matter denial. Great stone faces ... impossible to read, thought Brady.

"Also," Brady continued, " if you read Section 30 of the 1863 act, it points out specifically that persons who are in the service of the United States government should be tried by court martial or military commission. We punish our own citizens in uniform, but not those who are not in uniform." Brady turned toward Beall.

"The man before you," he motioned to Beall, "is not in the uniform of a U.S. soldier, therefore commits a crime against society. His punishment belongs to civilian courts, not this one."

What an irony, thought Beall. If I were a civilian tried for these so called crimes, I'd at worst get a prison sentence. But because I'm a military man, and because the Union government is too stubborn to recognize the Confederacy, I might have to die as a convicted spy.

As Brady continued, he studied the faces of the commission. They were taking more notes, but their faces still gave away no reaction to his arguments. Brady reached into his coat pocket and pulled out his eye glasses. He perched them on the bridge of his nose and began again, looking at the court over the top of the lenses.

"My second point is that Captain Beall is charged as a spy and a guerrilla within our lines. First ... I ask the court to consider the phrase "within our lines." What does that mean? This war is being fought all over the map. Where are those lines?"

Brady picked a packet of papers from his table and searched for his place.

"Second, in regard to charges of being a spy and a guerrilla. According to Major General Halleck, in his treatise, *International Law and the Laws of War*, says,

> . . . spies are persons who, in disguise or under false pre-
> tenses insinuate themselves among the enemy in order to
> discern the state of his affairs, to pry into his designs and
> then communicate to their employer the information thus
> obtained.

"It is the disguise or false pretense that constitutes the crime." He placed the treatise back on the table and turned to face the court.

"In 1806 Congress passed a law that said spies found lurking in or about the fortifications or encampments of the army of the United States who are not citizens of the U.S. should face court martial and subsequent death if convicted. If our government does not recognize the Confederacy as an independent country, then Captain Beall is still a citizen here, and this law does not apply to him. Also the law states that the person is in disguise. Being in civilian garb does not constitute being in disguise. There is no proof that my client even had a uniform, that he ever owned a uniform, or wore one. I suppose that you gentlemen know that in the south there generally is no uniform, and has not been for two or three years ... yet, I believe, if I am correctly informed, where an officer of the Confederate government has been captured by our side, he has not had on a uniform. In fact, when General Johnson was captured by Hancock, he had no uniform on. He was dressed in civilian attire ... and he was within our lines. He was not charged as a spy. "

Brady paused to sip some water from a glass on his table, but it was more for dramatic effect than need of refreshment. Make your point, then pause, let them think about it, then go on ... with feeling.

"Captain Beall did not, I emphasize, did ... not ... go into Ohio or New York to act as a spy. If he acted in a military capacity, it was an act of war, not spying!"

The men of the court rustled papers and glanced at one another. Brady moved on. "Captain Beall is also charged with acting in violation of the laws of war as a guerrilla. The Judge Advocate asserts that acting as a guerrilla may be deemed a military offense like acting as a spy. The character and actions of a guerrilla in this present rebellion is well understood as the same as that of a spy. The mere mention of the term guerrilla brings with it the definition of a crime." Brady smiled and motioned toward Major Bolles.

"I have the pleasure of knowing the Judge Advocate well. He is a very able lawyer. I don't think there is a man alive that would surpass his genius and eloquence. Those deprived of hearing him in the court room have been deprived of a great intellectual treat. I am sure that the Judge Advocate with all his brilliance has explained to this court what a guerrilla is, and by his definition my client is a guerrilla! However, I am not sure that the current definition of a guerrilla is a fair one, considering the circumstances of this case."

Brady knew that if Beall were judged by existing law and definitions he hadn't a chance. The court had to realize that the old rules and laws applied to past wars could not apply to this one. This current war was so different from wars in the past. Past wars had a foreign enemy. Lines of battle were clearer. The definitions of who was a spy or guerrilla more definite. Not this war. Clearly half of both armies had no uniforms. Were they all spies and guerrillas?

"The soldiers who brought Captain Beall to trial this morning regard him as a villain, a murderer. Yet, what they do not yet understand is that all men sent into the field under the command of superiors are called on to be murderers. If my mother or sisters reputations were defamed in my presence, and in that moment of passion I would slay the perpetrator, I would be guilty of murder for sure, but the court would look at my past record and the circumstances of the act and would surely grant me some measure of mercy.

We accuse my client of putting the lives of innocent people at risk," he paused, "yet we send armed battalions into the south to tear up railroads, burn towns and destroy private property. Innocent civilians get hurt or killed ... as in the recent foray by General Sherman in Georgia. Yet we do not consider his army's actions as criminal. He is not a guerrilla. The only aspect of the definition of guerrilla that yet comes into question is that of a guerrilla committing acts of war ... with no authority."

Again Brady paused to let the point sink in. He took a paper from the table and held it up.

"You gentlemen have before you a document labeled Exhibit F, which is a treatise sent to our government in relation to the pending extradition of Bennet Burley from Canada. As was testified to before, Mr. Burley was with Beall on the lakes as second in command. In it you will note that President Jefferson Davis in his own hand states unequivocally that Burley acted under the express authority of the Confederate States government. He, by our definition, is therefore not a guerrilla. Since Beall commanded that very expedition, surely he had the same authority as Burley! We have sought to get similar proof of authority expressly for Beall, but somehow Captain Beall's letters of request for said documents was never delivered!"

Brady knew that the letters to be sent had never left the desk of General Dix. He did not want to antagonize the court by saying so, but he was almost certain that the commission members were aware of it, too. He moved on, pulling his glasses up to his eyes.

"A little earlier I referred to the writings of our own General Halleck. In his book, on page 306, he states:

> Partisan and guerrilla troops are bands of self organized and self controlled men, who carry on war against the public enemy without being under the control of the state. They have no commission or enlistments, nor are they enrolled as any part of the military force of the state. If authorized and employed by the state they become a portion of its troops and the state is as much responsible for its acts as any other part of its army. There are no longer partisans or guerrillas in the proper sense of those terms for they are no longer self controlled, but carry on hostilities under the direction and authority of the state.

"If that be so," Brady paused, "you cannot convict any man as a guerrilla who holds a commission in the service of the Confederate government, and perpetrates an act of war in that capacity. You will find that Captain Beall was acting as an officer of the Confederate government, either in command of soldiers on the lakes or under the command of a Confederate officer, Colonel Martin, on the railroad outside Dunkirk,

New York."

Brady cleared his throat and sipped more water. "The act of attempting to take the *U.S.S. Michigan* on Lake Erie was an act of war against the U.S. government."

Bolles jumped up and protested. "There is no proof that they actually intended to take the *Michigan!*"

"Oh, yes there is," Brady countered, "By the statement of your own witness, Mr. Walter O. Ashley ... that was the exact purpose of the trip!"

One of the members of the court leaned over to General Warren and whispered, "Yes, Ashley did say that was the purpose." Bolles sat down, resigned to defeat on that point. Brady continued.

"Once they had the *Michigan*, Beall was to extricate Confederate prisoners from Johnson's Island prison. That is what I call a military expedition. And it was legalized warfare." He hoped the court would agree.

"Now, the expedition near Dunkirk, New York, to derail trains was proven by no witness except the young Mr. Anderson. Now, who is Anderson? He is an accomplice. Accomplice's testimony is often accepted out of necessity for public justice. We must realize that Mr. Anderson's testimony is an act of turning traitor to his own associate. We all have known from boyhood ... that is the lowest form of perfidy. I realize that based on his testimony alone you could convict, but it is stated by McArthur on Court Martial that the witness, Mr. Anderson, must be corroborating something that directly implicates him." Brady extended his hand into the air with a sweeping motion, "Now, what exactly was the object of stopping the express train? There is no one from the railroad who can testify to it. We really don't know what happened to that train. We don't even know if anyone was injured. According to Anderson's testimony there was no attempt made to take possession of anything on board. The carpet bag found in Beall's and Anderson's possession at the time of arrest? Beall did not say it was his. Anderson said it belonged to Beall. Anderson is an eighteen-year-old boy who was told by his superiors that they were going to rob the express car. On that we have only his word ... the word of a frightened eighteen-year-old who will escape punishment if he testifies against a fellow soldier. Captain Beall contends that Anderson was told that by

Colonel Martin so that only those of the party who needed to would know the real mission ... to help Confederate officers being held prisoner to escape during transport from Sandusky to Boston. Again, a military mission."

Brady moved to the exhibit table and picked up a small paper book bound with a string. He held it up for the court to see and spoke. This time the forcefulness was gone. In gentle tones he began.

"Finally, let me remind you that in Captain Beall's diary he tells of how he left his mother and sisters unwillingly. He felt a duty to them, but the call of a higher duty, to his state of Virginia and to his country. He did what any honorable man would do ... he served his country." Brady placed the diary back with the other exhibits.

"Therefore, I think, we have two distinct questions here. Is the accused a spy? Is he a guerrilla? What proof is there for the purpose of establishing of these charges?

In the one case we say he was within our lines ... if we had any lines at all, acting as a spy. His actions, testified to here, are inconsistent with spying. In the other case it appears he was not a guerrilla because he was a commissioned officer of the Confederate service acting as any other man would in an act of war. However wrong the South may be, is there any one of you on the commission who believes that Captain Beall's actions were any less moral than those of our own men ... many of whom are considered to be heroes.

Many mothers have lost sons in this war. Those boys have fought and died for ideals and because of a sense of honor and duty to country. No matter how misguided you think his cause, do not convict Captain Beall because he is a southerner. If you must convict, do it only because you are convinced that the law is clear on this and that the law demands it. Thank you."

No witnesses, no documentation. Only the law, such as it was. Brady had done the best that he could by Beall. And Beall knew it. Both silently sensed it didn't matter. The court was a mere formality, a means to an end. They could only hope that the members of the commission were open-minded and willing to examine their personal beliefs and not those of their commanding officer.

As James T. Brady wearily sat down, General Warren looked to Major

Bolles. The Judge Advocate studied his notes. "Major, are you ready to proceed?" inquired Warren.

"Yes, sir," he answered, not taking his eyes off the notes. Bolles stood slowly, an air of deep concern on his face. He began his speech to the court.

"Mr. President and Gentlemen of the Commission: It would not be proper, even if it were possible, for me to imitate the eloquence of the counsel for the accused. Mr. Brady has a right to be eloquent. He is counsel for the accused. I am the Judge Advocate. As you know, I do not act solely as a prosecutor here. My job is not to seek conviction, but to see that the facts of the case are laid out as accurately as possible and that justice in this case is done. To accomplish that I will address many points that have been brought up by Mr. Brady.

Before I begin to deal with matters of fact, let me clear up some allusions that have been made before the court. First, the issue of the fires in New York were never brought up in this case. No facts linking Captain Beall to those fires were ever introduced. As you know, the court cannot, and I'm sure would not go beyond the scope of the facts presented in this case.

Second, some reference has been made to the defendant's ancestry, education and family wealth. No evidence has been brought forth to prove that either. But we are asked to believe it is true. Why? So that the United States government can have some sympathy for the accused perhaps? Yes, we are asked to believe without evidence the statements of a man who upon his arrest lied to the officers saying he had been a prisoner at Point Lookout when the facts show clearly he was not."

Bolles stared into the eyes of the commission members and leaned across his table toward them. Softly he said, "It has been argued that the accused is honorable, deeply religious and tender of conscience. We are asked to believe statements made in his diary as proof. I ask, is a man who would attempt to derail a train, putting lives of many innocent people at risk, able to thank God, as he does in his diary, that 'he has never committed any outcrying sin'?" Bolles paused to let his point be absorbed.

"The court is also asked to show some forbearance because of his hearty and conscientious belief that the cause in which he was engaged, the rebel cause, is righteous and just. Yet on page eleven of his own diary he says that among his consolations was that he never of his own accord left the home of his mother and sisters. I quote, 'I never voluntarily left them.' So his service to the Confederacy must be involuntary! And we are asked to agree he was a firm believer in the rebel cause."

Beall jerked forward, wanting to cry out against Bolles, but Brady put his hand on Beall's arm. Both knew what was meant by the statement in the diary. Bolles was twisting the meaning. Both hoped the commission could see that, but neither man was comfortable.

Major Bolles continued, "Two papers have been put into evidence by the accused ... his letter of appointment as Master's Mate in the rebel navy, and the letter written by President Davis in regard to Bennet Burley's role in the Lake Erie expedition. I am willing to admit that Beall was a rebel officer and that all he did was authorized by Mr. Davis, because my view is that all he did either on the lake or along the railroad, commission or no commission, were violations of the laws of war." Bolles picked up a volume from the table, opened it and read:

> A soldier is bound to obey the lawful commands of his superior officer.

Bolles scanned the faces of the court. "The ninth article of war punishes him for refusing to do so. It also says:

> . . . a superior officer cannot require or compel any soldier to act as a spy or assassin.

If such a command was given by Mr. Davis and obeyed by Captain Beall, then both are criminals and deserve punishment."

Bolles could see his words were having an effect. The eyes of each member of the commission followed his every word. A few took notes as he spoke. He continued.

"We are asked to believe that these acts were legitimate warfare, yet all the prisoner's conduct while in our jurisdiction repels the idea of legitimate warfare. He says he seized the *Philo Parsons* as an act of war ... that his intention was to free prisoners at Johnson's Island. But for this act he produces no order from a superior officer. The evidence in this case does not show that he actually had any such order."

Bolles moved on gaining emotional momentum. All eyes were on him. Beall and Brady sat silently. Beall coughed and studied the members of the commission for some sign of disagreement. There was none.

"What the evidence shows is that the prisoner seized the *Philo Parsons* dressed in civilian attire, held civilian passengers hostage, and ordered Mr. Walter Ashley to surrender the ships papers and about ninety dollars which was split between Beall and Burley."

"I object!" Brady was on his feet. "Mr. Ashley did not know how much money there was, and he was not positive that the money was split between them. In fact, that was said to be the ship's money, not Ashley's personal money. Therefore a part of the contraband of war."

"That depends on if one believes that this was a legitimate act of war," retorted Bolles. "The government contends that it was not!"

General Warren intervened, "Your objection is over-ruled. Continue, Major." Brady slumped back into his chair and shook his head.

"As I was saying, gentlemen, this event has been portrayed as an act of war and the robbery has been portrayed as part of that act. If this was an act of war, why is it that these men and the *Philo Parsons* got no closer to Johnson's Island and the *U.S.S. Michigan* than fourteen miles? Captain Beall contends that this act of war was sanctioned by his government, but the only proof offered is a letter from Mr. Davis that may well have been written to cover the actions of Beall and his men after the fact."

Bolles paused and sipped some water. "You have also been asked to reject the testimony of George Anderson in regard to that outrageous event near Buffalo because he was an accomplice. The court has been reminded that the law says to regard such testimony with suspicion. There is no arbitrary rule on the subject. According to *Benet's Military Law*, page 242-243, you are at liberty to believe it or not, and on that basis you may convict the accused. I refer you to the letter Captain Beall sent to Mr. Daniel Lucas. Captain Beall describes himself as an officer in the Confederate Navy, that he is no spy or guerrilla. You may believe this or not believe it." Bolles looked to his table and shuffled some papers around.

"At this stage of the case I would like to address the remarks made by the learned Mr. Brady about the meaning of the words "within our lines." There can be no doubt in the military mind that any man who enters the loyal states from an insurgent state for hostile purposes is within our lines. Any rebel who comes from a neutral country and crosses into the United States in the guise of a peaceful citizen is within our lines. Within our lines means any spot where the enemy may do us mischief, be it by commandeering a boat on the lake in Ohio, or interfering with railroads outside Buffalo, or if rebels entered New York City with designs on burning it down. They are all within our lines."

"Major Bolles," General Warren interrupted, "The issue has been raised about the propriety of trial by commission. What does the law say as to the jurisdiction of this commission in this case?"

"I was in the process of leading up to that, sir." Bolles grabbed the book on his table and thumbed through the pages quickly. "According to *Revised Army Regulations*, page 542,

> . . .all persons who in time of war or of rebellion against the supreme authority of the United States, shall be found lurking, or acting as spies, in or about any of the fortifications, posts, quarters, and encampments of any of the armies of the United States or elsewhere, shall be triable by a general court martial, or military commission, and shall, upon conviction, suffer death.

"By this definition anyone lurking or acting and found within the broad limits of the United States is amenable to a military commission like the court I now have the honor to address. Gentlemen of the Court, if these crimes had been committed in peace time they would certainly be tried in a civilian court, but even though the nature of this war is different than those of the past, the same rule of law applies. In this case it is very clear that personal advantage was not the motive that led to the seizure of the steamboat or the attempt on the railroad. The motive was to destroy commerce on the lakes, to inflict great injury on their Yankee enemies. The acts are acts of war, and the accused has no Constitutional right to a jury trial."

Bolles sipped more water and picked up another volume from his table. "Now if it pleases the court I will go on to the charge of acting as a guerrilla. I will not spend time explaining the definition of a guerrilla.

Mr. Brady has already ably done that. In the introduction to *The Study of International Law,"* Bolles held it up for the court to see, "it is stated that war is waged between governments by persons whom they authorize, and is not waged against the passive inhabitants of a country. It goes on to say that guerrilla parties do not enjoy the full benefit of the laws of war. They are annoying and insidious, and they put on and off with ease the character of a soldier. Is that not what Captain Beall and his crew did? They posed as civilians and then claim to have exposed themselves as soldiers. They acted without regard to the safety and health of passive citizens and put many civilian lives in danger."

Brady busied himself taking notes on Bolles' points. The law was clear, he thought, but the case was not, nor were the issues of this whole damned war. Beall wondered about Colonel Hill in Detroit. If their government was so concerned about threats to the safety of civilians, why had he allowed the *Philo Parsons* depart at all that morning with civilians on board?

"And now, Mr. President and gentlemen of the commission," Bolles continued, "I come to the final part of this most interesting and important trial. What has the evidence proved? I submit to the court that we have proved that the accused was and is a rebel officer, that he was within our lines in disguise, that he with the help of other rebel soldiers in disguise seized two steamboats, the *Philo Parsons* and the *Island Queen* in September, scuttling and sinking the latter, that they stole money and destroyed freight on the *Philo Parsons*.

We have also proved that in December he came from Canada to Buffalo in disguise and attempted unsuccessfully to throw a railroad train from its track and was caught attempting to escape back to Canada." Bolles paused to let his points be fully absorbed by the commission members. "It must have been apparent to you, gentlemen of the commission, that in the conduct of the defense the accused was utterly embarrassed, perplexed and at a loss to know how to protect himself, and that he was compelled to resort to two distinct, incongruous, and contradicting lines of defense ... at one time seeking to escape from the jurisdiction of this court by treating his acts as mere civil offenses. And at another time claiming the protection of the laws of war as a legitimate and regular belligerent, acting in obedience to the lawful commands of his superiors.

Neither of these lines of defense, I respectfully submit, can stand for one moment against the charge and pressure of the law and the facts. All the evidence in this case tends to show that the accused was part and parcel of a widespread scheme of unlawful and irregular warfare along our whole Canadian line whose purpose was in any and every way, except by open and honest hostility, to endanger the lives, destroy the property, and weaken the strength of those Yankee citizens whom these rebels so bitterly hate.

This piracy on the lakes, and the outrage on the railroad were part of a system of irregular warfare under the fear of which no man, woman, or child can sleep with any feeling of security. Gentlemen, you sit here today, and I stand here today as the representatives of recognized and honorable warfare, to see that such outrages shall not escape unpunished." Exhausted, yet pleased with his performance, Bolles concluded his address.

General Warren looked first to Captain Beall and Brady, then to Major Bolles. "Gentlemen, the commission has heard the evidence and at this time will retire to make its decision." The officers of the commission gathered their papers and exited the room single file. No one spoke, none looked back at Beall. Bolles followed them silently. Beall and Brady sat for a moment without speaking. As the guards approached to take Beall away, Brady asked if he could have a moment. The guards retreated.

"Captain Beall, I won't deceive you. It does not look good. I think you know that. If this were a civilian court I would say you might get the benefit of the doubt, but every man on that commission owes his future career to General Dix. That career will depend on his vote in this matter. Best you prepare for the worst, John." He patted Beall on the back as the guards approached for the second time.

James Brady knew that the law was clear, but how that law was applied to a case as unusual as this was not all that clear. How would the court decide? How would each member interpret the facts? How would they individually vote? He knew the answer to the big question already. Poor Beall was the final pawn in a chess game played in the waning days of this war. His execution would send a clear message to the South that to press this war further from a new front was folly. Beall was the message.

Six officers were now convening to decide the fate of his client. In normal circumstances the commission members would review all the evidence and each member would make his decision. A vote would be taken. It would take at least four votes of the six on the court to convict. Once a conviction or acquittal was obtained, all records, notes and vote results would be destroyed. No one outside was to know if the vote was close or unanimous. No individual commission member could be held accountable for his vote. For public record it was simply the decision of the court. Brady's guess was that the vote would be unanimous. It would not be a legal decision. It would be political.

18

Lincoln Bows to Pressure

On Monday evening, February thirteenth, Captain Wright Rives made his way to John Beall's cell. In all his life he could not remember a duty he dreaded doing as much as this one. The turnkey opened the door and Rives entered. Beall was reading the *Bible*. He looked up as Rives entered. The pain in Rives' eyes told the story. His voice was gentle and sad.

"Captain Beall, I have with me the findings of the court." He handed them to Beall who read them over carefully. Rives stood in the doorway and watched until Beall was finished, "I'm very sorry, Captain Beall. Is there anything I can do?"

Beall looked up from the table and asked, "What will they do with my body?"

"Your friends may come for you and bury you according to your wishes."

"Thank you, Captain. I'll tend to the arrangements. Can you deliver some letters if I prepare them?"

"Yes, sir, I'll see they are sent. Again, I'm sorry." With that said, Rives slipped out of the cell and the door closed behind him.

Beall sat and stared at the door. The order stated that he was to be transferred to Fort Columbus on Governor's Island for purposes of execution. He was a condemned man. On Saturday, the eighteenth, he would be executed, some time between noon and two p.m. said the court's decree. What a sham the trial was. Of course he could produce no witnesses! How could he? The only ones who knew his true intentions could not come forward, nor would he expose them to the fate that had just befallen him. If he had exposed Cole, Hines, Martin, Headley and the others, he might have saved himself, but he could not bring himself to do that. Maybe someday, he thought, when this is over, the truth will come out and I will be judged differently.

Tuesday morning came after a sleepless night. Beall's first act of the early morning was to write two letters. He wanted to be sure to get these sent before he was transferred to Fort Columbus. The first letter was to his good friend in Baltimore, James A. L. McClure.

Dear James,

Last evening I was informed of the finding and sentence of the commission in my case. Captain Wright Rives, of General Dix's staff, promised to procure you a copy of the record of my trial. I ask you who are my friend to attach to it this statement:

"Some of the evidence is true, some false. I am not a Spy or a guerrilla. The execution of this sentence will be murder."

And at some time when it is convenient please forward that record and statement to my friends. I wish you to also find out the expenses of the trial, and forward it to me at once, so that I can give Mr. Brady a check for that amount. Captain Rives assured me that my friends could have my body. For my family's sake, please get my body from Fort Columbus and have it plainly buried, not to be removed to my native state till this unhappy war is over. Then my friends can bury me as their wishes dictate. Let me again thank you for your kindness, and believe me to be now, as in days of yore, your attached friend.

John Y. Beall

His second letter was to his brother, Will. Beall assured him that he had been tried unjustly and that by the time Will got the letter, he would have been executed. As he wrote, Beall remembered his boyhood with Will and all his friends. He asked Will to tell them he had not committed any crime against society. No thirst for blood or money made him do it. He served his country and he would die for his country.

> ...Should you be spared through this strife, stay with mother, and be a comfort to her old age. Endure the hardships of the campaign as a man. In my trunk and box you can get plenty of clothes. Give my love to mother and the girls, too. May God bless you all and ever more, is my prayer and wish to you.

> John Y. Beall

On Wednesday morning James McClure, a friend and classmate of Beall's at the University of Virginia, received a telegram from Fort Lafayette informing him of the sentence. He immediately retained attorney Andrew Sterret Ridgely of Baltimore to prepare an appeal to President Lincoln. Ridgely, McClure, and Ridgely's associate Albert Ritchie, who also had been a classmate of Beall's, spent all day Wednesday and most of the night preparing the appeal. During the afternoon McClure got a telegram from Beall's long time friend, Daniel Lucas, asking McClure to use every means possible to prevent the execution.

On Thursday the sixteenth, McClure received Beall's letter. He was impressed by the sincerity and honesty of it. There is nothing, he thought, that could better show the character of Beall than this letter in Beall's own hand. It had to be included with the appeal to the president. McClure responded immediately by telegraph through Captain Rives. He told Beall he would see that the letter was delivered, but that he wanted to use it first as part of the appeal.

Unfortunately, by the time Beall's letter arrived, Ridgely had already left for Washington with the appeal. Ritchie rushed to catch the next train for Washington so that Ridgely could present the letter with the appeal. But Ritchie was too late. Ridgely had already seen the president and returned to Baltimore. Unable to see the president himself,

Ritchie returned on the night train frustrated and dejected.

Both Ritchie and McClure met with Andrew Ridgely that night. They were not encouraged. Friends in Washington had appealed to Lincoln even before Ridgely arrived, but it looked to Ridgely like the president would not interfere with General Dix's orders.

It was decided on Thursday night to make a visit to the home of Francis L. Wheatly. Wheatly had had for years a great deal of influence in Washington political circles. Perhaps he could get through to Lincoln. They got him out of bed and desperately pleaded their case. Wheatly agreed to go with them to Washington in the morning.

Wheatly and Ritchie went to Washington Friday morning and met with some other men who had come in from New York. All acutely felt the anxiety of the moment. After some discussion, they agreed that one of the president's oldest friends in Washington might be just the person to talk sense to Lincoln. They contacted Oliver Browning, former Senator from Illinois. They did not know that, as they spoke, the president's office was being besieged with appeals for mercy on Beall.

While Browning prepared an appeal in his office, Albert Ritchie and the others went up to Capitol Hill to Congress. They knocked on doors and stopped busy congressmen in the corridors. Most were sympathetic to their cause. Those who weren't were at least willing to support a stay of execution for a time, and so noted that next to their signatures. By now just about everyone had heard of Beall's case. They managed to get ninety signatures on an application asking for a commutation of the sentence.

Late Friday afternoon Browning, Ritchie and Dan Lucas arrived at the White House office of the president. Only Browning, an old friend of Lincoln from Illinois, was allowed in. Ritchie and Lucas sat outside near Lincoln's secretary's desk and waited nervously.

Senator Browning's interview with Lincoln lasted one hour. When he emerged from the office he told Ritchie and Lucas that he felt sure the execution would not be carried out the next day, but he was unsure for how long it would be delayed.

That same evening Andrew Ridgely again hurried back to Washington by train. He, Ritchie, and the others all met in Browning's law office just after dusk and discussed what other measures might be used to save Beall.

On Saturday morning they got word that the execution had indeed been delayed, but they did not know for how long. Senator Browning tried again that day to see the president, but Lincoln was taking no appointments. By Saturday afternoon Ritchie and the others met with Browning for the last time and asked for a frank assessment of Beall's chances for a commutation. Browning told them he believed there was little hope of that coming from Lincoln. He felt the key to commutation lay with General John A. Dix. If they could get Dix to agree to a commutation, Lincoln would probably go along.

Wheatly and Ritchie returned to Baltimore, leaving Ridgely and Browning in Washington with the assurance that nothing to save Beall would be left undone. From Baltimore, Ritchie, Wheatly and Lucas contacted friends in New York. They would go to General Dix, present their case, and hope he would agree to approve commutation, or at least, recommend it to Lincoln.

Early Monday morning McClure left for Washington to meet with Oliver Browning and Andrew Ridgely. Albert Ritchie stayed behind to get letters of support from other influential people. If it was necessary to go to New York, these letters would be presented in his appeal to General Dix. Monday evening Ritchie received a telegram from New York that gave him some hope. There was, in fact, talk of commutation.

It was not yet nine o'clock on Tuesday morning, and already the office of the President of the United States had been swamped with visitors requesting an audience to plead on behalf of Captain Beall. Lincoln had heard enough. His secretary was instructed to tell anyone who arrived that, without exception, the president was seeing no one this morning in regard to Beall.

Lincoln sat in his office trying to go over reports. He was perplexed. Perhaps there was some way to resolve this Beall situation, he thought. The man certainly had a lot of admirers. What a waste it would be to execute a man so intelligent and educated. Imagine the contributions to society a person of his social class could make if allowed a productive lifetime. He had just about convinced himself to grant the commutation. Lincoln was not a vindictive man. It would be wholly against his nature.

Lincoln looked at his pocket watch. Stanton and Seward should be here any minute, he thought. This Beall issue needed to finally be resolved, and he seemed to feel that clemency at least was in order. What good would one more man's death do to hasten the end to this blasted war anyway? Still, he needed to hear what two of his most important cabinet members had to say.

Seward and Stanton's carriage arrived at the rear White House doorway at nine-fifteen. They took the back stairs, hoping to avoid the crowds of visitors and reporters that invariably congregated out in front. Stanton took the lead up the stairway to the second floor, Seward only steps behind.

"Just remember, William, follow my lead. We need to present a united front on this issue. The president needs to feel some heat this morning. I know he's wavering on Beall. He's dying to grant clemency. It just can't happen, dammit. Just stick with me on this and we'll get this whole issue over with once and for all this morning."

"I spoke with General Dix," said Seward breathlessly as he climbed the second flight of stairs. "He says that as far as he's concerned, he won't be the one to grant clemency. Only the president can do that."

"Precisely the problem, Seward, precisely the problem. That idiot of a president is too damned soft on those Confederates ... always has been, I say," scowled Stanton. "First it was piracy on the Chesapeake, then on Lake Erie, train wreck in Dunkirk ... and probably one of the ones who set those damned fires in New York if the truth were known. He's just plain got to hang ... and that's all there is to it."

Access to the president's office via the back stairs was through a small hallway. At the end of the hall were a door and a sentry. It was through this private entrance that the president allowed those with whom he had appointments to enter his office unseen by the public. They approached the door to the oval office. Seeing them, the sentry came to attention.

"Stanton and Seward to see the president," said Stanton.

"Yes, sir, just one moment." The sentry entered to announce them, leaving the two behind in the hallway.

"We'd have all been a far sight better off if we'd have hanged a few more," whispered Stanton. It grated on his every nerve how the president had gone so easy on these people. Every time some crying mother came to his office, he'd grant another damned pardon. That man is an imbecile! he thought.

The sentry returned, "The president will see you now, gentlemen." He opened the door and held it as they passed through.

"Mr. President," said Stanton cheerfully as he shook Lincoln's large hand, "Good to see you this morning, sir!"

Seward stepped forward and shook, "Mr. President," he said slightly bowing his head.

"What can I do for you gentlemen this fine morning?" the president asked. He knew quite well why they were here, but best to let them blow off a little steam. Lincoln motioned for them to sit, and walked around his desk to his own chair.

"Mr. President, we are here ... as you probably know ... on the matter of Captain Beall." said Stanton. "We are quite aware of the great number of requests you have had lately for clemency."

"Yes, indeed, there have been many. It's been like a circus parade," said Lincoln. "What's on your mind?"

"Well, sir, we would like to know what you intend to do to resolve the matter," said Seward.

Lincoln rubbed his long fingers over his face and paused to think, "I've given a good deal of thought to the matter, lately, and I am inclined to grant the request for commutation, at least." He could see Stanton begin to squirm in his seat. "Beall's mother was here, you know. A delightful lady, and so sad, the poor woman. Despite the desperation of her son's situation, she showed remarkable restraint and dignity. It was no easy thing for her to make a trip all this way. She has great fortitude. Her daughter came with her. She was very convincing as well. This Captain Beall must be quite a young man for so many to come to his aid, and I might add from both North and South."

"Mr. President, I think commutation, or any clemency at all, would be a grave error on your part. This war is almost over. To go easy on this man now would in as much tell the South that we will tolerate anything from them," said Stanton, his voice raised slightly. "Jefferson Davis must know in no uncertain terms that we will tolerate no more from them."

It was Seward's turn. He knew that if Stanton kept talking, he'd get angrier and say something that might really push Lincoln into a corner. Now was the time to be diplomatic. Lincoln was an easy going man, but he could be very stubborn, too. Once he made his mind up, there was no changing it.

"Mr. President, what we should be examining here goes beyond whether Captain Beall should be granted any kind of clemency. The point is, if the South can get away with what they have done, if they even feel one bit encouraged to continue, half of the civilian population of the states around the lakes will be outraged. Their lives and property will be at even greater risk. The other half are in a mood right now where they just might join in the southern cause! Are we to put our loyal citizens in physical peril for the sake of one man's life? And ... perhaps risk yet another move for secession among the disloyal of the north? We're lucky to have kept New York, for God's sake!

"That is exactly right, Mr. President," interjected Stanton, "those bastard Copperheads out in Ohio who helped him ... not to mention the ones up in New York. We just cannot tolerate their activities any longer either."

"But if our Republic is to survive, will it rise or fall on this one man's life?" asked Lincoln.

"I don't think that there is any doubt that we can defeat the South at this point. It's just a matter of time," said Seward. "But what your concern should be, Mr. President, is the political implications at risk here. The Democratic Party is divided over the war, have been for some time. I don't have to tell you that. There are thousands of people out there who'd just as soon see a political settlement to this war."

"He's right," said Stanton. "If you don't do anything about Beall and his kind now, just wait and see what develops next. Any more of these attacks in the northern states and the demand for a settlement will spread like wildfire. What's to be gained if we've fought a war, lost hundreds of thousands of lives, and just let the South go in the end through some fool agreement?" Stanton was now on his feet pacing. "If you let Beall go, that is exactly what the Copperheads will think. That is exactly what Jeff Davis will think."

Lincoln stroked his beard and pushed back on his chair. "You know, the good book says to love thine enemy, to forgive, turn the other cheek. Don't you think after all this tragedy we couldn't bring a little forgiveness to Captain Beall ... for his mother's sake, at least?"

Now Seward stood, unable to contain himself. "Mr. President, I implore you. Do not grant clemency! There is nothing to be gained by it, all you can do is lose."

"There is the life of one, perhaps misguided young man ... and his family," answered Lincoln.

That was exactly the problem, thought Stanton. Lincoln had always showed too damned much mercy. Stanton had a long and unforgiving memory. He'd seen Lincoln pardon thousands during the war so far, and where had it gotten him? You jackass! he thought. The war drags on and on, and the people who oppose it become more and more brazen in their help for the South. It was bad enough they opposed the war, but to outright help the opposition!

"Sir," exclaimed Stanton, "the good of the country is more important than this one man! We ... You ...must think of the good of the Union!" Stanton had lost his temper. Lincoln was playing with words and Stanton despised that. He was devoted to the Union, almost a fanatic about it. To hear the President of the United States place the value of a damned Confederate's life ahead of what was good for the Union was more than he could take. "Mr. President, if you are serious about sparing Beall's life then you'll have to do it without me." He paused as Lincoln looked up startled. "I cannot stand by and allow the Union to be further injured by a decision that I feel would be absolutely foolhardy. I will have to tender my resignation, sir!"

Lincoln stared at the fuming Stanton. Perhaps he had underestimated the man's resolve. He knew Stanton was not a man to be trifled with. He was shrewd, ruthless, tough, and most of all vindictive. Those qualities did not always endear him to the people at the War Department, but Lincoln knew there was not a better man for the job to be found. He did not want to . . . no, could not risk losing Stanton at this late stage of the war. And he certainly could not afford to make him a political enemy.

"And what about you, Seward, what do you have to say?" Lincoln asked.

Seward looked to Stanton who was now slumped in his chair, and then back to Lincoln. He was shocked to hear Stanton's threat to resign. There had been no hint of that as a possibility from Stanton on the way over to the White House.

"Mr. President, I must tell you, that I agree with all that Mr. Stanton has said. I feel that to grant clemency to Beall would do irreparable harm the the Union right now. It is possible that this war could be over in a matter of months. Why risk having to bow to political pressure for a settlement at this late date? The Union is more important than that. It must be preserved." Seward hesitated, coming to a decision he did not really want to make. "If it would take my resignation to change your mind on this matter, then yes ... I would do it. This one man's life cannot be worth the damage that might be done to the public good or to the Union. I cannot support such a decision. Yes," he said quietly, "I ... I would resign."

"Well, gentlemen, I must tell you ... this comes as quite a shock to me," said Lincoln, "I will have to give some very serious consideration to the import of what you have both said. Expect to hear from me by this afternoon, this evening at the latest."

By Tuesday evening discouraging news arrived. The execution was on again. The truth was, rumors were flying, and no one really knew what was happening. Albert Ritchie had to know the truth. He decided to leave for New York on Wednesday night to find out for himself how the case stood. When he arrived in New York on Thursday morning, he was shocked to read in the papers that the execution was to be carried out the next day! He went directly to the office of the newspaper, and getting no definite answers, made for the office of General Dix as fast as he could. The story was true. The order for execution had been given. Ritchie got an interview with General Dix and presented his letters of appeal.

"General Dix, my name is Albert Ritchie. As you know there has been a great deal of effort made to spare the life of Captain Beall." He pulled some envelopes from his satchel. "These are letters that I have been asked to present to you requesting clemency for Captain Beall. As you can see, some very prominent people have become involved on his behalf." He knew that Dix had political aspirations himself, and hoped that Dix would be swayed by the prestigious reputations of the people trying to help Beall.

Dix was pleasant but firm. "Mr. Ritchie, I can appreciate the efforts you and your friends have made of behalf of Captain Beall, but as far as I am concerned there is not one gleam of hope in getting me to change my mind. Your only hope is in Washington. President Lincoln has the last word."

Ritchie handed the letters to Dix and asked, "Would it be possible to get a pass to see Captain Beall, sir?"

"Yes, of course." Dix answered. "I have been strict about giving out passes to see Beall, but it's only because I don't want outsiders intruding. You may tell his friends that I will be glad to grant passes to anyone who wishes to see him."

That General Dix would freely grant passes to any of Beall's friends was a lie. Mrs. Mary Mildred Sullivan had picked up the New York *Times* and read about a Captain John Yates Beall, who had been convicted of crimes in both Ohio and New York. She recalled having heard about the raid in Ohio back in September, but attached no importance to the name. Now the *Times* carried further information about the criminal, and she recognized him to be a schoolmate of her sister's from the University of Virginia. Mrs. Sullivan, having known John Beall well as a student, immediately tried to make arrangements to visit. On her first trip to For Lafayette, she was told she could not see Beall. He had been transferred to Governor's Island. Permission had to be granted by General Dix. The following day she went back to Fort Lafayette to get Dix's permission. He let her wait two hours before he would see her, and then informed her that he would not grant permission unless Beall specifically asked for her to visit. She would need to write Beall, requesting to see him, said Dix. She left empty handed. Beall received her note on February fourteenth, and he could not have been more surprised. Yes, of course, he would send a note to Dix requesting a visit. Then back to Dix's office, another long wait, and finally grudging permission. Her persistence was finally rewarded. Dix was not happy then, and in truth he was not happy now, but he granted Ritchie a pass.

Leaving Dix's office, Ritchie telegraphed both Washington and Baltimore with the news. He told McClure in Baltimore to send Ridgely and Wheatly to Washington for one more try at the president, and for him to come to New York to be with Beall if all hope died.

Ridgely and Wheatly went to Washington immediately and set about a massive effort to get Lincoln to change his mind. Late Thursday evening Andrew Ridgely, accompanied by John S. Gittings and Montgomery Blair, former Postmaster General, sent a message to the president that they would like a meeting. They were flatly told that if the meeting pertained to the case of Captain Beall that Lincoln would not grant an interview.

James T. Brady also arrived in Washington on Thursday evening. Early Friday morning Brady, Francis Blair, who was Montgomery Blair's brother, and a well-known attorney in his own right, and Wheatly called on Lincoln at the White House. By the time they arrived, there had already been two other groups to see Lincoln on the same mission. Lincoln's private secretary, who by now had lost all patience, told Brady that the case of Captain Beall was closed and the president could not be seen in reference to it. All hope for clemency now appeared to be exhausted. Neither Dix nor Lincoln would have any part of it.

19

Day of Execution

If General Dix was anything, he was meticulous. Beall's execution, scheduled for Friday, February eighteenth, had to be postponed. Dix discovered that there was a minor error in the wording of the charges against Beall. He wanted no possibility of legal recourse by Beall or his associates to avoid what the general regarded as the inevitable. Fortunately, the reprieve allowed his mother enough time to travel from Charles Town for a final visit.

Janet Beall came to her son's cell accompanied by several officers. As she entered the small room, John quickly arose and went to her. They held each other for some time without speaking. He felt that he had to comfort her. "Mother, mother, I 'm so glad you were able to come. I think of you so often."

Mrs. Beall gently pushed him away from her and looked him over. His eyes were clear and sharp. She did her best to smile. It was a sad smile. "John, I have missed you so! Why does it all have to come to this?" She laid her head on his chest.

He kissed her cheek and said, "Sit down, let's talk for a while." Trying to avoid the obvious issue of his impending death, he asked about his sisters and brother. The sisters were all fine. Willie was now a prisoner of war, but she had heard he was going to be released soon. As far as she knew he was in good health. The farm was still there, untouched by the war.

"John, there isn't much time, they told me they'd come for me shortly. I just want you to know that I am proud of you, and I know that what you have been accused of is wrong. I know the kind of a man you are, and whatever you did, I know you did for your country."

"Thank you, mother, it's good to know that you still believe in me." he said.

"Oh, John, I'm not the only one. You can't imagine the number of people who are protesting this sentence, both in Washington and New York." She folded her hands in her lap to keep them from shaking. "Has there been any word of a pardon, yet?"

"No," he replied, "they are thirsty for my blood. I doubt that a pardon is coming."

"Well, I haven't given up yet," she said with all the confidence she could muster. "It is still possible that either President Lincoln or General Dix will have a change of heart. Mr. Ritchie said that there has been talk of a possible commutation."

Beall knew what that would mean. Life in prison. He would prefer to die rather than spend the rest of his life in prison. But there was no point in saying so to her. Let her have hope. It was all that was left for her now. He had seen from the moment she entered his cell that she was a strong woman, up to the task that lay before her. He knew that it did not matter to her whether he died on the field of battle or on the scaffold. She just did not want to lose him, and would not give up trying until all hope was lost. She was that kind of woman.

Though it was difficult for both, they kept their composure and talked about family and the past, remembering the good times before the war. He had hoped to comfort her, but it was he who received strength from her.

And then the time was over. They came for her. "Mrs. Beall, I'm sorry, it's time for you to go," said Major Cogswell. He looked to Beall and silently shook his head, sorry to have to end the meeting. John held his mother for a short time, they whispered private expressions of love for each other.

"Mother, please remember me to Martha, will you? Tell her I love her and think of her always?"

"Yes, dear, I will."

They said their goodbyes and she left. Mrs. Beall walked swiftly up the corridor and out of the cell block until she was sure John could not hear. Only then did she break down. She had been strong for her son, but now she sobbed uncontrollably.

The next few days, between the eighteenth and twenty-fourth of February, friends came and went. All offered that there was a faint hope that he could be saved from the gallows. Some said that perhaps Lincoln or Dix would relent at the last hour and commute his sentence to prison. Beall held no hope for that. One of his visitors, desperate to help him, had brought him a new pair of boots. Sewn into the uppers, he said, were two tiny saw blades. If John could saw through the bars and escape, the friend said, he would have a boat waiting to pick Beall up. It was impossible and Beall knew it. But it showed how much his friends cared and how desperate they were to save him. Besides, even if he could escape the cell, the ice on the bay would have prevented an escape by boat. Beall knew, however, that the tiny blades had another purpose if he chose to cheat the hangman.

Between visits from friends, Beall spent his days reading the *Bible*. He made notations in the margins about the verses he had read. Not for himself, but for Martha. He had written a letter to Albert Ritchie, asking him to purchase some pins and a locket into which his picture could be placed. The pins were to be sent to his mother and sisters. The locket, containing a clip of his hair, was to be sent secretly to Martha O'Bryan after his death, along with his *Bible* and a personal letter.

On Thursday, the day before the execution date, Albert Ritchie arrived at Fort Columbus to see Beall. As he walked to the entrance of the fort, he met the Reverend Joshua VanDyke. He had just left Beall, and they paused to speak.

"You were right about him, Mr. Ritchie. A finer man and a finer Christian I've never met. He will surely be in my prayers. Let me know if there is anything more I can do, will you?" He patted Ritchie on the arm and headed down the steps to the waiting ferry.

"For a man they're about to murder, they are pretty concerned about your health, John," said Ritchie as he entered the cell, trying hard to be in good humor.

Beall had begun to write another letter, but put down his pencil.

"Why do you say that, Albert?"

Ritchie glanced over his shoulder and motioned toward the door with his hand, "Major Cogswell made me promise that I wouldn't give you anything with which you could take your own life."

Beall threw his left foot over his right knee, tapping it with his finger. "In my shoe here," he said in a hushed tone, "I have had all this time two little steel saws with which I could have opened a vein at any moment had I wished to do so." He grinned, enjoying the irony of it, "And I would like you to remind me of it in the morning!"

Let's hope that something has changed by tomorrow morning." said Ritchie. "We haven't given up hope yet. James is going to see General Dix this afternoon to plead your case again. The old man has been besieged with requests for clemency. So far he's held fast, but until all hope is lost, I assure you, everything in our power is being done to save you, John." said Ritchie. "By the way, I saw Reverend VanDyke on my way in. He was very impressed by you."

"Yes, we had a long talk ... nice man. Thank you for asking him to come, Albert."

"He's a good man, I'm glad he was able to come. I hope he was of some comfort to you." said Ritchie.

As Albert Ritchie visited with Beall, James McClure went to the office of General Dix to ask permission to visit Beall. He had not seen him since Beall was moved from Fort Lafayette to Fort Columbus on Governor's Island. McClure took the opportunity to plead one last time for Beall.

"General Dix, I am aware that you have been besieged with requests for clemency for Captain Beall, but I am impelled to make yet another plea for mercy. I know John Beall probably better than anyone. We were roommates in college, and the best of friends. I know you to be a man of fairness and high principle, a man who knows and respects the law. But ... more than the law ... what I ask you to think about is justice. If you knew Beall as I do, you would realize that he, much like yourself, is a man of very high principle. He has lived his entire life based on the highest and strictest moral values. It is precisely because of these values and morals that Beall served the southern cause. It may not have been your cause...indeed it was one that I know you opposed vehemently. But can you understand, can you respect, that those who hold a different opinion from your own, do so based on the same high codes as those on which you base your own beliefs?

"Mr. McClure," Dix said with an honest air of compassion, "I sincerely believe that all you say about Beall is true. You see, I have read his diary. I am convinced by his own words that he is a man of integrity. However, I am also as sincerely convinced that he is guilty of violating laws of war, for which he must be punished. What good will the law be if it is not enforced? What harm do we do to the public safety if we excuse those who violate those laws, no matter how well intentioned they may think they are? No, I am sorry. I cannot grant clemency in this case."

McClure was demoralized. He knew that all hope was lost if Dix's mind could not be changed. "May I at least visit Captain Beall?" he asked.

"Yes, sir, I will give you a pass to visit him for Friday morning." said Dix. "Now, if you'll excuse me..." He led McClure to the door.

Albert Ritchie spent Thursday evening with Beall, not leaving until midnight. Wanting to be there first thing in the morning, he had gotten permission to sleep over at the fort. He hoped McClure would be there early so they all could spend Beall's last hours together.

Beall was kept up all night by the same throbbing toothache he'd had in Buffalo. He needed laudanum, but was afraid to ask. The request might make his jailers think that he wanted to kill himself. He didn't want to risk being restrained or watched. He needed what little freedom and privacy he had in his last hours.

As dawn broke, Beall arose and dressed with unusual care and neatness. He wore a white linen shirt with a collar, a black silk cravat tied neatly around his neck. At nine o'clock the photographer he had invited arrived at his cell. A final picture was taken, one that would be sent to each of his loved ones. Between ten and eleven o'clock McClure arrived at the fort and met Ritchie. They got to Beall's cell at eleven. The execution was scheduled for between twelve and two o'clock. The men were left to spend an uninterrupted hour with him. They talked calmly, reminiscing about old times and old friends. Beall recounted his adventure on Lake Erie and went over the episodes on the Dunkirk and Buffalo railroad. He spoke and laughed, occasionally rubbing his hands together as he had a habit of doing. He told his friends again that he wanted to be buried in Baltimore until the war was over. Then take him back to Charles Town. He dictated his epitaph to McClure, "Died in defense of his country."

As the hour passed, McClure glanced at his watch. Beall caught the movement and asked, "What time is it?"

"It's a few minutes after twelve, John," McClure said reluctantly. The men all knew that time was short.

Major Cogswell came in to say goodbye. No word had come from Dix or Lincoln. Probably none was coming. Cogswell felt a good bit on sympathy for Beall, having himself been a prisoner in Richmond earlier in the war. He had become more than a jailer. He had been drawn into Beall's circle of friends. As Cogswell left, Dr. Weston, chaplain of the 7th New York regiment entered. With him was an attendant who brought Beall his last meal, a bowl of soup and two slices of toast. Beall looked at the food. "Would you all like to share this with me? I won't eat it all." Neither man was hungry, but they shared this last communion with their friend.

The men had just finished eating when a guard came to the door. "Gentlemen, I'm going to have to ask you to leave for a while. When I'm finished, I'll come and bring you back here."

Within a few minutes a second officer appeared and entered the cell. Beall knew it was finally time to prepare. He pulled on his vest and coat, and meticulously put on a pair of yellow dog-skin gloves. Neither he nor the guards spoke. The first officer pulled Beall's hands gently behind him and attached manacles to his wrists and upper arms. The other slipped a blue-black military cape over his shoulders. It fell so low that only the yellow fingertips of his gloves were visible. On his head they placed a black hood which they rolled up over his eyebrows. Its turban like folds would later be lowered over his face. Beall trembled slightly. His muscles began to tighten with nervousness. He looked at the guards and said, "All I ask is that there be no unnecessary consumption of time in the execution, for after all, it will be to me a mere muscular effort."

Dr. Weston, McClure and Ritchie returned for a final few moments. They saw his pale face and clear blue eyes. They were not the eyes of fear. They beamed. Weston asked that they bow their heads for a moment of prayer. When he finished, he touched Beall gently on the shoulder and left the cell. John Beall was now prepared both physically and spiritually. McClure awkwardly extended his hand to shake Beall's, but Beall could not because of his manacles. McClure had not noticed and felt his face redden with embarrassment. Beall smiled and shook his head as if to say, don't worry, I understand. He saw the humor in the situation even then. Now it was time to go.

At a few minutes after twelve noon Captain John Yates Beall was led out of his cell, down the corridor to the sally port, and out into the yard of Fort Columbus by Provost Marshal Murray and his assistant, Mr. Tallman. Dr. Weston joined the procession at Beall's side. He held Beall's arm with his left hand to both steady and comfort him, and carried a *Bible* in his right.

For days the skies over New York had been overcast, but that morning the clouds had dispersed and the sun had broken through. The procession headed slowly and deliberately west across the yard toward the gallows accompanied by the slow cadence of the garrison drummer.

As they passed through the column of soldiers lining their way, bayonets glinting in the sunlight, there were quiet whispers of encouragement. A few soldiers wept silently. This prisoner may have been the enemy, but not a man you could hate. Many here who had gotten to know him admired his courage. Few wanted to see him die.

The Provost Marshal ordered the column to halt midway across the yard. A signal from the men at the gallows indicated all was not ready. Beall took the time to breathe in the fresh salt sea air. He could see the hills of Staten Island and the heights of New Jersey. He saw the waves in the harbor and raised his eyes to the sun, saying to no one in particular, "This is the last time I shall seen the sun." In a few minutes the death march resumed.

As the entourage approached the gallows, Beall spotted the rough pine box setting off to the side of the gallows, but his eyes were caught and held by the rope of the gallows. The gallows on which Beall was about to die did not have the usual trap door through which the body falls. It was a new design that through the use of the weights and pulleys, the body was jerked abruptly upward from his feet into the air.

The quick action immediately dislocated the vertebrae in the neck, cutting the spinal cord. No pain. Instantaneous death.

The men climbed the few narrow stairs of the wooden platform. Beall was walked to his position. A chair had been placed directly beneath the noose for Beall to sit on as the charges were read. He sat for a moment, but then stood and pushed the chair aside with his foot. Albert Ritchie looked around nervously in hope of some message of last minute reprieve. McClure's stomach burned, he felt ill.

The post Adjutant began to speak loudly, reading the charges against Beall, the findings of the court, and General Dix's order of execution. Finding the recitation extremely long, Beall pulled the chair back over with his foot and sat down. In doing so he turned his back to the Adjutant in defiance and sat facing south. He avoided looking at anyone around him. As he heard each of the specific charges against him, and General Dix's disposition on the case, he slowly shook his head and grimaced derisively. The crowd of on lookers began to get restless. The executioner, impatient to do his work, and very aware of how cruel it was to Beall to drag out the inevitable, called out, "Cut it short, cut it short! The Captain wants to be swung off quick!" Reporters in the crowd rumbled their agreement. At the end of the long recitation Beall stood up again. Dr. Weston approached. As he did, Beall bowed his head. Weston stood before Beall and pronounced his benediction.

" The grace of our Lord Jesus Christ, the love of God, and the fellowship of the Holy Spirit, be with you and sustain you." He patted Beall gently on the arm and left the gallows.

Now, Provost Marshall Murray and his assistant approached. Murray asked, "Captain Beall, do you have any last words?"

Beall replied in a crisp voice loud enough for all to hear, "I protest this execution. It is absolute murder ... brutal murder! I die in the service of my country!"

Murray and Tallman stepped back and took positions to the rear of Beall. The executioner, out of mercy for Beall, was eager to get the job done. He threw back Beall's cape and placed the noose around his neck, pulling it up tight. He attached the noose to an iron ring at the end of the gallows rope. Beall quietly reminded the executioner about what to do with his body after death. This done, the executioner pulled the hood over Beall's head and stepped to his position behind an enclosure that housed the system of weights and pulleys. Onlookers stood in silence. Only the wind and lapping of the waves beyond the yard could be heard.

The Provost Marshal gave the signal and the executioner did his deadly work. The weights inside the enclosure dropped. Beall's body jerked straight up into the air, suspending him three feet above the platform. Some said they could hear his neck snap. It was over in seconds.

McClure stood at attention, tears rolling down his cheeks. For a few moments Beall's shoulders shuddered and then he was still. Ritchie turned away. He could not watch. He quietly repeated a phrase in his head ... "vengeance is mine, sayeth the Lord ... vengeance is mine."

Captain John Yates Beall hanged there for twenty minutes in accordance with the law. Union troops, there to witness the execution, began to silently file out as his body was lowered and the post surgeon declared him dead. No one spoke. None felt victory. The United States government had just completed its first execution of a spy since the American Revolution.

John Beall's body was placed in the simple pine coffin. McClure and Ritchie arranged to have his body carried by train that day to Greenwood Cemetery in Baltimore where, according to his wishes, he was to be buried until the war ended. The pins bearing his picture were delivered to his friends, and his *Bible*, a locket containing his picture and a lock of his hair, and a final letter would be taken to his fiancée, Martha O'Bryan, in Nashville.

Lincoln was saddened by the news of the death, but felt there was nothing he could do. General Dix closed the book on the case, feeling justice had finally been done. The South would now know that he meant business.

The war would be over by April 12, 1865, when his family and friends would gather again to bring John Beall home, home to Charles Town, home to the family plot in the shady, quiet, northwest corner of the Zion Episcopal church cemetery . His stone read as he wished it to, "Died in Defense of his Country."

After Word

What Happened to the Others After the War?

The Civil War had lasted four years and took over six hundred thousand lives. There were great personal tragedies on both sides as a result. Captain John Yates Beall was executed on February 24, 1865. He was thirty years old when he died, and confident that despite the ultimate personal cost, he had been true to his sense of honor in not betraying his friends or his cause.

President Abraham Lincoln was murdered while attending the play, *Our American Cousin* at Ford's Theater on the night of April 14, 1865. He regretted the execution of Beall, but had succumbed to the political pressures of the time. Three weeks later his assassin, the famous actor, John Wilkes Booth, died in a Virginia tobacco warehouse. The evidence is unclear about Booth's motive. For a time the United States government believed there had been a plot by the Confederate government to kill Lincoln, but eventually gave up on that theory for lack of evidence. Confederate operatives in Canada had apparently covered their tracks well. While there is no clear and irrefutable evidence, it would seem that Booth, secretly a courier for the Confederate Secret Service throughout the war, knew of John Yates Beall, and might have killed Lincoln out of revenge.

Of the three Confederate Commissioners in Canada, all continued to be successful men after the war. Jacob Thompson, who had lived lavishly in Toronto, and mishandled thousands of Confederate dollars, was indicted in 1865 by the United States government for his possible connection in the murder of Lincoln. This was a personal hurt to Thompson. He had considered Lincoln a friend, having served in Congress with him long before the war. Thompson fled Canada for England and later Paris, France where he lived for three years at the Grand Hotel. Surrounded by rumors that he embezzled Confederate money, he returned twelve thousand English pounds to Judah Benjamin, former Confederate Secretary of State, who was living in London. No one knows what happened to the rest of the money. In 1868 Thompson returned to his home in Oxford, Mississippi, only to find it had been destroyed by Federal troops. He moved north to Memphis where he enjoyed business success until he died a very rich man in 1885.

Clement C. Clay, a graduate of the University of Alabama, and son of the Governor of that state, became a lawyer and had served in Congress before the war in both the House of Representatives and the Senate. Just before the end of the war he returned south. When he heard that a warrant had been issued for his arrest in connection with Lincoln's assassination, he refused to flee. Instead he rode one hundred-seventy miles on horseback to Macon, Georgia, and surrendered to government authorities. He was taken to Fort Monroe where he was kept in solitary confinement for one year. No trial was ever held and he was released, a broken man, both spiritually and physically. He continued to practice law until his death at age sixty-six in 1882.

The third and least active of the three commissioners was James P. Holcolm. He had left Canada in the summer of 1864 to deliver secret government documents to Confederate ministers in London and Paris. Having lost the documents in a boating accident, he returned to Richmond. After the war he became active in literary and education activities, running a private school for the children of prominent local families in Bedford County and later at Capon Springs, West Virginia, where he died at age fifty-three in 1873.

Jefferson Davis, President of the Confederate States, heard of Lee's surrender and made plans to flee south. At Irwin, Georgia, he was arrested by Federal cavalry and was held prisoner to two years at Fort Monroe where his family was permitted to share his quarters. He was never brought to trial, and was finally released on May 13, 1867. His health and home were gone as was his fortune. At age seventy Davis became involved in several failing business ventures and was provided a home by a friend of his wife, Mrs. Sarah Dorsey, on the Gulf of Mexico called *Beauvior*. There he wrote *The Rise and Fall of the Confederate Government*. Though Mississippi wanted him to run for the United States Senate, he refused to ask the United States government for a pardon. Davis died at age eighty-two in New Orleans.

General John Adams Dix retired from the military after the war and went on to a successful political career. He served as minister to France from 1866 to 1869. In 1872, despite the fact that he was still a Democrat, Dix was nominated to run for governor of New York by the Republicans, where he defeated Horace Greeley by fifty-three thousand votes. He served competently as governor, but in an age of reform, failed to adequately deal with corrupt practices in the state's political system, and was defeated for reelection in 1874 by Samuel Tilden. He spent the last years of his life in retirement in New York City where he died in 1879.

James T. Brady, who had acted as John Yates Beall's attorney at no charge, later served as defense counsel for General Cole, who had been accused of murder. The pressure of the trial finally got to him, and probably contributed to his death. He became exhausted both mentally and physically, collapsing after the trial was over. Known as a lawyer's lawyer, he poured over every minute detail of each case. Brady had tried fifty-two murder cases and lost only two. A believer in state's rights and sympathetic to the Copperhead movement during the war, he was convinced, until his death in 1869 at age fifty-four, that General Dix had been biased toward both himself and John Yates Beall.

Thomas Henry Hines, who had served as aide to Jacob Thompson, remained in Canada until 1867. He studied law under John C. Breckenridge and married his sweetheart, Nan, who had joined him in Toronto when the war was over. When he returned south he served as editor of the Memphis *Daily Appeal* and then moved to Bowling Green, Kentucky where he practiced law and became a judge, being elected to several positions including Chief Justice of the Kentucky Supreme Court in 1884. In 1886 he wrote an article in the magazine, *Southern Bivouac*, which defended the actions taken by John Yates Beall and the others in Canada as honorable and consistent with the specific instructions he had from President Jefferson Davis. He believed that Beall's execution stemmed from the consternation felt by the United States government over Confederate activities in Canada and along the lakes. They wanted to discourage anyone else from imitating what Beall and the others had done. Hines practiced law until his death at age sixty in 1898.

Colonel Robert Martin was arrested and taken temporarily to a Louisville, Kentucky prison. While there he confided to two inmates that he had known about the plans for Lincoln's assassination. From Louisville he was transferred to Fort Lafayette in New York to be tried for his part in the attempted train derailment episode outside Dunkirk, New York. Trial never took place. Martin was pardoned and released by President Andrew Johnson in 1866.

Charles H. Cole, who acted as an oil tycoon in Sandusky, Ohio, while preparing for the attack on Johnson's' Island prison, turned state's evidence to save himself from the gallows. The government found that they really had no case for spying against Cole other than his own questionable admissions. They could, however, try him on treasonable conspiracy, violations of the law of war in trying to seize government property, violation of his oath of allegiance, and violation of his parole when released previously as a prisoner of war. Cole was first imprisoned at Johnson's' Island, and then transferred to Fort Lafayette in September of 1864. A cellmate, Major Robert Stiles of Richmond, Virginia, asserted that Cole was a real villain, and that he had probably deserted both armies. On February 5, 1866 on a writ of habeas corpus Cole was brought into court where it was determined not to try him. He was released from prison on February 10, 1866. Once released from prison, Cole briefly visited the home of Daniel Beddinger Lucas, John Beall's oldest friend, whose conclusions about Cole's character were similar to those of Major Stiles. Cole was never heard from again. It is believed that he went to Texas to ranch or get into mining interests, or that he went to Mexico.

Beall's second in command, Bennet Graham Burley, mistakenly arrested for Beall in Guelph, Ontario, was brought back to Port Clinton, Ohio, on charges of assault, robbery of forty dollars, and the theft of a watch from Walter Ashley while aboard the *Philo Parsons*. Ashley had never mentioned the watch at John Beall's trial. Judge Fitch of the Ottawa County Court decided that the jury should accept the fact that the occurrence on the *Philo Parsons* was indeed a military mission and that Burley should be treated as a prisoner of war even if the United States government would not admit to the legitimacy of the southern government. The trial jury could not decide his guilt unanimously, resulting in a mistrial. They disagreed on whether the money and property were taken for the southern cause or for personal gain. While awaiting a new trial, Burley escaped jail with the help of sympathetic citizens of Sandusky, and returned to Canada in September of 1865. From Canada, Burley left for Scotland where he later married and became a war correspondent for the London *Daily Telegraph*. As a reporter, now spelling his name Burleigh, he covered the first Egyptian war, the French campaign in Madagascar, and the South African War from 1899 to 1902. He also reported on the Boar War and the Russo-Japanese War. Burleigh authored several books on the conflicts in Africa including *Desert Warfare, the Two Campaigns: Madagascar and Ashanti, Khartoum Campaign, 1898, Sirda and Khalifa,* and *the Natal Campaign.* An ardent socialist, Burleigh campaigned several times for Parliament in Glasgow, Scotland. Burley died in 1914, just before the beginning of World War I.

At least two men's treachery led either directly or indirectly to John Yates Beall's death, Godfrey J. Hyams and George S. Anderson. Godfrey Hyams, who posed as friend to Jacob Thompson, had moved to Canada when his property was confiscated by Union troops. There he had met with Confederates and gained their confidence. Hyams learned their plans, and then betrayed them by selling their names and information over a period of time to Union officials for sixty thousand dollars. He later provided damaging testimony about Bennet Young and the St. Albans raiders. Hyams became involved in the plot with Dr. Luke Blackburn to spread yellow fever in Washington, D.C., and later testified about the plot. There was not enough evidence to try him, so he was released to return south.

George Smith Anderson, who had been with John Beall when arrested, turned state's evidence to save his own life. Barely eighteen years old, he testified at Beall's trial and provided damaging, but inaccurate evidence that led to Beall's conviction. In return for his testimony Anderson was released in August of 1865 after serving only seven months in prison. Upon his release, he returned home to Pittsylvania County, Virginia. He later attended Richmond College and the Southern Baptist Theological Seminary. Ordained a minister in 1872, Anderson preached in Florida and married Isabel Hunt Spigener. He went on to preach in West Springs, South Carolina, where four of his nine children were born. Anderson became a publisher of Sunday school literature, was associated with Furman University, and wrote two books on religion. He lived a long and fruitful life, but admitted that for years he looked over his shoulder, always fearful that someone would take revenge for his betrayal of John Yates Beall. Dr. George Smith Anderson was ninety-six years old when he died in 1943.

Most of the men in this story either were or became married after the war. With few exceptions they led long, prosperous, and successful lives, despite their sometimes less than honorable wartime activities. This was not the case for John Yates Beall and his fiancée, Martha O'Bryan. Their engagement and plans for marriage were ended by the gallows rope. Martha was devastated by John's death. She was not permitted to attend the trial, nor was she able to travel the great distance across Union lines to see him before the execution. After the war she visited John Beall's mother and his grave in Charles Town. Martha never married, and to the day she died wore mourning clothes and the locket with his picture around her neck. Though a devoutly Christian woman, she could not forgive Lincoln for allowing John Beall to hang. For the rest of her life, she would not tolerate the mention of the name Lincoln in her presence, nor would she even use pennies bearing his likeness.

Returning to Nashville, Martha opened both a boarding school on Spruce Street, and a day school at the corner of Ninth and Broad. By the 1880's Martha's health was failing and she sold the boarding school. Its new owner renamed it the Nashville College for Young Ladies. Though she retired from teaching, retirement from service was not in her make-up. Martha O'Bryan became more deeply involved in church and charity work. She traveled the streets of Nashville on foot until her brothers George and Joseph bought her a horse and buggy, collecting donations for the needy. The conditions she saw among the poor and working classes of Nashville disturbed her so much that in 1894 she began an organization through her Presbyterian church called the Gleaners. It became the mission of the Gleaners to teach poor women how to cook and keep a clean house for their families. She and the Gleaners collected old clothes and food from the more affluent residents of Nashville and delivered them to the poor. To raise additional money for their cause, the Gleaners also served a weekly businessmen's luncheon. "Miss Martha," as she was affectionately known, died at age seventy-five in 1910 after a long period of declining health. She devoted her life and work to the honor of John Yates Beall, but her work did not stop with her passing. Today in Nashville, Tennessee, a community center, the *Martha O'Bryan Center*, continues the work Martha O'Bryan started.

Captain John Yates Beall died in 1865, some said as a victim of his own honor. But that honor did not die. It lived on through the life and works of Martha O'Bryan and those Nashville citizens who have been inspired to follow her example.

What can be said for the legacy of those who put their own welfare above duty and honor to their cause and country? Nothing. Most have all but been forgotten. Perhaps through his unfair death, Captain John Yates Beall proved that honor is more eternal than self after all.

Bibliographic Essay

Research

The writing of *Victim of Honor* is the result of much travel and research. In Ohio, the location for the planned attack on Johnson's Island
prison, I consulted the Follett House Museum and microfilm records
of the Sandusky Register 1861-1865, located at the Sandusky Public Library. Insight and guidance from local historian, Roger Long, of Port
Clinton, Ohio, was most helpful. Also consulted was the the Bowling
Green State University local history collection, and the local history
collection at the Rutherford B. Hayes Presidential Center, in Fremont,
Ohio. I also interviewed Judy Cumming at the Lonz Winery on Middle
Bass Island, and Joan E. Copeland of Port Clinton, Ohio (current own-
er of the *Philo Parson's* Captain, Sylvester Atwood's home on Middle
Bass Island). Also consulted were several local history books, including
Charles Frohman's, *Rebels on Lake Erie*, and *Memoir of John Yates Beall*, by
Daniel Beddinger Lucas, which included much of Beall's private and
personal coorespondence.

In Virginia, I was in search of information about Captain Beall's personal life and discovered that Mrs. Ann Bretsch of Charles Town was
the current owner of Captain Beall's homestead. Interviews with her,
and visits to the home were followed by interviews with other residents of Charlestown, West Virginia, including Don Wood, Chair of

the Charles Town Historical Society, who made documents available to me, and Blackie and Betty Davis, who supplied me with personal letters either by Beall or about him. They are Beall family members. Most helpful to me in gathering information in Charles Town was Robert Pratt who introduced me to many knowledgeable local residents. Also consulted were the Shepardstown College Library, and the Sons of the Confederacy and Daughters of the Confederacy. Additionally, articles were found in the archives of both the Martinsburg, West Virginia *Morning Herald* and the Martinsburg *Journal*. More information and direction was gathered from the Shepardstown Chamber of Commerce and Professor of history, Dr. John Stahley of Shepardstown College. Other Virginia sources include the Belle Boyd House in Martinsburg, West Virginia, and the Museum of the Confederacy, in Richmond, Virginia.

Helpful in gathering material on life in Richmond during the war were the Virginia State Library, the Virginia Historical Society, and the Valentine Museum, all in Richmond, Virginia. For official records regarding all aspects of the story, I consulted the Official Records of the Confederate and Union Armies and Navies, at the National Archives in Washington, D.C.

Additionally, regarding the battle for Harper's Ferry that resulted in Beall being wounded in 1861, I researched articles provided by the Harper's Ferry National Historical Park, the Archives at the Harper's Ferry Center and the Harper's Ferry Historical Association. Particularly helpful were records held by the Charles Town Public Library's local history room, the Jefferson County Museum, and the records held by the Zion Episcopal Church of Charles Town, West Virginia.

The material in the story regarding John Y. Beall and Martha O'Bryan was gathered primarily in Nashville, Tennessee, her hometown. Most helpful were the Nashville Historical Society, the Tennessee State Historical Commission, the Tennessee State Archives, and the Nashville City Archives. Insight into her personality and her family were provided by Joan Armour, a volunteer at the Martha O'Bryan Center, Cindy Husband, a great-great grandniece, Lucinda O'Bryan Tribue, and Steve Driver, who currently owns the O'Bryan house and is knowledgeable about the family history. I am also indebted to an article written by Carol Kaplan, entitled "Remember the Ladies", a tribute to successful and well known Nashville women. Finally, I consulted the Nashville Archives, reading the papers of Martha's brother Joseph, "The Joseph Branch O'Bryan Papers", and "The Fanny O'Bryan Papers".

The part of the book that deals with John Beall and the attempt to rescue generals from the train outside of Dunkirk, New York and his subsequent arrest in Niagara Falls, New York was gathered at the Buffalo and Erie County Historical Society, the Niagara Falls Public Library's local history department, and the New York City Historical Society and Archives.

George S. Anderson, the boy who was arrested with Beall, and whose confession and testimony led to Beall's conviction was born in Pittsylvania County, Virginia. There I was able to interview descendants and others who were knowledgeable about Anderson's life. John Anderson, great-great grandson of George, was especially helpful, but other information was obtained at the Virginia-North Carolina Genealogical Society in Danville, Virginia, Richard Anderson, and Dale Foster at the Auburn University Library Special Collections department. Also consulted were records regarding George Anderson held by Furman University, the Pittsylvania County, Virginia Court House, and the Virginia Genealogical Society, and the Thomas Hines Papers, at the University of Kentucky, Margarite King Library.

For general information, I consulted numerous books on the subject of Civil War spying, secret service and military engagements too numerous to mention. I am indebted to them all and trust that I have accurately portrayed the events within this book.